Sedipar Trilogy

Tracy A. Daigrepont

Copyright © 2024 by Tracy A. Daigrepont

All rights reserved.

No portion of this book may be reproduced in any form without written permission from the publisher or author, except as permitted by U.S. copyright law.

Contents

Dedication	VIII
Character List	IX
Map of Sedipar	X
1. Glimpse of Perfection	1
2. The Boys	7
3. The Trio	13
4. Surrounded by Dysfunction	16
5. What Used to Be	23
6. Boogie Nights	27
7. Summer's Over	40
8. First Kiss	43
9. Reunited With Lies	47
10. Homecoming Shenanigans	52
11. Every Girls Dream	62
12. The Bonfire	72
13. The Grand Annual Event	78
14. Masquerade Madness	86

15.	Football Is Life	91
16.	Unexpected Visit	96
17.	Some Things are for the Best	105
18.	Web of Deception	111
19.	Family Discussion	124
20.	Tampering With the Truth	128
21.	Range of Emotions	139
22.	Biological Father	145
23.	The Aftermath	149
24.	The Breakup	160
25.	The Truth Will Hurt	166
26.	Party at the Abyss	176
27.	The Accident	190
28.	Lifeless	195
29.	When Reality Sets In	204
30.	Much To Be Desired	214
31.	Flatline	222
32.	Regret	226
33.	Solitude	230
34.	Subdued	234
35.	Selfish Motives	237
36.	On Edge	242
37.	Across the Tracks	250
38.	Awakening	258

39.	Holding Back	265
40.	Raging Emotions	275
41.	A Different Perspective	284
42.	Ready or Not	295
43.	Secrets That Surface	307
44.	Confrontation	316
45.	Tug of War	328
46.	Defeat	340
47.	Caught Up in the Moment	352
48.	Off the Deep End	364
49.	Moments of Truth	380
50.	Nowhere to Hide	393
51.	Exposing the Truth	406
52.	Shattered Secrets	417
53.	Breakthrough	433
54.	Burdens Released	444
55.	Liberated	453
56.	Defining Moment	459
57.	Worth the Wait	465
58.	The Twilight Zone	478
59.	Silver Lining	486
60.	The Blame Game	497
61.	Friday Night Lights	502
62.	Uninvited Host	511

63.	Homecoming With a Twist	522
64.	Jailtime	531
65.	Torn	545
66.	Failed Attempts	553
67.	There's Your Motive	563
68.	Like Mother, Like Daughter	569
69.	Queen of Denial	577
70.	Shocking Truth	582
71.	The Next Best Thing	588
72.	The Betrayal	595
73.	The Only Way Out	608
74.	Divulged Secrets	612
75.	Confronting the Obvious	627
76.	Christmas on Bayou Fueob	632
77.	Mic Drop	641
78.	A Mess of Things	650
79.	A Pink Sapphire Promise	657
80.	Devious Ways	660
81.	A Step Closer	668
82.	Leaving Sedipar	674
83.	Crumbling	680
84.	Sadie Hawkins Disaster	687
85.	Better Left Unsaid	696
86.	New Beginnings	702

87.	A Fresh Start	710
88.	Batter Up!	715
89.	Nothing Else to Lose	729
90.	About the Author	733

Dedication

This novel is dedicated to so many family and friends who have been supportive of my author journey.

My spouse, TJ, and daughters, Kennedy, Hannah and Addison, I love each of you a thousand times more than you will ever know and I love how each of you have rooted for me and supported my newfound journey in writing.

My mom, Pam, taught me everything I needed to know and more about life, being a mom, appreciating what you have, and giving to others selflessly. I love you!

My sister, Michelle, has been one of my number one reader fans since I published my first novel. I love you!

My phenomenal editors are Jenn Jakes, Aunt Carolyn, my sweet friends Amy and Diane, and my cousin Eva. You ladies rock and are phenomenal proofreaders! I love every one of you dearly.

And finally, and certainly not least, my readers. I feel so blessed to have connected with each of you and it warms my heart to know you loved my trilogy.

Character List

The Corbins:
Tucker, Isabella, Nessie, Beau
The Callaways:
Mason, Melissa, Owen, Charlotte
The Beales:
Kent, Allison, Jackson
The Adams:
Trisha, Tennie, Brice
The Taylors:
Carl, Barbara, Whitney
Charlotte's Friends:
Stella

Whitney
Beau's Friends:
Blaine

Jackson

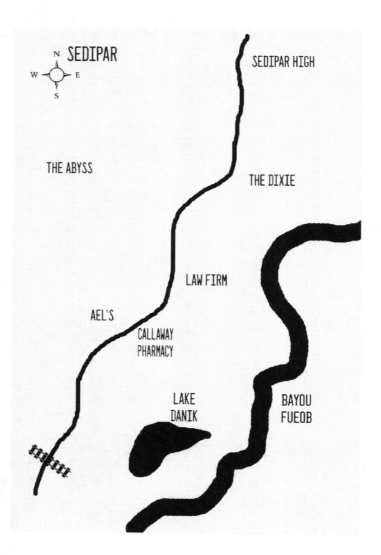

Chapter One

Glimpse of Perfection

I awoke to the annoying blare of my alarm that I mistakenly set the night before because of my school routine. It was summer for crying out loud! While still half asleep, I reached over to my nightstand and fumbled to turn off the alarm. I nestled back under my covers and attempted to fall back to sleep, but it was no use. I sat up in bed and grabbed my journal. Flipping to the last page I wrote: Nessie's Summer – 1993 – Sedipar, Louisiana.

"Every day is a new day. It is better to be lucky.
But I would rather be exact.
Then when luck comes you're ready."

This was scribbled in the back of my journal, a quote from Hemingway that I lived fearlessly by. As I closed the pages, the word "exact" resonated deeply within me. I am a realist. I call things as I see them which leaves minimal time for emotions to develop.

Often, I sat nestled in the seating area of my bedroom bay window switching between reading and admiring the most impressive two-hundred-year-old southern live oak in our backyard. Mesmerized by its large sweeping branches and overall majestic presence, I would sit for hours captivated by its beauty. When our climate would allow and mosquitoes wouldn't "pack me off," I would open the bay windows and embrace the sweet sounds of a southern summer night.

Unfortunately, between the humidity and flying bloodsuckers, this was a rare occasion.

"Nessie!" Isabella––aka my mother––called from downstairs as I quickly threw my library books into a book bag. You're wondering why I call her by her name. It's simple: she'd have to act like a mom to be called one. She barely knows I'm alive––ironic for a 'caregiving' doctor––much less has ever acted like a parent. This goes for Tucker, my father, too.

Tucker, Isabella, and I are not super close, but we are as close as any fifteen-year-old daughter can be to her parents. They both work late most nights, and I usually see them for just a few minutes when grabbing a snack from the kitchen after finishing my homework. We don't share many special memories as my childhood is summed up nicely with one word...Nanny. She filled the gap that Isabella chose to ignore...the loving mother part. I'm not overly sensitive about it anymore. It's just easier not to care.

I still send Nanny Christmas and birthday cards though.

Since I'm past the point of wishing my family life was normal, I typically focus on how Tucker and Isabella's strong work ethic and drive support my taste in designer everything. After all, Tucker's sternness in the courtroom did afford me the beautiful, black Christian Louis Vuitton pumps he purchased for me at Saks for missing my junior high graduation.

No, I'm not shallow. He missed my graduation for a client meeting! Okay, maybe I am a little shallow...*I bit my lip*...but not really.

Anyway, I knew the reason Isabella was calling me. Owen was likely pacing the front porch waiting to go to the town library.

"I'm coming!" I shouted as I entered the foyer and waved toward Isabella as I ran out the front door. As predicted, Owen stood waiting on the porch steps.

"You're never on time, Nessie," Owen said as he shut his car door.

As I jumped into the front seat I casually responded, "I'm as punctual as I prefer to be."

Owen, and I graduated eighth grade a few weeks ago, and while most kids our age are stoked about the summer and how they plan to spend every amazing hour sleeping in until noon or lying out by the pool catching a tan, our primary focus is on reading what we want, when we want and however long we want. We have been best friends since elementary school and have spent more time in libraries than in our homes.

This summer we're also excited about Owen having his license. Owen's cousin in Alabama wanted to move to Louisiana just to get his license at fifteen. *Sucker.*

Owen's parents had recently bought him a brand-new Range Rover classic for his fifteenth birthday, and he was excited to drive it around town. I rolled the window down to feel the sun on my face and my hair blew freely in the wind. This summer was going to be our best one yet!

***

Owen is a realist like me – nothing like his sister Charlotte – although they are twins. There is NO doubt Owen got his sweet demeanor from Melissa, his mom. He has the sweetest soul of anyone I know. He's that friend that you can sit on the phone with for hours not saying more than a few words every ten minutes, but you're comforted knowing they're with you. That's Owen to me. My Owen. Nothing romantic – we are simply friend-soulmates. Since Kindergarten, everyone has thought we 'liked' each other, but he's nothing more than a very close friend – almost like a brother. Frankly speaking, he knows me better and cares more about me than my real brother Beau does.

Owen is quiet and stays to himself other than when he hangs out with me. Often, he studies with Jackson, but that is the extent of their friendship. I pick at him a lot about the vibe he sends out to others with his quirky black frame glasses and serious stature.

"You're so over the top serious," I constantly tell him, and he just shrugs his shoulders and softly laughs.

He champions everything academically focused and spends every waking extra moment he has in the library...with me. Girls in school seem fascinated by his tall frame and dark brown eyes, however, he doesn't seem interested. He's socially awkward and disengages easily in conversation if cornered. I've saved him numerous times throughout our elementary existence to which he owes me...indefinitely. He is the yin to my yang, and we connect. It's easy, painless, and comfortable.

Owen just gets me.

***

"Let's stop by The Dixie before we get to the library," I said recognizing the new freedom we had via his license.

We pulled into The Dixie and grabbed a bite to eat. I had been craving their signature burger and curly fries – and I planned to get us both a soft-serve vanilla cone for the road.

We laughed and talked about our reading plan for the summer as friends from school began to crowd around us filling The Dixie parking lot.

Charlotte, Whitney, and Stella – the trio – appeared suddenly which invoked everyone's attention – as planned - when they strutted up to the order window in their bikini tops and short blue-jean bottoms. "Three chocolate shakes and three fries to go," Stella ordered from the window as Whitney applied more lip gloss and Charlotte scanned The Dixie for any sight of Beau.

"This place is lame today," Whitney said as she stole a French fry from our table.

Charlotte looked at me and smirked slightly but was immediately pulled back into Whitney's conversation. Charlotte was every boy's dream girl – she's perfect in every way – and I was almost certain she had a thing for my brother.

I quickly smirked back at her, then looked back down at my burger.

"I hope there are some cute guys this year in high school." Whitney scanned The Dixie parking lot.

Stella rolled her eyes at Whitney's' comment because she knew it didn't matter who Whitney might sink her claws into, it would never be for any long period of time. "Whit, girl, you know all the guys. You went to school with all of them during elementary."

Walking back toward Charlotte's car, Whitney noticed several guys checking her out and waved at them, blowing each one a kiss.

Stella always gets annoyed with Whitney's exaggerated efforts to be noticed. "Get in the car before we leave your butt here!" Stella said while Whitney finally climbed into the front seat.

I watched the trio speed away as I sat listening to Owen ramble on about some newly released nonfiction series. My mind wandered to Charlotte taking the time to acknowledge me just a few minutes before. After all, we had been in each other's classes since kindergarten, and she hardly knew I existed.

I faced it a long time ago that I am a nerd, and well, Charlotte has always been one of the most popular girls in school. I could go on kidding myself that she wanted to befriend me, however, I know she just wants to get closer to my brother. I give her kudos for trying – get in good with the sister and she's golden. However, I am not that naïve.

My last name is prominent in our small town which gives me clout and speaks "rich" as the name rolls off people's tongues. Apparently, I'm "going big places" and will "set things on fire" per various residents of the town. Can my last name have such a dramatic impact on how successful I'll be? It's a little nauseating if you ask me, but I'm just an annoying fifteen-year-old who has an opinion about everything.

But I am more than just my last name, and I will prove that one day.

Still, everyone knows us Corbin's, and if you don't know us then you haven't been in this town long. But being the rich family in town doesn't make us perfect. Far from it.

And nothing could prepare our family for what was to come.

Chapter Two

The Boys

Early morning practice was the only thing Beau hated about football. Coach didn't give the team much reprieve over the summer. Conditioning was his primary focus which meant early morning runs and lifting weights.

After a late-night partying, Beau grabbed his football gear and jumped in his Corvette and headed to school. Coach had the guys stretch and then lift a few weights before running three miles around the school.

Beau and Jackson arrived before everyone else and began bench pressing to get warmed up. Jackson was surprised to see Beau walk in the weight room. "Man, after last night I didn't expect to see you here so early!" Jackson laughed as he grabbed his towel and wrapped it around the back of his neck.

Beau looked at Jackson and put his bag into his gym locker. "Yeah, yeah, I hear ya. I didn't get too messed up last night since I knew we had to run this morning."

Blaine entered the weight room about thirty minutes late, struggling to stay awake. "Dude last night was awesome!" he said as he walked up to Beau.

"Yeah, it was fun – but we are paying for it now." Beau struggled to reset the bar.

"Man, there are a lot of hotties coming into school this year," Blaine said while attempting to do a few sit-ups. Feeling dizzy, he scooted back and leaned against the wall. "The room is still spinning a bit, dude. I'm not sure I can run three miles this morning."

Beau and Jackson shook their heads at Blaine thinking about all the keg stands and cigarettes he entertained last night kicking his tail this morning. "Oh well," Beau replied. "You better find the energy because you know Coach is going to kick our ass if he finds out we went out last night."

Beau stood up and admired himself in the mirror as he did a few bicep curls. He knew he was hot and that every girl wanted him.

Jackson continued his reps of curls while Blaine leaned against the mirror trying to recover.

***

"Two laps around the track, fifty pushups, and do that rep three times," Coach said to Jackson since he was the first one lined up on the track. Jackson was always the first one to get to practice, the first one on the line, the first one to the game – he was never late for anything.

Beau and Blaine joined Jackson at the starting line on the track and poked fun at Jackson acting so eager to run.

"Dude, you can relax that "always perfect" attitude and live a little." Blaine laughed. Jackson ignored Blaine as he was accustomed to his snide comments and continued focusing on his conditioning.

"Just try to finish the laps this time, Blaine," Jackson responded as Coach blew the whistle.

Jackson is backup quarterback, which means he rides the sidelines quite a bit and doesn't see much playing time, however, he could run all the plays with his eyes closed.

"Let's go, Jaaaacksonnnn!" his dad, Kent, yelled from the sidelines. Jackson ran a few plays with the second string. Kent regularly watched practices and snuck in a few coaching moments when Coach wasn't looking. Jackson didn't get distracted by him yelling from the sidelines, however, he wished he wouldn't come to practice and nag him. His dad had his football fame and glory while in high school. Jackson didn't need Kent reliving his dream through him.

***

Jackson is not a regular jock type. He's best friends with Beau and Blaine and has been since elementary school. Jackson and Beau have one thing in common – football. Jackson moved to Sedipar in third grade and instantly became best buds with Beau due to their infatuation with the sport. Through junior high school, Jackson longed to be selected as quarterback, however, the coach always picked Beau. Jackson's main role was to step in should Beau become injured. Unfortunately for Jackson that meant watching the game from the sidelines and being ready should Coach need him. Jackson longed to show Coach his ability.

Not only was Jackson athletic, but he had a strong desire to follow in his mom's footsteps in the legal profession. Jackson had strong aspirations to attend Tulane after graduation and study to become an attorney. He certainly had the grades to make that happen in addition to a high pre-ACT score. While he focused most of his time on football, his academics never suffered. He was a member of most school committees and clubs and took part in extracurricular activities.

Over the years, Jackson joined a variety of clubs and volunteered for activities after school when they didn't conflict with football, which was rare. While he wants to contribute, he does have an ulterior motive for always volunteering. That motive is Charlotte Callaway. Jackson occasionally studied with Owen at the Callaway's home, hopeful to have the opportunity to visit with Charlotte.

While Beau has openly expressed his infatuation with Charlotte, Jackson secretly longs for her to be his girlfriend and has for quite some time. Charlotte, of course, is always in the spotlight and at times Jackson felt convinced that maybe he had a chance. But with Beau always charging forward to sweep her off her feet, Jackson knows he can't compete.

And he wouldn't do anything to sabotage his best friend's relationship.

***

Blaine Ferrell gets the "hot head" award for our school. We all joke that he was born looking at himself in the mirror. As much as anyone hates to admit it, Blaine is hot and has every reason to think so highly of himself – regardless of how irritating he is. His body is perfect. His tall, strong, muscular frame is hard to miss. His hair is light brown and softened with blond highlights. He has the deepest brown eyes that paralyze most girls when he talks to them.

He uses his tall, muscular frame to his advantage on the field as a middle linebacker. This position is perfect for him. His height and ability to read offensive plays make him the best middle linebacker Sedipar has ever seen.

Blaine and Beau have been best friends for quite a while and have played football together since elementary school.

When Jackson moved to Sedipar, Blaine and Beau realized his passion for football was strong and they pulled Jackson into their group. The three are now inseparable most days, and for them to start on the high school team as sophomores speaks to their athleticism.

Blaine would like to skip school more often; however, football practice requirements keep him in line. His academics are less than average. He doesn't aspire to play football after high school, which would be the only reason for him to attend college – and he's not attending college. He doesn't focus much on his grades. Jackson tries to help him with tests and homework for him to graduate high school, but Blaine blows Jackson off quite a bit and recenters his focus on practicing football or chasing girls.

Blaine's parents own quite a bit of farmland on the outskirts of town, and his dream is to run the family farm one day. The knowledge he has learned since his childhood has more than prepared him to take on the farm one day. While not playing football or practicing football, he spends his other "free time" working on the farm. He's planted and harvested more crops than most of us have probably eaten in our lifetime. His only dream is to become a farmer like his dad.

On weekends, Blaine doesn't miss an opportunity to party with friends. He's the prankster of the group, and if something seems wrong or goes afoul, we all know Blaine isn't far. His parents bought him a used black Ford F-150 4x4 over the summer. He had the truck customized with loud pipes, shiny rims and, of course, loudspeakers. Everyone benefits from his speakers since they are the source of music at the Abyss, random barren dirt roads or the country airport runway where everyone hangs out over the weekend.

As a bonus, Blaine's uncle owns an Exxon station about twenty miles southwest of Sedipar, and unbeknownst to his uncle, Blaine carefully had been extracting cases of various alcoholic beverages from the store's supply shed to share with friends over the weekend.

Blaine will never settle down with any girl for any long period of time. He enjoys the chase, then moves on to someone else.

Chapter Three

The Trio

Charlotte likes the spotlight and gets annoyed when all eyes are not focused on her. She enjoys the companionship of her two best friends, Whitney Taylor, and Stella Atkinson. All three have been besties since elementary school and while there is jealousy among them, they stick together. Whitney is the epitome of the preppy girl who demands the floor when she enters the room and can count her true friends on one, maybe two, fingers.

Charlotte and Whitney have always seemed to step on top of one another to keep climbing to the top of the social status bar.

Who should the prettiest in class go to? Hands down, Charlotte drove every boy in town crazy and she knew it. She never followed through committing to a serious relationship with anyone and lightly flirted back with all of the guys who wooed over her.

But she really only wanted to grab one guy's attention – and that guy was Beau.

Whitney, on the other hand, was more of a teaser and rumor had it that she almost went all the way with a guy over the past summer. Of course, she never shared anything, and no one dared to ask her. Whitney's long, blonde, straight hair coupled with her blue eyes made her stand out in any crowd. Her beauty was all she had going for her. Her grades in school were never good because she despised school more than anything. The only part of school she looked forward to was making her striking appearance as she entered the front doors. After the bell rang, she transported herself somewhere other than the classroom.

Whitney was adopted by the Taylors and had never met her paternal parents. Part of her ego is that the Taylors give her everything she wants when she wants it. She is their only child, so, naturally, they spoil her, but OMG.

Whitney and Charlotte spent most of the summer practicing stunts and cheers to get ready for high school cheer team tryouts. Whitney cheered most of her life just like Charlotte had. Both had spent many weekends at dance and cheer competitions over the years. Whitney had a small crush on Beau, what girl didn't, but she knew Charlotte had her eyes fixed on him too.

***

Stella Atkinson keeps things very real. Stella is the third leg of the Charlotte – Whitney trio, but she always holds her own. Stella has never been into academics or sports. She's not into cheer like her best friends, which seemed odd to many since the three were inseparable.

Stella's an only child and she liked it that way. When she felt like being alone, she had no trouble zoning out in her bedroom listing to music from her record player. Other times when she needed girl time, Charlotte and Whitney would pile in her bed and they would gossip all night until the early hours of the morning. The girls loved spending time at Stella's, especially during the summer since she had an inground pool. Stella's dad had put it in when they built the house and the girls spent many summers lying out by the pool listening to the radio.

Stella's main interest was Jackson. This year, as a freshman, she would get to see him again in the halls of the high school. The sophomores and freshmen shared most of the classrooms in one hall and she secretly hoped that her locker would be close to his.

She was infatuated with his freckles that fell across his nose on both cheeks coupled with his deep brown eyes that penetrated her soul – when he looked her way. His sweet, baby face screamed innocence while his rock-hard abs and large biceps made Stella want to defy that innocence.

Jackson had never paid much attention to Stella, but she hoped since they would be at the same school this coming year, she might have a chance to get to know him better. She also hoped that at a party over the past summer, they'd cross paths, but he rarely went to parties and when he did, he stayed close to Beau and Blaine. Stella would be on a mission the first day of school to scout out Jackson. Nothing usually got in Stella's way – except the fact that Jackson secretly had feelings for Charlotte.

Chapter Four

Surrounded by Dysfunction

As Beau's sister, I was less impressed with his "greatness." The girls adored his dusty blonde hair that naturally parted perfectly down the middle. Beau – aka Mr. Perfect - had melted every girl's heart in this town, but he hadn't settled for any of them. He spent every waking minute either in front of the mirror looking at his biceps or refining them in the gym. His name is plastered all over the school walls with mantras of "Corbin for the WIN" and "Beau Knows." He plays football perfectly and says all the right things at the right time. He gets whatever he asks for at any given moment. In all his existence, I don't think anyone had ever told Beau "no."

Tucker and Isabella undeniably regard Beau as the prodigy child. Their continuous pampering of him drives me crazy. Freshman year he had over 4,200 passing yards so they awarded him with a brand new, bright red, 93' Corvette ZR-1.

Did he really need something else to help him get noticed?

I'm pretty sure his ego swelled the width of Lake Pontchartrain with that souped-up motor under the hood.

The old saying, "chip off the old block" perfectly describes Tucker and Beau. Beau's athleticism is attributed solely to Tucker who was a football star in high school and signed with LSU his senior year on a football scholarship. It is obvious to everyone that Tucker lives vicariously through Beau, pushing him to be the best and to live out his dream of getting to play in Tiger Stadium.

Beau is Isabella's pride and joy – not due to football – but just because he's her beautiful son. Of course, he soaks in all the attention and dreams of leaving the little town of Sedipar and moving to Baton Rouge and living on his own.

While he thinks he has it all figured out and nothing can deter his perfectly laid-out plans, I know his one weakness. Beau may be rough around the edges and upholds the role of super cool guy with a big jock ego, but I know his one secret.

He only truly wants one girl, and that girl is Charlotte Callaway.

***

"Your honor, I object!" Tucker shouted sternly to the judge as the prosecution cross-examined Tucker's witness.

"Overruled!" the judge replied while the prosecuting attorney continued questioning Tucker's witness.

Tucker despised when prosecutors from outside of Sedipar tried to manipulate what he referred to as his courtroom – even though it was the judge's courtroom. Tucker had been a defense attorney practicing in his hometown since graduating from law school. He has a stern side that few people see other than in the courtroom. This sternness enables him to be very successful in defending his clients.

Tucker quickly left the courtroom once the ruling was delivered. Isabella needed him to pick up a few prescriptions from the neighborhood pharmacy before it closed.

"Allison," Tucker said as he handed a few files to his paralegal, "can you please take these back by the office for me? I won't have time to swing by there before Callaway's closes."

Allison is Jackson's mom. She and Mr. Beale – Kent – own the town garage. They moved back to Sedipar when Jackson was young. And as luck would have it, about the same time Tucker needed help at the law firm.

"Sure." She placed the files in her briefcase and snapped the latches. "Tough one today?" she asked as they walked out the front door of the courthouse.

"Yeah, you can say that again. I thought I was going to lose this one, but it turned around in my favor at the end."

Walking out of the courthouse, Tucker was congratulated by various old friends who were frequent spectators of the courtroom.

"Way to put it to 'em,'" one man said as Tucker shook his hand while walking down the front steps of the courthouse.

Tucker looked back at the man and humbly replied, "Oh, thank you, but I'm just doing my job!" He was never boastful, and the town appreciated his genuineness.

He loosened his tie casually while walking to his car parked along the curb. Even without the wealth tag, Tucker would remain the center of attention just by his genuine demeanor.

***

The clinic's lobby was filled with everything from screaming babies to sniffles and coughs from the dreaded summer cold. The nurses scrambled to clear out each room and disinfect prior to the next patient entering. It was a revolving door.

Looking down at her watch, Isabella sighed. It was only half past one. *It seems like lunch was ages ago,* she thought while she pulled a patient's chart from the door, knocked, and walked in.

"What brings you into the clinic today Miss…Callaway?" Isabella questioned as she took a seat on her stool. Isabella was startled by seeing "Callaway" – a name she despised.

Charlotte was surprised when Dr. Corbin entered the room since her appointment was scheduled with Dr. Dawson.

"Where's Dr. Dawson?" Charlotte asked as Isabella pulled her pen from her coat pocket.

"He had an emergency, and I took his patients this afternoon," Isabella responded coldly while reviewing the chart, pulling the folded yellow sticky note free. Looking over the glasses perched on her nose, she asked, "Is there a problem seeing me instead of Dr. Dawson?"

Isabella wanted to tell her just to wait for Dr. Dawson. She couldn't stand any of the Callaways…especially Mason. But having his pretty little daughter here was enough to put her in a bad mood.

Charlotte immediately felt tension building in the room which made her even more uncomfortable. But she had hoped to have sex and she didn't want to get pregnant! She gulped and glanced at Isabella. "Well, yes…I mean, no…ma'am, it isn't a problem."

Isabella nodded and unfolded the bottom part of the sticky note.

Birth control request.

She folded the sticky note up and closed the folder.

So, Mason's daughter was a tramp. Not surprising.

Clearing her throat, she asked, "Have you ever been on any kind of birth control, Charlotte?"

The girl's face turned bright pink. "No' ma'am. I'm still a virgin but …"

"I see. OK, well, let's do a quick exam and then I'll get you the prescription." Isabella started gathering the tools and a paper gown. "It won't take long."

And the sooner she could be rid of a Callaway, the better.

***

Isabella has earned every bit of respect in the medical field for her dedication to Cross Bayou Regional Clinic. She's a physician at the clinic leading several nurses and administrative staff. Dr. Dawson owns the clinic and has been the only provider in town for as long as anyone can remember. Isabella's dream since high school was to be a physician, and even then, she volunteered her free time at Dr. Dawson's clinic.

Isabella had ambitions to go to medical school alongside Tucker at LSU, however, her high school pregnancy was a bit of a detour. Her desire to become a physician centered largely around giving back to the community. While on the surface, it may have appeared she was being generous, everyone knew Isabella's focus was solely on becoming the poster child of the "giveback." Her intentions were jaded by her unavoidable desire to be the center of attention.

Dr. Dawson is Isabella's biggest fan - other than Tucker. He was there from the beginning seeing Isabella through the pregnancy, delivering Beau, *and* giving Isabella a job at the clinic. Isabella always felt a strong connection with Dr. Dawson, and the feeling was mutual. A few years after Beau was born, Dr. Dawson helped her get through medical school with hopes she would take over his practice – and that happened. Since she obtained her medical certification Dr. Dawson only sees existing patients a few days a week.

Basically, Isabella runs the show.

***

I would be one of the last in my class to get my license which required me to bum rides with friends or inconvenience one of my family members to drive me.

The library was hosting a book show today, and I promised Owen I would meet him. Beau had already left the house for summer conditioning practice at school and Tucker was in court all day. My only remaining source of transportation was Isabella.

Sigh.

Did other girls my age desperately dread talking to their mom like I do?

Most likely not, I thought to myself as I rounded the wall leading into the kitchen.

Isabella was standing behind the kitchen bar area with her long, blonde hair neatly placed into the most perfect sleek ponytail.

"You're up early," she said, placing her coffee cup on the table.

Walking past her to grab some juice from the fridge, I replied, "Yeah, I need to be somewhere this morning."

Isabella sat down at the table taking a few sips of her coffee not responding to my obvious need for a ride. After she took a few more sips of her coffee, she pushed away from the table. "Speaking of time – I'm late! I've got to get to the office soon. I have a full day of patients, and I forgot Dr. Dawson is out half a day today."

Before I could elaborate on where I needed to be and at what time, Isabella had already left the room. Shortly after, I heard the front door close.

I sighed as I stood behind the kitchen counter. My family life was so dysfunctional. There was no, "Have a good day sweetheart" or "Do you need me to take you somewhere?" Isabella remained laser-focused on one thing – her job and her patients. While my expectations remained low that she would one day become the mother I never had, a small piece of me held on to hope that one day I might become more important to her.

Unfortunately, I knew better and wasn't holding my breath waiting for her to shift her focus to her family.

Chapter Five

What Used to Be

Tucker and Isabella were high school sweethearts. With their first kiss, both knew they would spend the rest of their lives together. Hearing Tucker tell the story *repeatedly* about how amazingly beautiful Isabella was cheering from the sidelines is painful. She caught his attention, and he never let go of her. Their sweet, high school, fairytale love continued through senior year.

You know how things typically end up with high school romances, right? Well, most of the time the relationship doesn't survive once college plans are made in opposite directions. In Tucker and Isabella's case, neither had the chance to make the college decision. Isabella got pregnant in the spring of their senior year. Tucker's big plans to play LSU football and walk in his father's footsteps were no longer in reach. The bright lights of Tiger Stadium quickly faded as diapers and bottles soon became his reality.

Shortly after Beau was born, Isabella was "surprised" with a second pregnancy – me. I'm sure that I was the last thing Tucker and Isabella wanted since they had begun planning out finishing community college and starting their careers.

Tucker graduated from Southern Law School years later. My grandfather didn't over-celebrate Tucker's graduation because his alma mater bled purple and gold for LSU. I'm not sure why this mattered in the end? After all, Tucker received a law degree. Grandfather fell ill shortly after Tucker moved back to Sedipar– Grandfather had timed it perfectly. Tucker built up the practice and has continued to ensure it thrived in our small town just like Grandfather did.

***

Mason, Tucker, and Isabella were inseparable through grade school. High school changed the dynamics of their friendship though as Tucker and Isabella became more intimate and developed into a love story.

Mason became more disconnected over time and disgruntled with how they ousted him over their "romance." He quickly became more focused on academics in his newly found spare time. He was student council president, straight A student, and of course, valedictorian of the senior class. While he wasn't anything short of smarty pants, he had the looks to go along with it and was a little cocky about it.

Mason's stomach would turn as he watched Isabella run and jump into Tucker's outstretched arms. He would catch her, grab her legs, and spin her around, kissing her like no one else was watching. Secretly, Mason was jealous–jealous of the way Isabella looked at Tucker so intently.

Mason kept this crush to himself – or so he thought. He might have decided it best to look the other way, but she was cunning and full of herself and her desire to be noticed and wanted by everyone didn't fade.

Mason graduated from Sedipar High and left the town to attend pharmacy school in New York, and once he graduated, he quickly returned home to the family business – with his new wife Melissa by his side.

***

Melissa was the comforter of the family. It is hard to fathom what attracted her to Mason, but she was one hundred percent committed to him and her family.

Melissa Callaway was "drafted" back to our town after falling in love with Mason in Manhattan. She worked as a publicist with a fancy corner office in downtown Manhattan. One evening she stumbled across Mason at a local tavern, and they talked for hours until drinks turned into coffee in the wee hours of the morning. She had her life together with a stable income, a two-bedroom flat, and years of experience – but she was missing one thing – and that was true love. The moment she saw Mason's eyes meet hers across the tavern – her heart melted.

Mason proposed to Melissa shortly after they discovered she was pregnant, and they were married only weeks later at a cathedral in New Jersey. They soon learned that the baby they were expecting was two – they were having twins! Months later, Charlotte was born minutes before Owen, and they were just perfect.

A few years passed and Mason graduated from pharmacy school at the University of Buffalo, Melissa quit her job, packed up their New York apartment, and headed south to Louisiana to begin a new life together as a family of four.

After settling into Sedipar and helping Mason at the family-owned pharmacy, Melissa took ownership of the books and ran the register.

When Damon Callaway passed away and the legacy was left to Mason, she eagerly took over running everything except for administering medicine.

Melissa might be a transplant to the South, but she has every bit of Southern grace and a wholesome Southern soul that everyone in this town seeks out. It's hard to fathom that she wasn't born and raised here.

Chapter Six

Boogie Nights

1976 senior homecoming. The disco hype was all over the school. All Sedipar High was anxiously awaiting Saturday night's festivities. If you didn't have a date, you probably were going solo at this point.

Tucker Corbin and Isabella Ducaine were voted homecoming king and queen. How appropriate it was for them to become Sedipar High royalty.

They were the hottest couple, and everyone aspired to be them. They were perfect. Well, at least everyone thought they were perfect based on their impeccable looks and the way they fit together seamlessly. He was enamored with her long blonde hair and perfect body. But beyond her looks, he loved her for who she was, true love, a forever love.

Tucker was the captain of the football team and Isabella was the captain of the cheerleaders – perfect fit, right? Any referee could've easily called that play. They had dated since freshman year, and Tucker was committed at first glance when he first saw Isabella on the sidelines practicing a cheer. Her perfect blonde curls bouncing on the sidelines mesmerized him from the field. Her very short cheer skirt and long tan legs probably didn't hurt either.

One day during practice, Isabella fell flat on her face during a stunt. When she raised her head in shame from the ground, Tucker was standing there offering his hand, then scooped her up and took her to the sideline bench. Immediately they both felt a connection as he wiped away the dirt scuffs from her face. He leaned in for a kiss and touched gently around her lips thinking slyly this was his opportunity, but she quickly pulled away. For that quick second he felt such desperation and then she said, "Only if you promise it's not our last kiss." Then she pulled his chin toward hers and kissed him back.

From that moment on, they were inseparable. Friday nights were spent cheering on Tucker at the football game and after the game hanging out at The Dixie with friends. He was madly in love with her, and everyone thought the feeling was mutual. She couldn't keep her hands off him-- especially when all the other girls were looking. She always wanted the spotlight so there was some speculation whether she held his heart as close as he held hers. Some wondered if it was for show but in his mind, she was the one.

***

The homecoming theme was "Boogie Nights."

Everything was perfectly planned down to each minute of the night. The dance was to be held in the cafeteria, but a water leak forced the dance into the gymnasium. Something about sweaty lockers and old pine flooring waxed to perfection didn't speak "homecoming" but that was the only option. Nonetheless, the dance was three Saturdays away, and everyone was focused on the homecoming game and their confirmed date. Even though they were formally a couple, Isabella insisted that Tucker ask her to the dance and make it memorable. He had planned a romantic dinner on the cliff of the Abyss one evening with a bottle of white wine he snatched from his parents' collection.

Tucker picked her up Saturday evening and they drove out to the Abyss.

When they drove up to the cliff area, she cried out, "It's so amazing! I can't believe you did all of this for me. I had no idea!" He had carefully laid out an old blanket across the ground, bordered by candles that flickered in the soft wind. Two Dixie burger bags set across from each other – one with a pink ribbon securing a note with "Isabella" on the exterior.

She darted out of the truck once Tucker parked and picked up her bag with the note. It read: *My beautiful Isabella. Will you be my date for the senior homecoming? You're already my queen. I want to hold you close and sweep you off your feet. Love always, Tucker.*

Isabella's eyes pooled with tears as she looked up at him standing on the blanket and began kissing him passionately. He quickly became so entranced with her kiss and tight hold on him that he lost focus of the candles and *Whoosh!* Tucker's foot accidentally knocked over several candles igniting the blanket.

"Fire!!!" she screamed.

"Shit! Isabella, move, move..." he frantically picked up the blanket toppling the other candle which landed into a thick patch of pine needles. *Whoosh!* A once intimate picnic had quickly turned into an inferno. She ran frantically toward the truck while he tried to contain the fire. Luckily, the area was sandy as it was repeatedly trampled on by teenagers on weekends, so the fire couldn't go far.

Sirens could soon be heard through the forest and flashing lights appeared amidst the fire. Campers nearby noticed the fire and called

911 from the check-in station. Mason Callaway volunteered at the fire department and was part of the crew that responded. When Mason saw Tucker and Isabella were alone and the remnants of what he assumed to be a date night, he laughed to himself. Mason still had a thing for Isabella. His feelings were not as strong as they were freshman year, however, he still felt a little sick to his stomach anytime he saw them panting all over each other.

"Hey, Mason, man, glad y'all made it." Tucker pointed at the fire-singed blanket. "The wind picked up quickly and W*hoosh* went the candlestick. I guess I should've prepared better for that!"

The chief of the fire department looked toward Tucker, and, glancing back at Mason with a cunning smirk, walked to put the fire out. Mason nodded and helped the chief with the equipment.

Tucker had removed his T-shirt in his attempt to put out the fire and Isabella caught herself staring at his muscular body. She longed for him to hold her close now more than ever before. Tucker moved away from Mason and the chief and centered his attention on Isabella, holding her close to his chest, his letter jacket folded around her while leaning against the tailgate of his truck.

As they finally watched the lights from the trucks fade in the distance, the only remnant of their picnic dinner was the imprint the fire left on the ground. Tucker caressed Isabella's body as she fell in closer to his chest apologizing for how the night had ended before it even began. "Baby, I'm sorry. I know this was supposed to be a special night for us, and I ruined it. I had everything planned out so perfectly..."

Seeing the despair in his eyes, Isabella reached for Tucker's face and pulled his lips close to hers, and whispered, "Stop apologizing. The night is perfect under the stars with you holding me close." Both of their bodies became weightless as he laid Isabella back into the bed of the truck positioning his body on top of her.

Tucker pulled her closer kissing her neck and up to ear. "I love you, Isabella Ducaine. Will you be my homecoming date?"

She reached for his hand and placed it near the buttons on her blouse insinuating for him to free them.

"Are you sure you want to do this?" Tucker questioned while she continued to pull his body closer kissing his neck while wrapping her legs around his torso.

Her fingers stroked across the muscles in his back as she whispered, "Yes, I want you more than anything."

He had been waiting for this moment since they started dating. He wanted to have all of Isabella from the moment he laid eyes on her. He had respected her desire to wait and never pushed her. Secretly he'd hoped that tonight things might go in his favor with the candles and picnic, however, that hope had quickly dissolved with the fire disaster.

Now, she looked more beautiful than ever, her perfect skin glistened under the moonlight as he slowly removed her skirt and finished unbuttoning her blouse. Her pale pink bra and matching panties made his heartbeat faster while she began to remove his belt and unbutton his jeans.

Tucker pulled Isabella's bra straps down exposing her breasts and while fondling them he whispered in her ear once more, "Are you sure you want to?"

She was caught in the moment and responded by pulling his body into hers. The feeling was like nothing she'd ever felt before.

Why have I waited so long for this? she thought as Tucker moaned and pushed his body into hers softly and passionately. His perfect body weighed her down into the truck bed while his hands carefully touched all over her body.

The moonlight peeked through the tall trees shining light on their naked bodies in the back of the truck. Tucker pulled a blanket from the cab of his truck to cover them as they lay holding each other closely. Then without saying a word they made love again under the moonlight.

***

Homecoming week was finally here! Sedipar was slated to play the Avoyelles Panthers homecoming night, and the boys were pumped.

Tucker threw six touchdown passes and the team had four interceptions. The Sedipar Mustangs won the homecoming game – hands down – 62-25. While every football game is intense with emotion and all the feelings that come with Friday night lights, Tucker couldn't wait to get off the field that night and celebrate with Isabella and kick off homecoming weekend.

She waited patiently for him to exit the locker room after the game. "You played a good game, superstar," Isabella said as she grabbed him and pulled him in for a kiss.

"Let's go have some fun!" He opened the passenger door of the truck, and she hopped in.

"Where to?" Isabella slid in closer to Tucker on the bench seat of his truck.

"The Dixie. I'm starving. Then, back to my place?" He stretched his arm around Isabella's body holding her close. She rested her head on his shoulder as they drove down Main Street.

They met up with friends at The Dixie and hung out in the parking lot for a while. Mason was parked across from them and was drinking beer and hollering at girls driving through the parking lot. Around ten thirty, Isabella was getting tired thinking about the long day of hair and makeup that faced her the next morning.

As she leaned up against the wall of The Dixie, Tucker pressed his body against hers, running his fingers through her hair and kissed her forehead. As much as he wanted to remain in that moment, he knew she was tired and reluctantly whispered to her, "I'll take you home."

Their friends gave them a hard time since the party was going to continue at the Abyss, but Tucker knew Isabella wasn't up for it. They walked hand in hand back toward the truck. As she stepped up to get in, she heard from across the parking lot, "Hey, Isabella!" Mason yelled. "You and Tucker gonna' continue that love-making inferno y'all started last Friday night?"

Mason took a sip of his beer and laughed. Tucker turned and gave Mason a stare. He shut her door and walked across the parking lot. Mason put out his hand with a beer extended as if to call a truce. Tucker knocked the beer out of Mason's hand and pushed him up against his car.

"Mason, man, if I knew any better, I'd think you're just looking for trouble. You need to stay out of my business. Leave Isabella out of this!" Realizing that Mason had consumed a few too many beers, Tucker broke his hold and stepped away. "I know we aren't friends like we used to be, but dammit, I thought you were better than this. Neither I nor Isabella deserves our business spread all over town."

The crowd, who were at first disengaged, thinking the argument was just a small-town tiff between two old friends immediately gained interest. As everyone stood closer, all eyes were fixed on Tucker and Mason, until Isabella pushed through the crowd and stood in the center.

She boldly said, "For your information, I had sex with Tucker right there in the back of his truck last Friday, and it was amazing." Smiling slyly, she started to walk off, but instead turned back to face Mason.

Walking up to him, she put her hands around his waist and whispered in his ear, "Well, to be honest, we had sex *four* times."

As she turned around and faced Tucker, he stared at her in disbelief. She walked past him and stopped briefly to grab his hand, attempting to get him to follow her. He was furious and resisted her, throwing her hand away from him as he walked back to the truck.

"What in the world has gotten into you?" he shouted as he peeled out of The Dixie parking lot. "That was nobody's business but ours and you just confirmed it to the whole damn town!"

Tucker stared at Isabella as she scooted in closer, placing her hand on the back of his head, and running her fingers through his hair. He jerked his head away saying, "I just don't know what to think. That was personal. Why did you feel the need to tell everyone, especially Mason? *Mason*, of all people!"

When he pulled into the driveway, she scooted to the passenger side of the truck. She stared at him as he continued focusing intently out the windshield while gripping the steering wheel.

"Just get out!" he yelled.

She slammed the door and didn't look back while running into the house.

***

Tucker didn't call the next morning.

Isabella patiently waited until noon before trying to reach him. She called him several times after lunch, but there was no answer. She waited most of the day, putting off getting ready for the dance hoping Tucker would show up at her doorstep. Around four, Isabella decided she wasn't wasting her senior homecoming at home.

Her dress was long, sequined, bright pink and fit snugly to her body showing off every curve. *If Tucker could see me now,* she thought as she admired herself in the mirror. The dance started at seven and most couples were meeting up for pictures and eating dinner before. A few couples went the fancy route driving to the neighboring town for a sit-down meal while the majority hung out at The Dixie.

Isabella decided to meet some friends there since Tucker had stood her up. She still hadn't heard from him and gave one last try on his house phone but still no answer.

Ditching homecoming... Really, Tucker...ditching me at that! How dare you! Isabella thought as she drove into the parking lot of The Dixie.

Tucker wasn't anywhere to be seen.

Several moms were taking pictures of the various groups when Isabella walked up to the crowd. She felt a tap on her shoulder, and it was Mason. "Gorgeous," he said to her when she turned around.

Her heart wanted it to be Tucker regardless of how mad she was at him.

"Mason." Isabella sighed and turned back around to the crowd.

He grabbed Isabella's hand. "Look, I know you're probably mad at me, and I get it. I had a few beers and shouldn't have said what I said. Come on, you guys forgive me already. By the way, where's Tucker?"

"Good question." She rolled her eyes as she walked toward her group of friends.

Mason continued to follow her and grabbed her hand again asking, "Well if Tucker isn't taking you to the dance and he isn't here, I'd sure love to take you. As friends, if that's okay?"

Isabella, keeping her hand in Mason's hand, turned. "Boy, you got some nerve! First, you make a big spectacle about me and Tucker in front of all our friends and now you're asking me to go the dance with you?" She turned back toward her car, pulling her hand out of Mason's. He followed her.

"Look, Isabella. You may or may not know this, but I've liked you for a long time. I never pursued anything more than friendship because I saw how much Tucker loved you. I've waited a long time for an opportunity like this to get closer to you, and I'm not going to let it pass by me. Not when it's sitting right in front of me."

Mason leaned against her, softly pressing her back against the car door. "Give me a chance, please?" He pressed in closer to her.

"I can't, Mason," she replied. "I gave my heart to Tucker." Isabella desperately searched the parking lot hoping Tucker had swallowed his pride and was there to surprise her. "I shouldn't even have come here," she said as she tried to escape from Mason's hold, but he wouldn't move.

"I feel like such an idiot – putting on this stupid dress coming here. Look at everyone – all happy – taking pictures with their dates. And look at me – I'm...alone." She felt overwhelmed with self-pity.

Mason noticed that Isabella's resistance had begun to soften, and he thought, *If I ever had a chance with her, now is the time.*

He softly cupped her face. "I get it, Isabella. I see how much you care for Tucker, but he isn't here. He didn't show up for you." Mason moved his hands down to her waist, leaned in closer and whispered, "Just come ride with me. We don't have to go to this stupid dance. We can hang out like old friends. Nothing more than that. Just give me a chance."

As he remained close, she looked at her friends holding their dates closely. She thought, *How could this have gotten so messed up? This was our year, senior year, senior homecoming - mine and Tucker's. But he didn't care to respond all day – leaving me all alone..."* Isabella knew in her heart that *"yes"* was the wrong answer, but something inside her was screaming, *just go.*

She locked eyes with Mason and replied, "Why the hell not!? Let's go before I change my mind."

***

Mason's family owned quite a bit of land near Lake Danik. He drove out to one of his favorite places where the trees met the stars. It was a beautiful evening, especially since Isabella was there with him. He parked the car near the edge of the water, and they walked to sit by the lake's edge. He pulled two beers from the ice chest and handed one to her.

"This is one of my most favorite places to come and stare across the lake. It's like nothing else matters when I'm out here. The world fades away and all the problems seem to escape me."

Isabella took a sip of her beer and her head fell on Mason's shoulder. Her mind kept reliving the events of the day and how Tucker had avoided her. Looking out over the water and up at the clear, night sky, a sense of peace fell over her. "Mason, I'm glad I'm here and not at that stupid dance. Thank you for helping me avoid the thousand questions people are dying to ask about me and Tucker. I guess it's over. I just don't know what to think at this point." She took another sip of beer as Mason grabbed another one out of the ice chest.

They sat and talked for hours–– mostly reminiscing about their past friendship. Mason yearned to have Isabella by his side, even if they were only friends and nothing intimate. He stared at the water as Isabella continued resting her head on his shoulder, then said, "It's funny how we were all such good friends up until high school then life just got in the way. I miss those days, a lot."

They continued drinking and reminiscing about the "old days" and all the mischief and fun they had along the way.

A wealth of feelings ensued Isabella as the memories of Tucker flashed through her mind. Taking a sip of her beer, she said, "Such good times and now look at us. We are about to graduate and start a new chapter. I thought my chapter would be with Tucker." She stared at the empty bottles of beer on the ground and dug her heels into the mud. "Screw it. You know, I'm tired of the pity party." Looking toward Mason she asked, "Do you have any cigarettes?"

Mason reached into his jacket pocket and pulled out a pack of Marlboro Lights. "Girl, when did you start smoking?"

Isabella responded by snatching a cigarette from him and leaning in closer to light it. "I don't smoke, but tonight is a new night. Let's toast to the moon!" She raised her beer and cigarette at the sky.

Following her lead, Mason took a long drag off his cigarette and raised both arms to the sky.

"To our rekindled friendship and new beginnings!" Isabella yelled as she tried to stand up. Not realizing that her heel had stabbed part of her dress into the damp ground, she lost her balance and fell forward.

Mason, hiding his laugh, hurried to her side. "Are you alright?" he asked while he attempted to lift her from the ground.

As he reached down, she grabbed him around the waist and pulled him on top of her. He responded by leaning in closer and softly pressing his lips against hers. To his surprise, she kissed him back.

He kissed her neck as his hands felt every inch of her body they could find. Isabella didn't resist. She pulled him closer, retaining her hold. He wanted her badly, but he wasn't going to pressure her and ruin the moment. But his mind continued to race with thoughts of making love to her, and it was getting harder for him to resist the urge.

Isabella's touch became more intense, and she kissed Mason back with deep intent. He knew if things continued it would be difficult for him to stop. Still, as much as he wanted her, he didn't want to take advantage of her.

He pulled himself up and lay next to her. His emotions were rampant as his fingers lightly followed her collarbone and moved to her chest.

She closed her eyes enjoying his soft touch. Watching him intently follow every curve of her body with his fingers, she touched his face and pulled him into her for a kiss. The grassy embankment sparkled under the full moonlight as Isabella whispered, "Make love to me, Mason."

Caught in the moment, he carefully slid his hands up the side of her dress, caressing her body. Isabella didn't resist and pulled him in closer to her with her back pressed against the ground. She worked her hands slowly near his belt to loosen off his jeans. Her pink dress found its way thrown near the water's edge and their naked bodies pressed against each other with the moon casting shadows on the bank.

Chapter Seven

Summer's Over

August's humidity had made its way to Sedipar which meant the school year was about to start up.

Everything was ready for the incoming freshmen. The auditorium stage was set up with chairs for the various school officials, teachers, and our principal to lead us through two hours of "meet the school."

Beau, Blaine, and Jackson had to be at school forty-five minutes before orientation and Blaine was still griping about having to be there. The athletic department had set up several tables in the gym with information on the various sports offered at the school.

Blaine found a football behind a set of bleachers and yelled, "Heads up!" to Beau as they began throwing the football across the gym. Jackson, however, continued helping Coach put out registration forms and pamphlets on the sports.

"Yo, Beau!" Blaine cockily yelled from the other end of the court sending a long pass straight into Beau's arms or so he thought.

Coach stepped in, intercepted the pass, and motioned for Beau and Blaine to head back over to help. "Guys, you're here to help and not play football. If you want to practice, I can set you up with some run time on the field this evening after orientation is over."

"Yes, sir," they both said in tandem and stood by the doors entering the gym to greet students.

***

Outside, Charlotte and Stella pulled up ready to make their fashionable entrance. Walking down to where Charlotte parked, Stella laughed, "Char, your car is double parked, babe."

Charlotte had just gotten her license and was still learning how to maneuver her new BMW. "Oh, Stella, it's fine. I don't want anyone parking by me anyway." She rolled her eyes and slammed the door.

Whitney followed them closely and parked a few spaces down. Charlotte slapped the trunk of Whitney's new black Toyota Supra her parents got for her over the summer.

"Come on, Whit! I see Beau's car here so I'm sure Blaine is here too. Let's accidentally bump into them," said Charlotte grinning while latching arms with Stella and Whitney, and they pranced into the school in their miniskirts and cowgirl boots.

***

The halls were filled with new freshmen telling stories of summer, and nervous parents eagerly awaiting their children's next chapter: high school. As parents and students filled the auditorium and took their seats, Beau and Blaine stood near the back entrance of the auditorium.

Beau scanned the room for Charlotte.

She's somewhere in this crowd.

As he glanced toward the left, he noticed her looking back at him and their eyes locked.

"Look," whispered Charlotte to Stella. "I mean, don't look now! But they are looking this way and OMG do they know how gorgeous they are?" Charlotte shifted in her seat leaning on Whitney while Stella leaned over her lap giggling. They were taking bets on who would go talk to them first.

"Ladies," a deep voice said as Whitney felt a hand lay on her thigh and smelled the most amazing cologne. Blaine had squatted down next to her and though he removed his hand from her leg, he remained in the aisle trying to make conversation. His timing was awful since the program was about to start.

The principal asked everyone to get in their seats. Blaine winked at the trio and said he would be in the back if they needed anything. When Blaine walked to the back of the auditorium, Charlotte peeked across Whitney's shoulder trying to get a better look at Beau.

As Charlotte glanced his way, he remained leaned up against the back wall with his arms crossed. Charlotte smirked as their eyes locked.

The student council president asked everyone to stand for the National Anthem. Afterwards, everyone began to sit, and Charlotte turned around hoping to find Beau still staring her way, but to her dismay, he was gone.

Chapter Eight

First Kiss

Charlotte followed Whitney after being dismissed from the auditorium out into the main hallway of the school. "Where to next, Whit?" she asked as Whitney began dragging her down to the gym.

Deep, thunderous chanting could be heard down the main hall of the school coming from the gym. Only the football team could make such noise. Stella followed behind secretly laughing at her two best friends' hopeless hearts. As they rounded the lobby gym doors, Charlotte and Whitney flirted with the row of football players that were lined up along the gym door.

"Hey, boys!" Whitney cheered while pulling Charlotte through the tunnel of football players.

Charlotte hoped to look up and see Beau at the end of the welcome line, but he wasn't there. Stella, following closely behind, hoped to catch Jackson's attention, but he glazed over her and went to help at the table once Charlotte and Whitney passed by. Blaine was waiting inside the gym and motioned for Charlotte and Whitney to come over.

"Girls, y'all are in luck because we are going out to the Abyss tonight to celebrate the first day back at school. Y'all should come." Blaine leaned in closer to Charlotte and whispered, "Maybe we could spend some time alone, just me and you tonight? I'd love to hang out, maybe have a few drinks, you know, see where it takes us."

Whitney rolled her eyes and stepped between Charlotte and Blaine. She grabbed his waist and pulled him closer. "Take me instead. She's not interested in you."

Stepping away, Charlotte couldn't decide if she was thankful Whitney stepped in or mad that Whitney so easily drew Blaine's attention away.

"Well, aren't they just hitting things off quick?" said Stella sarcastically as she watched from the bleachers still hoping Jackson would look her way.

"I guess so," replied Charlotte. "They are perfect for one another since neither can - nor want - to settle down. Commitment is not exactly part of their vocabulary."

***

They left the gym heading through the main hall of the school, Charlotte imagining Beau was waiting for her back by the auditorium door. To her dismay the auditorium was empty. Her heart started aching when she didn't see him there.

Gosh, why am I crushing on this guy so hard? Get it together, Charlotte.

They walked out to their cars, and Charlotte noticed a car parked very close to her car.

"What the hell!?" she shouted as she walked frantically toward her car but suddenly paused and a grin fell across her face.

Beau had positioned himself between the ridiculously small space left between Charlotte's car and his Corvette. He was casually leaning against his Vette, smiling.

He was always cocky but smooth. Leaning confidently against his car, he hoped deep down that she had feelings for him like he had for her, and that he hadn't wedged himself in this tight space for no reason. He had strategically parked his corvette right on the line next to her car forcing her to split the space with him.

"You're crazy, Beau Corbin! If you put a scratch on my car..." Charlotte started as she got closer. He grabbed onto her waist and pulled her close. With one touch of his hands, her tone faded into a whisper. "You disappeared tonight," she said gazing into his eyes and softly caressing his arm.

He pulled her closer with one hand and with the other reached up to move her hair away from her ear then leaned in and whispered, "I've been waiting for you here the entire time. The question is where have you been, Miss Callaway?"

Charlotte didn't give in easily usually, but something about Beau made her knees weak. She was infatuated with everything about him and had been dreaming about this moment for what seemed like an eternity.

Resisting the urge, Charlotte attempted to play hard to get. "I'm not that easy you know." She pushed back from him turned toward her car. As she reached for her keys to unlock her door she said, "Besides, how do you know I don't already have a boyfriend?"

Beau pushed himself up from against his car and placed one hand on Charlotte's door, leaning up close against her back. He whispered in her ear, "I'm the only boyfriend you need, Charlotte Callaway. Quit making me work so hard for a kiss."

She faced him, bit her lip, and gazed into his eyes considering this was the moment she had dreamt about all summer.

She thought again, *Why am I playing hard to get?*

She tried to push away once again when she felt his strong arms grab her and pull her in closer.

Holding Charlotte felt so natural to Beau. He had longed to kiss her and now was his chance. He slowly pulled her hair away from her neck kissing it sweetly as his arms squeezed around her waist.

Charlotte was mesmerized by his persistence. She knew she couldn't continue to resist her deep feelings for him. As he kissed her neck, she whispered, "I have a boyfriend."

Beau's lips continued to lightly kiss her neck, not seeming to be bothered by Charlotte's words. Her breath became deeper as he ran his fingers around the top of her miniskirt. His lips found their way closer to hers and he whispered, "Then let him kiss you," as her lips softly touched his and kissed him back.

Chapter Nine

Reunited With Lies

Tucker didn't sleep most of the night after dropping off Isabella. As he lay in bed, he thought, *How could she be so thoughtless and share such a perfect, memorable night? Our night...with everyone...especially Mason!*

Tucker was frustrated with her to the point he didn't want to see her, but his heart kept flooding his mind with images from the night at the Abyss. He loved her more than his own life, and he hated how last night had ended. It was their senior homecoming and they both had waited for this night to come, but his mind was made up that he wasn't going.

Morning came too quickly as Tucker finally fell asleep around four. Sun rays peeked through the window of his room around ten, and he responded by pulling his pillow over his head to hide from the light. He tossed and turned for a while in his bed while his mind kept replaying Isabella whispering into Mason's ear.

Dammit, Isabella, he thought. *Mason of all people.*

Tucker almost went by Isabella's house ten times to apologize, but his pride kept stepping in the way. He decided to go fishing instead to clear his mind. He gathered all his gear and drove out to Lake Danik.

His parents were gone for the weekend on a business trip, so he had the house to himself. *My luck*, he thought as he cast the line into the water. *My parents are gone for the night, and I'm here alone.*

Tucker spent all day at the lake thinking about what happened the night before and the longer he was without Isabella he began feeling bad for being so hard on her. Slowly, his resentment toward her turned into a desire to find her, wrap his arms around her, and tell her he was sorry.

He tried calling Isabella when he returned home from fishing, but her mom answered and said she had already left for the dance.

So, she decided to go, I guess. He sat for a bit pondering whether he should just surprise her at the dance and take a chance that she had moved past their fight.

If I just have a minute to talk to her, I know she will understand.

***

Dressed in a navy coat jacket and navy dress pants, Tucker made his way out of the door with Isabella's pink corsage hoping to find her desperately waiting for him in the gym.

He didn't see her car in the parking lot at the dance. *Maybe she rode with someone else*, he thought while he walked through the crowd of people. As he made his way to the back of the gym where the stage was set up, he saw some of her friends. "Hey, have y'all seen Isabella? Did she happen to ride with one of y'all?"

"No, we haven't seen her tonight. We did see her get out a couple hours ago at The Dixie, but we left right after to set up the photo booth for the dance," they replied as they turned back to the stage putting away some boxes.

Tucker wondered where in the world she could be. After making another pass around the gym and not seeing her, he decided to drive over to The Dixie to see if she was there. As he drove into the parking lot, he saw her car parked in the back behind the building. But Isabella was nowhere to be found. He asked a few friends that were hanging around the parking lot and no one had seen her that evening. He parked next to her car and stayed there for an hour or so knowing she would be coming back to claim her car eventually.

Hours later, Tucker heard soft tapping on the passenger side window. On the other side of the soft tap was a beautiful blonde in a sequined pink dress staring pitifully through the window.

"Tucker! What in the world are you doing?" exclaimed Isabella through the glass. "Open the door!"

He wiped his eyes to clear his vision, leaned over, and unlocked the passenger door. Isabella scooted onto the bench seat of his truck.

"What time is it?" he asked.

"Two in the morning," she replied as she scooted in closer to him. He leaned up and wrapped both arms around the steering wheel.

"Where have you been?" Tucker asked her pointedly.

"I was just out with friends." She looked down at the floorboard of the truck.

"Out...with friends?" he said, confused. "Isabella, your friends were at the homecoming dance. I saw them when I went looking for you at the school. You weren't there."

She leaned into Tucker, grabbing his arm, and pulling it down from the steering wheel to hers. *He went looking for me*, she thought.

"Well, I'm here now." She touched her lips softly on his.

Tucker began to kiss her back, then quickly pulled away.

"No, this doesn't feel right, Isabella. Answer me – I have a right to know – where were you?" he asked as he pulled away from her.

Ashamed, but fearful he would find out from Mason, she explained that she had ridden to the lake with him, and they had a few drinks. "I promise, Tucker, nothing happened! We just had a few drinks, that's all!" she cried while he opened the door of his truck and kicked his boots in the dirt on the ground.

"Dammit, Isabella, why are you drawn to him? First, you tell Mason all about our sex life and then you spend *our* homecoming night *with* him?" Tucker continued looking toward the ground as Isabella stepped out of the truck behind him and wrapped her arms around his waist.

"Please turn around and look at me," she said. "Nothing happened, I swear. You have to believe me. I love you, and I'm sorry I messed up our homecoming."

His heart was broken knowing Isabella spent their senior homecoming night with Mason. Tucker wanted to believe her. His plans for the evening were to leave the dance and spend a romantic evening at his house since his parents were away. The night had certainly taken a different route.

"Baby, what are you thinking? Please talk to me!" she said caressing his arm and waist.

Tucker turned to her and, leaning in close, kissed Isabella more passionately than he had before. "I love you, more than you apparently know. I've sat here for hours waiting for you. I know I was an asshole last night and I'm sorry. But Mason…of all people you could've chosen to be with. You chose Mason!?" He held her face softly in his hands.

A tear rolled down Isabella's cheek as a small part of her screamed, *Tell him!* but she knew it would break his heart. "I love you more than anything too. I promise nothing happened between me and Mason tonight. I swear. I went with him as a friend to the lake, and we had a few beers and hung out."

As much as Tucker wanted to push Isabella away, his heart pulled him closer to her and his body pressed against hers while they fell back onto the seat of his truck.

Chapter Ten

Homecoming Shenanigans

Beau and Charlotte had become inseparable. Wherever she was, he wasn't too far away. They were the perfect couple, and they both knew it. Between Friday night football games and hanging out at The Dixie with friends, every weekend night during football season was predictable. The trio had divided with Charlotte's attention focused solely on Beau.

They still hung out, just not as much as they did before he came into the picture.

Homecoming was getting closer, and Charlotte was stressing about what color dress she wanted to wear. Holding up two dresses Charlotte bought from B's boutique in Marksville a few weeks prior she looked at Whitney and Stella in her bedroom mirror.

"What color should I go with girls?" Charlotte pulled the royal blue one closer to her body and pretended to dance in the mirror and then exchanged it for the slinkier baby pink one with the cut-out back, then threw them both back on the bed.

Shrugging with indecision, she fell back onto the mattress. "The night has to be perfect, and it all starts with my dress. Beau needs to be mesmerized when he first sees me walk down those steps."

"Well, we all know he's mesmerized by you even without a formal dress," Stella responded sarcastically with a smug grin.

"Shut up!" Charlotte laughed as she threw one of her bed pillows at Stella who only ducked and giggled. Charlotte then picked up the baby pink one and went to try it on in her bathroom.

Stella put the royal blue dress up to her body and sashayed with it in front of the mirror. "I am asking the quarterback from Avoyelles High to bring me. Well, honestly, I'm going to *tell* him he has to go with me. We have been friends since daycare days, and well I don't have a boyfriend so..."

When Stella said she was telling someone to do something, that usually ended with her winning. She made it difficult for anyone to tell her no, except for Jackson. His ability to ignore her was a mystery and made her even more frustrated that she couldn't win him over. As she turned around to put the dress back on the bed, she noticed Whitney sitting on the floor staring into space.

"Whit, girl, you have been quiet. What is going on with you?"

Whitney smiled. "Oh, nothing is wrong. Just thinking about who I want to go to the dance with that's all." Whitney had never been open about her feelings for Beau, but Stella knew she liked him. *Who didn't like Beau?*

Charlotte and Whitney were close enough friends that Whitney was okay taking the back seat. Was she jealous? Absolutely. However, she cared enough not to jeopardize something truly special like their relationship. Besides, she could've asked any boy on the football team, and the answer would've been yes. The boys on the sidelines drooled over her during football games as she pranced on the track and waved at them, flirting the entire game. Whitney knew what she was doing.

"I'll probably go with Blaine anyway. I don't know why I'm even considering who I'll go with. He's so amazingly hot, and I melt inside when he holds me close. His hands are so strong and his muscles...I mean," Whitney forgot she was talking out loud until she realized Charlotte and Stella were staring at her shocked listening to her crush on Blaine.

"Whit! We didn't know you felt that way about Blaine!" Charlotte lay across her bed on her belly, facing Whitney on the floor.

"Well, I don't really, it's just that, well... he is pretty hot!" She laughed.

"But he's...Blaine. Mr. Hothead," Stella replied.

Whitney knew Blaine would never have a girlfriend. Who was she kidding? She never really wanted to settle down either. Her crushes spanned across the entire football team; however, she would never give any of them her entire heart.

She sat on the floor staring at her reflection in Charlotte's mirror thinking, *There is only one guy I think I could give my heart to, but unfortunately, that will never happen.*

***

The dance was only a few days away, and the halls in the high school were filled with green and white streamers, paper chains, and various banners labeled with "Beat the Bears" and "Mustangs Stomp 'Em'." The faculty despised homecoming week because the student's focus wasn't on Algebra, US History, or English. Rather, the halls of the school were filled with whispers of who had dumped whom and who was now going with someone else or who didn't get asked to the dance.

Beau and Charlotte started sharing a locker so they could see each other during the five brief minutes they had between classes. They didn't have any classes together so they savored every minute they could to sneak a quick kiss.

"Hey, Beau." I purposely interrupted him while his lips found their way down Charlotte's neck. "Gross, get a room!" I said while Beau casually turned to me.

"What, Nessie? What now? Let me guess. The school is on fire, and you want to save the day?"

Beau laughed while Charlotte quickly kissed his cheek and said, "I got to get to class."

Most days my grandmother picked me up since Beau had practice after school, but today I didn't have a ride. I had a late November birthday ––hence the last person in our freshman class to get their license.

"Remember you have to give me a ride home today after school. Grandma can't and––"

Cutting me off, he pushed me aside saying, "You have to find another ride. Coach called emergency practice this afternoon. Sorry."

He wasn't sorry. He had never been sorry one day in his life. Especially to me.

***

Whitney was always late to class and always got tardies. She typically used the excuse she was caught in the bathroom, or the office needed her. The faculty knew she was late due to primping in the mirror or flirting with every boy down the hall on the way to class. This time she was late trying to find Blaine to discuss final details about the exact shade of red she wanted in her corsage.

"Not too deep, Blaine, because it looks like Christmas. But then again not too soft because it'll resemble pink, and Char is wearing pink."

Blaine rolled his eyes. "Yeah, yeah, middle red ok. I got it." He pushed through the stragglers in the hall trying to make it to class.

"Make sure you pick the right one, Blaine. It has to be the perfect shade for my dress!" Whitney yelled while Blaine gave her a cheesy thumbs up and continued down the hall to class.

Guys suck, Whitney thought as the bell rang. She was late for class...again.

***

Stella's date from Avoyelles High had stopped by her house after school on his way to pick up his boutonniere and her corsage and asked if she wanted to ride along.

She chose to wear Charlotte's long royal blue dress and had picked out a royal blue and soft yellow combination for her corsage. "No, I think I'm going to pass," Stella replied.

While Stella was excited to go to homecoming with her friend, she longed for Jackson to change his mind and ask her to the dance. She thought about Jackson constantly. While she was at school, she tried to search for him and find ways to get next to him. At home, she tried to block him out, but his perfect face and genuine smile were all she kept seeing.

Jackson has to be wanting someone else, she thought. *What's so wrong with me that he wouldn't give me a chance?*

***

The team enjoyed a little fun after their Friday night win which provided some reprieve from the intense practices. Coach had given the team Saturday and Sunday off due to the homecoming dance and it felt like vacation to them.

After Friday night's game, the team was stoked to kick start their short reprieve from practice. While the team knew it wasn't permanent, they soaked up the small ounce of freedom they were given.

Beau couldn't wait to spend every minute with Charlotte. Other than seeing her at his locker and sneaking in a quick kiss, their relationship had been put on hold due to football.

She patiently waited for him to come out of the locker room after the game. Coach had centered the team's focus the past week on Friday night's game which left Charlotte alone and all in her feelings. Her emotions ran wild expecting their night to be perfect.

When Beau exited the locker room door, Charlotte ran toward him jumping into his arms. Dropping his football bag, he caught her, and they spun around holding each other close. *It feels so good to be back in his arms,* Charlotte thought as Beau held her tightly not relinquishing his hold.

"I've missed you so much, babe, and I'm sorry this week has sucked for you," he said while she slowly dropped her legs from around his waist. The rest of the team continued to exit the locker room jokingly laughing while Beau and Charlotte remained entranced staring at one another oblivious of the stares and jokes.

"Get a room you two." Blaine straightened his baseball cap as he stood by Whitney and Stella. Charlotte rolled her eyes at Blaine and, latching hands with Beau, walked to meet their friends.

"Everyone headed to The Dixie tonight?" Stella asked the group while fixating her eyes on Jackson who was standing behind Blaine.

"Well, hell yeah, Stella." Blaine picked up Whitney by her legs and threw her over his shoulder. "Y'all coming!?" he yelled as Whitney screamed for him to put her down.

Stella, determined to get closer to Jackson, found herself standing next to him as everyone retreated to their cars. *This is my perfect opportunity*, she thought. "Hey Jackson, want to ride with me over to The Dixie and hang out?"

Jackson, watching Beau and Charlotte fade into the distance replied, "Thanks, Stella, but I'm going to pass. It's been a long week. I'm going to head home."

As he walked away, Stella thought, *I'm the perfect match for him, and he just doesn't see it.*

"Your loss," she muttered as she turned and ran toward Blaine and Whitney who were still in the parking lot.

***

Beau and Charlotte enjoyed most of their night holding each other close and visiting with friends at The Dixie. It felt like old times again even though she knew it was temporary. Beau didn't want the night to end, but midnight rolled around soon, and she had to meet curfew.

He loved the drive out to her house as the road followed the curves of Bayou Fueob. Every curve that Beau's Corvette took gracefully,

Charlotte's head remained pressed against his shoulder with her arm around his waist.

When they pulled into the driveway, he stopped the car and put it into park. "Midnight, right on the dot," he said as he saw the time on his dash.

"Well, technically Dad wants me in the house at midnight not still sitting in the car with my boyfriend." She grinned.

Reaching his arm around her body attempting to coax her over to the driver seat, he motioned for her to sit on his lap.

Beau's hands found their way up the sides of her track shorts while he softly kissed along her collarbone and up her neck.

Charlotte's body felt weak as she had almost forgotten how amazing his touch and kiss felt. The last thing she wanted was for him to stop touching her or for this perfect night to end. Her hands found their way under his shirt purposefully feeling every inch of his muscular chest.

Was something really going to happen here? Charlotte wondered while Beau's hold became stronger. She felt his hands begin to pull up the bottom of her shirt. Her heart started racing, her mind going in circles. *This is about to happen...I'm about to lose my virginity to Beau Corbin.*

Now shirtless, her breasts hiding behind her lacey, light pink bra, she reached her arms to her back to release the bra clasp.

Beau's emotions were running wild as he placed his hands on hers and the pink bra fell to the floorboard. When she leaned in to kiss him, he heard the ring of his bag phone breaking through the faint sound of the car radio.

"Come here." He pulled on her waist, ignoring the sound of the call. For a moment, the only sound was the soft music coming from the radio as he leaned his seat backward and she fell on top of him.

The bag phone kept ringing again, over, and over, until, obviously frustrated, he pulled his seat back up and answered it.

"What!" he exclaimed as she covered her exposed chest with her shirt.

When she heard Isabella's voice echoing from the phone, "Beau, where are you?" She found her bra on the floorboard and jumped back to the passenger side of the car.

Beau could've thrown the phone out of his car at this point and seeing the disappointment on Charlotte's face made him even more angry.

Trying to calm his impulses and frustration, Beau finally replied, "Mom, really, it's twelve-thirty. I'm usually not home until after one. I gotta go," and he hung up the phone.

He leaned back in his seat and threw his hands at the steering wheel and screamed, "Dammit! That's so messed up." Reaching over the console, Beau took Charlotte's hand and said, "I'm sorry, babe. This is obviously not how I wanted this to end tonight."

She rubbed her hand across his, also disappointed that they were interrupted.

"Maybe it was an omen. Maybe things are moving too fast, and it wasn't the right time."

Looking down toward her lap, then back at him, she leaned in closer, placing her hands on his face and bringing his lips closer to hers, and said, "I will always love you, Beau Corbin. Tonight, was perfect. You're my forever love."

***

Mason carefully tip-toed into the kitchen around three in the morning. He couldn't sleep, and he knew why. His daughter's new *boyfriend*.

He'd never really talked much to Beau but if the little ass was anything like his mother, then Charlotte was only going to get hurt. And if he were being honest, he just couldn't stand that she was dating Isabella's son.

Walking toward the fridge to grab a bottle of water, he stumbled into a barstool spilling the contents of Charlotte's purse. Mason slammed his hands down on the kitchen counter, staring at the spilled contents on the kitchen floor. Cursing about his now-aching toe didn't compare to the blue streak he spewed when he gathered up the mess--and saw her packet of birth control pills.

Prescribed by none other than that bitch Isabella Corbin!

So, not only had she tried to ruin his life as a teenager, now she was trying to ruin his precious Charlotte's!

Fuming, he stuffed everything back into her purse and grabbed a beer instead of the bottle of water he'd come downstairs for.

Well, we'll just see about this, Isabella. We'll just see...

Chapter Eleven

Every Girls Dream

Charlotte had been dreaming of this day for a long time. Her first high school homecoming dance and it was made even sweeter since she had snagged the hottest boy at school to be her date. Most days she felt like a princess, and it regularly showed, but today seemed surreal. She had managed to wrap the quarterback's heart around her finger, and it felt amazing. That's every girl's dream, right? Nothing could mess up what they had going.

The trio met up the morning of the dance at the Callaway's house. Charlotte's mom Melissa had planned the perfect girl's day filled with brunch, getting their hair fixed at the salon in town followed by their makeup. She planned for the girls to feel like princesses for their first high school homecoming.

Mason was too frustrated to stay home amidst the chaos of homecoming preparation - and seeing Isabella's son in his home. As much as he wanted to confront Charlotte about the birth control pills and tell Melissa, he chose not to ruin the moment. He would find the right time to bring it up. Exhausted, he spent the remainder of the morning and most of the day sleeping on his secluded deer stand.

Stella and Whitney drove up at the same time. Hauling their bags and dresses up the porch steps they sweetly yelled, "Hey Mrs. M!"

Melissa laughed as she watched them haul their homecoming necessities up the stairs to Charlotte's room. It appeared like they were moving in. "Girls, let me know if y'all need any help up there," Melissa yelled from the base of the staircase.

"We are okay for now Mom," Charlotte replied.

Melissa took the girls to have brunch in town at AELs. The special of the day was bacon, scrambled eggs, pancakes and hashbrowns. The most important part of the special was always the dessert...AELs famous pecan pie!

As the girls sat down at the booth by the window, Charlotte noticed Isabella was sitting at a two-top with Dr. Dawson drinking coffee. They were in deep discussion while Isabella took notes on a paper tablet. Charlotte quickly turned around hoping Isabella wouldn't notice her.

As soon as Whitney sat down in the booth, she noticed Isabella across the room. "Mrs. Issie!" she exclaimed and ran over.

Isabella looked up from her coffee and embraced her. "My sweet girl, what are you doing here?"

"Oh, me, Char, and Stella are here with Mrs. M for brunch and then we are getting our hair fixed for the dance," Whitney said, oblivious that Isabella had to know Charlotte was going to the dance with Beau.

"Oh, yes, I seem to have forgotten about the dance. I've been so busy at work. I, unfortunately, let that slip by me." As she reached to take a sip of her coffee, she peered over to Whitney's table and noticed Charlotte, made quick eye contact, then looked back at her tablet. She then looked at Whitney, gave a sly smile, and said, "I'm sure you'll be beautiful tonight, sweetie. It has been so crazy lately that I don't recall whom my Beau is going with...?"

Whitney walked back over to the table and put a smile on her face despite her curiosity about why Isabella was being so hard on Charlotte.

"What was that all about?" Charlotte questioned Whitney as she stared out the window.

"Oh, nothing! Mrs. Issie was debating something with Dr. Dawson, and they asked my opinion," she lied.

Why did Isabella gaze over at me so hatefully then? Charlotte thought.

"Girl, she said you were going to be so gorgeous tonight, and Beau couldn't wait to see you." Whitney leaned into Charlotte smiling.

Charlotte smiled back but knew in her heart that Isabella was against her. Something just wasn't right.

***

After brunch, Melissa took them to the hairstylist for the afternoon, and the girls enjoyed being pampered with washes, color, curls, and a little teased hair. It felt great to be together again, the three of them, just like old times.

After their hair appointments, Melissa took the girls back to the house to put the final touches – their makeup. She'd hired a friend who was a makeup artist to make them more beautiful. The make-up artist had every shade of pink and red imaginable in every kind of product. The girls were mesmerized.

Stella stepped into the beautiful royal blue gown that followed every curve on her body. The back of the dress showed her back beautifully, and it fell perfectly off her hips, tapering toward the floor offering a nice slit up the right side exposing her leg.

"Stella! You're absolutely killing it tonight in that dress!" Whitney said as she walked from Charlotte's bathroom in only her bra, panties, and high heels. "I can't get dressed yet though." She plopped down on Charlotte's bed thinking about what Isabella had said at brunch. *She didn't mean anything by that, Whitney. Just let it go*, she told herself while getting up from the bed.

Charlotte made her way gracefully from her closet and faced Whitney and Stella in her very slim, baby-pink dress.

She undeniably looked like a queen, only without a crown. Her dress accentuated Charlotte's long, dark brown hair. Pink wispy fur wrapped around her chest and followed the slit that exposed her tanned leg.

She jokingly modeled for Stella and Whitney and then faced the mirror and thought, *I look amazing.*

Noticing it was almost five o'clock, Whitney finally slipped on her dark, burgundy dress. Her body had more curves than Charlotte and Stella combined. Her dress easily accentuated her well-endowed chest. Her blonde ringlets hung just appropriately at the base of her neck.

"*I can get any guy I want,*" Whitney said under her breath as she admired herself in the mirror.

***

Blaine had announced earlier in the week that he was having a bonfire at the farm following the homecoming dance. His parties were always the talk of the town before and after the party. His dad, along with some friends, helped him haul logs into the open field for the bonfire.

The land was often the site for parties since it was out of town – which meant it was off-radar for the police.

Blaine's parents weren't oblivious to what was going on at his parties. They wanted the kids to have fun – but responsible fun. They had one rule that everyone knew had to be followed: anyone who drank more than they should had to spend the night.

Blaine wasn't overly excited about the dance. He was only going because Whitney required him to, and he didn't want to jeopardize having her as his hot date for the party afterward. While the party was the only thing on his mind, he knew he had to focus on being a gentleman for a little while.

Blaine arrived at Charlotte's house around five-thirty as instructed by Whitney. When he got out of his car, he saw her walk onto the porch to meet him. As he met her on the top step, he set her corsage down on the porch rail, leaned in, and kissed her cheek, then softly said, "You look amazing, Whitney."

"You look pretty hot yourself!" she said laughing while he grabbed her around the waist and spun her around in the air.

"Put me down, Blaine! You're going to mess up my dress!"

He finally cooperated, setting her down. He removed her corsage from the plastic container sitting on the edge of the porch rail.

"I hope this is the right color," he said as he stretched the elastic and pulled it over her wrist.

She was amazed that he had selected the most perfect color that matched her dress.

"Wow! Blaine, you listened for once!" Whitney admired the beautiful crimson roses on her corsage.

I've finally done something right! he thought.

Still admiring her corsage, she didn't notice his continued stare.

She's freakin' so hot – and she's my date!

He stroked his hands along her dress. He couldn't help but pull her closer, and they fell into a deep kiss.

Stella walked out on the porch anxiously waiting for her date to arrive and saw Blaine and Whitney making out while leaning against the porch column.

"Gross, stop it!" she said, staring curiously down the drive hoping to see her date pulling up.

"Where's your man, Stella?" Blaine said jokingly.

"He's coming, Blaine," Stella replied rolling her eyes. "Just please stop petting my friend like that. Give Whit some room to breathe!"

He relinquished his hold on Whitney and walked down the steps onto the driveway when he saw Beau pulling up. The guys exchanged their ego-centered football handshake and headed back toward the porch.

As Beau walked up the porch steps, he caught a glimpse of Charlotte making her way down the foyer to the front door. For a moment, he was completely speechless.

Blaine, noticing Beau's obvious infatuation at seeing Charlotte, nudged him on the arm and laughingly said, "Snap out of it, man!" He couldn't fathom feeling so deeply for a girl––especially in his second year of high school. Leaning closer to Beau to get his attention, Blaine laughed out loud saying "Dude, you're ruined."

When Charlotte appeared through the doorway, Beau's heart melted. She was gorgeous. Her pink dress fit tightly to her perfect body accentuating every curve perfectly. Her soft, long brown curls danced happily on the edges of the pink fur that outlined her dress along her chest.

She spun in a circle upon Beau at the door and landed her arms around his neck. "What do you think, Mr. Corbin?" she asked as he wrapped his arms around her back pulling her in close.

"Beautiful, you're just beautiful, Miss Callaway." Beau gently kissed her lips. "This night is going to be perfect," he raised her arm to twirl her then pulled her back closer against his chest, "because I'm sharing it with you." For a moment, the world seemed to stop as they stood under the soft porch lights staring into each other's eyes. As he leaned in to kiss her again, they were interrupted by Whitney's scream.

"Put me down, Blaine!" she yelled as he threw her over his shoulder and jokingly tried to spin her in the air. He moved toward Beau and Charlotte, Whitney thrashing trying to escape his hold. "Stop joking around and put me down now!" She shouted again.

Beau led Charlotte to the other side of the porch hoping to have a few moments alone. "You look so beautiful...I can't take my eyes off of you." Charlotte felt his hands move alongside her hips as his lips touched hers. "I love you Beau...and yes...this night is going to be perfect." He took her corsage from the plastic box and placed it carefully on her wrist. "It's beautiful! Pink roses are my favorite! They are just perfect!" Her fingers carefully glazed over the top of each rose. Gazing into his eyes she whispered, "I love you so much." He kissed her softly once more. "They are perfect like you."

***

Whitney noticed Stella's date hadn't yet arrived and asked, "Stella, where's your date? It's getting close to six."

"Girl, don't even get me started. He knows how I feel about people being punctual," Stella replied. "And he's going to get a piece of my mind about this. It's BS that he's making me wait!"

About the time she finished her ranting, dim lights could be seen at the end of the driveway. "Well, he must have heard me talking about him!" She moved closer to the front porch steps to meet her date, but as the lights got close, she struggled to determine if it was her date or someone else.

When the vehicle moved closer to the house, Stella's heart began to flutter. To her surprise, Jackson stepped out of his Jeep Wrangler and, looking more handsome than ever, walked up to the porch.

"Jackson." Stella smiled as he casually looked her way and then kept walking up the steps past her.

"Hey, Stella," Jackson responded flatly.

What in the world is he doing here? Stella thought.

"Hey, man! What's up!" Stella could hear Beau and Blaine greeting Jackson in the background.

"Stella!" called Melissa from inside. "Honey, come inside. You have a phone call."

As Stella approached the front door, Jackson casually leaned up against the wall, his hands in his pant pockets. *He looks so hot*, Stella thought while she slowly walked past him wishing he would notice her. But he just stared ahead watching the rest of the group discuss the events of the night.

Stella returned to the porch minutes later and announced that her date was sick with the flu and had fallen asleep and forgotten to call her. *Just my luck*, Stella thought as she stared at the couples ready to celebrate the evening–together. She glanced at Jackson hoping he might comfort her and ask her to join him. "*Who am I kidding? He doesn't act like I exist.*"

Whitney and Charlotte knew that Stella could accept going to the dance alone, but the thought crossed their minds that it made sense for Jackson and Stella to go as friends.

Beau, noticing that Stella was trying to get Jackson's attention, pulled him aside saying, "Hey, man. She doesn't have a date tonight.

I'm not saying you two have to go as a date, but you could bring her, so she doesn't feel like the third wheel."

Jackson hadn't planned to attend the dance, however, Kent and Allison persuaded him to go. He could've kicked himself for agreeing now that he was faced with having to make small talk with Stella. "I didn't even plan to be here, Beau. Now I feel obligated to take her just because her date cancelled. This sucks."

The trio had gone back inside to freshen their makeup for pictures. "Do y'all think Jackson'll ask me or will we be weird like third wheels all night?" Stella asked Whitney & Charlotte while reapplying their lipstick in the powder room.

"He should ask you. I mean, it's not like y'all have to date or anything. He's technically a third wheel too, so it makes sense for y'all to ride together," Charlotte replied.

"I guess so." Stella shrugged. "It would be nice if he would just look at me. Damn, I can't figure him out!"

The trio walked into the living area, where Melissa had set up a backdrop for pictures. Beau and Charlotte went first followed by Whitney and Blaine and then multiple poses of just the girls. Jackson had stopped at the far end of the living room hoping to be forgotten. It was awkward when the couples made their way back to the front porch with Stella closely behind. Feeling relieved no one instigated a couple's picture with her, Jackson was the last to follow the group to the front porch.

"How are we riding?" Beau asked as everyone gathered their things.

Charlotte, seeing how uncomfortable Stella and Jackson were at this point, offered, "Why don't Jackson and Stella just ride with me and Beau in my car?"

Beau, frowning toward Charlotte, wasn't in agreement since he was hoping they could recreate what almost happened the night before.

"No, that isn't going to work. Sorry," Jackson quickly responded. "I'm not staying long at the after-party, and I'm sure y'all will be out late." He gave a half grin.

At this point, Stella was over it. She walked over to her car and said, "I'll meet y'all at the dance."

Chapter Twelve

The Bonfire

The dance captured the attention span of students for about one hour then naturally their focus shifted to the after-party at Blaine's. All the planning, dress shopping, shoes, hair and makeup, and deciphering who is going with whom - is that worth the hour, at most, that students end up spending at the dance? Sounds ridiculous, doesn't it?

Beau and Charlotte posed for a few pictures in front of the backdrop and then snuck into the hall to be alone. Holding hands, he softly squeezed hers signaling to move closer to him. Just as Beau was about to lean in and kiss her, Whitney burst through the gym doors.

"There y'all are!" she exclaimed, Blaine following closely behind. "Beau, I need you to tell Blaine we need to stay a little longer. He's obviously had enough of the dance and wants to get out of here."

"Damn right I do!" he said walking up behind Whitney. "There is a keg of beer waiting for all of us – right now – so, what are we still doing hanging at this lame dance?"

Beau laughed knowing nothing was going to change Blaine's mind at this point. Kissing Charlotte quickly on the lips he replied, "Let's take this party to Blaine's then."

Cars began to line the gravel driveway leading to the Ferrell Farm. Mr. Ferrell directed everyone to park in a pasture across the gravel drive. Around ten-thirty, most everyone had circled around the bonfire. Blaine had backed a few farm trucks up to the bonfire and lowered the tailgates to provide seating. It was a clear, cool October evening. The most perfect night for a bonfire.

Leaning against the tailgate of one of the trucks, Blaine pushed himself up to sit in the bed and grabbed another beer out of the ice chest. "Grab me one," Whitney yelled as she walked toward him.

Blaine, holding both beer cans in his hands, wrapped his arms around Whitney's waist and pulled her between his legs asking, "I got you a beer, so what are you going to do for me?"

Whitney rolled her eyes because she was used to Blaine's flirtatious nature. "Whatever, Blaine, give me the beer."

He set the beers aside and his hands found the back pockets of her jeans. Filling every inch of her pockets, he pulled her closer.

"You're persistent." Whitney softly kissed his neck.

His hands worked their way under the bottom edge of her blouse and his fingers began to slowly follow her curves upward. She pulled back slightly and planted each hand on the tailgate framing his torso.

She casually grabbed one of the beer cans and placed her index finger on his lips. "Maybe later."

As Whitney turned to walk away, Blaine jumped off the tailgate laughing and said, "Playing hard to get, are you?"

Dancing her way back to the fire, she turned back and yelled, "You bet your ass I am!"

***

Charlotte found herself in the most perfect spot lying in the bed of one of the trucks leaning up against Beau. Her small frame fit nicely wedged between his outstretched legs. His arms were tightly wrapped around her waist as they both looked up to the clear night sky.

This had to be the most perfect night ever.

Beau softly caressed her body while she lay against him soaking it all in. He tried hard to slow his impulses, but she made that almost impossible.

"This night is so perfect," she said, looking up at him while leaning her head against his chest.

Beau smiled as his hands grabbed her pulling her closer. "I agree. This night is perfect. I have the girl of my dreams lying here in my lap. I can kiss her when I want to and as much as I want to."

"Awe, you're so sweet," Charlotte said smiling back, dramatically putting her hands on her heart. Then she positioned herself on top of his body, leaned in closer, and said, "Well, you *think* you can kiss me whenever you want."

His hands cradled her hips. "We'll see about that!" And he pulled her closer.

"Uh, um," was heard faintly in the background while the melody from a slow country song filled the night air. Charlotte and Beau peeked up from the bed of the truck to see Blaine leaning over the side.

"Well, isn't this just a pretty sight?" Blaine said as he jumped into the bed. Holding up two beer cans, he clanked them together. "I hope I'm not interrupting anything, but you two have been at it over here for a while by yourself. Why don't y'all come over and join the rest of the party and have a beer?"

Knowing that Blaine wasn't going to leave them alone, Beau helped Charlotte slide to the edge of the tailgate. He looked back at Blaine, frustrated that he had interrupted them. It was nice to hold Charlotte close and kiss her at his pace and not be interrupted – at least until hot head showed up. Holding her close to his chest in his arms felt so perfect, like nothing he had ever felt.

As he looked back at her sitting on the tailgate, Beau knew there was something special about her that had him completely mesmerized.

***

After Blaine coerced them to come join the party, minutes later Beau saw Blaine and Whitney intensely kissing each other near the barn in the distance.

"Well, look at that," Beau said. Charlotte sat in his lap on one of the tailgates closest to the fire.

"You surprised?" Charlotte replied as he squeezed his arms tightly around her waist pulling her backward into the bed of the truck.

He finally had her back where he wanted her. Gazing into her eyes while she lay beneath him on the bed of the truck, her favorite song came on blaring across the speakers.

"Dance with me Beau, please," she whispered as she kissed his lips softly and pushed herself up.

Disappointed that once again another intimate moment was sabotaged, he stood up next to Charlotte in the bed of the truck as they danced to her favorite song. She realized quickly that he was struggling to dance. While he had exceptional skills on the football field, his dancing skills left more to be desired.

"What is so funny?" he asked, his arm latched around her waist.

Looking up at him, Charlotte smirked. "Your dancing, well, let's just say you definitely need to stick to the football field!"

"You think it is funny this quarterback can't dance, huh?" he replied as he picked her up and spun her around in the back of the truck. She struggled against his strong hold to break free.

"You're not getting away that easy." Beau laughed as he guided her slow descent to the bed of the truck closely nestled in his arms. Moving her hair to expose her ear, Charlotte felt her body tremble anticipating his sweet kiss. To her surprise, he softly whispered, "I think we have had enough of my dancing!"

She giggled and faced him. "Yeah, I think you make a good point." She felt Beau's strong hold on her waist as her hands cradled the back of his neck. Running her fingers in his hair she pulled his lips closer. "Besides, I'd rather do this instead."

***

It was near midnight and a few stragglers remaining at the party saw Blaine and Whitney making out near the side of the barn. Most were disinterested as they looked back toward the fire taking sips of their drink while holding their date closely. Blaine and Whitney seemed perfect for one another since they lived each day to the fullest and never planned for a second more. Everyone assumed they would end up "dating," but it would never be any more than that - if dating was even the correct reference. Blaine's reputation of being a player coupled with Whitney's undying love for herself certainly made for a perfect relationship storm.

Tonight, however, they had been committed to one another – from the dance to the party – Blaine had his hands all over Whitney most of the night. Leaning against the rough wooden wall, he pressed his strong, muscular body up against her as he kissed every inch of exposed skin on her chest. His fingers followed the rim of her jeans along her waist while she began to loosen his belt. She wanted him just as much as he longed for her…nothing romantic…just to be with someone.

He removed her top and continued kissing her chest while his fingers softly pulled down the straps from her bra. Her body became weaker when he removed the lacy cups exposing her breasts. He pulled her closer to his chest softly kissed her neck, then found her lips. Without saying a word, he could see that she wanted him as much as he wanted her.

Blaine led Whitney inside the barn and pulled a few horse blankets down from the top of the stable then laid them across the hay. He kissed her gently as he coaxed her onto the blankets.

Later, as car lights began to fade down the long gravel drive, Whitney found herself naked, lying securely in Blaine's arms.

Chapter Thirteen

The Grand Annual Event

The Grand Annual Event, to me, was nothing more than Isabella's conceited way of showing her flashiness to the town and her old friends that she was rich. I hated the event. While I had to contribute by smiling and welcoming guests to our home, I wanted to die inside. I hated attention drawn to myself not to mention my family. Money didn't make our family perfect, however, Isabella had managed to make the town believe we *were* the perfect family.

The event consisted of social elites from Isabella's doctor friends combined with many of Tucker's attorney friends. In my honest opinion, it was a reunion of a large group of rich, conceited people who bathed in wealth and stories of their continued prominence in society.

The Grand Annual Event was born out of a desire to visit New Orleans, aka NOLA, every fall. When their friends discovered Tucker and Isabella lived along the path to their destination, they extended their trip a few days to incorporate some time on the bayou. "What a marvelous place to hold our annual event," they would say while strolling through the backyard along Bayou Fueob, sipping on wine.

"Beau, you didn't say it was like a president was coming to visit!" Charlotte said, taking in all the catering and delivery trucks lining the long driveway to his home.

"It's mom's annual event this Saturday, and I'm just warning you, she's in beast planning mode. So don't take offense if she's short with you. She's been short with all of us - all week," he said as he got out of his car and went to open her door.

"Oh, stop! You kill me with your "gentleman-ness," she said and stole a quick kiss before heading inside.

They walked up to the front porch hand in hand where Isabella was pointing to florists on the placement of topiaries and ferns.

"Well, Beau, this must be Charlotte," Isabella said dryly, turning toward them. "I don't have much time to visit. I have to wrap up a few things here and be back at the clinic by four-thirty. Nice to...*meet you, Charlotte*." She passed by slightly breezing her shoulder.

Isabella gritted her teeth as she walked away. *How dare that girl show up here after coming in for birth control– just so she could sleep with Beau!* She'd have to tell Tucker to have a talk with him about using protection.

Charlotte immediately felt a sense of coldness from Isabella and, grabbing onto Beau's arm, said, "Your mom doesn't like me, does she?" She knew it had to be from the day at the clinic.

He smirked at her and reached his strong arms around her waist, pulling her close. "My mom doesn't like any of my girlfriends, but she'll love you once she gets to know you." Charlotte immediately pushed Beau away, slapping his pecks that were bulging out from his tight football shirt from practice.

"Really, all *your girlfriends*," she said mockingly, rolling her eyes.

She crossed her arms and kept them crossed as he moved in closer trying to break apart her stronghold across her chest.

"C'mon, you know you're my girl, the only one I love," Beau whispered into her ear.

Every time his lips got near her ear or neck her body melted. Even in his sweaty practice jersey, he seemed to take over every part of her body. Maybe it was his natural, undeniable charm?

Beau grabbed Charlotte's hand. As they walked into the house, he led her to the kitchen where Tucker was eating a sandwich.

"Hi, I bet you're Charlotte," said Tucker extending his arms out to hug her.

Charlotte felt Tucker's sincerity at once and a sense of peace fell over her. She gave him a hug as Beau went to the fridge to grab two waters and a few snacks.

"Mom's on a mission still," Beau said to Tucker who was now by the sink washing his plate, looking out the window.

"Yeah, you know this is what she does. She yearns for this event all year long and when it gets here, she runs herself ragged–and all her family crazy." Tucker grabbed a bottle of Chardonnay from the wine rack.

"I can hear y'all talking about me!" Isabella shouted as she made her way into the kitchen with her tablet. "You know Charlotte, I expect you to defend me when these boys talk behind my back," she dryly said glaring at Charlotte, waiting for her reaction. "After all, talking about what someone does behind their back isn't right – even if you wanted to."

"Oh, yes, ma'am, of course," replied Charlotte while discreetly motioning Beau to save her.

"Mom, really." He grabbed Charlotte's hand and walked past Isabella. "We weren't talking about you. We were just describing what this week has felt like for us."

Isabella rolled her eyes and smiled at Beau; she could never get mad at him.

***

Beau and Charlotte went up to his room and sat on his bed. "I'm sorry about Mom." He moved closer on the bed toward her attempting to kiss her. She stared blankly at the bedroom wall.

"Hey, what's wrong, babe? I know my mom can be a lot–"

She cut him off. "It's not that. I can handle it, I guess. She just continues to act like she doesn't know me."

"What do you mean by that?" he asked as he leaned closer to her. Charlotte didn't want to share the clinic visit, so she changed the subject.

"I guess she's just protective of her *'sweet little Beau,'*" she said jokingly pushing against his hold on her. "I am disappointed that I didn't get an invite to the event though. Whit mentioned it today at school and was surprised I didn't know anything about it." Charlotte rested her head on Beau's shoulder.

"Whitney got an invite, and you didn't?" he asked, looking toward Charlotte puzzled.

She played with the frayed ends of her shirt. "Yeah, Whit showed it to me, addressed directly to her from your mom. She said she's been going for several years as your guest. I didn't plan to bring it up to you..." that's why I acted surprised when we drove up to your house today."

Beau stood up, his hands on his sides, pondering what in the world his mom was thinking not inviting Charlotte. "Look babe, I'm sure it is an honest misunderstanding. Mom knows you're my date, and that you're coming. Whitney's parents are friends, and Mom always includes them. Since Whitney is around my age, she's always seated us together for dinner. Otherwise, I would be seated with Nessie."

"I just wish she liked me. I know she doesn't," Charlotte said lying back on his bed.

As soon as she fell back on his mattress, Beau, realizing his opportunity, jumped on top of her holding her hands softly above her head, and kissed her.

"Can we please stop talking about my mom and focus on this?" His lips moved down her neck while his hands fondled the rim of her shorts. "You're beautiful, Miss Callaway," he whispered to her kissing every inch of her skin his lips could touch.

As Beau's lips found their way across her body, thoughts of the event and Isabella faded from Charlotte's mind. Every kiss felt so perfect, and her body became weightless lying on his bed. Her hands lost their way into his tousled hair, and she softly pulled him closer to kiss her. Her breathing became deeper, and her heart raced while his hand found its way under her shirt. As his body pressed closer to hers, her body became weaker as traces of sandalwood and amber from his Eternity cologne lingered on his football shirt from practice.

His lips met hers again and he kissed her deeply while his hand fondled her breast. His lips followed her jaw line to her ear and whispered, "You're so gorgeous, and I want you more than anything."

Charlotte's heart continued to race as she looked up into Beau's eyes. "What are you waiting for then?"

He swallowed deeply while his fingers danced along the top of her track shorts and slowly removed them.

She closed her eyes as she felt his body lying on top of hers. As she wrapped her arms around his muscular body, her fingers danced around the rim of his shorts hoping to remove them.

Could this really be happening?

Their blissful moment was interrupted once again by her dreadful voice. "Beau! I need you to take out the trash and feed Jasper!"

At the sound of Isabella's voice, Beau's body pressed closer to Charlotte's, and he continued kissing her.

To his dismay, Isabella continued hollering from downstairs.

"Dammit, Mom!" he yelled angrily as his eyes drifted over Charlotte's naked body. *Mom has to ruin every intimate moment for us,* Beau thought as he kissed Charlotte softly, then fell to her side.

Charlotte pulled the comforter over her while searching for her clothes. He knelt on the bed close to her. "Can you just stay here and wait for me...please? Even though we didn't get to...well...I still want to lay here and hold you."

She looked back toward him and placed her hand on his cheek. "Baby, I love you more than anything, and I want nothing more than to lay here and you hold me, but this doesn't feel right anymore...not here at least." Charlotte grabbed her clothes as Beau rounded the bed to wait for her.

Isabella shouted again loudly from below. "Beau!!!" Beau begrudgingly replied, "Okay, Mom. I'm coming! Just give me a minute!"

They made their way downstairs and met Tucker and Isabella in the living room.

"Beau, we have a lot of stuff to get done before Saturday, and I really need your help around here." Isabella cut her eyes toward Charlotte.

Getting the feeling Isabella was insinuating for her to leave, Charlotte said, "I'm going to go now. I have some things to do at home as well."

***

"Thank you again Mr. and Mrs. Corbin for having me over. I guess I'll see you Saturday for the big event." Charlotte couldn't get to the front door quickly enough.

Isabella looked at Charlotte a fake concern suddenly on her face, then said to Beau, "Well, honey, I invited Whitney as she has always been your guest. I honestly didn't think to invite Charlotte being, well, that you're a 'new item'."

Charlotte was fuming inside and couldn't fathom what she was hearing. She was about to respond when Tucker interrupted. "Well, I'm sure it was an honest misunderstanding, and Charlotte you're most welcome to attend as Beau's date if that is his intention. We would love to have you."

Beau looked at Charlotte and then back toward Isabella then grabbed her hand and coldly said, "Mom, *Charlotte* is my date. Change Whitney's seat to a different table," and he walked past her, leading Charlotte out to the porch.

"Babe, I'm so sorry," he said as they walked outside. "Mom is sometimes harsh, but she does have a lot on her mind. Things will settle down once the event is over."

Charlotte rested her head on Beau's chest hoping it was true, and Isabella didn't utterly despise her. She didn't want to bring up what happened at AELs the other day with Whitney. She had tried to push this out of her mind, desperately hoping that Isabella would like her. But this evening Isabella made it very clear that she *hated* her. Was it because she asked for birth control? Shouldn't she be glad her son's girlfriend was on the pill?

"Beau, I think your mom hates me because she wrote my birth control script." Charlotte remained leaning against his chest hoping he wouldn't get mad that she kept this from him.

"Wait...you're on birth control...and my mom...why didn't you tell me?" He pulled back from her so he could see her face. "That's something you should tell your boyfriend don't you think? I mean, I would like to have known...and my mom knew before me!"

Charlotte kept her arms wrapped tightly around his waist hoping her hold on him would soften his reaction. "Beau, I didn't intend to keep it from you. It is just weird that your mom wrote it. I went to see Dr. Dawson, but he was out that day. It just kind of happened."

He knew Charlotte had been struggling with Isabella's resentment and couldn't blame her for not telling him. "I'm not mad, babe, I just wish you would've told me. No wonder my mom is acting strange. You should've said something sooner to me."

"I should probably go now with everything going on around here." She pulled away from Beau's chest and started down the steps of the porch.

He reached for her hand and walked her to his car. As they drove away, Charlotte peeked back across the front porch and saw Isabella in the foyer window watching them leave.

Chapter Fourteen

Masquerade Madness

The theme Isabella chose for The Grand Annual Event was "Masquerade Madness." How fitting to celebrate the upcoming carnival season with a pre-masquerade ball in November. The Corbin's driveway was lined with beautiful luminaires lighting up the paved path adorned with Mardi Gras masks filled with carnival colors...purple, green, and gold.

Isabella began shouting out orders early. Attempting to dodge her wrath, Beau arrived at Charlotte's house before Isabella could pull him into "event duty".

By the time they made it back to his house, guests were making their way inside the house. Beau drove past the valet to park in the garage and noticed Whitney's parents were just arriving. He caught a glimpse of their car parked at the front of the house. Trying to be discreet, he searched to see if Whitney was with them, but she didn't get out of the car. *Whew! Maybe she won't show up.*

Beau walked hand in hand with Charlotte up the walkway to the back side of the house.

This was the largest crowd the event had ever brought in. Beau went to the bar to grab drinks while Charlotte admired the beautiful lights strung through the old, antique oaks. Carnival colors sprinkled over guests enjoying their time dancing to the band. The tables were decorated lavishly with huge lanterns boasting Mardi Gras medallions and beads.

Charlotte walked along the brick pavers path alongside the backside of the house and saw Isabella on top of the porch steps. *I guess I should go and say hi*, Charlotte thought. *That way at least I tried.*

As she rounded the large fern that framed the steps, she heard Whitney laugh. "Mrs. Issie, that's hysterical." Both Whitney and Isabella's cackles echoed across the back porch. It was too late for Charlotte to run at this point, but she wanted so badly to climb back into Beau's car and go home. But there was no doubt Isabella had spotted her and there was no turning back.

As Charlotte started to make her way up the steps, she felt Beau's hand grab her waist. He handed her a small glass of white wine as they continued up the steps to face his mother together.

Isabella pulled her arm from Whitney's and said, "Well, well, Beau honey, you decided to grace us with your presence? And Charlotte--it's Charlotte, right? You did decide to come now, didn't you?"

Charlotte thought she had prepared for this moment of truth with Isabella. Now, with Whitney standing arm in arm with her, chatting away like old friends, she lost her strength.

She loved Beau more than anything and realizing the control Isabella seemed to have on him, she chalked up her pride and responded, "Yes ma'am. It's Charlotte. Beau asked me to come as his date."

Looking out amongst the festivities in the back yard she tried to focus on the positive saying "It's beautiful. You did an amazing job!"

"Of course, it is amazing, Char," Whitney replied as she walked down two steps to where they were standing. "Mrs. Issie is the perfect planner of everything. She always has been."

Whitney smiled looking back up at Isabella. "Oh, darling Whitney, you must stop pampering my ego." She placed her empty wine glass on a tray and grabbed another.

Whitney grabbed Charlotte's arm and led her down the steps to the parquet dance floor. "Char, I've been waiting for you to get here to dance with me! This band is amazing!" She pulled Charlotte onto the dance floor.

***

"Mom, really…you *know* her name is Charlotte," Beau said directly looking at Isabella who smirked cunningly.

You wrote her birth control prescription.

"Honey, I can't remember everyone's name that comes around here. Honestly, I just met her and you expect me to know her life history!" Isabella took a long sip of her wine waiting for Beau to respond. *Actually, I met her at my practice, and she wanted to get on birth control pills to sink her claws into you.*

"Charlotte is my girlfriend, and she makes me happy," Beau said as he searched to find her on the dance floor. "Not only is she beautiful on the outside –*damn she looks so hot in that dress*– "she has a wonderful heart, and she loves me back."

Isabella began to roll her eyes but stopped herself since she could tell he was becoming irritated.

"Mom, just *try* to be nice. Once you get to know her better you will love her just as much as I do. Can you do that for me, please? If you can't, well, it doesn't matter because she isn't going anywhere." Beau grabbed another beer from the caterer passing by and walked out to the dance floor to steal Charlotte away from Whitney.

Isabella watched him latch onto his prized golden possession. *A Callaway, Beau – of all girls you could have – it had to be a Callaway.*

Isabella gulped the rest of her wine, then turned to greet more guests.

***

Ten minutes later, the one person she never wanted to see at her home ––and *never* invited to any of her parties––elbowed his way up the walk, a chilling, evil grin on his face. *Mason Callaway.*

"Fancy party you got going on here, Isabella." Mason swept his arm toward the crowd.

She could smell whiskey on his breath.

"Yes, just some of our friends. Which you're *not*. So, you need to leave."

He smiled. "Oh, now...we used to be friends. All three of us. But particularly you and me."

Isabella grabbed his arm and dragged him to the side of the porch. "How dare you show up here and bring that up!" she hissed.

"And how dare *you* put my fifteen-year-old daughter on birth control without speaking to her mother about it." He backed her up against the wall of the house. "I'm sick and tired of you thinking you're the queen of this town. I think it's time to knock you off your high-horse and–"

"What's going on here?" Tucker pulled Mason back, then pushed him away.

Mason scoffed. "You always were naive, but especially when it came to her. "If you only knew –"

"Shut up, Mason. Tucker, make him leave! He's ruining my party."

Tucker advanced on him. "Get out. Now. The sheriff is here, and I *will* have him throw you out in front of everyone."

Mason held up his hands. "Fine, fine. But this isn't over, Isabella. You're gonna get yours and it's way past time." He turned and bumped Tucker's shoulder on the way out.

"What in the hell was that about?" Tucker narrowed his gaze at Isabella.

"How should I know?" She waved her hand as if shooing a fly away. "He was drunk. And obviously, he hasn't grown up at all since high school." She took a deep breath. "Come on, let's get back out there before someone asks where we are."

She continued entertaining her guests with perfect poise, hoping to forget what just happened.

But a sick feeling settled in her stomach and wouldn't go away.

Mason was going to cause trouble again.

His little "angel" of a daughter wasn't as innocent as he thought.

Chapter Fifteen

Football Is Life

While Beau and Charlotte's relationship grew stronger so did the coach's pull for Beau to practice. As the season was in full swing, district games were on the horizon and Coach wanted one thing – to win.

Beau loved football more than anything, well at least before Charlotte popped into his life. He practiced every day after school until six-thirty. Coach secured every Saturday morning with daybreak runs followed by practice drills until noon. Sundays were slated for rest unless Coach felt like the team didn't work hard enough in practice that week. Most Sundays the team could be found on the field. Yeah, Coach was infatuated with winning.

At first, Charlotte accepted his absence and decided if she couldn't see him after school and have him to herself, then she would just sit on the sidelines after cheer practice and wait for him. Each day, like clockwork, Coach would end practice with three sets of three reps of harness runs. Groans would be heard from across the field as the guys set out the tires to be used as resistance, attached their harnesses around their upper bodies, and attempted to explode into a sprint. She used this cue to pack up her things from the bleachers and wait by the fence for him.

Beau's favorite part of practice was getting to cover her with sweat and dirt he had collected during practice when he'd pick her up and spin her around with her legs wrapped around his waist.

As time passed, she was in the stands less often waiting for practice to end. She would wave to him when cheer practice was over and blow him a kiss secretly wishing he would run off the field chasing her. That never happened of course - the running off-the-field part. She had decided that she couldn't keep hanging out every day at practice for only five minutes with him – that's all she really got was five minutes to hold him close, kiss him, and discuss their day – then he had to head home to shower, do homework, and rest up to do it all over again.

She appreciated his intense love of the game and his dedication, but what about their relationship?

Did it mean anything to him anymore? she often wondered.

She thought back to the first time they kissed in front of the school at orientation. He had mesmerized her with his intent focus on her which is what she desired – football had taken that from her.

***

Beau began to feel like Charlotte was becoming more distant as she didn't wait for him at their shared locker and often ate her lunch in the classroom. Today, he hoped to see her on the field at practice to try to make things right.

As he walked onto the field, he heard chanting from the sidelines and smiled as he heard her voice, "Let's do it again ladies. This time, listen to the count."

Looking over to find her amidst the sea of high ponytails and cheer skirts, Coach yelled from the field interrupting his search. "Beau, you going to practice today or not?" He ran onto the field hoping he'd have another chance to find her before cheer practice ended.

Later, Coach let the team have a five-minute water break. Seizing the opportunity to talk to her, Beau ran over to the sidelines.

"Babe," he yelled to her while running toward the fence bordering the field during a water break. She had just finished leading a stunt and hearing Beau call her name she walked over to the fence to meet him. Leaning over the fence casually he said, "I miss you, babe, a lot. I know football has taken most of my time, but you're on my mind constantly."

With her arms crossed and not budging, she looked away and then back at him. "I miss you too. I want things to be back to how they were when we could leave school and just... be together. I know football is your thing, but I thought *I* was your thing too. Don't I count anymore?"

About the time she leaned closer across the fence, Coach yelled, "Beau! Water break is over!"

He quickly pulled her closer across the fence and said, "You'll *always* be my everything. My one true, forever love. You know I love you."

As he ran back to the field, he turned to her while putting his helmet on. He touched his jersey near his heart and pointed his index finger back toward her.

Charlotte knew he had feelings for her still, but his words didn't make up for his absence.

***

Jackson longed to be QB. Beau was a killer on the field, but Jackson was right behind him eager to fill his spot when needed. Jackson had been second pick for quarterback behind Beau since elementary football. Jackson was a great football player even though he spent most of his time on the sidelines waiting for his chance to be put in. As backup, Jackson couldn't help but feel slighted most days since he knew he had the ability to lead the team.

Not only did Jackson feel overlooked in football, but he was also accustomed to being the third wheel when it came to Beau and Blaine. While they included Jackson in everything, he felt like he sometimes didn't belong.

Jackson had a lot going for him.

While football was his life and first focus, his academics came in at a remarkably close second. He wasn't the typical football jock who ditched classes and barely passed tests. When he committed to something he cared about, he went all in. Whether it was football or school, he was going to give one hundred and ten percent. Period.

***

Stella found herself watching practice from the sidelines to get closer to Jackson. Her infatuation with him had grown stronger. She was still struggling to wrap her head around why he ignored her.

Who ignores Stella Atkinson?

After watching Charlotte and Whitney practice cheer, she jumped down from the bleachers and met them on the track.

"So, girls, what's the plan for this weekend?"

"Honestly, I'm not sure." Charlotte grabbed her water bottle and cheer bag and threw the strap across her shoulder. "For all I know,

Beau might just keep playing his stupid football game all the way through the rest of sophomore year."

Whitney could tell Charlotte was upset and motioned for Stella to help her be supportive. Stella, however, avoided emotions as much as possible, so Whitney knew it was up to her to comfort Charlotte.

Stella walked toward the sidelines to continue focusing on Jackson.

"Char," Whitney said placing her arms around her friend trying to comfort her. "Beau wants nothing more than to be with you. The season'll be over soon, and things will be right back to how they were before football took over his life. You'll see. Things'll get better."

Chapter Sixteen

Unexpected Visit

"Dr. Corbin!!" The receptionist called as she ran down the hallway.

Isabella stood, wondering what emergency had come in.

"Dr. Corbin, you better come outside right now!" The woman was shaking her head and her face was flushed red. "Now!"

Isabella hurried to the front lobby and out the door, a dozen scenarios running through her head.

Heart attack in the parking lot? Someone fainted from the humidity?

But nothing could've prepared her for what she saw.

Hundreds of flyers littered the sidewalk at the clinic door and blew like leaves into the street. She grabbed one and flipped it over to read...and her world tilted, a sick feeling dropped like a rock into her stomach.

Isabella's picture and bright red ink filled the white space.

THIS WOMAN PROMOTES TEEN SEX! ARE YOUR CHILDREN SAFE IN HER CARE?

Her heart stopped beating for a second, then her brain kicked into high gear.

"Get a trash bag!" she yelled to a nurse's aide standing by the door. "Help me pick these up!" she told the receptionist who had followed her out.

"Who would've done such a thing?" the woman asked, grabbing handfuls of the vile papers.

Isabella took a deep breath and shook her head, pasting a look of calm on her face that she definitely didn't feel. "Someone who is obviously delusional and crazy…"

She ran across the street to pick up the flyers that had landed on the bank of Bayou Fueob and to give herself some time to figure out what she would say to the staff.

Yeah, some crazy person, all right. Mason Crazy-Callaway. And he is going to pay.

***

Whitney had been feeling ill the last few days with nausea setting in every morning when she first woke.

Ugh, a stomach bug. Just what I need.

But as each day passed and the nausea continued only in the morning, she became worried.

Her period was seven days late which never happened.

She skipped third hour and showed up at the clinic requesting to see Isabella. She sat in the lobby for about an hour watching the revolving door of patients get called back. Finally, she heard her name being called from the receptionist's desk.

"Yes, ma'am," Whitney responded.

"Dr. Corbin will see you now in her office," the receptionist said.

"What can I do for you dear?" Isabella said, staring across her desk at Whitney. Isabella could tell something was wrong. Whitney wasn't her usual perky self.

Looking down toward her lap and fidgeting with her dress, Whitney whispered, "I didn't know who else to go to with this. I'm embarrassed and scared."

Isabella stood up from her chair behind the desk and sat in the chair next to Whitney. Grabbing her hand, Isabella said, "Whitney, you know you can tell me anything. What is it, dear?" Many things were running through Isabella's mind at this point, none of which were what Whitney was about to share with her.

"I think I'm pregnant, Mrs. Issie," she softly cried and leaned into Isabella's arms.

Shocked, Isabella pulled her in to comfort her. "Okay, well, that's a lot to take in. I understand that you're scared. Let's start with a few simple questions. Have you taken a home pregnancy test?"

Whitney leaned back in her chair and reached for her purse. She pulled out three pregnancy tests and held them up where Isabella could see them. All three reflected she was pregnant.

"Okay, so that is the first step. Sometimes though the over-the-counter tests are false positives. I can run a simple urine test and we'll know for sure. Let me go grab the supplies." Isabella exited her office.

Whitney remained in the chair still stunned. *How in the world am I going to do this – tell my parents – go to school – take care of a baby?*

Isabella quickly returned with the supplies needed for the sample and led her down the hall to another room. Time seemed to stand still. Whitney knew in her heart that it was probably true.

Three positive home tests, Whit?

Minutes had passed by, but the time seemed to stand still. Whitney was growing impatient when finally, Isabella entered the room. Holding a chart, she sat down next to Whitney and took her hand.

"Whitney, you *are* pregnant. I assume you're about four weeks gestation hence the nausea and fatigue." Tears began to fall down Whitney's face as she re-ran the words through her head, YOU ARE PREGNANT.

Isabella knew Whitney was overwhelmed and let her have some space telling her to lie down on her office couch if she wanted. After about thirty minutes, Isabella came back into the room to check on her.

"I can have this baby," Whitney said caressing her belly. "I'm not scared, Mrs. Issie. I can't be. I messed up, and I own it. I know it is going to be tough, but Blaine will be –"

Isabella cut Whitney off. "Blaine Ferrell? Whitney! I thought you had more sense than that, girl. Every woman in town knows that boy is only after one thing. Why in the world would you think differently?"

Whitney leaned forward in the chair, then looked back at Isabella, and replied, "It just felt right. I know that sounds silly, but it did. He held me so close, and it felt so perfect. It just happened."

Isabella loved Blaine like her own son, however, she knew he was only after the chase.

"Whitney, honey, you can talk to Blaine about this, but I want you to be prepared that he likely is not going to be supportive."

"Well, maybe he has changed his ways." Whitney headed toward the door. "I appreciate you so much, Mrs. Issie. Please keep this between us until I'm ready to share with everyone."

"Of course," replied Isabella. "Your secret is safe with me."

***

Tucker's law firm simulated a larger firm in a big city, not due to the size, but rather the client base. Some say Allison helped attract business to the firm since she had quite a few connections in the city. Others attributed his success to his charming wit and ruthless ability in the courtroom.

Allison practically ran the law firm for him with her eyes closed. She was the perfect addition to the business as she skillfully prepared for court cases with her amazing organizational skills. Not long after Allison and Kent moved back to Sedipar, Isabella befriended Allison. They didn't have much in common other than their sons being in the same grade in school coupled with their son's love for football, which fostered their friendship. The women spent most of their Saturdays cheering on their boys at tournaments for various football leagues.

Isabella rarely left the clinic during work as her days were filled with back-to-back patients which didn't leave her with much free time. Occasionally, she would schedule a lunch break and surprise Tucker with a lunch from AELs. While most days his schedule left little room for lunch breaks, he graciously rearranged his calendar for Isabella which often meant working late to catch up.

***

"Honey," Tucker said noticing she was ignoring her lunch. "Just put it out of your mind for thirty minutes and enjoy your lunch. We don't have proof it was him. I mean, lots of kids have sex. It could be any angry parent."

Isabella rolled her eyes with obvious frustration as she focused again on her salad.

"And to top off my *wonderful* morning, you'll never believe this." Tucker reluctantly stopped eating his ham sandwich from AEL's, listening intently while she told him about a pregnant teen. As she pushed her salad away from her, she continued, "I obviously can't identify her due to HIPPA, but she's fifteen and scared shitless." She sighed. "I had to get out of the office and detach from this madness. What is happening in our world today? They get younger and younger it seems. And can you imagine how this will look on me if anyone saw those horrible flyers and now when this girl starts showing?"

"Oh gosh," Allison cried as she walked into the conference room, hearing the last part of Isabella's rant. "I would *die* if my Jackson came home saying he got some girl pregnant. Kids today just don't understand the consequences of their actions."

"Well, see then, it could have been this girl's parents wh--" Tucker looked up. "Allison, can you excuse us for just a minute?"

After she closed the door, Tucker continued, "It could have been this girl's parents who made those flyers. But lots of teenagers have sex. As we well know." He grinned.

Isabella looked toward Tucker, reminiscing about the end of their senior year when her baby bump had started to protrude and was slightly noticeable at senior graduation. Their situation was completely different though – at least that's what she told herself.

But it was time to come clean because she wasn't going to let Mason Callaway get the better of her.

She shook her head as she refreshed her lipstick. "I know who put the flyers there. And I know why, and worse, it involves Beau."

Ten minutes later, Tucker ran his fingers through his hair trying to digest all she had told him. "So, Mason is mad because Charlotte came to you for birth control?" He shook his head. "I don't know..."

Isabella looked at him and stood. "Well, *I know* and I'm going to do something about it. You can come along as my husband or lawyer or both. Or stay here, but I'm going to put a stop to this slander before he ruins my career!"

***

Mason wasn't working at the pharmacy that day, so Isabella and Tucker drove out to his home. Upon arriving, Mason met them on the front steps of his lake home and greeted them. "Well, what do I owe this most pleasant surprise?"

"Go to hell, Mason!" Isabella replied slamming the passenger door and walking toward the house. Stopping a few feet in front of him, Isabella shouted, "I know you dropped those flyers all over the front of the clinic! That's slander and I ought to sue you!"

"Is that right, Isabella? Well, you have it all figured out, don't you?" Mason replied with a sly grin.

Tucker tried stepping in to diffuse the situation. "Look, Mason, cut the crap. We know you're upset that Charlotte is on birth control without your consent. We get it...we'd be upset if Nessie did this and was sexually active."

Mason took a sip of his coffee and started walking alongside the porch to an Adirondack chair near the corner. "I guess I could sit here and deny the fact that I didn't have anything to do with it, but I won't."

Isabella stepped up on the porch and leaned against the porch railing. "Shouldn't you just be glad she's using protection? We sure as hell don't want Beau getting her pregnant."

Mason looked out into his front yard and smiled to himself. "So, what do you want from me now, Isabella? An apology?"

Isabella could feel her heart pounding faster. "What's this *really* about, Mason? Because I chose Tucker instead of you?"

She heard Tucker groan beside her. But the words were already out.

Mason leaned forward in his chair and set his coffee mug on the side table. "You know, Isabella, your ego knows no limits. You have been entitled your entire life and most of the time you hurt people along the way to get what you want. This was my chance to hurt you and hopefully break some of that overconfidence and self-pride."

Isabella, now fuming with madness, leaned in closer toward Mason and softly whispered, "Oh, Mason, why don't you just tell me the truth about why you did it? It wasn't that you hated me for being so ruthless to others. You despised me because I resisted you. It was always so clear you wanted me for yourself, and you *forced* yourself on me that one night. You didn't want to let me go. I loved Tucker. You never got over that!"

Mason looked back toward Isabella with disgust. "Wow, Isabella, now that is low." He walked to the end of the porch, then spun around, his face tight with anger. "That night by the lake, *you* instigated everything! You're really something...turning all of this around on me. Mason – the bad guy – forced himself on the innocent Isabella Ducaine! *Yeah right*!"

He stood and walked past her to the front door. "It is not even worth fighting you over it at this point. Get off my land!" He slammed the front door of his house behind him.

Isabella stood motionless, surprised by Mason's attack on her, then she felt Tucker's hand on her arm.

"Did I just hear what I think I heard!?" Tucker stared at Isabella for answers. "You had sex with Mason? When did this happen?" He paced back and forth on the porch.

Looking at Isabella, he threw his hands up in the air. "Well? I'm waiting!"

Isabella took a deep breath and calmly folded her arms. "High school, Tucker. It was high school."

"High school...high school, Isabella?! That really narrows it down for me! I deserve more than that!" He continued pacing along the front porch. "*When* the hell in high school? Or did you forget that small detail like you forgot to tell me you cheated on me with one of my best friends?" Tucker wouldn't look at her face.

Isabella lowered her gaze and reluctantly replied, "It was homecoming night."

She could see the devastation on his face as he walked to the car.

Shortly after, Tucker's taillights faded into the distance.

She swore she could hear Mason's laughter through the wall.

Chapter Seventeen

Some Things are for the Best

Whitney had avoided Blaine for a week, still building up the nerve to tell him she was pregnant. A part of her kept thinking, *This is a dream, snap out of it,* but the morning sickness that had set in was a constant reminder it was true.

The only person Whitney had shared the news with was Isabella, although she had come close to telling Stella and Charlotte, but decided Blaine should find out first.

"You coming to the party this weekend at the Abyss?" asked Stella as they rounded the corner to first-hour class. Whitney knew if she didn't drink at the party, everyone would draw conclusions, which she wanted to avoid.

"No, my parents and I are out of town this weekend," she lied and walked briskly to her class before Stella could probe with more questions. As Whitney entered the doorway to her classroom, Blaine passed right by her brushing her shoulder but kept walking. She watched him walk further down the hall past her classroom and noticed he was bombarded by a few guys on the football team. She felt relieved; she had escaped another moment of truth.

"You not coming to cheer practice, Whit?" Charlotte asked later when Whitney walked toward the student parking area.

"No, Char, I'm not feeling good. I'll call you later."

Charlotte waved and headed back toward the gym for practice.

***

Whitney had been acting strange since Blaine's party. Charlotte was concerned that she was hiding something from her. As she entered the gym, she noticed Blaine and Beau standing near the bleachers. She ran over to them hoping to question Blaine about Whitney.

"Seems like you two were pretty close the night of your party," Charlotte said as Beau stood behind her.

"Yeah, man," Beau said with his arm around her waist. "Y'all were almost as close as me and Charlotte, right babe?" He snuck a quick kiss on Charlotte's neck.

Blaine shrugged and laughed back at them both saying, "Y'all are gross, all happy and crap. None of that is real dude. Y'all need to relax all that cheesy love stuff."

Charlotte became easily agitated with Blaine. Everything was a joke to him.

"I'm serious, Blaine, have you talked to Whitney? I just saw her, and she said she wasn't feeling well. She hasn't seemed like herself lately." Charlotte glared at him. "Please go check on her after practice. I mean it."

Blaine responded by rolling his eyes and mocking Charlotte as she turned to run back to the girl's locker room.

***

Whitney made it home and immediately fell asleep. It was almost seven that evening when her mom called from downstairs to say that Blaine was on the phone.

"Tell him I'll talk to him tomorrow at school," Whitney yelled as she rolled over in her bed.

The last person I want to talk to right now is Blaine. Ugh, I've got to get it together and tell him.

Around eight-thirty, she awoke to an overwhelming feeling of nausea and ran to the bathroom. After vomiting, she sat on the cold tile floor leaning up against the vanity cabinet. She felt exhausted, and even though she had slept all afternoon, she was still tired. She thought a bath might feel nice; however, exhaustion dissuaded her.

As she leaned toward the mirror above her vanity, she felt a strange sensation followed by a great deal of pressure. As she looked down at the floor, her bathroom tile was covered with blood. Forced to contain her emotions so her parents wouldn't hear, Whitney screamed inside with fear as she mopped up the floor with a towel.

Feeling alone and scared, with only one person she could confide in who knew her secret, Whitney dialed Isabella's number.

"Hello," answered Isabella.

"Mrs. Issie...*sniff*...um, this is Whitney," she said in a soft, frail voice. "I'm scared and I need your help."

"Whitney, what's going on?" Isabella could hear the desperation in the girl's voice.

"I think I just lost the baby," Whitney whispered as her tears rolled furiously down her face.

"Oh, honey, I'm so sorry. Take a deep breath and tell me what happened."

Isabella listened and provided support to Whitney to help calm her down.

"Come by the clinic tomorrow for an exam. Everything will be okay. I promise. It's *going to be ok.*"

***

We were down to the last few games of district, which caused Beau and Charlotte to become more distant because these games were critical. Jackson had seen more playing time in the last few games due to higher scores. This provided Beau with some reprieve, and Coach wanted to save Beau for each district game. Jackson played extremely well and displayed various skills that surprised Coach.

"Good game, Jackson." Coach patted Jackson on the back as he came running off the field. While the win was attributed to Beau, Jackson felt the glory when the game was over. Beau, while jealous, smiled watching Jackson get lifted by the team with the crowd cheering him on.

Good for him!

Beau ran out on the field following closely behind Coach.

Everyone in the stands came rushing to the field after the game as usual. Beau searched for Charlotte in the crowd, longing to have her by his side, but he couldn't find her. He stood beside Coach while the rest of the team lifted Jackson again carrying him around the field.

While he focused on Jackson soaking in all the attention, he scanned the crowd again for Charlotte. Suddenly, he felt a hand touch his side and he knew it was Charlotte's.

"Hey, handsome," she said as he pulled her in close and kissed her. It felt so good holding her in his arms. Her soft touch and sweet perfume made him weak. He lifted her off the ground and spun her around on the field.

"I've been looking for you. You're all I needed to complete the night," Beau said wrapping his arms tightly around her.

***

Stella found her way onto the field in hopes of getting closer to Jackson and telling him how great he played. However, as she got closer to him, she couldn't help but notice his intent stare...Jackson's focus was locked on Charlotte as Beau held her in his arms. As the team lowered him back to the ground, Stella thought, *What the hell do I have to lose? I'm tired of him ignoring me.*

As she got closer to Jackson, she noticed he had not taken his eyes off Charlotte. This wasn't an innocent "Hey! I'm glad my friends are in love" kind of stare. Jackson's look was intent and deep with envy as he watched Charlotte playfully dance and spin holding Beau's hand.

It was at this moment Stella understood why Jackson had blown her off so many times. He was fixated on Charlotte like every other guy seemed to be in this damn school.

Forget him. I'm so over him.

***

Whitney had gotten to the clinic early hoping Isabella would fit her in. She didn't sleep much the night before with all the stress of losing the baby.

Isabella finally arrived at the clinic around ten and saw Whitney waiting in the lobby.

"Oh, honey, I'm sorry." Isabella walked through the clinic lobby. "Come, follow me into my office."

"How are you feeling?" She placed her purse down and sat behind her desk.

"I don't know, Mrs. Issie." Whitney fidgeted with the strap to her purse. "One part of me is super relieved that I don't have this weight hanging on me –- like having to tell Blaine he's going to be a father –- and my parents that they'll be grandparents sooner than they planned. Then, I feel guilty that I caused this. The baby didn't deserve for this to happen."

Hearing the desperation in Whitney's voice troubled Isabella. "Look, honey," Isabella walked around her desk and placed her hands on Whitney's lap to comfort her, "this is not your fault. While you didn't make the best decision having unprotected sex, you did not have any influence on what happened to the baby. This happens quite often in young pregnancies."

Whitney knew that Blaine wasn't her lifetime soulmate but having sex with him felt right. "I own sleeping with Blaine, and honestly I'm past that." She stood from her chair. "What I can't shake is losing this baby, Mrs. Issie. It's like a piece of my soul exited on the floor last night. I kept dreaming about it."

Isabella stood up and pulled her into a hug. "Whitney, honey, time will heal your body and your heart. Let's go get you checked out to be sure you're okay health-wise." She led Whitney to the exam room.

Chapter Eighteen

Web of Deception

Recently I began spending more time at the library.
How was that even possible?

Call me crazy, but our "perfect" family turning even more dysfunctional, was a bit more than I could take at fifteen. The last two weeks were spent hanging out as late as possible with Owen at the library. Our town library is unique. It occupied the bottom floor of the historic old high school that was closed in 1967. In our opinion, it offered a level of tranquility you couldn't imagine.

And now that I had my driver's license, I escaped from the cuckoo's nest any time I could.

"Sooo...our parents..." he opened a fresh, crisp book he found in the history section.

Fresh crisp books – that was one of my favorite parts about being at the library late – all the new books were put out and we got first dibs on them. I loved the smell of a new book and the stern spine that hadn't yet been disturbed.

"Yeah, I don't want to talk about it." I buried my head in my book. He knew better than to ask me questions and put me on the spot, but the news of Tucker, Isabella, and Mason had spread across town quickly.

Owen sat quietly at the end of the table and didn't say another word. I guess I should've felt odd since his dad was the central force that had driven a wedge between Isabella and Tucker. But I didn't blame Owen for Mason's mistakes just like he did not blame me for Isabella's.

My friendship with Owen was worth more than Isabella and Tucker staying together. Neither one of us wanted to expel much energy on their mistakes.

As Owen sat across from me at the table, I tried to keep the focus on my book, however, my mind kept reliving Isabella's confession to Tucker. It was one of the lowest blows she had ever delivered to anyone.

Not that I needed to pick sides in this feud, but I one hundred percent sided with Tucker. No, my choice has nothing to do with the fact that Isabella cheated on Tucker. The sole reason is that I despise Isabella.

While she is my mother, she has offered me nothing more than criticism over the years.

I resented her long before this confession.

***

I stayed at the camp house with Tucker a few nights when I knew I couldn't stomach being around Isabella. Since he had moved out, she focused her free time on myself and Beau, which meant my home life had become even more awkward. Her hovering was more than I could bear. She tried to be considerate of Beau and my feelings since we were both certainly caught in the middle; however, her selfishness and arrogance wouldn't allow her to genuinely care for our feelings for very long. The constant questioning about "how was our day" or "anything exciting happen at school" might have seemed normal for most mothers, but not Isabella. Her questions appeared innocent on the surface, a desperate attempt to chat with us, but I knew her motive was purely for personal gain.

Tucker was glad to see me at the camp and needed the company. A part of me wished that he would come home and kick Isabella out of the house since the land *and* the house was part of his family legacy. He had every right to do it, but that thought had never crossed his mind. I knew deep down Isabella was the love of his life, and he wouldn't destroy her.

I didn't mind staying at the camp house with Tucker because he didn't pressure me with questions or probe me to tell him how I felt or ask what I was thinking. He had a genuine heart, and I always wondered how he fell in love with Isabella in the first place.

"Your mom and I are just in a tough place right now," Tucker said and that was the gist of our conversation about it.

"Nessie, you can stay here as long as you like." He grabbed my hand softly and smiled. "Your mom doesn't like you being here I'm sure, but I've been lonely all by myself and certainly appreciate the company." I could tell his anger had faded some over the last few days, but he wasn't ready to face Isabella yet.

As he got up from the table, I stared out the window gazing at the water, thinking how peaceful the view made me feel.

"Thanks. I'd much rather be here than back home getting drilled each day about who mentioned her name at school." I was reluctant to leave as I knew this amazing sense of peace would vanish when I returned home.

"I do need to spend tonight at home though because I have a study group at the library until late. It's a shorter drive home from the library. I'll be back here tomorrow night, ok?"

"No problem. Have fun at your study group. I'll see you tomorrow night." Tucker kissed the top of my head and headed out the door to work.

***

Tucker hadn't spoken to Isabella since her confession. She had tried her best to corner him and make him talk to her, but he was purposely avoiding her. For once, she felt alone and afraid that she had lost the one good thing in her life that made sense – Tucker.

She called the camp phone repeatedly, and he wouldn't pick up.

She left multiple messages trying to explain why this happened and that she still loved him.

Tucker never returned her call.

Weeks passed and she heard nothing from him. When she made her usual appearance at the firm for lunch, he was never there.

Allison felt sorry for Isabella each day as she came in with lunch, and regretfully Allison had to tell her he had left for the day or had gone home for lunch.

Isabella knew she had wronged him. However, he wasn't giving her the chance to explain which she felt was unfair. It was such a long time ago.

***

"Mom," yelled Beau from his upstairs room, "I need to get that sponsorship form signed by Dad's office. It is due by Thursday." Isabella grabbed the form from the kitchen table where Tucker had last sat and examined the empty signature line on the form. He had completed the form but didn't sign it.

I can take care of that easy enough. Isabella grabbed a pen and signed Tucker's name.

"Here you go," Isabella said as Beau hurriedly grabbed his book sack and football gear.

"Thanks, Mom." Beau started heading for the door. "Hey, Charlotte is coming over tonight to hang out. With football taking up most of my time lately, I haven't seen her much. I miss her. Anything special for dinner tonight?"

Isabella smiled tightly. "I have a late night, so I doubt I'll have anything prepared. I suggest you stop by The Dixie on your way through."

Isabella watched Beau leave the driveway.

My next task is to break those two up. No Callaway is going to be part of this family ever if I have anything to do with it.

When she walked out the door and grabbed her keys, she noticed the small camp house key. Isabella placed the key in her purse and closed the door.

***

Charlotte followed Beau home directly from school and couldn't wait to spend some alone time with him. School was dismissed early due to a pipe bursting and all practices were canceled.

"Nessie still at school?" Charlotte asked while walking toward the garage door.

"She's at the library if I had to guess." Beau grabbed Charlotte's hand and walked into the kitchen. "We have the house to ourselves until Mom gets home later tonight."

Charlotte smiled at the idea of finally being alone with Beau, but the mere mention of Isabella's name made her cringe.

Ugh, why does Isabella have to be Beau's mom?

As soon as they entered the house, he grabbed her legs, and she latched them around his waist. He picked her up and she slid onto the top of the kitchen counter. As her legs fell on each side of his body, he positioned himself snugly between them. While kissing her neck, he slowly unzipped her cheer hoodie and pulled one sleeve down to expose her shoulder. He kissed along her collarbone while his fingers followed the top ridge of her camisole.

She held onto him tightly while her hands followed his solid back muscles down to the top ridge of his jeans where her fingers danced along the edge softly flirting with his bare skin. He picked her up and carried her to the sofa in the living room. His kiss became stronger as his body pressed harder against hers. He removed her camisole and bra while continuing to kiss every inch of her bare skin.

"Beau, you sure no one is coming home?" Charlotte asked him as he began running his fingers near the side seam of her leggings. "Babe, it is just us, I promise." He removed her leggings, leaving her clothed in only her red lacey panties.

"I want you so bad," Beau said while his tongue flirted with Charlotte's belly button and then followed her panty line across her abdomen.

Her hands found their way to his belt as they loosened the buckle and then removed his shirt.

Charlotte lay still while Beau caressed her thighs and ran his fingers up the side of her panties at her hips.

"Do you want to do this?" he asked hoping the answer would be 'yes'.

Charlotte pulled Beau's face closer to hers and nuzzled her face close to his ear and whispered, "Of course. I want you more than anything."

His hands worked smoothly to remove her panties and he tossed them on the floor next to the sofa.

As his body began to press against hers, she placed her hand on his chest to stop him. "Beau, you do have a condom, don't you?"

Beau ran his fingers alongside her side caressing her skin softly. "Not downstairs, babe," he replied continuing to kiss her lips trying to make her forget.

"Well, can you get it? I'd rather be safe than sorry. With everything going on I've missed a couple of my pills." Charlotte softly pushed against him signaling him to stop.

Beau wanted nothing more than to have Charlotte at that very moment, but he could tell she wasn't comfortable.

"I'll go get one." Beau reluctantly put his boxer shorts on and ran upstairs.

Charlotte felt relieved and laid back on the sofa, grabbing a blanket for cover. As she touched her lips remembering his soft kiss and closed her eyes hoping to hold on to every moment of the bliss she had just experienced, she heard the carport door open. Fumbling to find her clothes scattered across the floor, she succumbed to lying perfectly still under the blanket hoping not to be noticed.

***

When I opened the door from the carport and entered the kitchen, Beau greeted me, in his skimpy boxer shorts, making his way back to Charlotte, lying naked on our sofa.

To both of their surprise, my study date had ended early so here I was –- staring at my half-naked brother and his naked girlfriend –-obviously about to have sex. Feeling awkward in your own home isn't something most people likely deal with, but it was a constant for me.

Trying not to look at either of them and desperate to leave the room, I kept my gaze to the floor, and said, "You have a room for that," and went upstairs.

I closed my door hoping to shut everything that I saw out of my mind forever.

***

Isabella drove up the driveway and noticed Charlotte's car.

Ugh, I forgot she was going to be here. I've got to break these two up somehow.

"Hey, Mom," Beau said from the living room as she placed her purse on the kitchen counter. Isabella noticed Charlotte close up against Beau's chest on the sofa watching football on TV.

"Hi, Beau, good day at school?" Isabella asked while pouring a glass of wine, then heading into the living room.

"Like any other day." Beau's focus remained on the TV.

Isabella sat in the chair across from them making Charlotte uncomfortable. She tried to sit up and push away from his chest, but he grabbed her arm.

"Babe, where do you think you're going?" He laughed as he pulled her back against him.

"Well, maybe she doesn't want to be so close, Beau. Let the girl go if she wants to sit up." She took a long, slow sip of wine.

Isabella made most people feel uncomfortable, but Charlotte felt her wrath more than anyone.

The evening had been so wonderful before she came home. It felt amazing being held in Beau's arms while he kissed her softly. While their intimate moment had been sabotaged again, just having him close to her felt amazing.

But Isabella's glare unnerved Charlotte, and regardless how wonderful it felt with Beau holding her, she wanted to leave.

"I should go. It's getting late," she whispered looking up at him and kissing his lips lightly.

"Thank you for tonight. It felt so great being close to you." Beau whispered in her ear. He could tell Isabella had made her uncomfortable.

As Charlotte grabbed her book sack and purse, Isabella slyly grinned Charlotte's way. "Thanks for having me, Mrs. Corbin," Charlotte said walking toward the front door. Beau followed closely hoping to secure one more kiss from her before the night was over.

Isabella stood up from her chair and, taking a sip of her wine, turned, and replied, "Goodbye, Mason's daughter."

***

The next evening, Tucker returned to the camp house late since he was in trial most of the day in a neighboring town and had to review testimony with Allison afterward at the office. As he entered the garage, he noticed the kitchen light was left on. Nessie had called and said her group study meeting was rescheduled and she wouldn't be staying the night so he knew it wasn't her - and there was no car in sight.

He put his briefcase down and took off his coat. *That's odd. I guess I left the light on this morning when I left.*

When Tucker rounded the hall toward his bedroom, he noticed the lights were dimmed and he recognized the sweet smell of Isabella's perfume. As he entered the room, there were rose petals placed strategically across the bed that spelled, "I love you." He followed the rose petals into the bathroom where he found his jetted tub full of bubbling hot water with rose petals floating on the top.

It has to be Isabella obviously, but where is she? He closed the bathroom door and headed back to the kitchen.

When he entered the living area, he saw her leaning over the kitchen counter with two glasses of wine sitting in front of her. "Hi," she said as she picked up both glasses of wine and walked toward him. "Have a glass of wine with me, please," she whispered handing him the wine.

"Isabella, how the hell did you get in here?" He set the glass of wine on the side table. "I don't want to have a glass of wine with you. I don't even want you here!" He was furious that she had invaded his space.

"Honey..." She lightly touched his arm rubbing it softly.

"No, we are not going to do this!" He pushed her hand away. "You have no right to barge in here when I requested space from you. I haven't returned your call because I don't want to talk to you."

Isabella wasn't rejected often and almost always got her way. But she wasn't giving up on their marriage and continued to try to get Tucker to talk to her.

"I realize you're angry at me, and you have every right to be. But we can't work through this if you don't give me a chance to explain.

I thought we could enjoy some nice wine together and talk. I made a nice bath for us if you're willing."

Tucker stared intently at her. He couldn't believe she thought a few glasses of wine and a rose petal bath would win him over.

"Isabella, you slept with one of my best friends and never told me. What in the world do you think I am supposed to do? Why would you not have told me this back then?" He was getting more frustrated as each word came out. *Why am I even entertaining her at this point? I should make her leave.*

An hour or so passed and they sat in silence. "Tucker, look, I'm sorry that I didn't tell you. I wanted so badly to tell you that night you waited near my car, but I couldn't bear to break your heart. It felt so amazing to be in your arms and spend homecoming night together like we originally planned."

Tucker looked up and across the room, fuming. "You bitch!" he yelled. "That night? The night I couldn't find you at the dance, and I waited for you at The Dixie by your car, you and Mason had sex! You *repeatedly* said nothing happened, and I believed you!"

Isabella walked closer and tried to console him, but he pushed her away again. "I couldn't tell you. Honestly, I didn't love Mason. But you deserted me, Tucker. You didn't answer my calls all day. I thought you hated me. Mason just happened along and asked me to go for a ride..."

Tucker turned toward her as he leaned against the kitchen counter. "I apologized for that a long time ago. Hell, Isabella, I fell asleep by your car and waited for you. I wouldn't have waited knowing you had slept with Mason."

"Tucker," she continued, "we can continue to go back and forth on this and frankly we aren't going to get anywhere. Besides, there is something else I wanted to tell you."

He sat on the bar stool with his head in his hands.

What else could she have to tell me?"

Isabella sat on the bar stool across from him. "This is extremely hard for me to say. You won't believe that I kept this from you all this time to protect you, but I didn't want to hurt you."

"Dammit, just say it – enough with the secrets!" Tucker beat his fist on the counter.

"The night I was with Mason wasn't consensual. He asked me to go out to Lake Danik with him and have a few drinks. At first, I rejected him and just wanted to go home. I couldn't find you anywhere and you hadn't answered my calls. Anyway, Mason coaxed me into riding with him out to the lake. We drank quite a bit and Mason started getting too close. The last thing I remember was him being on top of me near the water's edge, and all I could think about was him stopping. I drank quite a bit that night, Tucker, but I remember that feeling of helplessness. Tucker, Mason raped me."

As Isabella finished the words "raped me" Tucker stood up from the bar stool and threw his hands in the air. "Son of a bitch! Isabella, why in the hell wouldn't you have told me this?" He continued screaming while he stomped in circles on the kitchen floor.

"My parents were furious and filed charges against Mason, but after a few weeks, they had the charges dismissed. No one other than my parents ever knew."

"I can't hear any more of this!" Tucker yelled. "I don't even know what to believe from you anymore. How and why could you have kept this from me? Is this just a plea or a last-minute cry for help?"

Isabella sat in disbelief as Tucker screamed at her and for once she just listened, sitting quietly, letting him vent because she still had something else to tell him.

"All I can say is I'm sorry, Tucker. I truly am sorry for all of this. I know I can't take any of it back, and I am sorry you're hurting. I know you're upset with me and if you can't be with me or we need continued space, I'll give you that. However, there is one more thing I need to tell you."

Looking back at Isabella, Tucker threw his hands up in the air. "Well, you're just full of surprises lately. Hit me with it! I can't even imagine something worse than what you just told me."

Isabella placed the wine glass on the counter and walked toward Tucker. Forcing him to hold her hand, a tear rolled down her face.

"Beau is not your son, Tucker. Beau is Mason's."

Chapter Nineteen

Family Discussion

A rainstorm set in over Sedipar for the following three days and saturated the town. Bayou Fueob's banks were feeling the pressure from the excessive rain. The water was at levels no one had seen before, and the local farmers were desperate for it to cease. Some streets in town were flooded after the first day of rain and several homeowners were trapped inside due to rising water. The severe downpour of rain and cloudy skies didn't help the melancholy mood that had set over the town.

Tucker had called me the day after Isabella "surprised" him at the camp house. He wanted me to hear it from him and be there when he told Beau - if Isabella didn't get to Beau first.

I had so many questions for Isabella. While her first confession had caused quite a bit of commotion, her latest admittance that Beau wasn't Tucker's son was a huge blow. I couldn't wrap my head around how she kept this a secret for so long. As much as I wanted to understand why, I wanted to avoid her more.

Tucker came to the house after school and was waiting for Beau and me to get home. The rain had postponed the last district game, so Beau didn't have practice after school.

Tucker had called me early that morning and shared the news. School was a blur for most of the day because all I could concentrate on was what Beau would say.

I got home around three fifteen and noticed Beau wasn't home yet. When I walked inside, Tucker was sitting at the bar in the kitchen.

"Hey, Nessie," Tucker smiled as I put my stuff down by the door.

"Hey," I replied as I grabbed a bottle of water from the fridge. "I haven't seen or heard from Beau since I called him last night to tell him I needed to meet with both of you." Tucker fidgeted nervously with the coaster on the counter.

"I saw him at school today and he seemed ok." I sat next to Tucker at the bar.

I wanted to ask questions, but I didn't want to stress him out more than he already was.

***

Beau came home around four-thirty, followed by Isabella. Tucker wasn't expecting *her* to be home so early.

When Beau entered the door, Tucker stood up to meet him.

"Son...Beau...uh..." Struggling to find the right words, he sat back down to recollect his thoughts.

"Save it, Tucker," Isabella said as she placed some grocery bags on the counter. "I already told him. He knows everything. He needs time alone."

Tucker glared at Isabella while putting up the groceries.

Beau walked toward the living room and sat on the sofa. Tucker got up and followed Beau. He remained silent since he wasn't sure what Beau was thinking.

"Dad," Beau said as he looked at Tucker. "Is this all true?"

Tucker felt a weight inside him like he had never felt before. "Well, it seems your mom thinks so, and she's the one who would know."

Isabella had fixed a glass of wine and joined them in the living room. "Beau, honey, you have been through a lot this afternoon. Why don't you go upstairs and get a shower and relax?"

I could tell Beau was beginning to get irritated with Isabella. "Mom, I'm fine. I don't want a shower. I want to talk about this!"

I joined them all in the living room only to be a buffer for the guys. Beau sat quietly for a while as Tucker and Isabella glared at one another. She casually took sips from her wine glass like nothing was wrong.

Tucker wanted to be there for Beau, but he couldn't stay in the room with Isabella much longer. He looked at Beau. "We can certainly get to the truth of this easily. We'll do a paternity test and decide the truth based on facts and be done with this."

Isabella tried to interject, and Beau stopped her. "Mom, stop! Enough! I want a test to prove it. I'm sorry, but all of this is too much to digest and honestly, I don't know who to believe at this point."

Tucker could feel Beau's frustration as they both stood up and paced around the living room. Isabella sat quietly for once taken aback that Beau had silenced her.

I stayed silent as usual, taking everything in.

Tucker placed his arm around Beau's shoulder while walking back toward the kitchen. "I can get Allison to begin working on that tomorrow."

Isabella's emotions were rampant as I watched her fidget with the stem of her wine glass. Each rotation of the stem became quicker as she lost control and the glass crashed to the floor.

"Dammit!" she yelled as she picked up the larger pieces of glass. "I'm just not following either of your logic here." She walked past Tucker and Beau to dispose of the glass in the trash.

"Why waste time on the test?" She turned directly to Beau, cupping her hands around his face. "Honey, I don't want to drag you any further along with this. A test will only drag out negative emotions and to what avail – a test telling you that Mason is your dad?"

Beau pulled away from Isabella, annoyed by her unusual caring behavior. "I want the test, Mom. Dad can help, so you won't be burdened by it."

Isabella rolled her eyes and glanced at Tucker who was standing with his hands rested on both hips and staring at the floor.

As Beau started to walk away, the phone rang. It was Charlotte.

"Hey, babe. Yeah, I know. I've been waiting for you to call." Beau walked up the stairs to his bedroom.

Tucker came over to me, still sitting in the living room, and kissed my cheek. "I love you, Nessie. I'll see you tomorrow at the camp house?"

I wanted to leave with him and spend the night at the camp house to avoid the wrath of Isabella that would ensue after he left, but I couldn't leave Beau alone. He was an absolute pain in my butt most of the time, however, I felt his misery and wanted to support him if he needed me.

As Tucker left through the garage, I heard Isabella on the phone with the carpet cleaner company demanding someone to come out first thing in the morning to remove the wine stain.

Chapter Twenty

Tampering With the Truth

Allison received word from Tucker the next morning to get things moving on Beau's paternity test. She couldn't believe things had taken an even greater turn for the worse.

First, Isabella's confession that she slept with Mason on homecoming night, and now this huge blow of news that Beau wasn't Tucker's son. She couldn't imagine how Tucker was feeling right now.

He hadn't been in the office for the last several days. He decided to take some personal time off. He came by the firm briefly to provide his DNA sample to Allison before leaving town. He had entrusted her to collect the DNA samples from Beau and Mason.

She carefully locked the kits in a cabinet in Tucker's office.

As he closed his office door, he turned back toward her and said, "There isn't anyone else I would feel comfortable leaving this with. Under no circumstances should you allow anyone in my office while I am away."

***

Beau stopped by the firm after school and provided his sample. As Allison placed his sample in the bag, she turned back to Beau and noticed him staring out the office window. "I know things are tough right now, and I'm sorry. I can't imagine what you're feeling."

Beau leaned forward in the chair with his arms resting on his legs and sunk his head between his legs.

"Thank you, Mrs. Allison. I appreciate that. I just feel lost. I can't concentrate on anything else other than getting these results. My relationship with Charlotte is obviously in jeopardy being that she might be my half-sister." Beau rubbed his chin in frustration as he heard the words "half-sister" come from his mouth.

When he stood up to leave, he looked at Allison. "When is Mason coming in?"

"Today. I heard from him earlier this morning, and he confirmed he'll come by this evening when he finishes at the pharmacy. As for your mom, I have not heard back from her. We honestly do not need her sample since the father is in question."

Beau wasn't surprised that Isabella wasn't cooperating because she had been very vocal that she didn't think we needed a paternity test.

***

Isabella stopped by the firm mid-afternoon looking for Tucker. Allison was organizing a few things in Tucker's office when Isabella walked in.

"Ali, where is Tucker? The receptionist said he took personal time?" Isabella asked as she leaned against the door frame.

Realizing that any answer Allison shared wouldn't be sufficient, she shrugged. "Yes, he took a few days just to get away from everything and clear his mind."

Isabella stood with her hand on her hip and rolled her eyes. "Get away from everything! Get away from everything?" Isabella yelled. "How in the hell does he get to "get away from everything" when the rest of us are living through this nightmare trying to find our way? He just leaves town when things go south?"

Allison didn't respond because she was certain Isabella wouldn't appreciate her answer.

You created this nightmare everyone is living, Isabella.

Attempting to change the subject from Tucker, Allison told her that Beau had come by earlier, and she collected his sample.

Isabella huffed. "I just hate that Tucker pressured Beau to do this stupid test. We could all be healing right now, but instead, we are prolonging things. Beau was so adamant about testing once Tucker talked to him. I thought I had him convinced to leave well enough alone."

Remembering Tucker's request to not let anyone in his office, she tried to get Isabella to leave. "You coming?" Allison asked looking toward her as she stood in the entryway of Tucker's office.

"No, I'm going to sit here for a moment."

Allison reluctantly left her in Tucker's office wondering how she would coax Isabella out. As she walked back to her office, she replayed Tucker's request in her mind.

Under no circumstances should you allow anyone in my office while I am away.

While heading back to Tucker's office, Allison heard the words "Mason Callaway" coming from the receptionist area.

Seriously? What horrible timing, Mason. Isabella is here. Ugh. I thought you were coming later.

"Mason!" Allison said softly as she rounded the corner of the receptionist's desk. "You're earlier than expected."

"I'm sorry. We had a lull at the pharmacy so I figured I would head over now and get this done. Is now an inconvenient time?" Mason asked.

If you only knew.

Signaling Mason to follow her, she replied nicely, "No, absolutely not. Follow me this way. It won't take more than a few minutes."

Mason sat down while Allison grabbed the sample material.

"I still can't believe I'm sitting here to determine if I have another son." He looked down at the floor as she sat across from him in a chair.

"I get it, Mason. All of this is just bizarre."

Mason at once looked up. "Which part? You said, "all of this"? Which part is bizarre?"

Allison cringed inside as she realized what she had said. "Mason, I'm sorry. I didn't mean anything by that. I just meant I agree that it is bizarre, that's all."

Mason sat back in his chair and unbuttoned his coat jacket.

"You think Isabella was too good for Mason Callaway?" he asked sarcastically.

Allison had always defended Mason when Tucker and Isabella would tell stories about him. She always thought Mason was a kind soul who fell victim to high school innocence and parted ways with this small town. She now saw a different side of him and regretted defending him.

What an asshole!

After his snide remark, she hurriedly gathered the kit to get him out of the office.

She collected the sample and escorted him back to the front of the office. Appearing to be annoyed and eager to leave, Mason raised his hand in the air when she tried to explain when the results would be back.

"Just call me," Mason said as he kept walking toward the exit.

***

Allison headed back to gather Mason's kit and noticed Isabella standing outside Tucker's office, leaning against the wall, smoking a cigarette.

"Isabella, we do not smoke in the office. Put that out!" Allison ran up to Isabella attempting to take her cigarette.

"Uh, I don't think so. I *own* this place. I can smoke inside if I choose." Isabella took a long drag from her cigarette.

"When did you start smoking?"

"Ali, dammit. Let me be. If I feel like smoking, I'll smoke. That is the end of it." Isabella finished her last long drag and put it out on the carpet right outside Tucker's door. "I need to visit the ladies' room and then I'll get out of your hair."

Allison quickly picked up the cigarette butt from the floor and discarded it.

She entered Tucker's office and unlocked the cabinet to place Mason's kit inside. Isabella returned to Tucker's office catching Allison as she hurriedly closed the file drawer.

"Oh, sorry to startle you. I forgot my makeup bag. I need to freshen myself up." Seeing how startled Allison was upon her entering the room, Isabella asked, "What on earth is so important in this office that you have to lock it up?"

She had tried so hard to avoid anyone knowing where she was storing the kits. "Oh, nothing. They are just checks Tucker likes to keep locked up."

"Hmm." Isabella smirked and grabbed her makeup bag then walked toward the restroom.

***

It was almost six-thirty when Allison was locking up the office. She had let the staff leave for the evening about an hour ago. As she turned out the office lights and headed to the front of the office, she noticed Isabella sitting in one of the lobby chairs drinking a glass of wine.

"Join me?" Isabella asked.

"What on earth are you still doing here?"

Isabella smiled her sarcastic half-grin and patted the chair next to her for Allison to sit down.

"Come, sit down," she said while repeatedly tapping the seat of the chair next to her.

Allison sat regardless of the feeling in her gut that was telling her to leave.

"I can sit down for a few minutes, but I promised Kent and Jackson I would be home for dinner."

Isabella laughed at that picturesque image. "Do families really do that kind of stuff?"

"Yes, Isabella, they do. Well, we do at least."

"Look, I just wanted to have a few glasses of wine with a friend. I do not have many friends in this town, and I really need someone right now."

Allison had never seen this vulnerable side of Isabella before. "Of course, I can stay for a while, but then I have to head home."

Isabella grabbed a wine glass off the floor for Allison and poured a glass.

"What a shit show," Isabella said taking a sip of wine and fumbling for her lighter. Lighting her cigarette and taking a drag, she exhaled and sat back in the oversized armchair.

"I honestly never thought this would come out – about me and Mason. I mean, he and I were not a thing. I didn't want anything to do with him other than being his friend. He begged and begged me to go to the lake that evening. We did have fun reminiscing about the past. The night was pleasant until Mason pushed himself on top of me and wouldn't stop."

Taking another long drag of her cigarette, Isabella looked at Allison and said, "You're thinking that Mason and I had some romantic fling that was ruined by me and Tucker getting back together. That's not the case. Mason raped me, Allison."

Isabella took another sip of her wine and reached for the bottle on the floor to refill her empty glass.

"Let me help you." Allison could tell Isabella was struggling to grab the bottle. Pouring her only a sip more, she set the bottle next to her chair.

"Look, I'm really sorry. I knew something had to make you despise Mason all these years, but I had no idea he did that. What an asshole!"

Isabella lit another cigarette while Allison took a sip of her wine.

"I filed a rape charge against Mason that no one ever found out about. Only my parents and the sheriff knew. I never told Tucker or anyone else. I was so ashamed he did that to me. My parents and I didn't want anyone else to know, so we dropped the charges. I wanted nothing else to do with Mason at that point. Tucker and I reunited and have been together ever since. Things just worked out like they were supposed to."

Isabella took another long drag from her cigarette and said, "I didn't mean to hurt anyone by this. Honestly, I planned to keep this to myself until Mason spread those flyers and attacked me professionally. I was so infuriated with him that I lost control. I knew nothing good would come out of this if I told Tucker. Look where we are now."

Allison sat back unsure of what to reply at this point. "Isabella, what a terrible thing to have to deal with at eighteen years old! And to have to live with that all this time all bottled up within you."

"There were many days I came so close to telling Tucker, but things were perfect for us. I would question myself about the damage this would do to our relationship and his heart – not to mention Beau. And for what?

Allison grabbed Isabella's hand to comfort her. "Well, no more secrets. We'll figure out who is Beau's father and no matter what happens, Tucker will always be there for Beau. I know it."

As more wine was consumed, Allison kicked her high heels off and drew her feet up on the chair. "What a freaking day." She gossiped with Isabella about her day as she drank one glass of wine after another until both women were laughing hysterically and found themselves sitting on the floor leaning up against the chairs.

"Pass me one of those cigarettes." Allison clicked the lighter and inhaled. "I don't even smoke." She inhaled deeply and then coughed.

"Me either!" Isabella laughed while twisting her cigarette into the carpet beneath her. "This town has a way of sucking you in, you know. I grew up here and fell in love with my high school sweetheart – hit a few bumps in the road with a teenage pregnancy – but we did well for ourselves in the end, or I think we did."

Isabella started dancing around the reception area like music was playing, spilling wine at each step she took. Without a care, she continued dancing.

Allison stood up and tried to join Isabella, but the multiple glasses of wine had impaired her as she fell to her feet, laughing. Thinking back over the events of the day and specifically how Mason had acted toward her, she became irritated. "Mason was such an ass today. I'm sorry for all those times that I defended him. He obviously *is* full of himself." Allison finally succumbed to her drunkenness and lay sprawled out on the floor.

At the sound of Mason's name, Isabella stopped dancing. "Wait, Mason came by today? Was I here when he came by?"

Realizing she had let that information slip out in front of Isabella, Allison pretended not to hear her.

"Ali!!!" Isabella yelled knowing she was purposely avoiding answering.

Allison sat up from the floor and leaned her back against the chair. Unsure of what the best response would be at this point, she decided to tell the truth.

"Mason came by to give his sample for the paternity test. He had planned to come after work, but he was able to slip away for a moment. And...you were in Tucker's office."

"Dammit," Isabella said irritated. "I haven't gotten the chance to talk to him since the other night. I also wanted to let him know I told Tucker about him forcing himself on me."

She left the lobby area and walked back to Tucker's office. "Where is his sample, Ali? Show me where his sample is."

Allison, attempting to follow down the hall, replied, "Isabella, you know I can't share that with you. Even if I could, I've already sealed the bags to be sent to the lab. There is strict scrutiny on the tests. They cannot be tampered with, or we'll have to start everything over."

Isabella entered Tucker's office and turned back to look at Allison. "What kind of person do you think I am? Are you insinuating that I would tamper with my son's paternity test?"

"Oh, no, I wasn't insinuating anything. I'm just saying the bags are sealed and we shouldn't handle them."

Dizziness overcame Allison as she found her way to Tucker's office door. She might have been inebriated; however, she knew she needed to shift Isabella's focus from finding the kits.

"Maybe it is the wine or that it has been an incredibly long day, but I just remembered the kits aren't here, Isabella. They were picked up earlier and sent off to the lab. I was on a call when the receptionist messaged me to asked me what cabinet they were locked in. The receptionist brought them to the front and handed them to the lab courier."

Allison began feeling dizzier and the room appeared to spin.

Isabella suggested she lie down on the sofa in the waiting area outside Tucker's office.

As she laid back on the sofa, Isabella grabbed a blanket and covered her.

"Thanks, Isabella. I called Kent a while ago and told him I wouldn't be home in time for dinner. He said he would send Jackson to come get me in about an hour, so it is no need to hang around. Jackson has the extra key to the office. I'll be fine."

***

Isabella watched while Allison finally succumbed to the wine she consumed and started snoring.

"Finally!" Isabella didn't believe that the tests were picked up earlier. Allison was inebriated, which ultimately discredited her story. Isabella knew the tests were inside the file cabinet, but she wasn't sure where Tucker kept the key.

As she searched Tucker's office for the cabinet key, a paper fell off the desk and she bent down to pick it up. While kneeling, she noticed a little shiny key protruding out from the keyhole.

Too easy, Isabella thought as she opened the drawer and – *voila* – at the top of the stack were the kits.

"*Jackpot*," she said, opening the zipped bag, and removing the contents.

Looking back at the sofa, she made sure Allison remained asleep. Isabella placed Beau's sample back in the bag and left Mason's and Tucker's on the table.

This is my chance to break Beau and Charlotte up for good. I can't let this opportunity pass by me.

Isabella stared at Tucker's sample.

This is all Tucker's fault and none of this would have happened if he wouldn't have left me alone on homecoming night for Mason to swoop in. Damn both of them.

Realizing this would drive a wedge between Beau and Charlotte permanently, she swapped Tucker and Mason's samples and zipped the bags up.

Chapter Twenty-One

Range of Emotions

Beau and Charlotte's relationship resembled a rollercoaster.

Football had ended but that didn't mean much. Coach transitioned to conditioning for the off-season requiring the team to continue practice after school. Cheerleaders shifted their focus to basketball now that Friday nights weren't consumed with football games. Practicing after school kept them both busy so they only had a few hours at night to talk – and that was usually over the phone.

Beau had convinced himself that Isabella's confession wasn't true. He wasn't oblivious to the stares and gossiping as he walked next to Charlotte in the school halls, but he believed that the paternity test would prove that he wasn't Mason's son.

Charlotte, on the other hand, felt defeated. She loved Beau more than anything, but she couldn't let go of the trainwreck their relationship had endured. Isabella obviously hated her, her father had sex with her boyfriend's mother, and now her one true love could be her half-brother.

How could things be so messed up?

The thought that Beau could be her half-brother completely grossed her out. She kept telling herself that it couldn't be true, but what if it was? She had distanced herself, but he was making it difficult.

"Charlotte, babe!" Beau yelled running down the hall to catch up with her.

"I'm late for class. I can't talk right now."

Beau tried to grab her hand and pull her closer to him, but Charlotte backed away and resisted. "Not here. It doesn't feel right. I have to get to class."

He watched Charlotte walk down the hall and vanish around the corner.

Dammit! I need this test to come back now so she quits avoiding me!

Beau punched the locker door and headed back to the gym lockers to change for practice.

***

Allison was still recovering from her "eventful" evening well into the next afternoon. She had called in sick to the firm and slept most of the morning. Kent had prepared breakfast, but she felt queasy and hadn't eaten anything.

He shut down the shop around three that afternoon and headed home to check on her.

"I think it is safe to say you shouldn't drink wine again– you agree?" Kent said, laughing while changing from his work clothes.

"Ha, ha, funny." Allison sat up in bed. Reminiscing over the events of the night, she grimaced.

"Tucker would die if he knew Isabella was dancing in the lobby, smoking cigarettes and spilling wine all over the place." As the details of the past evening became clearer, Allison froze remembering the cigarettes and wine stains – did they bother to clean up? Then, her mind raced to the kits.

The tests! They are still in the cabinet. Tucker is going to kill me!

"Oh no, Kent. I have to call the office!" Allison frantically exclaimed. "We left a mess and...if that isn't bad enough...the paternity tests need to be picked up by the lab courier."

"Calm down, hun," Kent replied as he stood by the bathroom vanity. "Jackson said he cleaned up last night before he brought you home, and the receptionist called this morning asking where the kits were locked away. I told the office you would call when you awoke."

"That's even worse." Allison fell back on the bed and sank her head into the pillow.

Great, my high school son picked up after his drunken mother partied all night, how embarrassing. And Tucker – he'll never forgive me for any of this, especially when he learns Isabella was part of it.

Kent, trying to hide his laugh, headed into his closet to find his tennis shoes. "Honey, it's fine. Jackson did ask if you started smoking since there were quite a few cigarette butts on the floor—and,er, burn holes in the carpet."

"Stop it, Kent! You're not funny!" Allison said as she threw a pillow at him. "Isabella kept putting her butts out on the carpet. She said she owned the place...this is bad."

She picked up the phone, dialed the firm, and provided the receptionist with the location of the kits.

"Yes! The kits are on their way to the lab." Allison laid back on her pillow. Kent sat on the end of the bed as she hung up the phone with the office.

"I'm glad you enjoyed last night. You stay so busy all the time chasing after me and Jackson. You deserve to have some time for yourself – even though it was with Isabella." Allison crawled across the bed to get closer to Kent and placed her arms around his neck.

"What did I do to deserve such a good man?" She kissed his cheek.

"I love you," Kent said kissing her. "I just have one request – don't turn into Isabella if you can help it."

"Oh please!" She rolled her eyes. "She does have a lot going on right now."

Kent gave her a confused look.

"Well...she kind of created the mess that is going on right now in my opinion," he said. "I mean, don't you agree?"

"Last night, Isabella told me about what happened between her and Mason. It was a mistake." Kent raised his brows; now curious about what Isabella had shared. "She said Mason coaxed her out to the lake and then pressured her to have sex. Kent, Mason raped her."

Allison began to feel guilty that she was sharing Isabella's private confession, but she couldn't keep it to herself.

Kent wasn't surprised at Isabella's confession but found it hard to believe she was completely innocent. Thinking back to their high school days, Kent was familiar with Isabella's manipulative nature.

"Allison, I know your heart is in the right place and you feel sorry for Isabella. I get it. I just want you to be careful. She has always focused on one thing – herself. Everyone knows that. There is no doubt they had sex. He had his eye on Isabella for a long time and everyone knew he was jealous of Tucker. But everyone also knows that she would never be taken advantage of. I can promise you that."

Allison's head fell back against the headboard feeling confused. *Why do I feel so sorry for her then?*

* * *

Whitney had been distant for several weeks and both Stella and Charlotte knew something wasn't right. Even her attendance at school had become more regular than usual.

They cornered Whitney at lunch and coaxed her to sit with them like old times. Blaine, Jackson, and Beau tried to sit with them, but Stella pushed them away.

"Girl talk, guys." She rolled her eyes and turned her back to the guys.

They didn't seem to be jaded by Stella's refusal as their typical lunchtime conversation was centered around one thing – football.

"Whit," Charlotte said when the guys moved away from their table. "What on earth is going on with you? You blocked our calls. You quit coming to practice. We don't see you on the weekends. And you're at school every day! What's going on?"

Whitney fidgeted with a soggy French fry as she stirred it around in the ketchup on her lunch plate.

Stella lightly touched Whitney's arm to get her attention. Whitney looked up at Stella and then to Charlotte and said, "I'm just not ready to talk about it yet, girls."

They watched Whitney go back to stirring the French fry in the ketchup on her plate.

"Well, we are here for you when you're ready." Charlotte grabbed Whitney's hand and squeezed it softly. Stella leaned into Whitney and smiled letting her know they supported her.

As they finished their lunch and made their way to dump their lunch trays, Whitney noticed one of her classmates sitting close to Blaine at the lunch table. She was hanging on his arm and practically trying to sit on his lap. Blaine sat there soaking in the attention.

"Ugh," Whitney huffed and rolled her eyes while throwing her entire plate in the trash.

***

Isabella felt a sense of relief that the results of the paternity test would come back the way she wanted. Thinking back on the night before, she was grateful that Allison was so easy to influence. And she only somewhat regretted manipulating the only friend she had in town.

While her tactic with Allison was successful and the kits were mailed off to the lab for testing, one part of the night still bothered her: Jackson Beale.

Recalling the events of the night before, Isabella remembered the cold stare from him as she closed the cabinet drawer.

Surely, I'm overthinking it. He was picking up his inebriated mom from her office. I'm sure he was a little embarrassed... that's all.

While she told herself to chalk it up to paranoia, Isabella couldn't shake the uneasy feeling that Jackson was a risk.

Chapter Twenty-Two

Biological Father

The end of the week, Tucker returned to town expecting to hear the results of the paternity test. The last several days he had spent reminiscing about the past and how in love he and Isabella were when they were younger.

Given Isabella's strong personality and ego, many wondered how Tucker could've loved her so deeply. He typically was passive and always succumbed to Isabella and smoothed things over.

As his mind centered on the events of the last few weeks-- her having sex with Mason and Beau not being his son-- Tucker couldn't forgive her easily this time.

We slept together only a few weeks before she slept with Mason. That night was so special...at least it was to me.

Walking into the firm, he noticed the carpet stains and burnt spots in the lobby.

What on earth happened here?

Allison had arrived at the firm early that morning, knowing Tucker was back in town.

"Well, it's so great to see you!" she said as she walked behind him following him into his office.

"Yeah, I guess I'm glad to be back," Tucker responded. "What in the world happened in the lobby?" Allison took a seat across from his desk.

"It all started with your wife..." She walked Tucker through the events of that night.

"What in the hell was she doing here in the first place?"

Allison felt Tucker's anger. "She was looking for you."

"Me! What on earth did she want with me?" he questioned. "She knew I was leaving. I told Nessie she couldn't stay at the camp house alone since I was going out of town. I'm positive Nessie would've told Isabella."

Allison, now realizing Isabella hadn't been honest with her, became a bit frustrated. "She didn't say what she wanted. She ended up spending most of the day in your office." She raised her hands. "Before you say anything, I tried everything in my power to *remove her* from your office. But she kept reminding *me* that she partly owned this business, and she'd do as she pleased."

Tucker had only been back in town for an hour, and Isabella was already making him angry.

Seeing that Tucker's anger was building, Allison tried to diffuse it by telling him the kits had been sent off and expected back today per the lab.

He felt a sense of relief.

"That's at least a positive. I want to put all of this behind me. I'm glad Mason came in and cooperated. I wondered if he would even show up."

***

It was almost noon when the lab courier dropped the paternity results off at the courthouse. Tucker had instructed the results to be dropped off directly to the judge's office so that Isabella couldn't accuse Tucker of tampering. The judge's clerk left a message that the results had arrived. All parties were to be in the courtroom at three o'clock for the reading of the results.

Tucker's mind was racing in different directions all day and three o'clock couldn't get here soon enough.

Mason and Melissa arrived at the courthouse around two-thirty and sat in the back in hopes of avoiding Isabella. Melissa had been supportive of Mason and understood that everyone had a past. Secretly, she hoped Beau was Tucker's son. She knew how much Charlotte cared for Beau. They were both good kids and didn't deserve all this heartache and worry.

Melissa squeezed Mason's hand when Isabella entered the courtroom. Looking over toward them, Isabella glared and took a seat at the front of the courtroom next to Beau and me. Tucker sat across from us alone so once Isabella sat down, I decided to sit with him for support.

"Nessie, where are you going?" Isabella asked pointedly.

"I'm going to sit with Tucker – chill out." As if she had ever cared before.

Beau sat motionless, staring into space, and was oblivious to everything surrounding him.

Charlotte, Stella, and Whitney appeared – the trio arrived as one – and took seats behind Beau and Isabella. Charlotte reached over and touched Beau's shoulder to let him know she was there. Feeling her touch, Beau turned slightly and grabbed her hand resting on his shoulder.

"Thanks for coming," he said and turned back around.

Kent and Allison arrived right before the judge walked in, so they sat in the back of the room. To Allison's surprise, she didn't see Jackson. She knew he would want to be here to support Beau.

Where are you, Jackson?

It was now three on the dot and the bailiff yelled, "All rise," as the courtroom stood and watched the judge make his way to the bench.

"Today, the court will hear the results from a paternity test to determine the biological father of minor, Beau Corbin. The court will not hear testimony since all parties consented to the paternity testing." The bailiff brought the sealed envelope up to the bench handing it over to the judge. After opening, the judge placed his glasses down and asked Mason, Tucker, and Beau to rise.

"The paternity test to determine the biological father of minor Beau Corbin is conclusive. The test results can be contested should any party find fraudulent behavior is associated. Once read aloud, the biological father will assume the legal responsibility of the minor child and pay associated child support should the child not live with the legal father."

When the judge picked the letter up, Isabella held Beau's hand for support.

Beau looked over at Tucker who was staring eagerly at the judge to read the results. Beau felt Charlotte's hand again on his shoulder but stared directly at the judge waiting for the answer.

As the judge unfolded the letter and read the results, Beau remained silent. It was like the room was spinning around him as it filled with the sound of the gavel and whispers of the results.

Mason is my father, kept running through his head as he sat in disbelief.

Chapter Twenty-Three

The Aftermath

Whitney had decided she should tell Blaine about the baby. His baby.

Would he even care since I'm not pregnant anymore?

After playing tug of war in her mind about it, she finally decided Blaine had the right to know that he *was* a father – even though it was for a moment of time.

Since football was over, on Saturdays, Blaine worked on the farm.

She knew she would find him either on a tractor or near the horse corrals. As she drove down the long driveway to his house, something inside her kept telling her to turn around thinking that this wasn't a great idea. She resisted the urge and kept driving. When she got closer to the house, she saw Blaine working with the horses and parked near the front of the barn.

He looked up from over the saddle he had placed on his horse.

What is she doing here?

He took his gloves off and headed over to meet Whitney.

"Hey," Blaine said when he got closer to her car. "What's going on, babe? I think this is probably the only time you have come here during the day."

He laughed.

Whitney still found Blaine irresistible even with his sarcastic comments. After all, he did have a point. She hated the outdoors, and a bonfire beer party was about the only time she'd been to the farm.

"Hey," Whitney said as she stood a foot or so from him and placed her hands in the back pocket of her jeans.

"I haven't seen you around much lately," he said. "I was kind of getting worried you didn't like me anymore," he laughed, trying to lighten the mood.

"Blaine, can we be serious for once please?" Whitney moved closer to him. "I have something to tell you, and I don't want you to be mad at me for keeping it from you. I just felt I needed time to think things through."

He had never seen her so serious before. But instead of talking she just stared at the ground. Even the horse started getting impatient and stomped.

"Well...tell me! I've got horses to saddle, animals to feed, and then I gotta plow the backfield. It can't be that bad!"

Whitney started to have mixed emotions of anxiety and anger while her stomach turned hearing the words "I *was* pregnant" replay in her head while Blaine was angry that she was deterring him from his work. Her resistance to mouth the words "pregnant" was suddenly overshadowed by the fury building inside her induced by his response. But he deserved to know.

Taking a deep breath, she looked him in the eye. "I was pregnant, Blaine."

Whitney watched his face as he shook his head in disbelief and began backing away from her.

"What!? No way, babe – no way you're pregnant." Blaine continued shaking his head and looking away from her.

She moved in closer and grabbed his hand to regain his attention. Blaine pulled away and walked back to the barn.

"Great, Blaine, thanks for the support, jackass!" Whitney yelled. She quickly wiped the tear away to avoid showing any signs of weakness. "You don't get to just walk away!"

She continued yelling as she followed him into the barn. Forcing him to look at her she asked, "How do you think I've felt over the last several weeks, huh?"

"I've been alone dealing with this not knowing what the right path was."

Blaine was silent as he walked away from her to close several doors inside the barn to contain the horses.

As he closed the last stall door, he slowly walked back toward her.

"Wait a minute. You said *was* pregnant. Did I hear you right?" Blaine asked as he replayed the last few minutes in his mind. "Why did you say *was*?"

Whitney moved closer and this time he didn't back away. "You heard right. I *was* pregnant. I had a miscarriage. I lost our baby."

Blaine stared back at her motionless.

"Talk to me. Don't just stare at me and not say anything!" Whitney placed her arms around his waist.

Blaine didn't move nor respond to her touch as he stood staring and speechless.

Whitney rested her head on his shoulder ignoring the awful smells from inside the barn and avoiding the dried mud on his shirt. He didn't hold her back like she had imagined he would. She hoped that hearing the news of what she had been through he would console her.

"Blaine, say something. What are you thinking? Say something!" she demanded, looking up at his face.

"I don't know what I'm thinking honestly. One minute you're telling me you're pregnant and then telling me you're not."

Blaine backed away from Whitney's hold.

"How do you even know it was mine? I mean, I know we slept together in the barn after homecoming, but c'mon – was I the only one?"

Whitney held back tears of anger while she listened to Blaine directly accuse her of lying *and* sleeping around.

"What an asshole!" She tried to turn away and walk out of the barn.

Blaine grabbed her arm. "Wait...I'm just asking: how you know it was mine? I feel like that is a fair question!"

Whitney turned toward him with despair. "Because you were my first, Blaine. I haven't slept with anyone else. And just so you know in case there is an ounce of concern inside you– I'm fine."

Pulling her arm away from his hold, Whitney walked out of the barn back to her car. Blaine didn't follow her. He just stood and watched her walk away.

Whitney grabbed the handle of her car door while another car pulled up beside her. It was the classmate who was flirting with Blaine in the cafeteria. She got out of the car, waved at Whitney, then headed toward Blaine at the barn.

Whitney rolled her eyes and drove off.

How could I have been so stupid to fall for him so easily?

***

Charlotte hadn't heard from Beau for several days after the results were read. I hadn't seen much of Beau either and we live in the same house. He had become a recluse, and honestly, I didn't blame him.

Charlotte called the house several times a day only to hang up when Isabella answered. Charlotte wanted to hear Beau's voice more than anything, however she was relieved when he didn't answer because she wasn't sure what to say.

Her heart ached at the fact that Beau was her half-brother. Her mind would wander to them kissing and holding one another and it felt so perfect – and then she had to block it out.

We can't stay together–obviously, she kept repeating to herself, but her heart felt differently.

***

"Hey, honey. Just wanted to check on you." Melissa walked by her room and noticed her door was cracked open.

Charlotte knew her mom meant well and was only trying to comfort her, but she didn't feel like talking about it. "Thanks, Mom, I'm okay. I just wish Beau would answer or call me back. I just need to talk to him."

Sitting on the bed next to Charlotte, Melissa hugged her. "Honey, he just needs some time to think through all of this. I can't imagine what he's thinking and feeling. I feel so bad for him...for both of you."

Charlotte leaned on Melissa's shoulder as a tear rolled down her cheek. "Thanks, but nothing can make my heart stop hurting. I loved him. We had something special, and now I don't have a clue what happens next. He's going to sit down at dinner with me...?"

Charlotte struggled to hold in her emotions as the thought of Beau never holding her close again looped in her head.

Melissa held Charlotte closer and comforted her. "We'll figure this out one day at a time, honey."

***

Mason had retreated to his hunting camp giving time for the news to settle down, however, he knew things would never settle down easily with Isabella involved. With her at the helm, things were just getting started.

Beau didn't resemble him in any way which made it more difficult for Mason to fathom that he was Beau's father. However, the results had to be true, and now everyone had to face the facts.

That one stupid night. If my pride wouldn't have gotten the best of me, my family wouldn't be in this mess right now.

He cradled his whiskey tumbler and tossed the ice ball around in the almost empty glass and pondered how things would've been different if Isabella had chosen him instead of Tucker all those years ago.

I wanted Isabella more than anything that night, and she wanted me back. She instigated it.

He continued reliving the events of that night that ended so terribly – with Isabella back in Tucker's arms. Mason became more irritated as he recalled her accusing him of forcing himself on her.

She has lost her mind!

As he sat his tumbler down on the table, he laughed to himself.

Maybe I did win by losing Isabella to Tucker. After all, Isabella is a poison that destroys anything and everything in her path to get what she wants. I wouldn't want to be Tucker right now.

***

Tucker was one hundred percent certain that he couldn't forgive Isabella for the turmoil she had caused their family. Upon hearing that Mason was, in fact, Beau's biological father, Tucker knew that he couldn't be a part of her life any longer -- other than communicating with her about me.

I had instantaneously become the stick of glue that held the family together – if we were even a family at this point?

Tucker made the decision to draw up the divorce paperwork and Isabella was served a few weeks later.

He moved out to the camp house permanently and let Isabella have the house while I finished high school. While Tucker didn't like being alone, he loathed Isabella and couldn't be around her for any length of time. His drive to work from the camp house was quite a bit longer than from home, which provided him with more reflection time as he navigated the windy roads following the lake.

How could something so perfect that has lasted for so long turn so very wrong?

As Tucker drove into the firm one morning, he struggled with loving Beau as his son for sixteen years and now having to relinquish his role of father to Mason Callaway.

I'm not going to let go that easily. Beau is still my son.

Tucker parked his car in front of the firm and noticed Isabella's car parked a few spaces down from his car.

What in the hell is she doing here?

When he walked through the door, Isabella was sitting in the lobby.

"What the hell is this?" Isabella struck Tucker with a manila envelope.

Divorce papers.

Ignoring Isabella's strike and question, he kept walking toward his office with her following. She leaned against the frame of his door, staring, probing him for a response.

"If you think you're going to change my mind, you're wrong," Tucker said. "I loved you as my wife and mother of my children for a long time. I thought we were perfect. Hell, everyone in the town thought so. Sure, we had our difficulties, but who doesn't?" Tucker sat against his desk staring back at Isabella where she stood, her arms crossed.

"Isabella, through the years I've managed your mood swings and persistent nature to have everything precisely your way. I've sat back and let you run the show of life. The moment you shared that you and Mason were together was a huge blow. Perhaps it might have been different if you'd told me in a different setting other than during a debacle with Mason. In the heat of the moment, while lashing out at Mason, your secret was made public."

Tucker paused and stared, surprised that she hadn't interrupted him. "I just have to ask; did you honestly *want* me to find out?"

Isabella moved closer to Tucker and sat on the edge of the sofa. "No, Tucker...I mean yes..." For once Isabella struggled to respond. "What I meant to say is, I didn't want to hurt you or anyone. It was one night Tucker – one night – an awfully long time ago and it meant nothing to me. The best part of that night was when I saw you. I mean that. What good would it have done to tell you about Mason back then? Huh? You wouldn't have stayed with me, and we're perfect for each other – you know that."

Tucker softly laughed to himself and rubbed his chin. "There you go again– doing what you do best. Spinning this around in your favor – avoiding the truth. Whether you loved Mason or not –because I don't know what to believe at this point– you slept with him and lied to me about that night, *and then* kept it from me our entire marriage! Not to mention lying to me about Beau!"

"I did *not* want to sleep with him! I explained what happened! Mason forced himself on me!" Isabella's voice became more defensive.

Tucker grabbed his coffee mug from his desk. "Maybe. Maybe not. But we are over, Isabella. I can't do life with you anymore. There is nothing you can say or do at this point to mend what you have broken. Yes, I agree. We had a forever love. Sadly, you've ruined that."

Isabella shook her head. "No. It sounds like your heart just needs some time to heal. I'm willing to give you that time, honey."

Before Tucker could respond, she had turned around and walked out of the office.

Shaking his head at her continued persistence, Tucker looked down at his wedding ring. Removing the band from his finger, he placed it inside his desk drawer and said, "This is how I'll heal," and slammed the desk drawer.

***

My life had been turned upside down quite a bit over the last two months. I'm not overly emotional generally–rarely emotional at all – and the latest news had pulled at my heartstrings more than I thought it would. The idea that Isabella kept secrets from Tucker, and moreover our family, throughout their marriage disgusted me. With the potential loss of a brother and Tucker not living in our home, I naturally became more distant.

Due to all the commotion going on with the paternity test results, my reclusiveness went unnoticed. Lately, I found safe harbor in my bedroom. Rarely does Isabella come by to chat or check in. My retreat to my bedroom and being alone felt right to me.

When the paternity results were shared, I felt the need to hide...or change. I couldn't put my finger on it exactly, but I knew I needed space to figure things out. I had distanced myself from Owen as well, of which I wasn't proud. But I needed to figure some things out for myself and not be bombarded with questions from anyone.

School was difficult. The stares coupled with the questions looming in everyone's mind were becoming unbearable. Beau had not returned to school yet, so I felt the brunt of everything. As a straight-A student, I'd always chosen the front seat in the classroom, but lately I found myself sitting in the far back of the class hoping to be invisible. Isolating myself made me feel in control, and as each day passed, school became a little more bearable.

Home was a different story. Isabella was a tyrant – not much had changed. Her receipt of divorce papers had her head spinning, and she couldn't understand why Tucker wanted to end things.

Her phone conversations with Allison were nauseating. "I just don't see how he can throw all of what we built away!" and "How can he not love me for this – it was a mistake? I was honest thinking telling him was the right thing to do."

I'm sure Allison agreed on the other end of the line just to be nice.

Isabella didn't need comforting – she needed followers.

As days passed, I found myself spending more time at the camp house with Tucker. I knew he needed company and was truly lonely.

Most nights we both sat in silence while he watched TV, and I read my book. It was a comfortable silence that I appreciated.

He had made the right decision to divorce Isabella in my opinion, but he would have to be strong to deal with her through the wrath of filing it.

Chapter Twenty-Four

The Breakup

Since the paternity results were shared, Beau hadn't seen Charlotte — and he longed to hold her in his arms and kiss her — until he woke up from the nightmare that had become his life. His entire world had entered chaos mode – from losing his girlfriend and his dad at the same time.

One day back at school Beau already felt different without Charlotte by his side. She usually would wait for him near the student parking entrance each morning. As he pulled into the parking lot, he glanced toward the door where she typically stood eagerly waiting for him – and she wasn't there.

Walking into school, everyone was glad to see him. He was relieved the "news" didn't seem to be the gossip in the hallways. Blaine and Jackson joined his side while they walked down to their lockers.

When Beau opened his locker, he realized Charlotte had removed her things.

"Sorry, man," Jackson said noticing Beau's disappointment.

"She cleared her stuff out the other day, dude." Blaine slammed his locker and walked across the hall to his class.

Beau leaned his head against the cold metal, realizing this was going to be more difficult than he thought.

Jackson struggled to be more compassionate than Blaine. "Maybe you can talk to her today, man. But right now, we gotta get to class." Jackson shut his locker and Beau followed.

***

Charlotte was late for school. Driving into the parking lot, she noticed Beau's car. *He's back*, she thought as her heart jumped.

No. I have to stop.

But her heart was stubborn.

She had to go to the office to sign in since she was late, and her path took her by Beau's first-hour class. As Charlotte passed by, she didn't look inside hoping to avoid seeing him.

Beau swallowed the lump in his throat when he saw her pass and quickly looked back down at his paper.

This is going to be hard. She was my everything, and I've lost her.

After the bell rang, Beau hoped he'd have the chance to catch up with Charlotte in the hall, but he didn't see her. At lunch, she was nowhere to be found. He searched the cafeteria and outside where everyone visited until the bell rang.

She's avoiding me.

At the end of the day, he walked out to the student parking lot with Blaine and Jackson -- trailing behind the crowd of students because Coach had stopped them in the hall to talk about the next season.

"We're going to The Dixie, you coming?" Blaine asked, getting into his truck.

"Nah, I'm going to pass, man," Beau answered as he opened his car door.

The parking lot had cleared with only a few cars remaining – and then, he saw her. Charlotte was leaning against the driver's door of her car staring back at him. His heart began beating faster and he wasn't sure what to do next. Before he could decide, he noticed she was headed toward him.

"Hey," Charlotte said softly walking up to the passenger side of his car.

"Missed you today." Beau instantly thought, *Wrong thing to say*.

Charlotte smiled. "Can we talk, or do you need to be somewhere?"

"Nope, I wanted to talk to you today, but I couldn't find you," Beau replied. "Want to get in?"

Charlotte opened the door.

It felt different being in his car and not touching him or being close to him. She placed her hands in her lap deciding that was the safest place to secure them.

Beau felt bad that he hadn't called her and wanted to apologize. "Look, I'm sorry I haven't called. I didn't know what to say to you. It's just been a lot to take in, and I'm still trying to understand it. So much has changed in such a short time – my head is spinning."

Charlotte felt at ease sitting near Beau – like old times – just not as intimate. She heard the words "didn't call you" and "apologize" but was distracted by the sweet smell of his cologne and his lips that she had missed kissing.

Reaching for his hand and then stopping mid-way, Charlotte responded, "Beau, I can't imagine what you're thinking or feeling. I wanted to be there for you, but you pushed me away. I know you're hurting inside, but I am too. I felt all alone."

She looked down toward the floorboard as he reached over and grabbed her hand. "Thank you for waiting for me and coming over. I looked for you all day and didn't see you. I know this is weird and things are different between us now, but I still have feelings for you—which I know isn't right...or doesn't feel right."

Charlotte's emotions ran wild. While her heart was telling her to kiss him, her mind was telling her to leave.

"We had the perfect relationship until this blew up." She squeezed Beau's hand. "I think we both know where this goes, unfortunately."

Beau let go of Charlotte's hand. "I've been running this through my mind...and it doesn't make any sense. Something just doesn't feel right. I don't want to lose you, but I know we can't stay together."

Hitting the steering wheel with his hands Beau yelled, "Dammit!"

His action startled her. He shook his head and gave a crooked smile.

"Sorry. Look, I've been thinking. We should get the test re-submitted at a different facility. I think it is worth it. I don't want to lose you and if this does break us apart then I want to be confident in the reason."

Charlotte looked out the passenger window and closed her eyes, hoping she would wake up from this unbelievably bad dream. Opening her eyes and turning back towards Beau, she could see the anguish in his heart.

"Beau, I'm not sure that another test would make things better. Allison took ownership of the kits, and they were sent off securely to the lab. I trust in the process. I know you're grasping at straws for a way out of this, but prolonging the inevitable based on the hope that the test was false is only going to drag this out further."

Beau shook his head and looked out his window. She wanted him to be right and maybe another test would prove Tucker was his father, but she wasn't convinced that her heart could ride the rollercoaster of emotions that retesting would bring with it – only to find out it was Mason.

"I'm not dropping this, Charlotte," Beau said cranking his car. "I want another test for validation, and I'm hiring someone independent to do it. Then, I can move forward based on the results. I can't lose you over this. I'm going with my gut. Can you please give me some time to figure this out and we go from there? I love you too much to let you go this easily."

Charlotte longed for Beau to grab her in his arms and comfort her -- making everything okay -- but she knew that wasn't going to happen.

"I understand you wanting to get another test. I get it. I can't stop you and won't try to. However, in the meantime, I can't continue to pretend that one day this all goes away, and we can date again. That isn't fair to either one of us, Beau. My heart aches for you to hold me and kiss me like before – but it doesn't feel right." She looked away, saying, "I think for now, we need to part ways. It makes sense while we figure out the next steps. It hurts me so much to even say that."

Beau sat staring at Charlotte as the words "part ways" came off her lips.

"I don't know if I can part ways with you. You have been my life for the last six months. I love you more than anything."

"Beau, don't!" Charlotte exclaimed as a tear rolled off her cheek. Wiping it away quickly, she turned to him. "I loved you too, but it has to be over."

He reached across the console and grabbed her arm. "It's not over until I get the new test results! You'll see this is all a misunderstanding. I hope you love me enough to wait for that."

Charlotte pulled free from Beau's hold on her arm and ran from his car.

Watching him leave the student parking lot, Charlotte said, "My heart hopes you're right, Beau Corbin."

Chapter Twenty-Five

The Truth Will Hurt

Beau was determined to order another paternity test and that's all he focused on. After discussing it with Tucker, he felt even more inclined to move forward with it.

Tucker didn't object to Beau having another test taken, but he wanted Beau to understand that simply requesting a new test solely due to his skepticism would be difficult to convince the judge without justification.

"Son," Tucker said. He was accustomed to calling Beau, but now it felt odd hearing those words aloud. "I just want you to be aware of the roadblocks. This won't happen overnight. Frankly, while unfortunate, I believe the test is honorable.

I trusted Allison with keeping the results locked away – although...never mind, she said they were locked up and then a lab courier picked them up and delivered them to the court."

Beau still couldn't explain why but he felt like something wasn't right. "Dad, I get it. I'm willing to take the chance. I don't care what a judge says, something just doesn't feel right. An independent test will reveal the truth."

***

Since the night Jackson picked up Allison from the firm, he couldn't forget the way Isabella looked shaken when she saw him at the door of Tucker's office.

What was she doing in his office?

Jackson hadn't said anything to Allison, but it kept running across his mind.

What if she did something to the tests?

Isabella wouldn't stoop that low knowing the news would break her family apart – would she?

The more he thought about her being in Tucker's office that night, he decided to just let it go.

***

All Beau could talk about at school was getting the second test results. Jackson and Blaine couldn't get a word in edgewise.

"I just have to get Mason to agree to do it again," Beau said as he leaned back in his desk chair.

Jackson, sitting behind Beau, leaned forward. "Man, you really want to reopen the gossip? It is sort of dying out at school. You wait for another test and what if the answer's the same? What did you gain?"

Beau understood where Jackson was coming from, but it was the same reasoning everyone else had given him.

"I'm doing it, man. I have to know if it's true. Dad – Tucker, not Mason, said if I can prove fraud then it has more weight to go back to court." Beau turned toward the front of the class.

"Fraud?" Jackson asked not following.

Beau replied, "Yeah, fraud. There could be any number of things that could've happened to that sample. I'm getting a completely independent sample and using a different testing facility that is not affiliated with anyone we know."

Jackson looked at Blaine who wasn't paying attention to their conversation but flirting with the girl sitting next to him.

Jackson shrugged his shoulders.

Maybe this is my chance to finally get closer to Charlotte. After the second test shows Mason is his dad, he'll have to give up. I feel bad for Beau, but he had his chance and fate decided differently for them.

***

Jackson stopped by the firm after school to drop something off to Allison. "How was school?" she asked as he entered her office. "Okay, I guess. It was just a normal day – nothing special." He plopped onto the sofa in her office.

"I've just got a few more things to do here, and I should be home earlier than usual. I can stop by the market and grab something to cook." She placed a few files back in a cabinet.

"Hello, Jackson," Tucker said walking in.

"Hey, Mr. Corbin," Jackson replied.

"Allison, can you walk with me for a minute, please?" Tucker asked.

She followed him into the hall. Jackson sat on the sofa waiting for her to return. He could hear whispering from the hall and then the sound became fainter. Finally, he decided to wait in the lobby for her to finish with Tucker.

As he got closer to Tucker's office, he overheard Allison saying, "I put them in the bottom of the filing cabinet each time I completed a sample. And yes, I locked the cabinet each time and always kept the key on me. No one else had access to the cabinet. There is one extra key, and I was the only one who knew where it was kept."

"The next day when the courier picked up the kits, I was at home sick, so the receptionist had to use the extra key to get into the cabinet. I told her where it was when the courier arrived at the office."

Jackson tried not to look in as he crossed in front of Tucker's office. "Bye, Mom, I'll see you at home." He waved and kept walking.

"See you at home, son," Allison replied as she continued her discussion with Tucker.

When Jackson left through the front door of the firm he thought, *Maybe my curiosity about Isabella being in Tucker's office isn't bizarre. That was the same filing cabinet Isabella was standing near when I startled her.*

***

With help from Tucker, Beau found a paternity testing facility an hour from Sedipar that would take samples at their location only. They did not accept pick-ups from labs.

Beau and Tucker had scheduled an appointment for the following Monday at the facility. Tucker had tried contacting Mason, but he was still out of town. Melissa expected him to return the following week.

Melissa said Mason would cooperate because he had some skepticism about the results. When Isabella was involved, Mason had little confidence.

Tucker had discussed with Allison the second paternity test which brought up the questions about the kits and where she had stored them. The night Allison and Isabella stayed late at the firm was mostly a blur. Allison remembered singing and Isabella dancing as they both had too much wine. She didn't remember Jackson driving her home.

I guess I blacked out during the time Isabella put me on the sofa and Jackson picked me up. What in the world did Isabella do during that time? Jackson came into the firm to get me so maybe he can shed some light?

Initially, Allison was confident in the paternity test, and had reservations when Tucker explained that Beau was seeking to take another one. She feared by prolonging the inevitable, Beau would never heal.

However, after Tucker's pointed questions about the kits, she thought, *Could Isabella have tampered with the kits somehow?*

***

Beau and Charlotte, while not officially together, remained friends and talked quite a bit at school. She preferred to minimize their interaction as it proved difficult for her to be around him and not get close to him. Charlotte had convinced herself if she pushed him away and spent less time with him, her feelings would diminish over time. Beau was convinced otherwise and wanted to remain friends.

He shared the news with Charlotte that he and Tucker were going to the independent testing facility the following Monday. With Mason being out of town, there would be a delay with the results, but he was one step closer to the truth – so he thought.

"Maybe we should all celebrate at the Abyss this weekend," Charlotte said while putting her books in her locker and closing the door.

"Do you want to ride with me?" Beau quickly asked. "Not as a date though, friends," he added.

Charlotte shook her head. "I'm going to see if the girls want to meet up, but thanks."

Beau had class across the hall but before walking into the classroom said, "Yeah, I get it."

During class, Charlotte spread the word about going to the Abyss Saturday night. Everyone was exhausted and needed a break.

"It feels like forever since we all hung out." Stella plopped in the chair behind Charlotte.

"I definitely could use some girl laughs," Whitney said as she put lip gloss on. "I need to talk to y'all after school if y'all have a minute."

"Sure, Whit, we can meet you in the parking lot after school."

Whitney hadn't shared her news about the miscarriage with Stella and Charlotte and knew she had to tell them before Blaine told everyone.

After school, the trio met up near Stella's car and Whitney told them about the baby, the miscarriage, and then about Blaine.

"What an asshole!" Stella responded hearing how Blaine reacted.

"Oh, Whit, I can't believe you didn't tell us so we could've supported you!" Charlotte was upset that Whitney kept this to herself to deal with alone.

Whitney explained that she had planned to tell them before the miscarriage, but felt she needed to tell Blaine first. Then the miscarriage happened, and she didn't know if telling anyone about it would even matter. After time passed, she realized she needed to let Blaine know. Now she regretted her decision based on the way he reacted.

He had moved on to someone else and wasn't bothered that she had gone through everything alone. "Anyways...I'm better now...especially after telling my besties. I've moved on. It feels good talking to y'all."

"It has been too long ladies!" Stella said hugging both Whitney and Charlotte.

***

Blaine and Whitney hadn't spoken since she told him her news. He obviously *had* moved on with his new "victim," and Whitney was okay with it.

It was odd seeing Blaine in the hall with his arm wrapped around another girl. But, Whitney knew it was for the best since he showed his true colors, not taking responsibility nor acting like he cared about her feelings.

Blaine passed by Whitney in the hall, barely smiled at her, then quickly looked away. Whitney didn't feel comfortable even being his friend at this point since they never truly had closure.

On the last bell, she hurried to the locker room in the gym to grab her bag. On her way out she ran into Blaine leaning up against his new girlfriend along the gym wall. Placing her bag on her shoulder, she casually walked over and interrupted them. Clearing her throat to get their attention and looking directly at him, Whitney asked, "Blaine, can I have you for a minute please?"

The girlfriend gave Whitney a nasty stare as Blaine kissed her again and slapped her back end. "See you in a little while at The Dixie," he said as she left the gym.

Whitney rolled her eyes in disgust.

He will break your heart soon – don't get too attached.

"Blaine, look, I just want to clear the air."

He laughed under his breath. "Clear the air about what?"

Whitney rolled her eyes and tried to hold her anger. "Blaine, quit playing stupid. My pregnancy. My miscarriage. *Your* baby. Does that clear it all up for you?"

Blaine stepped back toward the bleachers and sat down on the bottom row. Leaning forward with his arms resting on his legs he looked up and said, "Whitney, I don't know what to say. I could say I'm sorry. You want me to apologize for having sex with you? We both wanted it."

Before Blaine could continue, Whitney stopped him. "I can't believe that is your focus – we both wanted to have sex! Yes, you're right. But both of us made the choice to have unprotected sex, and I got pregnant. I own that. You should too! And to top things off, I lost the baby and had to deal with that tragedy – alone!"

Whitney stood shaking in front of Blaine who sat motionless on the bleachers. "When I told you what happened you didn't ask one question about how I felt or what I went through or if I was okay. You just wanted to know if the baby was yours. That was cruel and selfish. Blaine, I went through a lot of emotions and navigated it alone because I was scared and didn't know who to tell. You were so hurtful."

Blaine could see she was upset and tried to calm her down. "I'm sorry that I wasn't there. I didn't know – you didn't tell me so I *could* help."

Well, maybe Blaine does have a conscience and a heart.

Whitney was slightly convinced he might have a heart until Blaine continued, "But hey, things work out like they are supposed to. I mean, it sucks you lost the baby, for sure, but things are back to normal now. I'm sorry you had to go through all of that alone, but it's in the past. You seem to have moved on, and I have too."

At that moment in time, Whitney realized clearing the air would never happen with him. He would never get it. He would never understand. She made the decision then to clear her life of Blaine Ferrell, for good.

***

Jackson was upstairs in his room when Allison came home from work. "Jackson, honey, can you come downstairs when you get a minute?" she yelled from the base of the staircase.

Jackson came downstairs minutes later and found her in the living room.

"Hey, Mom, what's up?" he asked as he sat on the sofa next to her.

"Just curious about the night you picked me up from the firm." He took a deep breath realizing what was coming.

"Do you happen to remember if Isabella was still in the office when you got there?" Allison asked.

Jackson fidgeted with the tassels on the throw pillow as he framed his response. "Yeah, she was there. Why?"

"Oh, no reason, I'm just curious. Do you recall *where* she was at in the office when you came in?" she asked.

"Uh, umm...no, not really." He looked away.

"So, you don't recall where she was in the office, but you remember seeing her?" she asked again.

"Mom, I feel like I'm on trial here!" He laughed while tossing the pillow off his lap. "I mean, I guess she was back there with you waiting for me to get there. Isn't that what friends are supposed to do?" He hoped his answer would suffice.

Allison, still not convinced Isabella was there solely to befriend her replied, "Yeah, I suppose so. I remember her giving me a blanket and telling me to rest. Of course, I was in no shape to reason with her on letting me sleep versus calling you then to get me. Unfortunately, I don't remember much about that night -- which I'm not proud of."

Jackson could tell Allison wasn't buying his story, but he had made the decision not to get in the middle of this and did *not* plan to share any information. "Mom, you texted me that night and said to get you within the next hour. So, that's what I did."

"Oh, yes, I guess so... again, I don't remember much. So, embarrassing!" Allison placed her head in her hands. Looking back up at Jackson she said, "You don't remember seeing her by any filing cabinet in Tucker's office?"

Jackson felt a lump in his throat. He knew the answer to the question was "yes", but he was on a path to finally getting an opportunity to spend time with Charlotte. He couldn't give up so easily.

"No, ma'am."

"Okay then, well, that's all I was curious about. Thanks, honey," Allison said as she went back into the kitchen.

As Jackson walked back upstairs to his room, he felt both relieved and frustrated at the same time.

Chapter Twenty-Six

Party at the Abyss

Everyone was excited about the big party at the Abyss this weekend. It had been a while since everyone was able to just hang out-since Blaine's HOCO party. And with football season over, Friday nights were far less inviting.

The final bell rang dismissing students to enjoy their weekend. Blaine, Beau, and Jackson exited the building into the student parking area and met up with a few other team members hanging around Blaine's truck.

The trio saw the guys congregating near Blaine's truck and walked over. Charlotte felt Whitney hesitate as she slowed her pace. "I can't go over there y'all. Blaine made me so mad in the gym the other day, and honestly, I just can't be friends with him."

Charlotte and Stella turned back toward Whitney. "We get it," Charlotte said. "Let's go by The Dixie and get some fries and hang out a bit."

"Thanks, girls," Whitney said feeling relieved.

As the trio walked into the parking lot, Beau waved. Charlotte waved back quickly and kept walking to her car.

Jackson watched Beau as he broke away from the group and headed to meet the girls. "Hey, where are y'all going? We were all talking about tonight trying to get a game plan." Beau looked at Charlotte hoping she had changed her mind about going with him.

"We are going to The Dixie to grab some food before we get ready for the party tonight." Charlotte found it so hard not to make eye contact with Beau.

"All right then, I guess I'll see y'all at the party!" Beau said as he slowly turned away and headed back to Blaine's truck.

***

There were few people at The Dixie when the trio pulled up. Charlotte placed the order in the window as Stella and Whitney sat at the tables underneath the awning.

"Blaine is such an asshole," Whitney said as she noticed him pull into the parking lot.

"Yep." Stella watched Blaine get out of his truck to check his tires. Blaine never looked toward them nor came over. He hopped back in his truck and left.

"He infuriates me – the way he doesn't care. He just *does not* get it. I keep thinking I'm past it and over it, but when I see him, my emotions go crazy wanting to kiss him and strangle him at the same time!" Whitney had told herself to let go of Blaine and move forward, but it had proved harder than she imagined.

Charlotte came back with their food and drinks, and they talked about plans for that night.

"I can meet y'all before and we can follow each other out there," Charlotte said.

"Sounds good! Stella, you want to ride with me?" Whitney asked as she crumbled the paper that held her burger and threw it in the trash.

"Sure thing, Whit," Stella replied. "Pick me up around nine."

***

Blaine picked Beau up around seven-thirty and they headed to Blaine's house to grab some firewood. As they loaded up the truck, he noticed Beau wasn't his usual self.

"Man, you gotta quit thinking about Charlotte. I know y'all had a thing, but she's like your half-sister – which sounds really weird by the way," Blaine said continuing to load the truck.

Beau kept throwing wood into the back of the truck, blocking out what Blaine had just said.

Just wait until we get this second paternity test.

Seeing that Beau was ignoring him, Blaine grabbed the piece of wood from his hand to get his attention. "Look, you've got your entire life in front of you. Charlotte wasn't the one. Fate has proven that. We have the next three years of high school to play football and chase girls. Me and you, man. You wouldn't have wanted to be tied down with just one girl the rest of high school, would you?"

The more Blaine talked about moving on from Charlotte the angrier Beau felt. But he knew Blaine wouldn't stop pressing until he said *something*.

"Look, I get it. I appreciate your "support," but I love her man. I don't think the paternity test was accurate. Something in my gut tells me it was wrong. I can't give up on her not knowing the truth. Until I get this second result back, I'm not letting Charlotte go. I have to go with my gut."

Blaine flipped up the tailgate once they finished loading the last few pieces of wood and they both jumped back in the truck. As they headed down the driveway, Blaine looked over at Beau and handed him a beer.

"Here, man – this'll make it all better!" Beau grabbed the beer, opened the can, and almost finished it in three gulps.

"Give me another one," he said as Blaine opened the ice chest on the floorboard and handed him another.

"Hell yeah!" Blaine yelled, tossing the empty can out of his window. He watched in his rearview as it fell into the back bed of the truck.

As they drove out to the Abyss –and under the influence of a few beers– Beau continued focusing his discussion on the second paternity test and how Mason couldn't be his father.

"You're killin' my buzz, bro," Blaine said as he rounded a curve heading to the Abyss.

"Sorry." Beau looked out the passenger window, staring at the trees.

Blaine wasn't the best at showing emotions – other than his natural ability to flirt with girls– but he had never seen Beau this way before and wanted tonight to be fun.

"Look, I know I'm not the best person to get advice from in the relationship department. Hell, I sure messed things up with Whitney – not that I planned on anything serious with her." As Blaine took the last sip of his beer, he reached out the window, tossing another can into the bed of his truck. Grabbing another beer from the ice chest on the floorboard, Blaine said "I really screwed things up with her. You know we got together the night of the homecoming dance. It was great. I knew she wanted me because she flirted with me all night. I pulled her away to the barn and we ended up out there most of the night."

"Yeah, I think the entire school knows y'all slept together Blaine," Beau said.

"Whatever, man," Blaine replied. "Everyone else was practically doing the same thing around the fire."

Beau reminisced on that night with Charlotte and how perfect it had been...Charlotte's body lying up against his as he held her close in the bed of the truck and that feeling of wanting her so badly. He lost track of the conversation with Blaine.

But Blaine continued to talk about Whitney and her acting weird and Beau's reminiscing was halted when he heard the word "pregnant."

"Hold up– did you just say pregnant?"

Blaine looked at Beau and laughingly said, "Yeah, man. I said pregnant. You faded out on me for a while."

"Yeah, I guess I did, but who is pregnant?"

"Whitney." Blaine took another curve along the windy back road. "Well, she *was*, I guess I should say. She lost the baby a few weeks ago." Finishing another beer, Blaine shouted out the window, "Hell yeah!" when he saw all the headlights from cars pulling into the Abyss.

"Blaine – man – what the hell?" Beau responded, confused by the news. "Is Whitney, okay? Does she need help?" Beau could tell that Blaine had moved on and wasn't concerned much about the Whitney conversation.

If Blaine felt any regret, it quickly vanished upon arriving at the party.

"Blaine, you didn't just ignore the fact that Whitney was pregnant. Did you?"

Blaine grabbed the ice chest from the seat and looked back at Beau. "No, I didn't ignore her. She came to talk to me *after* all of this happened. She didn't have the decency to tell me she was pregnant *until after* she lost the baby. She's pissed now because I wasn't sensitive to her feelings or didn't care about her. It wasn't like we were going to get married or anything. It was a fun night – we both wanted it – and she's not pregnant anymore. So that's that."

Beau sat in the truck trying to dissect what Blaine had just shared with him.

Charlotte was right about Whitney. Something had been going on, Beau thought as Blaine closed the driver's side door and walked toward the party.

***

The Abyss was the perfect spot for parties – deep in the woods, secluded- providing the perfect place for noisy teenagers seeking to hang out. I was never much of a partier and while the Abyss was a beautiful place filled with serenity during the day – perfect for reading – at nighttime, the drunkenness, topped with masculine egos, childish flirting, and drama made it less inviting.

Tucker had called Beau and me earlier and asked if we wanted to come by for dinner. Beau already made plans to head to the party with Blaine, but I took Tucker up on the invite.

As I drove out to the camp house, I thought, *Why did it take my parents splitting up for a connection to form with Tucker – Dad?* If I were close to anyone in our family now, it would be him. Over the last few weeks, I had seen a different side to him, a softer side, a caring side – caring toward me.

When I drove into the driveway, Isabella was walking to her car. She waved at me. It didn't surprise me that she immediately hopped into her car and sped away without saying a word.

"Well, you must have said something that ticked her off," I said as I walked through the door and placed my purse on the counter.

"You know your mom, Nessie. Unfortunately, she stays ticked off most days." Tucker got up from his chair in the living room and headed toward the kitchen.

"I'm not sure if she was ever truly happy." I sat on the barstool. Standing across from me drinking a glass of wine, he smirked. "No partying for you tonight?"

Laughing at his response, I pulled out one of my books and waved it in his face, and said sarcastically, "This is my party tonight, Tu...Dad"

He smiled. Looking happier than I'd seen him since Isabella's secret came out.

He was an excellent cook when he felt like cooking. Tonight, he had made his famous fish couvillion, and I could smell the fresh bell peppers and onions as he sauteed them in butter. I sat and talked while he cooked dinner, and it felt nice.

All the years living in the house together, I could count on my fingers how many times this had occurred before. Maybe I hadn't given him a fair chance all these years *or* maybe it was just Isabella?

We made small talk about several books I was reading as he finished cooking dinner.

Around nine we started watching a movie about an attorney who had lost a case that caused him to lose his job, resulting in him moving to California to start over. Tucker seemed interested in the movie, so I agreed to stay and watch it. But I became bored after about an hour and pulled out my book. I got caught up in my book and realized another hour and a half had passed. He was sleeping. The credits to the movie were rolling so I turned off the TV. I didn't want to wake him since he looked comfortable so I left a note I would be back tomorrow and gathered my things.

As I drove away from the camp house, a light drizzle started. The rain wasn't heavy but aggravating enough to make it difficult to see the road. When I neared town, I decided to stop in the library.

Sitting at the desk alone, I smiled.

This is the beginning of a new chapter with Dad. We can start over.

***

The trio arrived at the Abyss around nine-thirty, and everyone could tell Charlotte had been drinking. They had gathered at Stella's house before and they had snuck cocktails.

"Heyyyy," Charlotte slurred as she walked up dancing and holding a cup filled with alcohol. Several classmates greeted her as they headed to the bonfire.

Stella and Whitney followed closely behind. Stella caught a glimpse of Jackson sitting on the tailgate of a truck laughing and talking with Beau and Blaine. She grabbed Whitney's hand to walk toward Jackson but seeing Blaine, Whitney hesitated.

"Whit, you can't avoid him the rest of high school. Walk by him and show him you're tough and don't need him."

Whitney thought about it for a minute. "You're right. I'm better than him anyway."

Blaine caught a glimpse of Whitney heading his way and thought, *Here we go again*, but was surprised when she walked by and playfully said, "Hey boys!" and kept walking.

Stella and Whitney found Charlotte sitting on a tailgate across the bonfire from the guys. It was obvious that she'd had more to drink than Stella and Whitney.

Whitney had taken Charlotte's car keys at Stella's house because Charlotte argued about driving.

"I gotta take my car y'all. I need to leave earlier than everyone tonight. I have something in the morning early so I can't stay out late." Whitney finally coaxed Charlotte into letting her drive to the party.

"I can just grab a ride with Stella home, no biggie," Whitney said knowing Charlotte wouldn't be in any condition to drive later either. She'd probably be passed out before midnight.

"My besties!" Charlotte yelled as Stella and Whitney walked up to the tailgate where she was sitting. Putting her arms around both, Charlotte spilled some of her drink on Whitney.

"Oh shit, my new blouse!" Whitney said. Irritated, she walked back to Stella's car.

"Oh, Whit, c'mon! It's just pineapple juice and rum! It's mostly clear!" Charlotte yelled as she stumbled to sit on the tailgate.

Stella helped Charlotte sit down and she asked for more to drink. "Charlotte, honestly, babe, you don't need anymore."

Charlotte placed her fingers on Stella's lips and laughed. "Shhh. You...don't get to tell me what to do."

Whitney reappeared with a new shirt she found in Stella's car. Blaine noticed her walking back to the group and started toward her.

"Where've you been?" Blaine asked, smiling at her.

"I had to change my blouse – Charlotte is wasted and spilled her drink on me."

Looking over across the bonfire, Blaine saw Charlotte stumbling in the crowd. "Yeah, she looks pretty messed up tonight. Guess she felt like doing it up good."

"Yep," Whitney responded dryly as she watched Charlotte lose her balance while Stella caught her. "I need to go – my friends need me."

Blaine watched Whitney walk back over to her friends.

Damn, she's so hot. Maybe she'll give me another chance.

***

Beau had noticed Charlotte was more rambunctious than normal and longed to be beside her, but he respected her request to keep his distance. Deep down he wanted her to come over and talk to him. While he tried not to be obvious, he had been watching her closely making sure no one got close to her. She never drank this much, and he became worried about her.

Standing near the bonfire, Whitney approached him and handed him a beer. "Here you go – you look like you could use another one."

"Thanks, Whitney. Perfect timing," Beau smiled.

Staring toward the fire and watching the flames, she said, "You know, it's funny how everything can seem to fall in line so perfectly and then – Wham! – something happens to knock it all off track."

Beau took a sip of his beer and nodded. "Tell me about it. Unfortunately, I had everything in line and then one day it is all a mess." He wanted to ask Whitney how she was doing, but he didn't want to put her on the spot. Blaine didn't tell him not to say anything, but it wasn't his business to pry.

"You may want to come over and check on Charlotte. I noticed you're keeping an eye on her. I know it must feel strange not being with her. I'm sorry." She placed her hand on Beau's arm. "She's drunk. I think we are about to take her home."

Beau looked over at Charlotte. "Nah, she doesn't want me around. She was clear on that. She told me she wanted to be by herself. Can y'all just make sure she gets home safely please?"

Whitney replied, "Sure thing," and walked back to stand near Stella and Charlotte.

Beau navigated back through the crowd and found Jackson. "Where's Blaine?"

Jackson pointed. "Over there."

As Beau looked across the bonfire, he saw Blaine leaned up against a truck bed kissing some girl. Shaking his head, Beau looked at Jackson. "He'll never change, will he?"

Charlotte had made her way near Beau and Jackson. Jackson caught a glimpse of her stumbling in the crowd.

"Charlotte is messed up tonight," Jackson said to Beau as he watched her stumble toward them.

"Yeah, she drank too much for sure. I asked Whitney to be sure she made it home safely," Beau replied.

As Charlotte had her way through the crowd, she bumped into a senior who had crushed on her since the beginning of school. He put his arms around her waist and pulled her forcefully to him. "Where do you think you're going?"

"Just walking around checking out the party." She felt herself sway back and forth and her head began to spin. "I think I need to sit down for a minute."

"You look amazing tonight, Charlotte," the senior whispered in her ear, and then his lips softly kissed hers.

She was caught off guard and pushed him away, but he pulled her in closer. She started to push back against him but became dizzier and lost her balance. As she fell toward the ground, she felt someone grab her from behind and catch her fall. She could see a faint image above her then she passed out.

Charlotte's body felt so light, almost weightless, as she seemed to float through the air. She could hear faint noises in the background but couldn't make out any of the words. Between the smell of smoke from the bonfire coupled with the alcohol that she spilled when she fell, she struggled to find the source of the faint smell of *his* cologne. Beau's cologne.

Her eyes fluttered open and she saw a blurry image of the dark, night sky and then his image became clear. It was Beau carrying her away from the party.

***

As he pulled her car into her driveway, Charlotte began to wake. She had dozed off again as he drove her home from the party.

"Hey," Beau said softly as she opened her eyes and leaned her head back against the seat.

"What happened?" she questioned placing her hands over her face. "I don't remember much of anything. I feel terrible." She closed her eyes again.

"You passed out." Beau stared through the windshield.

"I brought you home, and Stella and Whitney are going to meet me at my house to get your car and bring it back here. Do you want me to walk you inside?"

Everything was such a blur and Charlotte was confused. "Were you at the party?"

"Yeah, I was there."

"Gosh, I really pulled a good one, didn't I? I feel like I'm going to vomit."

Beau reached over Charlotte's lap and opened the passenger door, and she leaned out to get fresh air.

"This is better, thanks." Charlotte closed her eyes again. Her head began to spin with her eyes closed so she forced them to remain open.

"I didn't see you at the party."

Beau kept looking straight ahead resisting the urge to look her way. "I was there with Jackson and Blaine. You didn't want me to be with you tonight – remember? – so I kept my distance."

"Beau, I didn't mean you couldn't come talk to me. I would've talked to you if I would've seen you."

He fought the urge to grab her hand and pull her close to him. "Well, you seemed to be having fun – *maybe* a little too much fun." Beau gave her a sly smile.

Charlotte reached over and slapped his jacket and leaned back in her seat.

"How did we end up here?" Charlotte bit her lip hoping the nausea would subside.

"I saw that guy kiss you and watched you push him away – and then he pulled you back toward him. I could tell you didn't want to be a part of it. As I got closer, you lost your balance and fell. I caught you and – here we are." Beau swallowed hard, waiting for Charlotte to curse him for interfering with that guy. He waited for her to tell him that he had no business watching over her – that they weren't together anymore.

Charlotte found Beau's hand resting on the console and grabbed it. She wrapped her fingers inside his and leaned closer to him in her seat. "That's great – I don't remember much of that other than him kissing me. Thank you for being there for me. But you do understand that I'm not yours to save anymore. You don't have to worry about me."

Beau hoped that by some small chance, her holding his hand meant she might have changed her mind, but her words said otherwise.

"When I asked you how we ended up here, I meant here in this mess – broken and alone. I know you're holding on to this second test, and while I wish we had the results today that Mason is not your dad – we don't. It hurts too much continuing to wait for answers when we already have the answer."

Beau, feeling frustrated the test had become the center of their conversation again, replied, "I'm doing the test, Charlotte – it is scheduled. Consider it done."

She strengthened her hold on Beau's hand. "I just hate seeing you like this and honestly think the second test is just prolonging things. I loved you with all my heart and it broke me to know we can't be together. Things are different now, and we have to accept that."

Beau squeezed Charlotte's hand not wanting to let go. "You say that now but wait until the results come back. I promise you; the first test wasn't right. I feel it in my gut."

She turned back toward the car door, feeling queasier than before. "Thanks for driving me home. I guess I'll see you later. You're meeting Stella and Whit with my car, right?"

"Yeah, they're meeting me at my house. I still love you Charlotte – nothing will change that– ever."

Beau watched her shut the door and stumble up the porch steps to the front door.

Chapter Twenty-Seven

The Accident

Around midnight, there were only a handful of teenagers still hanging around what remained of the fire since curfews had forced many of them home.

The off and on rain showers also made the party less inviting.

The bonfire had lost its energy and the ground quickly became soggy.

Stella and Whitney were pulling out of the gravel road when Blaine stumbled to the passenger side of Stella's car.

Knocking on the window, he yelled, "I need to talk to you, Whitney."

Looking at Blaine while rolling down the window, she said, "We are in a hurry to meet Beau. You have five seconds, Blaine – that's all you got. And...it starts now."

He grabbed onto the side of the door and leaned down closer to Whitney. "Babe, I'm sorry for everything I said and did. I was wondering if you wanted to stay here and hang out with me longer? I can take you home."

Whitney began to roll up the window. "Go to hell, Blaine. You know we are over. And you're drunk. Go home!"

Blaine moved his hands off the door and Stella sped away.

Blaine stumbled around trying to find his truck. A football team member saw Blaine getting in the driver's seat. "No, man, I can't let you drive. I'll take you home, and my buddies will follow."

"Hell no!" Blaine said pushing the guy back. "I'm fine to drive, bro." Blaine cranked up the truck and slowly made his way down the gravel road.

***

Beau left Charlotte's house feeling even more determined to get the test results. As he drove back to his house, he thought, *I know she still loves me and wants that second test as much as I do. I can't be apart from her. I'm no good without her by my side. She means everything to me.*

The weather had gotten worse since he dropped Charlotte off. The wipers were going back and forth furiously trying to keep up with the rain. With each curve he took, the rain became heavier.

He couldn't help but replay the events of the night. His mind kept repeating her words. *Things are different now and we have to accept that.*

"Dammit," Beau said striking the steering wheel with his hands.

As Beau slowed to round the next curve, he was blinded by headlights and shielded his hand above his face to block them. Instinct made Beau pull the steering wheel to the right to avoid whatever was now invading his lane. For a moment he felt the car leave the ground –he felt weightless – and then he blacked out.

***

Down the road past the curve, a black Ford F-150 sat idling in the middle of the road. The rain began to pick up again and the taillights in the rearview mirror that were once visible began to fade away.

Blaine sat leaning on the steering wheel trying to recall what had just happened. He looked around trying to find what caused him to be parked in the middle of the road.

"Snap out of it, Blaine, you're just seeing things," he said and put the truck in gear and drove away.

***

Minutes later an ambulance, volunteer fire department, and every police car in Sedipar arrived at the scene. The fire chief, noting the damage, reported, "It looks like we have a one-vehicle accident. I'm unsure of survivors at this point." Looking down the embankment, the small sedan was wedged between several cypress trees that stopped its entrance into the Bayou Fueob. The taillights were blinking furiously on the car, and it smelled like it was leaking gas.

As the response team made their way down, they saw a male driver.

"I've located one male who appears to be pinned inside the vehicle with substantial head injuries." The team member placed the radio down to allow the receiver to answer.

"One male. Pinned in vehicle. Head injury. Can you confirm status?" the receiver asked.

The EMT paused, then, "He does not appear to be responsive at this point. At this point, it may just be recovery. We need to get him out of the vehicle to further assess."

They worked to extract Beau from the car.

***

Meanwhile, Stella and Whitney were headed to meet Beau at his house to get Charlotte's car. As they approached the scene of the accident and saw the lights, they pulled to the side of the road and walked closer to see what had happened.

The traffic was blocked due to the emergency vehicles on the road. Stella and Whitney joined the crowd of onlookers as everyone tried to figure out what had happened. The police were not talking to anyone.

***

I was heading back from the library when I saw the cars and lights flashing. I pulled over on the side of the road like everyone else and walked toward the scene. I saw Stella and Whitney standing together and walked up to see if they knew what was going on.

"No, we don't know anything." Whitney looked back at the sheriff.

I tried peeking around the crowd to get a glimpse of anything but the police cars, fire truck and ambulance had everything blocked. The rain continued to fall lightly as we waited for someone to explain to us what was going on.

I made my way to the other side of the crowd hoping to be able to see something. I heard the sheriff's radio go off and he turned to respond to dispatch. I couldn't see anything from this side, so I went and stood near Stella and Whitney.

The rain began to pick up again and the crowd slowly began breaking up and heading back to their vehicles. Stella, Whitney, and I, still wanting to know what happened, stood in the rain.

We watched the fire truck leave – and next the police cars – followed by the ambulance. The sheriff had relaxed a bit now that the crowd had thinned and walked closer back toward the scene.

When the responders cleared the area, the three of us watched the tow truck pull a car from the embankment. It was at that moment we saw "CHAR97" on the license plate.

The rain began to fall harder forcing us to run back to our vehicles.

It can't be... I thought, running back to my car.

Stella and Whitney were running alongside me frantic and upset. Whitney shouted, crying hysterically, "We can't lose both of them!"

As they reached their car, before I could ask a question, I watched their car speed away.

***

I sat motionless watching the rain continue to gain momentum while it poured down my windshield. Tears fueled by confusion began to flood my face, matching the fierceness of the rain that was now pounding my car.

Speculation is dangerous but I was going to find out who was in that ambulance.

Chapter Twenty-Eight

Lifeless

"One hundred and fifty-five, fifty-six, fifty-seven..." quietly left my lips as I stared helplessly down the narrow hall of the emergency room. The small squares of vinyl tile that adorned the hospital hall floor had consumed me over the last half hour after I'd burst through the ER doors while the EMTs unloaded the patient.

My words were choked and breathless as I nearly hyperventilated. "I think...that ambulance...just brought my brother in...! And...his girlfriend may have been with him. I'm not sure!" A kind nurse calmed me down and confirmed what my gut already knew.

Beau wrecked the car. But where was Charlotte?

The medical staff told me to take a seat in the waiting area, so I called Dad and waited. *And waited.*

The emergency room of Parish Regional Hospital left much to be desired. The carpet in the waiting area was in desperate need of a deep clean as coffee stains covered most of the surface. The chairs were donations from larger medical facilities that were on their third or fourth renovation. The wooden armrests provided me with some distraction as I read the various messages that had been scribed into each.

I watched doctors and nurses scurry down the hall toward the operating room. I leaned over in my chair, looking at the doors while they quickly opened and shut hoping to catch a glimpse of something – hopefully more answers.

Finally, exhaustion got the best of me, and I dozed off leaning my head against the wall. Just when I felt my body relax, I heard Dad's voice.

"I got here as fast as I could, Nessie." His hand rested on my shoulder.

"Do you have any more details? Has anyone told you what happened?"

"No, nothing." I slowly opened my eyes - and set up straight to stretch. Thinking back over the events of the night while Stella and Whitney's comment, "*We can't lose both of them,*" replayed in my head like an annoying needle looping on a record.

The few minutes of sleep helped, however, my mind continued to battle my body by refusing to relax.

Dad sat next to me as I explained what I saw at the accident site, which wasn't much other than Charlotte's car, made obvious by the license plate. I continued trying to connect the dots however a few things were not adding up.

Why was Beau driving? He was supposed to be at the Abyss which is on the opposite side of town. Why would he be on this side of town...in Charlotte's car? I thought, searching for answers.

"I guess Beau took Charlotte home – that's why Stella and Whitney were freaking out about losing both Beau and Charlotte," I softly murmured-- however, I was apparently louder than intended.

"What did you just say? Losing Beau...?" echoed across the small waiting room as I heard *her* voice. Isabella. I assumed Dad called her.

Things were complicated enough without having to deal with *her*.

"Nessie! I asked you a question. Why did you say *losing* Beau? He isn't...?"

"He's still alive, Isabella," Dad said.

She took a deep breath, then shook her head. "What does Charlotte have to do with this?" Isabella angrily walked toward me.

Dad stood up, putting his hand out protectively, "Isabella, just settle down. The doctor hasn't come out yet. Quit interrogating Nessie. We are all trying to make sense of this mess. No one has even confirmed Charlotte was involved, right?" he asked me.

I shook my head. "Whitney and Stella went to her house. They'll call as soon as they know something."

Isabella rolled her eyes. "Nothing surprises me if a Callaway is involved. What in the hell was he doing with Charlotte in the first place?"

I dryly replied, "We don't *know* they were together. We don't know *anything* yet."

Desperate to avoid Isabella's pointed questions and stares, I stood. "I'm going to stretch my legs." I got up and walked down the hall.

"Wait up, Nessie. I'll walk with you." Dad joined me, leaving Isabella in the waiting room alone.

Just as we approached the corner of the hall, we heard the operating doors open, and a group of doctors headed to the waiting area.

We turned around hoping they were coming to share details. I noticed their faces were long, expressionless, and silent.

Dad grabbed my hand as we got closer to the doctors and whispered, "This doesn't look good, Nessie."

***

Blaine made it home and ended up passing out in his truck. The next morning was a blur as he found himself sprawled out across the seat of his truck. When he attempted to sit up, his head began to pound, and nausea set in. He heard the tractor crank from behind the barn and knew his father would shortly be over expecting him to get to work.

Yeah, that's not happening today.

Lying back down on the seat Blaine closed his eyes hoping his throbbing headache might subside.

Guess I got pretty drunk, he thought as he tried to recall the party from the night before. He remembered driving out to the Abyss with Beau and talking about Whitney but everything after that was a huge blur.

Blaine's father drove past the truck shaking his head. "Sleep this one off, son."

As he began to drift back off to sleep, he was awakened by a light tap on the driver's side window.

"Blaine, honey. Tucker Corbin is on the phone for you," Blaine's mother said. "You need to come in and get a shower anyway. You pulled a good one last night it seems." She left him in the truck as she walked back to the house.

***

Beau lay lifeless on the operating table while doctors frantically scurried around removing his blood-soaked clothes and prepping him for surgery. His breathing was shallow, and he had lost a tremendous amount of blood.

Rescuers at the accident scene noted there was likely severe head trauma, and the surgeon now had a clear view of the deep laceration that was the culprit of the bleeding.

"Cerebral laceration...currently unresponsive...not responding to any stimulation," the surgeon blurted out as he continued his assessment. "It appears he also has spinal fractures. Let's get him to radiology for a CT."

"Any family in the waiting area?" the surgeon asked. A nurse nodded. "Yes, a..." she glanced at the paperwork, "sister. Corbin is the last name. She's been sitting out there since the ambulance brought him in."

Upon hearing the last name, the surgeon quickly glanced at Beau and then looked down at the floor in dismay as he moved closer to the door. As he expected, Isabella was waiting in the hallway.

Gently nodding toward her, he gave her a sad smile. "Dr. Corbin. I've just learned that the patient we have been assessing is your son. He's currently..."

"Oh, cut to the chase Dr. ..." Isabella replied dryly searching for his name tag. "I don't have time for any of this. I need to get in that operating room. He needs his mother. I want to see his chart...now!"

"Dr. Corbin," the surgeon replied, "he has significant bleeding and swelling on his brain in addition to spinal fractures. We have sent him for a CT scan and we'll follow with surgery. He's unresponsive currently and on a ventilator."

My heart sank again as Dad held me closer. While Beau and I were never close and he was a complete pain in my butt, he was still my brother – I guess he's my brother – nonetheless, I loved him and didn't want to lose him.

"I want to see him!" Isabella exclaimed walking toward the doors.

The surgeon followed closely behind replying, "Dr. Corbin, while I understand you want to be with your son, I think it is best you remain out here with your family. You have every right as a physician to enter that operating room, however, I strongly discourage you."

Isabella continued walking toward the door ignoring the surgeon's suggestion.

The surgeon quickly followed her. Before he could get through the door, Dad approached him. "Was my son the only one brought in from the accident?"

The surgeon nodded. "Just him."

***

Mason and Melissa entered, running frantically up to the receptionist desk. Dad noticed them bust through the doors.

"Mason," he said coldly as he continued walking past them and headed back toward me in the waiting room.

When the receptionist hung up the phone, Mason asked, "Where's my daughter? Charlotte Callaway? She's been admitted here in this hospital we were told."

Dad overheard Mason ask about Charlotte which piqued his curiosity.

The surgeon said only Beau was being treated for injuries.

As the receptionist scanned the admittance list, Mason looked back at us and walked over. "Tucker, have you heard or seen any sign of Charlotte?" Mason asked as Melissa stood back at the desk waiting for the receptionist to provide answers. "No, I haven't."

Mason swore. "We've been out of town since midday Friday, and we got a call from the wrecker service this morning that Charlotte's car had been involved in an accident after midnight and the driver was taken here. We haven't been able to contact Charlotte since we got the call. We stopped here first to see if she was admitted and then planned to go by the house."

While Dad couldn't stand Mason at this point, he could tell he was plagued with worry. He knew he had to tell Mason that Beau was driving Charlotte's car. "I don't have a clue where Charlotte is, but I can tell you that she wasn't involved in the accident last night. Beau was driving Charlotte's car."

"Beau? Beau was driving her car. What on earth...then...where is Charlotte?" Mason stood in shock as Melissa hurried over from the receptionist area.

"Charlotte isn't here, Mason." Melissa said grabbing Mason's arm. "Let's go to the house and see if she's there." Mason pulled away. "Wait, you said Beau was driving?"

"Yes, Beau was driving. The surgeon just confirmed that he was the only patient admitted from the accident." Dad grabbed my hand seeking support as Mason and Melissa continued questioning him.

Hearing the news for the first time, Melissa held on to Mason's waist and laid her head on his chest. "Beau...was...is he okay?" Melissa asked as she felt some relief that Charlotte wasn't involved but now her focus moved to Beau.

"We don't know at this point," Dad replied. "He is back in radiology getting a CT scan. He had significant head injuries and spinal fractures. He's currently non-responsive. Isabella went back a few minutes ago."

Melissa began to feel weak, so Mason helped her to a chair in the lobby area. "Sit here, honey," Mason said. "I'll go grab you a coffee."

"Walk with me, Tucker, please." Mason motioned for him to follow. Reluctantly Dad followed down the hall toward the cafeteria.

"Man, I'm trying to wrap my head around all of this," he said as Dad stared at the floor.

"Yeah, I know. I've been sitting here for over an hour waiting on answers...and we have nothing other than a definite head injury, spinal fractures, and he's not talking." Dad continued, "You know it was raining off and on last night. I've preached to them about going slow on those back roads especially at night and around those dreadful curves."

"Was there another car involved?" Mason asked.

Dad shook his head no. "I don't think so, however, we haven't spoken with the police yet. I assume that's coming next, and you and Melissa should be here."

By the time they got back to me and Melissa in the waiting area, Mason felt obligated to wait for more news on Beau but was still concerned that Charlotte hadn't contacted them. He asked me to drive Melissa back to their house to see if Charlotte was there.

Torn between wanting to see Beau but having to deal with Isabella, I agreed to drive Melissa home. "Whitney and Stella were going to your house. But..."

"They wouldn't be able to get in if Charlotte's not there."

"They'll assume the worst." Melissa told Mason as she headed to the front of the hospital. "I know Nessie probably wants to wait here..."

"It's fine, really," I replied as Dad mouthed "thank you" and turned back, facing the emergency room doors.

***

Driving back to Charlotte's house, Melissa remained quiet as she stared out the passenger window.

When we passed the site of the accident, I briefly glanced to my left at Bayou Fueob as my mind flashed back to Charlotte's car being pulled from the embankment. Beau's face is all I could see as I imagined him lying on the operating room table, lifeless, fighting for his life. I wiped a tear as it rolled down my cheek thinking this could not be the way life ended for Beau.

And then my favorite Hemingway quote came to my mind, "Every day is a new day. It is better to be lucky."

My heart hung on the words "a new day" hoping that the new day would bring a positive recovery.

Was Beau continuing to win in life based only on luck? Perhaps his luck was beginning to run short.

Nothing exciting typically happens in our little hometown of Sedipar.

Lately, I had begun to think otherwise.

Chapter Twenty-Nine

When Reality Sets In

Charlotte tossed and turned in her bed trying to escape the nagging headache that plagued her from last night's drinking bout.

Ugh, I can't sleep with this throbbing.

She attempted to bury her head under her pillow for relief.

Why did I drink so much last night?

Rolling over in her bed, she rubbed her eyes hoping the clock was wrong.

Three-thirty. I just knew it was only one or so in the morning.

Attempting to walk to the bathroom, the entire room seemed to spin, and she fell back on the bed.

Lying back down hoping the nausea and dizziness would subside, she closed her eyes. The spinning failed to cease. Feeling miserable and helpless, she sat back up and forced herself out of bed.

Making her way into her bathroom, she drew water for a hot bath and found her favorite station on the radio. She quickly slipped into the deep tub and closed her eyes.

***

Stella and Whitney knocked on the front door hoping for Charlotte to greet them.

"Girl, it's so dark...she must be passed out." Stella propped up against the front porch column staring back at the front door. Whitney continued ringing the doorbell and knocked furiously yelling Charlotte's name- hoping desperately to find her home and safe.

"Owen's car is here. He must be in some deep sleep to not hear us knocking," Whitney said as she peeked through the porch windows.

"His room is on the back side of the house. You know he uses that sound machine that resembles a jet engine. He can't hear anything with that noise going." Stella had given Whitney a reprieve from knocking.

After ten minutes had passed with no answer, both girls, feeling helpless, took a seat on the front porch rocking chairs.

"Whit, I hate leaving her. I know she has to be inside. What if she needs our help, and she's unable to move? We have to get inside." Stella began pacing the front porch.

"There's no way for us to get inside, but we're not leaving her. We're going to sit in these rockers until Mrs. 'M' gets here." Both girls tucked their legs up into the rockers and attempted to get comfortable.

Downstairs, the answering machine picked up and Melissa's voice frantically called for Charlotte. "Charlotte, honey, if you're home, please pick up the phone! I need to hear your voice and know you're okay. Call me back once you get this!"

***

News of the accident traveled quickly around town and every breakfast table was filled with gossip over what *could* have happened.

Blaine stopped by the gas station before heading to the hospital. As he placed a Coke on the counter, he noticed the news channel covering the accident on the TV.

"Such a shame, you know," the cashier said shaking his head as he handed Blaine his change.

"What's a shame?" Blaine cockily replied. *Does he know something? Did someone see me there?*

"Oh, just that the poor boy is in such bad shape I heard. He hasn't woken up yet either. He sure was a lucky fellow," the cashier responded.

Blaine grabbed his things from the counter and stared back at the cashier. "You don't know Beau well," Blaine said harshly while forcefully pushing open the doors to exit the store.

When he got back in his truck, he slammed both hands on the steering wheel.

Man...you gotta wake up, Beau. You gotta wake up from this.

***

The nurses brought Beau back to the operating room where Isabella was patiently waiting for his return.

Seeing Beau on the operating table hooked to IVs with various tubes protruding from his body coupled with the ventilator sent Isabella to her knees. Seeing him in such an unstable state was too much for her to handle.

"Dr. Corbin!" the surgeon said excitedly as he caught Isabella in her fall. He nodded toward the doors insinuating for them to bring her into the waiting area.

Two nurses holding Isabella under her arms, walked her into the waiting area. Everyone looked toward them, desperate for an update on Beau.

Dad, driven by habit, immediately grabbed her hand, guiding her back to the waiting area. He could see the desperation on Isabella's face. She never showed much emotion so Dad knew it must be bad.

"Isabella," Dad softly whispered while positioning a chair in front of her. "Isabella, he said again, "look at me."

Quickly wiping the tear that rolled down her cheek she replied coldly, "It's not good....it doesn't look good at all for my sweet boy."

She pulled his hand up to her lips and attempted to caress her face.

He immediately pulled his hand away and stood up from the chair. "Isabella, I refuse to think that way. Beau is strong, and he's going to pull through this. We have to believe that!"

Mason hurried over toward them. "What did ya'll say about Beau? Did they see anything on the CT scan?"

Isabella shifted in her chair while focusing on the operating room doors. Dad looked down at the floor waiting for her to respond.

"Will someone please tell me what's going on with my son in there!" Mason yelled directing his frustration to Dad and Isabella. "I have every right to know what's going on!"

Dad walked away leaving Isabella to deal with Mason. After all, they had created this mess together.

"Isabella!" Mason raised his voice as she stared blankly down the hall. "Answer me, dammit!"

"I don't owe you anything," she finally responded as Mason stood over her.

"What?" He gave a sarcastic chuckle. "You don't owe me anything!? My son, who you kept from me for sixteen years, is lying on a table behind those doors, and you don't owe me anything?"

Stepping back from Isabella, he continued, "Put aside your hatred for me and think about our son."

Hearing the words 'our son' made Dad look at Mason with disgust. While Dad was coming to terms that Mason was Beau's father, obviously his heart was not ready to hear those words.

"Oh please, Mason," Isabella responded dryly. "He's *my* son not *our* son."

"To hell with this." Mason bolted for the operating doors.

Isabella yelled, "You can't go in!"

Mason spun around, his face red and veins standing out on his forehead. "Then tell me, dammit!"

She sighed and reluctantly shared, "Beau is in surgery. We won't know anything else until that's complete. All we can do at this point is wait."

***

Last night's rain had left the air heavy and stagnant. Lake Danik resembled a sauna with swirls of haze dancing above the water. The sound of bullfrogs croaking happily filled the silence as I pulled into the Callaway's driveway to drop Melissa off.

Melissa couldn't get to the front door fast enough.

Melissa became sidetracked struggling to unlock the door. When the door cracked open, she smiled back at Stella and Whitney. "Charlotte sure is lucky to have you both." The girls gathered in a quick group hug.

"We've been knocking and ringing the doorbell. Neither Charlotte nor Owen heard us apparently." Stella and Whitney looked defeated.

"Oh, you poor girls. The doorbell has been broken for weeks now. I'm sorry. Come in and get a cold glass of water." Melissa opened the door and the girls followed.

***

I watched them disappear inside the house. I waved sarcastically and murmured, *"And...you're welcome for the ride,"* as I backed out of the driveway. They weren't worried about me at this point.

As I drove back into town, I thought, *I'm so glad Dad and I have gotten closer. It's a shame it took an accident to make him realize that I matter...that it's not always about Beau. But, I'm grateful that we are closer and will embrace it...for as long as it lasts.*

My thoughts shifted back to Beau and what was to come. Who am I kidding? With Beau in the hospital and the uncertainty of his condition, I expected Dad to solely focus on Beau's recovery.

Beau wins again – *sigh. Why do I feel so selfish? Don't I deserve to feel needed and wanted?*

***

Melissa quickly ran up the staircase to Charlotte's room while Stella and Whitney waited downstairs.

"Charlotte!" Melissa yelled as she opened the bathroom door.

"Mom, what in the world!" Charlotte hurriedly grabbed her towel.

"Oh, thank goodness, honey!" Melissa said as she leaned against the vanity.

"What's going on?" Charlotte questioned as Melissa placed her hands over her face and cried. "Mom!!!??? What's going on!"

"I'm just so happy that you're okay, honey. My mind has been racing since we received the call...I had to know you were okay."

Realizing that Charlotte likely wanted her privacy, she continued, "I'll give you a minute. I'll wait outside. I'm just so relieved."

Charlotte's head still pounded as she stepped out of the tub. The hot bath hadn't made her headache subside and coupled with her mom's frantic behavior; her head hurt worse. She hurriedly put on her bathrobe eager to see what had her om in such a panic. As she walked out of the bathroom, Melissa was sitting on her bed.

"You know, as a parent, we often take for granted having our children close...underneath our roof. As you get older, things get a little scarier as you begin to navigate life without us." Melissa said as she arranged the pillows on Charlotte's bed.

"Mom, you're freaking me out with all this. What happened? What news?" Charlotte moved in closer to her on the bed.

"Honey, I honestly don't know how to tell you this..." Tears began to well up in her eyes.

"Mom! What is it? You can't keep whatever this is from me. I can handle it. Just tell me...is it Owen...or Dad...what happened!?" Charlotte anxiously waited for her to share whatever information had her so distraught.

"There was an accident," she whispered as she held Charlotte's hand. "And...and..."

"*Okay*...so there was an accident." Charlotte nodded insinuating for her to share the details. "Mom...who was in the accident?"

Softly caressing Charlotte's hand and looking up to her, Melissa mouthed, "Beau", as her eyes stared down at the floor trying to control the tears that had welled up again in her eyes.

"Beau....no...Mom...that's crazy...he couldn't have...you must be confused!" Charlotte jumped up from her bed. "That's insane, whoever told you that is wrong!"

Melissa tried to grab Charlotte's hand, but she pulled it away.

Charlotte paced her bedroom floor now more anxious to learn the details as reality set in that Beau might be hurt. "Tell me! All of it. Mom, what happened?"

"Honey, there was a car accident. And we know it's Beau because he's at the hospital likely in surgery by now," Melissa responded softly.

"Did anyone see him!? What happened Mom!? Has anyone talked to him!?" Charlotte said as she hurriedly changed out of her bathrobe and frantically searched for her car keys in the bowl on her dresser. "I always keep them here...that's weird...Mom, help me find my car keys! I have to see him!"

"Honey, can you please sit down for a second? There's more I need to tell you and it's going to be difficult to hear," Melissa said calmly.

"Okay, Mom, now you're really scaring me." Charlotte cupped her hands over her face. "He...is...alive...? Isn't he?"

Melissa nodded, "Yes, honey. He's alive, but he," Melissa was quickly interrupted by Charlotte.

"No, Mom, you don't get to say '*but*'. He's alive. That is all I need to know. I'm going to the hospital! Where are my keys!?"

Melissa stood and grabbed Charlotte's hands. "Honey, your keys are not here. Beau had the accident...in your car."

Charlotte turned toward her mom. "What? No...he couldn't have been in my car. I drove home last night alone from the party. We weren't together."

Charlotte closed her eyes as she relived the events of the night.

"At least I think I remember driving home," Charlotte whispered as she struggled to remember the party and how she got home. As she sat on the end of the bed facing the floor, she placed her hands against her face hoping the throbbing headache would subside long enough for her to remember.

"I know I went to the party with Whitney and Stella. I remember seeing Beau there, but the rest is blurry." She paced the floor frustrated that she couldn't remember the details. "I remember drinking a lot...which is why I have got this terrible headache."

"Well, apparently Beau must have driven you home. It's the only logical reason for him to have your car." She scooted closer to Charlotte and wrapped her arm around her to comfort her.

Charlotte sat motionless as the reality continued to sink in that Beau was in an accident. The pounding in her head was a continual reminder that she had drunk too much the night before thus causing Beau to drive her home.

Bursting into tears Charlotte rested her head on her mother's shoulder. "Mom, I'm the reason Beau is hurt. I'm the reason he's lying in that hospital...I did this!"

"No, Charlotte, you aren't going to do this. None of this will help Beau. Right now, we need to focus on getting him better. I can bring you to the hospital when you're ready."

Wiping her tears and looking back at Melissa she muttered, "Good, because I want to talk to him and tell him I'll wait for him. I'll wait for the second paternity test. I love him so much, Mom."

Melissa knew in her heart that Charlotte didn't need to hear more bad news, however, she felt it was necessary to tell her. "Honey...there's one more thing I haven't told you."

Charlotte looked down at the floor hoping everything was just a dream. "There's more?!"

Melissa, struggling to share the news, softly replied, "No one has been able to talk to Beau since he was brought to the hospital. He had significant head injuries...and...well, he's non-responsive."

Chapter Thirty

Much To Be Desired

Over the railroad tracks on the west side of Sedipar is Country Suites Trailer Park. A dilapidated, wooden fence attempts to set a barrier between the paved road and the trailer park. A rundown 1970's, Dijon mustard-colored, single-wide home sits in the rear of the park where Trisha Adams and her kids live.

The trailer has witnessed more drinking bouts and outraged tempers in the wee hours of the morning along with cigarette burns on the carpet. Duct tape strategically covers up the 6-inch-wide hole in the entry door from Trisha's drunken boyfriends.

Inside the trailer, the buzzing of an alarm pierced through the quiet. Brice Adams jumped out of bed and threw on his coveralls and work boots. He rarely enjoyed his weekend days as they were spent working at the shop. He was responsible, unlike his mother, and they needed the money to survive.

As he got dressed, he stared at his baseball MVP trophy sitting upright on his desk – his glory days on the baseball field flooded his mind.

Being back on that baseball field would be awesome.

Grabbing his keys, he made his way down the hall. His foot accidentally kicked several beer cans scattered across the carpet. As he entered the living room, he saw Trisha passed out across the sofa. He pulled a blanket from the recliner and covered her. That's when he noticed a pair of cowboy boots...which told him she had brought home another stranger. He grabbed the bat with frustration and walked toward the back of the trailer.

Opening the door to his mom's bedroom while holding his bat across his shoulder he shook one of the stranger's legs and shouted, "Hey, man – you gotta get out of here!"

"Shit! Where am I?" The stranger sat up confused.

"You're in my house, and you need to get your ass out right now! I got family here that is sleeping...and you don't belong." Brice backed away from the bed and leaned against the door.

The stranger stumbled out of bed and found his way to the living room. Grabbing his boots and shirt he stumbled out the front door as Brice slammed it behind him.

When are you going to grow up, Mom?

Brice closed the door to the trailer mumbling, "I hate living in this mess. Something's gotta change."

***

Brice Adams pulled up to the mechanic shop. Kent always greeted him as he entered through the shop doors. "Brice, good to see you this morning!"

"Hey, Mr. Beale. They say it's gonna' be a hot one!" Looking around at the cars needing their attention, Brice checked out the work orders and grabbed his tools. "I'm going to start on that one," Brice said pointing to a red farm truck.

Kent nodded. "You need any extra hours this week? I have some extra work on the schedule starting Wednesday."

"Yes sir! I will take you up on the extra hours." Brice looked around the shop anxiously and continued. "I do need to leave early today. I have to fix a few things at home."

"Everything ok?" Kent was concerned.

"Oh, yes, sir. It's just a few repairs I've been putting off."

"Repairs can be costly. I'm willing to give you an advance if you need." Brice shook his head, stubbing his work boot on the garage floor. "Nah, I'm ok. I don't need the advance, but thank you Mr. Beale."

Kent nodded. "Sure, no problem. Well, do you need a hand with anything?"

Brice shook his head. "No, I think I can do it myself. But thank you for offering."

Kent smiled to himself, *How in the world is this boy the son of Trisha Adams?* While he was apprehensive about hiring Brice last summer, he had been pleasantly surprised by Brice's work ethic and apparent desire to do better for himself. Like most kids, Brice had made a few poor decisions over the last year that landed him in juvenile detention for a month. Kent was proud that he had turned things around and was on a good path now.

One day that kid is going to be dealt a good hand.

***

Trisha woke up around eleven o'clock to the smell of breakfast lingering in the air. As she sat up on the sofa, she held her hands up to her face as rays of sunlight pierced through the trailer windows.

"Why is it so bright in here? It's too early in the morning." She fumbled to find her cigarettes.

"You're all out!" Tennie picked up the empty box of Marlboro Lights and threw them onto Trisha's lap.

"Heard you had company again last night," Tennie said sarcastically as she grabbed her purse from the kitchen table. "And oh, it's bright in here because it's like eleven in the morning. I made breakfast about three hours ago."

Tennie stared coldly at Trisha as she continued to cover her eyes from the bright light. "Mom, really...when are you going to get your shit together? Brice and I bust our asses each day to keep whatever is left of this family afloat while you spend all your money on booze and drugs."

Trisha looked back at Tennie fumbling her fingers across the table hoping to find another pack of cigarettes. "Why so loud Tennie girl?" she replied as her head fell in her hands. "My head feels swollen." Trisha continued searching for the box of Marlboros.

"I'm not loud. You're hungover."

"Dammit! Brice probably took my last one. That boy! He has some nerve kicking my friends out when he leaves for work early. That's why I can't keep anyone around here. Your brother runs them off!"

Tennie rolled her eyes. "Don't you even go there on Brice. He's the only reason we make ends meet. And as far as your 'friends' go, Brice doesn't run them off! You do!"

Before closing the door behind her, Tennie noticed Trisha passed out again on the sofa.

"Figures!" she slammed the door.

"Sleep it off Mom," Tennie mumbled under her breath as she headed to work her afternoon shift at the Dixie.

***

Tennie Adams might have despised her mom, but she was wild and crazy just like her. Her red, curly hair was tousled like a windstorm had caught it and whipped it around a gazillion times. Tennie had inherited the nickname 'Red' for obvious reasons and despised it. Rumor was her dad called her Red the moment she was born.

The Dixie Burger hired Tennie last summer with great reluctance. The latest gossip around town was she was on the brink of losing her job as she rarely showed up when scheduled. Unfortunately, Tennie focused most of her time on partying, football tailgates, and skip days. The local police were very familiar with Tennie and her circle of friends mainly because Tennie rarely says 'no' when someone said, "Hey, you want to try this?"

***

Driving through town, I passed by Kent's mechanic shop and noticed the tow truck parked behind the fenced area – with Charlotte's car.

I pulled into the drive, parked my car in front, and stared at the mangled car. My mind began to wander back to the accident and then the surgery...everything seemed muddled and blurred.

I rested my head against the steering wheel of the car wondering how Beau could have survived such a crash. As my eyes closed, my body immediately welcomed the quiet.

I savored a few moments of sleep when I was startled by a knock at my car window.

"You can't park here," I heard someone yell, but it was muffled through the window.

I pulled myself from the steering wheel and laid back in the driver's seat. Exhaustion had set in which clouded my response.

I rolled down the window to address the voice that kept repeating, "You can't park here," as if I couldn't hear him. My vision became clearer, and my heart fell to the floor. All of the worry, angst, and exhaustion suddenly left as I searched for my glasses I had tossed onto the passenger seat.

"You can't park here. I'm sorry. We need to be able to respond to calls, and you're blocking the drive."

OMG...it was him...Brice Adams. He can't see me like this and of all times to run into him!

Brice tends to cause my heart to flutter rapidly followed by fumbling of my words. The butterflies appeared as usual in my stomach when he leaned down closer toward me. I'm not myself when he gets close.

"Ummm...yeah...sorry...ummm...I get it. I just noticed Charlotte's car. I was on my way back to the hospital and something made me pull in." I could hardly get the words out. *Why does he do this to me?*

Just as I began to put the car in reverse, he placed his hands on the door, and his fingers wrapped around the frame. I became mesmerized by his beautiful green eyes as his bangs flitted between them.

For a moment I escaped the reality of our conversation until I heard my name fall from his sweet lips.

"Nessie – you with me?" Brice leaned in closer. "How is Beau?"

"Oh, yeah…um…I don't know honestly. I'm on my way back to the hospital now."

My confidence weakened. Why do I allow myself to become so entranced by him?

"Well, for starters – he's lucky. He was very close to…." Brice paused mid-sentence realizing that I might not be interested in the details of what could have been.

"I want to hear it, please. We haven't been given many details…please share what you know." I turned in my seat to face him and waited anxiously for his response.

Brice, looking down at the pavement, reluctantly continued. "Well…um, he was about one foot from going into Bayou Fueob. A tree stopped him. I'm glad because he was unconscious and likely would have…you know…um…drowned. When they pulled him out of the car, my focus was extracting the car. I don't know much from that point. I'm just sorry this happened to Beau. Man, I hate it for ya'll."

I sat back in my seat thinking about what Beau had been through. I closed my eyes and thought, *He wasn't responsive…he could have drowned.*

Brice backed away from my car and began walking to the garage. Mid-way he turned and shouted, "Nessie, you can stay here a few more minutes. I know your family has been through a lot." He stared back at me for a moment with a half grin then walked back to the garage.

Do I say thank you? Do I tell him I'll let him know about Beau? Are you crazy...you're not even friends! That would be weird.

Several scenarios flooded my mind on how to casually tell Brice that I would keep him updated – but in true 'Nessie' fashion – I rolled up my window and drove off without saying anything. Brice never looked up from the hood of the car he was examining.

Quit fantasizing about him...he hardly knows that you exist! He only talked to you because of the accident.

Chapter Thirty-One

Flatline

Beau was in surgery for almost five hours. It felt like two days had passed. I'd become numb to the ticking of the clock on the waiting room wall and frankly, time wasn't important.

I just wanted to see Beau.

The waiting room began filling up with members of the football team.

Stella and Whitney arrived arm in arm with Charlotte. Melissa followed closely behind.

Dad remained close avoiding Isabella as much as he could.

Hours after surgery, Beau was moved to the ICU, and visitors were allowed. Dad, myself, and Isabella rushed to the unit door upon hearing we could see him.

"Only two are allowed in at a time," the nurse commanded as she placed her hands forward to stop us.

"I'll go in first," Isabella dryly responded while looking at the nurse.

"Nessie?" Isabella looked at me insinuating to join her.

"No, I'll wait back here for now," I responded without making direct eye contact with her.

"I'll go in with Nessie." Dad quickly chimed in as he stood next to me. A sense of relief enveloped me knowing I'd avoided being stuck with Isabella.

We watched her walk toward Beau's room alone. Mason suddenly appeared through the doors and quickly caught up with her passing by me and Dad.

"I'm his father," Mason shared as he approached Isabella and the nurse. "I want to see my son."

Dad squeezed my hand firmly hearing Mason's words. There was no doubt he'd wanted to be first at Beau's side, however, he stood back allowing Isabella to rule the moment. Again. Now Mason was taking his place.

As they entered the room, Isabella placed her hands up to her face and sat down on the bed next to him. Beau's head was covered with white gauze and the only movement was the slight rise in his chest from the shallow breaths provided by the ventilator.

"Beau, it's Mom," Isabella whispered as she caressed his cheek. "Honey, the entire team is here...your family is here...we're all waiting for you to wake up."

Mason stood behind Isabella expressionless. He didn't approach the bed and stood near the corner of the room staring at Beau. As the nurse continued checking Beau's vitals, he asked, "How long do you think he will remain like this?"

Isabella glanced at the nurse and then back at Beau. Grabbing his hand and placing it near her lips, she replied, "She's *just* a nurse. What does she know? He's a fighter and will come out of this coma. I know it."

The nurse glared at Isabella and then looked at the floor not responding. Mason knew better than to challenge Isabella at this point and avoided asking more questions. As the nurse exited Beau's room, she reminded them of the ten minutes of visitation remaining.

Dad and I switched places with Isabella and Mason. We each took a seat on the side of Beau's bed. It was so difficult to see him completely still and silent.

"I can't believe this happened," Dad whispered under his breath as he held Beau's hand. "Son, you must pull out of this and return to us."

While I'm not sentimental and rarely show emotion, the night before in the waiting room coupled with the events of the day had certainly worn me down. Now, staring at my brother in a coma, my heart sank at the thought of losing him – for good.

The nurse came back to the door within what seemed like only seconds and said, "I'm sorry but visitation is over."

As Dad and I walked back toward the door, the patient monitor alarm sounded sending us both into a panic. My eyes quickly retreated to the monitor, and I noticed the EKG line was erratic and then flatlined.

Tears began to well in my eyes as nurses ran to Beau's side. Before we could make it out the door, the noise from the monitor ceased. I quickly stopped and took a deep breath in. As I turned around and glanced at the monitor, the EKG line was back to normal.

A nurse called the nurse's station to bring a new monitor into the room. "This one has been giving us fits for a week now. I'm sorry to scare ya'll!" As compassionate as the nurse tried to be with her apology, we were still shaken by the event.

We both breathed a huge sigh of relief as Dad wrapped his arm around me and walked back to the waiting area. The doctor approached us slowly, almost hesitant to share the news.

"Our main focus has been on stabilizing the bleeding from his brain, however, the scan showed several fractures in his vertebrae. We have stabilized him in order for his body to heal from the neurosurgery, however, I regret to share that he still will need surgery on his back."

As I stood closely behind Dad, I immediately felt my body weaken with defeat. Dad threw his hands in the air and punched the wall. I tried to comfort him, but he pushed me away. "Not now, Nessie! I need time to think. I need to be alone. Just leave me alone."

Chapter Thirty-Two

Regret

"I need to see him...this is all my fault!" Charlotte incessantly cried as Stella and Whitney consoled her. "He was so sweet taking care of me...making sure I made it home...I don't know if I'll be able to forgive myself if he doesn't wake up from this."

Due to limited visitation, the Trio decided to leave the hospital. Charlotte was devastated that she couldn't see him. "We'll take you back home and wait. You need to get some rest." Stella helped Charlotte up from the chair and noticed Jackson staring their way...at Charlotte.

Ugh...he won't give up on her will he? Geez...her boyfriend is fighting to recover, and he's still trying to sneak his way in.

As the Trio left the waiting area, Blaine followed Whitney to the front door of the hospital. Softly touching her arm, he asked, "Babe, you okay?"

"Get your hands off me, Blaine!" She pushed his hand away. "And don't call me 'babe' anymore. I'm not your *'babe'*. And don't ask me how I'm feeling. You had your chance to care...and you didn't. Now get away from us!"

Why can't anything in my life be normal? He had his chance with me...and he blew it.

"Damn, girl. Why are you so mad?! I just wanted to check on you...well...all of you really," he said as he shifted his focus on Charlotte.

Charlotte wiped her tears and attempted to respond, but Whitney cut her off and responded dryly, "How do you think she feels, Blaine? Beau is fighting for his life. She's been through enough. It's a little late to start caring and being compassionate."

Blaine threw his hands up in the air realizing defeat with Whitney. "Whatever!" He joined Jackson and the rest of the football team who had become restless as they paced the waiting room lobby. He fidgeted with his key ring thinking how a part of him longed to hold her again and tell her he was sorry, but his pride and ego always took over.

***

Dad watched as the team wandered aimlessly around the waiting room lobby with somber faces similar to when they lost a game – which wasn't often.

"Thank ya'll for being here to support Beau. It means a lot to us...and to Beau." Dad hated that they weren't able to see him. He resisted his emotions and continued.

"Unfortunately, the ICU won't allow visitors the rest of the day, so I'd hate for you guys to be miserable here in this waiting area. Why don't ya'll go home and get some sleep and come back tomorrow?"

"Well, maybe we will get the chance to visit him tomorrow," Blaine said to Jackson as they walked out of the hospital.

"Yeah, I guess so." Jackson felt relieved that visitation was limited.

***

The sheriff's office completed its routine investigation at the accident site with the final report indicating a single-vehicle accident and reckless driving as the cause. The tire marks from Charlotte's car had left a slight imprint on the pavement. It was evident that no other vehicle was involved.

On their way back to Charlotte's house, the Trio stopped by the accident site. The girls tried to persuade Charlotte not to stop. "It's a bad idea," Stella repeated, but Charlotte insisted.

The cypress tree and limbs that blocked Beau's entrance into Bayou Fueob held remnants of her front bumper still dangling in the air. As the girls approached the embankment, Charlotte's eyes became misty. "Oh...I don't know if I can do this now," she cried while cupping her hands over her face. "He...he could have drowned...I would've lost him forever." Whitney and Stella embraced her and tried to persuade her to go back to the car.

"What am I going to do without him, ya'll?" Charlotte rested her head against Whitney while Stella leaned closer for support. "He was my everything. He *is* my everything. He was supposed to get another test on Monday and was so hopeful that the results would prove we could be together. He was so adamant about getting those results back."

Thinking back over the events of the night as they became clearer, she remembered Beau's words, *I still love you Charlotte - nothing will change that - ever.*

Charlotte became flooded with emotions and pushed away from the girls' hold on her as she walked into the road. With her eyes shut tightly she screamed in agony raising her arms toward the sky. Turning back to the girls with tears streaming down her face, she fell to the pavement.

"I never told him I loved him back...I didn't respond. I just walked inside the house, and he left. Now it may be too late to tell him how I feel." The girls helped Charlotte up from the road and walked back to the car.

"Char, he knows you love him. You didn't have to say anything." Whitney tried to reassure her.

As they drove away, Whitney caught a glimpse of Blaine's truck pulling up behind them in the rearview mirror. He parked on the side of the road and faced the embankment where Beau wrecked.

I wonder what he is up to, Whitney thought as Blaine made a U-turn and sped away.

Chapter Thirty-Three

Solitude

The last several weeks had been a blur since the accident. School ended and things seemed to be somewhat normal – except for my home life. With Beau still in the hospital, my days were spent balancing Isabella's sporadic mood swings and Dad's newfound depression – confined within about eighty square feet.

Beau's condition hadn't improved or worsened so we took that as a win. Well...most of us did. Isabella called every neuro doctor from California to New York, and they all gave her the same answer - only time will tell.

Dad became more distant. I knew he was worried about Beau – we all were. His primary focus was Beau again, and he continually pushed me away. With Isabella constantly breathing down his neck and Mason lurking around Beau's room- solitude was rare.

While everyone's focus was once again on Beau, *not meaning that in a harsh way,* I found myself alone again.

After a few hours of confinement in Beau's room, I decided to get some fresh air and grab lunch.

"Anyone up for a burger? I'll grab a few from The Dixie." As I grabbed my purse, Isabella handed me a twenty. "Get me a salad. No dressing." She dryly turned away and faced Beau.

I almost threw her twenty back in her lap, but I controlled my reaction. "Sure, anyone else?" I scanned the room for Dad or Mason to speak up but there was only silence and stares.

"Dad...you want anything? You need to eat!" I stared his way and he continued ignoring me.

"Dad!" I raised my voice.

"Dammitt Nessie! I don't want anything to eat! I can't eat right now. Just leave and go home. We don't need you here. You're just in the way. Dad walked closer to Beau and sighed. "I just need Beau to wake up. Just wake up son. I've lost everything if you don't wake up."

The walls shattered around me. I tried holding my tears in as I left the room. When the door closed behind me, I cried.

I've never been enough for them. It's always been about Beau. I couldn't take it anymore.

***

Tennie had the day shift at The Dixie today. I noticed her sitting at the first table by the order window when I drove up.

"Great," I mumbled to myself as I opened the car door.

As I approached the order window, I saw Brice walk from around the corner. My knees instantly became weak and butterflies started churning in my stomach. I adjusted my glasses while looking down at the pavement.

As I stepped up onto the concrete walk from the parking lot, my tennis shoe brazed edge of the walkway and I tripped...and fell flat on my face...right in front of Brice.

Pure devastation.

"Oh my gosh...Miss Perfect little Nessie Corbin planted her sweet little face right here on the concrete!" *Smack!* Tennie clapped her hands together to give the full effect.

I lay there completely mortified...wanting to crawl under the walkway...hoping Brice didn't see.

But, he did.

"Nessie, you okay?" I heard his sweet voice calling my name as I lay in front of him embarrassed beyond existence. He picked up my glasses that had flown from my face due to my fall.

"Here's your glasses. I'll help you." His hands touched mine as he gently lifted me up and asked if I'd like to sit at their table.

"Well, hey, there Miss Graceful!" Tennie laughed mocking me.

"Be quiet, Tennie." Brice sat down next to me and finished eating.

I was at a complete loss for words. Tennie sat across from me continuing to poke fun at my clumsiness. "Miss Little Perfect isn't so perfect after all!" Bursting into laughter, she got up from the table and went back to the order window as customers were walking up.

Why does she hate me so much?

I remained mortified wanting to crawl under a rock.

Brice sat quietly finishing his lunch.

I brushed the dirt from my knees and hands that had braced my fall. *Great Nessie, you look like kindergartners who fall at recess!*

Here we were again. Me...knowing I needed to thank him...but I couldn't get the words out.

Why am I so afraid to talk to him?

I stared at the order window as Tennie shouted orders into the microphone. Looking back down at my skinned knees, I mustered up enough courage to say thank you.

Just as the words began to leave my mouth, he wasn't there to receive them. Brice was gone.

Chapter Thirty-Four

Subdued

Charlotte waited patiently outside Beau's room. She longed to be near him, hold his hand, talk to him – anything to be by his side – and tell him she was sorry.

Isabella received a page from the clinic and stepped out of the room to take the call at the nurse's station and saw Charlotte in the waiting area. She stopped abruptly.

"What in the hell are you doing here!?" Isabella's emotions raged as she glared at Charlotte. "You have no right to be here. *You* did this to him! You will *not* see Beau." To top things off, she yelled for security to escort Charlotte away.

Dad stepped in. "Isabella. Calm down. You're being ridiculous. She has every right to be here. The accident wasn't her fault." Dad pushed the door open and allowed her to enter.

"Thank you, Mr. Corbin." She smiled at Dad. Isabella watched Charlotte through the small window in the door.

***

It was difficult for her to see him this way.

She lightly touched Beau's hand maneuvering around the various IVs. His shallow breaths provided by the ventilator and the bandages covering his head were constant reminders that Beau wasn't really here...with her. Placing her head down on the bed, memories of Beau flooded her mind. She laughed remembering the time he attempted to dance in the back of the truck. The dancing memory made her smile.

Images from their first kiss...when she was so mad that someone parked so close to her car...only to find out it was Beau...waiting for her. His kiss was so perfect.

And cheering for him on the football field...to the sweaty hugs after the game...she longed for it to be that way again.

His tender touch and soft whispers of how much he loved her flooded her mind...*I may never feel any of that again.*

Dad knew she would appreciate a few minutes alone with Beau. "I'm going to grab a coffee down the hall. Want one?"

"No, I'm good. Thank you." She never took her eyes off Beau and latched her fingers into his.

Whispering softly to him, she pleaded, "Come back to me, Beau. I can't lose you. I need you to wake up!"

She placed a neatly wrapped, dried, pink rose on his chest. "I saved this from the corsage you gave me. You picked my favorite shade of pink...and roses are my favorite. I never told you pink was my favorite color – I guess you assumed from the color of my dress."

Tears rolled furiously down her cheek as she continued. "This is all my fault. You wouldn't be here if it weren't for me. I'm so sorry."

She didn't want to leave his side. Even though he couldn't respond, it felt good to be close to him. She closed her eyes and tried to remove the accident from her memory. Her heart kept reliving the sweet moments of their relationship over the last year, but her mind kept replacing the happy memories with the reality of the accident.

Charlotte stayed for several hours holding Beau's hand tightly with no response.

She refused to give up on him.

Chapter Thirty-Five

Selfish Motives

Jackson hadn't been to the hospital since the night of the accident. He found every reason not to go.

His friendship with Beau weakened as his feelings for Charlotte became stronger. With Beau in the hospital, Jackson was holding onto his chance to get closer to her.

As wrong as it felt, he was tired of brushing his feelings aside. He was fed up with always being the second choice. Now, he felt more compelled to seek happiness...and that happiness was Charlotte.

Summer conditioning was underway and most of his time was spent on the field. Coach had assigned him as starting quarterback in Beau's absence, and he was soaking up all the glory.

While his attention remained on the field, his heart longed to run into Charlotte as the cheer team practiced stunts each morning on the track. Unfortunately, she hadn't been at practice the last few days.

I guess she's at the hospital with him.

"Jackson! Get your head in the game son!" Coach yelled from the sidelines as Jackson lost focus. "This is your chance to show me what you've got, Jackson, and win!"

Jackson nodded.

***

Owen had called me numerous times over the past few days, and I chose not to respond.

I couldn't stand the hospital cell I'd been trapped in, and I defaulted to the library for solace.

But, he knew me too well and found me in my hiding spot. He cornered me and forced me to speak to him.

"Not today, Owen," I replied as he pulled the chair away from the table and sat next to me.

"C'mon, Nessie, you have to talk to me at some point. What's going on with you?" Owen said as he opened a book blatantly ignoring my wish to leave me alone. "It's almost like you're mad at me for something."

"I'm not in the mood to talk. I just want to be alone. And I'm not sorry about it either." A part of me felt bad for shutting him out, but I didn't want to be around anyone.

"Nessie, you can't just shut out your friends...well me...since I'm honestly the only friend you've got." Owen stared down at the pages of his book and continued. "I'm not asking for deep intellectual conversation, Nessie. I just miss us hanging out. I miss my friend."

I slammed my hands down onto the pages of my book and glared at him. "Really, Owen! Thanks for making me feel like crap now. I'm overwhelmed with so many different emotions."

He started to gather his things and closed his book. I knew I'd hurt him. I was never good at sugarcoating my feelings.

"Look, I'm just under a lot of pressure right now. I've been cooped up in a small hospital room with Isabella. Dad is dealing with various emotions, and Beau hasn't shown us any signs of improvement. Your Dad makes his daily appearance which usually ends in an argument between all three of them. I know it's not your fault, but I blame your family for all of this!" I stared back at Owen tapping my pencil eraser on the table.

"I get it. Do you think I'm not feeling the brunt of this too? We're all under a lot of stress right now. Charlotte mopes around the house most of the day, and Mom caters to her every need. Dad is either working at the pharmacy, visiting Beau at the hospital, or hiding at the hunting camp. You can't shut me out. We've always been there for each other. I need you."

Owen's sincerity and his unwavering addiction to our friendship had become nauseating to me. He wasn't listening. I wanted to be alone.

"I just want to be left alone," I said turning away from him.

I wanted to scream inside as I felt Owen lingering. After a few minutes of thick silence, he packed up his things and left the library.

I don't know what had come over me, but I yearned to be alone. Maybe some of Isabella's ruthlessness had rubbed off on me. Perhaps, it was Dad's newfound misery that had brought me down with him. Beau's condition certainly didn't help. Owen's presence weighed me down – a constant reminder of how crazy my family was.

Whatever the reason, I was tired of picking up loose ends and making everything better for everyone else. I couldn't escape it. And I needed more. More of something that wasn't...typical Nessie.

***

Coach went easy on the team at practice. The practices hadn't been the same without Beau. Jackson was doing okay as quarterback, but Blaine and Beau worked more naturally together.

Jackson threw a pass to one of the receivers and it was long. "Ugh!" Jackson yelled realizing the missed pass.

Blaine rested his hands on his knees to catch his breath as the receiver retrieved the football.

Man, Beau, you have got to come out of this soon.

As Blaine headed back to the locker room to change, his teammate approached the bench where he left his bag.

"Hey, bro, I wanted to see if you had an update on Beau. I didn't want to distract the team on the field." The teammate grabbed his gym bag and threw it over his shoulder.

"Not sure. Last I heard he was still on the vent. No change." Blaine removed his jersey and replaced it with a school t-shirt from his locker.

"Thanks, bro. Just keep us updated all right?" the teammate replied as he turned to walk away.

"Yeah, bro, will do." Blaine shut his locker door.

The teammate turned before leaving the locker room. "Hey, Blaine, I think we're all going out to the Abyss tonight since Coach didn't set early morning practice for tomorrow. Any way you could snag more beer from your uncle's store?"

"Yeah, bro, I got you," Blaine responded as they shared a cocky football handshake.

"Just don't drink it all before you get to the Abyss this time." The teammate laughed.

Blaine questioned him. "What you mean by that?"

"Dude, the last party at the Abyss. Man, you were wasted. We tried to stop you from getting into your truck, but you told us to back off and you drove away. I don't know how in the hell you got home!" The teammate kept walking.

Blaine followed behind hesitant to respond.

I remember waking up in my truck. Why can't I remember who drove me home?

***

Blaine headed back to the farm to get some work done before heading out to the Abyss that evening. Driving a tractor in the open field provided time for Blaine's mind to wander. As he pulled the plow, he thought about Whitney and how she'd moved on.

Probably best for both of us. We would've been a trainwreck together. It was already headed that way. But she sure looked really good that night. Man, you need to get her out of your mind!

Images of driving out to the Abyss with Beau popped into his head recalling laughing and having a few drinks.

His mind replayed the events of that night and the words his teammate said earlier, *I don't know how in the hell you drove home.*

As he neared the end of the turnrow, he quickly stopped, as visions of headlights blinding him and his truck skidding to a stop on the wet pavement crowded his mind.

It was me. I ran Beau off the road. I caused the accident.

Chapter Thirty-Six

On Edge

"Tennie!!! Brice!!!" Trisha yelled as she hauled her suitcase to the door. "I'm leaving...ya'll take care of things while I'm gone."

Tennie rolled her eyes as she entered the living room. "Yeah, Mom we get it." She walked into the kitchen and continued, "We always take care of everything even when you're here."

Tennie made note of the larger suitcase which meant she might be gone longer this time. "How long will you be gone?" Tennie asked sarcastically, not really caring about Trisha but more about the number of days the trailer would be open for parties.

"About a week and a half-maybe sooner." Trisha grabbed her purse and keys and opened the front door. "I'm late. They're waiting for me down at Charlee's Bar. The bar is expecting a shipment, and then we have to get on the road for Houston."

"Well...have fun!" Tennie replied sarcastically as she shut the door behind Trisha thinking, *Party at the trailer park tonight!*

***

With the recent news about Beau's condition coupled with being cooped up in a small hospital room with Dad, Isabella, and Mason – something had to give. The end of my freshman year had become like a rerun of my most despised TV show, and it appeared my summer was going to be a waiting game. I longed for Dad to acknowledge me. That brief moment in time when we connected was real, and I longed to feel it again.

I called the hospital to check in with Dad.

"Hey, how are things?" The other end of the phone was silent. "Dad?"

"Nessie, yes, I'm here. What do you need?" Dad's voice was cold and pointed.

Why is he taking this out on me!? "Um, well...I was just checking on you."

"Well, I don't need a babysitter. I'm fine." Dad hung up the phone.

Why do I even try? Why do I care? No one is worried about how I'm dealing with everything that has happened. My family keeps pushing me away – until they need something.

I had to leave the house. I decided to feed my sadness with pecan pie. I stopped by AEL's and ordered a piece to go. The cashier asked me about Beau, and I mumbled a few words that he was still the same. *Ugh...everywhere I go it's always about him.*

I drove around for a while down the back roads with my windows down.

When I got home, I savored every bite of my pecan pie. Something about AEL's pie always hit the spot.

Afterward, I soaked in a hot bath and nestled in my bed hoping to drown out everything. I slept until seven o'clock that evening.

***

Blaine stopped by the hospital earlier in the day to see Beau. His visit provided Dad and Isabella with a few hours to check in at work.

"Man, you gotta come back to us. Coach has Jackson running drills, and it just isn't the same without you as quarterback." Blaine leaned forward in the chair beside Beau's bed.

Blaine sat in silence most of his visit staring at the wall. He found it difficult to see Beau like this – lying in a bed, helpless.

Two hours passed, and Blaine couldn't stand sitting any longer. The guilt continued to build inside of him as the ventilator continued to breathe for Beau.

I'm sorry, bro. I did this to you. I'm the reason you ran off the road. I shouldn't have been driving that night. You have to make it out of this.

Mason pushed the door open as Blaine stood up from the chair.

"Blaine, son, nice of you to come by." Mason walked toward the sofa and stared out the window.

"Yeah, I just wanted to come to check on him – see if anything had changed." Blaine put his hands in his pockets and stood staring at Mason. "I was telling Beau we miss him on the field. Not sure if he can hear me or not though."

Mason turned around to face Blaine and responded, "Son, have you heard about his fractures?"

"No sir, what fractures?" Blaine responded confused.

"Apparently Beau has several fractures in his back, and they have delayed surgery due to the trauma on his brain. Son, he won't be playing football next year. I'm sure of that."

Blaine felt as if someone had punched him in the gut. He stared at the floor choked with words.

How could I have been so stupid! I'm the reason my best friend will never play football again.

***

"Your dad is in there with Beau," Blaine said as he leaned against the hospital wall with his head hung as Charlotte passed by.

"You okay Blaine?" Charlotte said stopping in front of him. She moved closer to make him look at her. "What's wrong? Did something happen?"

Realizing he was drawing attention to his emotions, he responded, "Nah, I just don't like seeing him like that. That's all." Blaine was never good at showing weakness. "But it's Beau...he'll come out of this soon."

Whitney and Stella followed Charlotte closely behind. Blaine caught a glimpse of Whitney and grinned at her. She quickly looked away avoiding him...*As if I owe you a smile, yeah right*...and rolled her eyes.

"Char, me and Whit are going to grab a bite to eat from the cafeteria and give you some time alone with Beau. Want something?" Stella's arm was wrapped in Whitney's as they stopped near Beau's room.

"No, I'm fine. And, thanks girls. I need both of you so much right now." Charlotte pulled them in for a quick hug before going into Beau's room.

***

When Charlotte entered the room, she saw Mason standing by the window. "Hey, Dad, I brought a few snacks and things from home for the room."

He walked over to her, hugged her while kissing the top of her head, and replied, "You need to be resting. There's no sense in you hanging out here. I told you I would call you the minute something changes."

"Dad, I can't leave his side. I want him to wake up more than anything." Charlotte leaned her head on Mason's chest as a tear rolled down her face. "I heard the news about his back, too. He's going to be devastated that he can't play football next year."

"I know, honey, he has a long road ahead of him. He's a tough boy though. We just have to take it day by day." He gave her another hug and stood next to her as they stared back toward Beau. "Honey, I don't know if it's best that you're here. You've been through so much, especially with the news that Beau is my son. I understand that you care about him, but..."

"Stop it, Dad." She quickly moved away from him. "You don't get to make that call. None of this was fair to me and Beau. We can't just turn off our feelings even though I agree it's the right thing to do."

As she stared at Beau following the various tubes and IVs hooked to his body, she fought the urge to burst into tears. "He was going to get another paternity test. I thought it was a terrible idea, but I should have supported him. At least we could find closure with the second test. Now...he's..." She moved closer to Beau and softly rubbed his hand noticing the pink rose that she left on his chest was in the trash can next to his bed.

Ughhh...Isabella. It could only have been Isabella.

She removed the pink rose from the trash can and placed it near Beau's side. Kissing his cheek, she whispered, "You have to wake up. I need to tell you that I'll wait for the test. I should have told you that night, but I was too stubborn. Please come back to me, Beau. Please."

***

"Any more thoughts about doing the second paternity test?" Allison knew this was put on hold for good reason, however, she battled with the notion that Isabella had tampered with them.

"Honestly, I haven't given it much thought. With Beau's health right now, that is the furthest thing from my mind. But, you know, I don't need a stupid test for me to be his father. I'm never relinquishing that role. Blood relative or not...I still will call the 'Dad card'." Dad continued flipping through the papers that Allison had organized for his signature.

Allison hadn't questioned Jackson again about the night at the firm. She felt like he was hiding something. Years of paralegal work and dealing with attorneys every day made it easy to determine when someone was keeping a secret.

She hadn't shared anything with Dad or with Kent...but it was eating at her.

I know Isabella did something that night, and Jackson saw her. Why won't he tell me? I can't let Isabella ruin everyone's lives. She played me for a fool, and I fell into her trap.

Jackson is going to have to share what he's been hiding.

***

I had a little more momentum after my nap and decided to swing back by the hospital. I picked up dinner from The Dixie.

"Here you go, Miss Perfect. That's two specials and a side of cheesy fries." Tennie handed me the bag with a sly smile.

"Thanks." I replied dryly as I snatched the bag from her hand.

"You look like crap, you know," Tennie cruelly responded. "I mean, I know your brother is in the hospital and you're under a lot of pressure. I get that. But, I don't think I've ever seen you like this."

I rolled my eyes knowing her words were not representative of her caring for me. She was ruthless and spiteful and just plain mean. "Whatever, Tennie."

"Oh, little Miss Perfect has an attitude today, doesn't she?" Placing both hands on the counter and leaning closer to the order window, intrigued by my direct response, she laughed to herself and murmured, "I kinda' like this new attitude of yours."

I wasn't sure how to take her. One minute she was degrading and poking fun at me and the next she was attempting to talk to me. I knew it was fake.

As I got closer to my car, I heard her voice over the intercom shouting, "Party at Country Estate Trailer Park tonight! My trailer! Ten o'clock till!"

I shut my car door and headed to the hospital.

***

When I got to the hospital, everyone had left except for Dad. I had to pry him from the room to eat his burger. "Dad, you won't be gone long. The nurse is watching him and will call us. You need to eat." I coaxed him to the cafeteria, and we sat in silence.

"I can't take much more. I need you to talk to me. I'm worried about you." I sat staring across the table as he finished eating his burger. "Nessie. It has just been a lot to take in. You've always been the strong one in the family. Beau has a long road ahead of him...and hell...where do I fit in all of this? I mean...I'm *not* his father." Dad shoved his chair from the table and started walking back to Beau's room.

I gathered our trash and ran behind him trying to catch up.

"Dad! Wait up!" I yelled as I attempted to catch him before he entered Beau's room.

"I'm just worried about you, that's all. You haven't been at the law firm much, and you can't live up here. Mason and Isabella..." I tried to continue, but he cut me off.

"Damn both of them!" Dad forcefully opened the door to Beau's room. "Mason has already taken my son...or who I thought was my son...I've lost my wife...and now you're challenging me. I just need to be alone."

I'd never seen this side of Dad before. He was unsure of himself and jaded with all sorts of emotions. I realized at that point I should back off. He didn't want me around.

I watched through the window on the door as Dad made his way back by Beau's side and laid his head down on the bed grabbing Beau's hand.

It has always been about Beau. I get it...in this moment with Beau's condition...it's natural, but Beau has always been my family's number one focus.

I leaned against the wall and closed my eyes. As doctors and nurses passed me in the hall, I tried to escape from all of it - hoping when I opened my eyes it would be a dream.

Surprisingly, images of Tennie filled my head with her sarcastic, mean laugh, and taunting comments. A feeling of revenge and rage suddenly came over me. My grin felt almost as evil as Tennie's when she mocked me for tripping at The Dixie.

I think I'll go to your party, Tennie. After all, you did invite me.

Chapter Thirty-Seven

Across the Tracks

I drove up to the trailer park around ten forty-five that night. I almost turned around five times and went home, but the image of Tennie's surprised face when I walked up to her party kept me intrigued.

I didn't recognize anyone as I walked up to the trailer...not that I expected to know anyone.

No shocker – I never went to parties. The majority of my weekends were spent at the library with Owen...this obviously wasn't the same crowd. And I rarely came across the tracks.

Two guys with tattoos covering their forearms brushed my arm with bottles of beer nudging me for a drink as I made my way up the steps to the door. "You look like you could use a beer."

"No thank you, uh..." I hesitated, not knowing what to say.

Obvious that I did not belong here, they whispered under their breath and laughed asking, "Where in the hell did you come from?"

Both guys took a long drag from their cigarettes and went back to their conversation.

I kept walking past them...embarrassed...and wishing I would've taken a beer to 'fit in'.

Really, Nessie...grow up...who says, 'no thank you' at a party?

I squeezed by a couple who were making out against the front door and walked into the living room. Lights were flashing and music was blaring.

Suddenly, I became more uncomfortable. *Maybe I should leave.* Then a hand grabbed my arm.

And I heard *her* voice.

"What in the *hell* is Miss Perfect doing at *my* party!?"

It was Tennie...an inebriated Tennie...which made things even worse.

Suddenly, I began second-guessing my newfound inner strength to combat her.

I wasn't sure how to respond. She kept poking at me waiting for a response. I stood there...silent.

"Why are you here? I don't remember inviting Miss Perfect." She rolled her eyes and nudged me again for a response. "Well!?"

"If you aren't going to talk...here, take a sip of this - and loosen up, geez!" Handing me a half-empty solo cup filled with alcohol, she turned away from me and danced into the crowd. I reluctantly held the cup with both hands.

I stood there looking around the room wondering what I was doing there. Obviously, I was not thinking...coming to Tennie's party.

She threw her hands in the air dancing and then turned back to me. "Well...are you just going to stand there and babysit it or are you gonna drink it?" I could tell Tennie was getting agitated with me quickly.

Now's my chance. Drop it and run! That was true Nessie fashion. The old Nessie.

While my mind urged me to flee, the same feeling of rage came over me again, and I thought, *What the hell?*

I downed the drink and tilted the empty cup back to her sarcastically.

Tennie's eyes widened. "Oh...I see...maybe you're not so perfect after all. Follow me." Tennie led me across the living room and out onto the back porch. Lawn chairs were scattered across the backyard.

"Come and sit. Have another drink." Tennie handed me a second cup – this one filled to the brim.

"Oh, no, I have to drive home. That one was enough for me," I replied with some hesitation as I knew once I resisted, she was going to flip on me. I waited.

Tennie pulled her tousled red hair into a ponytail as she sat back in the chair and cunningly laughed. "You know what's wrong with people like you? I've got you all figured out. You have everything handed to you. You don't have to work for a damn thing. You have no clue!"

I knew Tennie's hatred of me stemmed from several factors. My wealth tag, which was not my fault, and her hatred of school...which was the complete opposite of what I stood for. She'd made a career out of being a freshman which was brought on by excessive absences, failed classes, and flipping off teachers that gained her more suspensions than I could count. She worked a lot of hours at The Dixie to help her mom make ends meet. I was the last person she wanted at her party...moreover to hang out with.

Corbins were her enemy.

She leaned forward in her chair and continued with slurred speech. "You could be anywhere you wanted tonight...and you show up here...in this trailer park. I don't get it."

I could feel her words penetrate me as her dark, cold eyes stared me down waiting for my response.

Everything she said was true. I could be anywhere I wanted, and here I was sitting in a broken lawn chair drinking with Tennie Adams.

"You know what Tennie? Maybe you're right, and I just longed for something different." I took a sip of the drink and held the cup between my hands. "I can't explain why I'm here. Maybe there's a reason...maybe not. But I'm here."

She remained crouched in her chair studying me, then lit a cigarette and leaned forward. Continuing to stare my way, she shook her head. "I'm still not sure about you, Miss Perfect."

"Give me one of those." I motioned toward her to hand me a cigarette.

"Oh...Miss Perfect is living on the wild side tonight!" she laughed while tossing me the lighter and cigarette. I wasn't sure how to light it, but I figured it out.

I attempted to take a long drag from the cigarette which ended in a coughing spell. I'm not sure if it was the alcohol or the fact I was holding a cigarette that made me feel more empowered but I responded directly, "Well...for starters...maybe you can call me Nessie and not that stupid ass nickname you've branded me with. Or should I call you Red?"

What had gotten into me? I'm sitting here drinking and smoking a cigarette with Tennie Adams and cussing. And...I just stood up for myself with her. This must be a bad dream.

She stared at me blankly without mouthing a word. I suddenly became nervous. The empowerment I felt was slowly leaving me as I knew what was probably coming. But, to my surprise, she leaned back in her chair and screamed with her hands waving in the air, "Hell yeah, Miss Perfect is now the trailer park queen!"

She leaned closer, clanked her cup against mine and said, "Cheers...to the trailer park queen!" as we both chugged the alcohol in our cups.

***

An hour or so had passed and I found myself sitting inside on the living room sofa.

How did I get inside?

As I looked around the room, the lights made me more nauseated and dizzier. When I tried to get up, I lost my balance and fell back onto the cushion. I leaned my head against the sofa and closed my eyes.

"Wake up! We got fireworks!" Tennie said while shaking my arm repeatedly.

Laughing as she helped me up from the sofa, she cut her eyes at me and said, "Don't puke on me Miss Per...Nessie. That is where I draw the line."

The fireworks were amazing. The town was hosting an early July 4th celebration and we had front-row seats. As each one popped into the night sky, my eyes became heavy, and my nausea worsened. "I need to sit down."

Tennie remained captivated by the fireworks as I stumbled back to the chairs. But with each step, everything started to spin faster, and I felt lightheaded. As I felt myself spiraling to the ground, his arms wrapped around me – saving me - again.

It was *him*...Brice.

"Nessie!" Realizing that I was intoxicated he continued, "Are you drunk!" Brice held onto me and helped me sit down.

I was mortified. Once again, Brice had to rescue me. This time my choice of drinking alcohol was to blame, not my clumsiness...but it was still embarrassing. The nausea was more than I could stand. I'd never felt like this before. I stood up and tried to walk back to the trailer and...I lost it.

I puked right in the middle of Tennie's yard...in front of Brice.

I think everyone was too busy watching the fireworks to notice me. But, *he* was there. I was completely mortified and didn't want to turn around and face him. But when I turned to look behind me, Brice was not there.

Whew! He didn't see all of that.

As I walked back inside the trailer from the back porch, I found my way through the crowd to the front door. I had to get out of here.

"Uh, where do you think you're going?" Brice grabbed my hand pulling me away from the door. "You've had *way* too much to drink. You're not driving."

I felt my heart begin to beat rapidly as his hand continued to hold mine. "Oh, yeah, I...I wasn't going to drive...I was going to call..."

"I'll take you home. You can get your car tomorrow. It will be fine here." He reached for my keys in my pocket. "Come with me."

***

The car ride home was awkward. My buzz from the alcohol was starting to wear off, and I felt myself falling into the "old Nessie" routine...not saying a word. My eyes wandered sneaking peeks at his tanned, muscular arms extended toward the steering wheel. The A/C was on max which stirred around scents of his cologne that mesmerized me.

Did he know how hot he was?

As he took the curves around Bayou Fueob, he stared straight ahead out the windshield not saying a word.

So many questions filled my head during the silence. *Why isn't he talking? Why would he offer to bring me home if he wasn't interested in getting to know me?*

When he pulled up to the house, he stared at me with a half grin. "I didn't think you were a party girl. You really pulled a good one tonight."

"Guess I'm full of surprises!" I replied sarcastically, which came off ruder than I intended, but I was irritated that he waited until we pulled up at my house to talk to me.

"Okay, yeah, I'd say you surprised most of the party being there." He leaned on the console, and his beautiful green eyes locked with mine – but only for a moment.

"I'm just curious why you came. I mean, you and Tennie aren't friends, so what made you show up?" He quickly looked my way again.

I giggled to myself watching him struggle to make eye contact with me. "I don't know. I guess I've been through a lot at the hospital with my *so-called* family. I needed an out. Tennie's party was my out."

"Yeah, I'm sorry about Beau. I know it's been tough and all. But, Nessie, you have to be careful around Tennie. She's like a trap and will suck you in. Besides, you're a Corbin...Corbins don't belong in the trailer park." Brice kept looking forward out the windshield.

"It wasn't her fault. I felt like I needed something different. I need a change." I looked back at him as he stared into the distance.

And there it was again...my dreaded last name had to be brought into the conversation. "I have to ask. Why in the hell does my last name matter...honestly...it's just a name." I sunk deeper into the passenger seat as my buzz continued to wear off.

He didn't reply. He continued staring out the windshield.

Did I make him uncomfortable?

I looked back at him hoping for an answer, but he continued staring into the distance without responding. I watched as he swallowed deeply and quickly changed the subject. "I'll drop off your car on my way to work. One of the guys from the shop can help me."

Wishing the car ride might have ended with something more, I opened the passenger door and waved. "Thanks for the ride."

I shut the door and walked toward the porch as he drove off.

You're peculiar Brice Adams. Are you interested in me or not?

Chapter Thirty-Eight

Awakening

Where am I?
Beau's eyes darted around the room confused as he felt the annoying tube in his throat.

It was mid-morning and Dad had fallen asleep on the sofa. Isabella had taken a call from the nurse's station down the hall. The annoying beep of the machine stirred the silence.

The nurse checking Beau's vitals nudged Dad to wake up and pointed over to Beau whose eyes frantically searched for a familiar face.

"Son!" Dad jumped from the sofa and grabbed his hand.

Beau's eyes continued to race around the room as his blood pressure started to rise.

"It's natural to see this," the nurse explained. "The tube is enough to make him anxious now that he's awake. I've called the doctor to assess, and we might be able to remove it."

Isabella entered the room once she heard the commotion and ran over to Beau. "He's awake! My Beau is awake!"

The nurses and doctors took over the room and asked Isabella and Dad to give them space. After checking his vitals, the doctor approved removing the trach.

He pulled Dad and Isabella aside. "He's going to be confused, and we're not sure what he will remember. You will need to give him time and not pressure him. Also, we have stabilized his back due to the fractures so he may become agitated that he's unable to move his arms."

Isabella moved closer to Beau's side and held his hand. "Beau, honey, just try to relax." Beau stared back at Isabella helpless and wanting answers.

***

The trach was removed later that afternoon.

"What happened? Why am I in the hospital?" Beau pulled at the IVs.

Isabella knew he was uncomfortable. "Honey, you have to keep these in for now. I'll explain everything. You need to take it easy and rest."

"Rest...but I'm not tired," Beau searched the room, and saw Dad sitting in the corner.

"Dad...you have to tell me what happened. Why do I have all this stuff attached to me? Where am I?" Dad sat across from Isabella on the bed near Beau.

"Son, you just need to take it easy. We'll explain everything. I promise." Dad glared at Isabella and then back at Beau.

"Where is Charlotte? I need to see her. She's probably worried about me. We're all supposed to go to the Abyss tonight for a party."

Beau attempted to reach his arm toward the table for the phone...and he realized he couldn't move his arm. "Why can't I move?"

Isabella got up and walked to the door frustrated by Beau's comment regarding Charlotte. *Dammit...he can't get this girl out of his mind. I hoped he wouldn't remember her. I need to explain everything now.*

Seeing the pink rose in the trash can made her smile. *I'm glad I threw it away before Beau woke up.*

"Beau, the party was a few weeks ago. You've been here since the party." Dad reluctantly replied as he stared at the wall.

Irritated that Charlotte was still on Beau's mind, Isabella chimed in. "And, that Callaway girl is likely not coming to visit. With the paternity test and all, it's doubtful she will come to see you."

The room fell silent, and Beau stared at the ceiling confused by Isabella's comment. "What...did you say...paternity test? What do you mean?"

Isabella stared silently at Beau as he continued to pry for answers and yelled, "Dammit! Will someone please tell me what's going on!"

"I don't deserve to be yelled at and will not take this abuse. I'm only stating the facts." Isabella folded her arms across her chest and stared at Dad. Beau closed his eyes tightly.

Dad sat back in his chair and ran his fingers through his hair. Isabella never ceased to amaze him. "Isabella, that's enough. Why don't you go back to the office for a while? I think you've done enough damage here for one day."

"Well, I want to be the one to explain everything." Isabella didn't give up easily, however, her pager went off, and it was the clinic. The clinic was always her main focus and was the only thing that would take her attention away from Beau.

"I need to get back to the clinic. I'm taking call for Dr. Dawson, but I won't be gone long. I'll be back within an hour." Her tone changed as she faced Beau and said, "Honey, I'll explain everything. Some of it will be hard to swallow but you need to hear it."

***

Hours later, the Callaways came to the hospital once they heard the news that Beau was awake. Dad met them in the lobby to warn them that Beau couldn't remember anything that happened.

"The doctors are encouraging us to give him time." Dad glared at Isabella leaning over the nurse's station and continued. "Isabella has already shared too much. Now, Beau is even more agitated wanting answers."

Dad noticed Charlotte fidgeting with the stem of a dried, pink rose she planned to give to Beau.

Charlotte's desire to talk to Beau soon became a pit in her stomach since he was awake. As she held the stem of the rose she thought, *I'll be damned if she throws this one away.*

"He asked about you, Charlotte." Dad lightly placed his hand on her arm as she glanced up toward him. "He...did?"

"Yes, it was the first thing out of his mouth." Dad smiled.

Charlotte squeezed Melissa's hand as they walked to Beau's room. Charlotte began to feel less anxious about seeing him until she heard *her* dreadful voice.

"Where do *you* think *you're* going? The last thing he needs right now is to see the person that put him here!" Isabella placed herself between Charlotte and the door and scornfully continued, "He does not know what happened, and I promised him *I* would share everything with him."

Isabella noticed the pink rose Charlotte clutched in her hand. She couldn't resist. "And the rose, honestly, that will only confuse him. He doesn't remember anything."

Looking back at Dad, Isabella waved for him to come closer. "Beau needs his family right now. Visitors will have to wait until we're ready."

Mason was fuming inside and attempted to hold in his anger, but Isabella's last comment about being a 'visitor' was too much. "Visitors? Have you lost your damn mind, Isabella? I'm Beau's father, remember!? My family is *his* family. Get out of the damn way!"

Dad watched as Mason shoved Isabella aside and attempted to open the door. He stopped Mason and said, "Mason, while I don't agree with Isabella often, I do think we should slowly share with Beau what happened. I think if we all go in now, we'll bombard him, and it will be too much for him. For now, I think it's best that only me, you, and Isabella should go in and explain the accident.

Dad turned to Charlotte and said, "I know Beau wants to see you, but will you please give us a moment to get him up to speed on what happened?" Dad was always good at 'softening' things.

"Yes sir, I'll do whatever you think is best for Beau." Melissa walked back to the waiting area arm in arm with Charlotte.

Isabella rolled her eyes at Mason. "Don't touch me again you idiot. I'll be the one to tell him what happened." She entered the room with Dad and Mason following.

"Honey, I know you're confused and want answers. Just bear with me while I explain." Beau searched the room for Charlotte and didn't see her. "Where is Charlotte, Mom? I asked you to call her."

Regretfully, she replied, "I did call her, and she's on her way." She looked at Dad and Mason daring them to say anything different.

I'm not telling him she's in the waiting room now. I need to explain everything first.

"Why is Mr. Callaway here?" Mason shifted his stance and let Isabella reply.

"Just try to relax, Beau. I'll explain everything." Isabella sat down next to him on the bed.

***

Dad called me several times and left three messages on the machine about Beau. I ignored all of them as I felt terrible. My headache felt like a machine gun going off in my head. The pounding wouldn't stop. I pinched myself to be sure it wasn't a dream.

Why do people enjoy drinking so much if this is what it does to them? Maybe Brice was right. Tennie will suck me down with her.
Despite the terrible hangover, it was a fun night!

***

As I drove to the hospital, I rolled the windows down allowing the fresh country air to fill my car. The sunshine peeked its way through my sunroof, and I embraced it.

Dad met me at the front of the hospital and filled me in. I saw Charlotte sitting miserably in the waiting room. Dad had told me Isabella would let her in to see Beau. A small part of me felt sorry for her.

When we got closer to Beau's room, Isabella came out and put her hands out to stop us. "He needs time. He's still shaken and upset and doesn't want to see anyone. He needs to rest."

"Isabella, you can't keep us from seeing him. We're his family, and he needs us now more than anything." Dad and Mason attempted to combat Isabella's orders.

"Absolutely not. I've asked the nurses not to allow anyone in his room. He wants to be alone." Isabella responded coldly and walked back to the nurse's station. "It's what Beau wants."

I leaned against the door and peeked through the glass. Beau looked miserable. Football and Charlotte were his entire world – everything he loved was ruined.

My emotions raged wanting to hug him and tell him how worried we all had been. I didn't care what Isabella said and I wanted to push her buttons. I turned the knob to open the door and he yelled, "Get out, Nessie! I don't want you in here."

The nurse came to the door and pushed me aside. "No visitors per Dr. Corbin."

Dad sighed as Mason retreated back to Melissa and Charlotte in the waiting room. Charlotte sadly leaned into Melissa's embrace as Mason shared that Beau didn't want any visitors.

"C'mon Nessie. Let's give him a minute. He will come around." Dad put his arm around me.

"I'm not so sure Dad. I've never seen him like this before." Isabella leaned on the nurse's station counter, and I glared back at her as we walked by.

She knew what she was doing – continuing to manipulate everyone to get what she wanted.

Chapter Thirty-Nine

Holding Back

A week had passed since Whitney and Stella had spoken to Charlotte, and she hadn't returned any of their calls. They decided to visit Beau without her since they heard the news he'd awakened.

The nurse stopped them as they approached his room.

"I'm sorry ladies. He doesn't want any visitors. Ya'll will have to come back later." The nurse held her stance in front of the door.

"Why...is something wrong?" Whitney was confused and stepped back from the nurse. Stella held her position and glared at the nurse with her arms crossed tightly across her chest. "Well, why can't we go in?" Stella demanded.

Before the nurse could react to Stella's boldness, Beau saw them through the glass in the door and buzzed the nurse's station. "Let them in."

The nurse continued to block the door making it impossible for them to enter. Stella stepped closer to the nurse. "Look, he's waving for us to come in."

Realizing the wrath that would unravel if Dr. Corbin found out she let someone in his room, but leaning on the patient's request, the nurse reluctantly moved out of the way. "Don't be too long now."

Whitney entered the room and was taken aback seeing him hooked up to the monitors and his arms strapped to the bed.

"What in the world have you gotten yourself into, Beau?" Stella joked.

"Ha...ha...real funny." Beau smiled for the first time since he'd awakened.

"What...you need a bodyguard now or something!?" Stella laughed as she sat down on the bed across from Whitney.

It was obvious Whitney was uncomfortable. She remained quiet staring at Beau strapped to the bed.

"Mom apparently thinks I need rest and has limited visitors. The last thing I *want* is rest. I'm miserable just laying here, but I don't really have a choice." Beau sighed as he pressed his head back against the pillow.

It didn't take him long to ask about Charlotte. "Have ya'll seen Charlotte? I miss her so much and well...after Mom caught me up on what happened...I need to talk to her."

It felt good to see Whitney and Stella, but he desperately had hoped Charlotte was with them.

"I haven't talked to her in over a week. You know, she came to the hospital the day you woke up. I haven't seen or talked to her since." Whitney fidgeted with the ring on her finger as her eyes focused on the straps restraining his arms, still making her uncomfortable.

Beau noticed.

"These things...yeah...they suck." Beau tried to lift his arms up and laughed. "I feel like I'm a prisoner."

"Yeah, that looks pretty miserable!" Stella responded.

"Guess ya'll heard my back is broken...I really did it up good didn't I?" Beau stared at the ceiling tiles.

Grabbing his hand, Whitney replied, "I'm sorry, Beau. I can't even imagine. All I know is that we have to get you better and out of this hospital."

Beau continued to stare up at the ceiling knowing his summer was not going to be spent as he'd planned. "The doctors told me I'll have surgery in a few weeks on my back, and I'll be in therapy for several weeks. The worst part is...I can't play football next year...maybe never."

"I'm so sorry Beau." Whitney stood up from the bed unsure of how to respond.

"If we see Charlotte, do you want us to tell her to come by? We've been trying to give her space. She won't return our calls, but we can try again." Stella looked toward Beau and smiled.

"Only if she wants to see me. Mom said she left the hospital upset the day I woke up and didn't want to see me. She must have changed her mind about us. It just doesn't make any sense." Beau stared out the window and continued, "I woke up wanting to hold her in my arms. Then Mom reminded me about the paternity test..."

"Are you getting the second paternity test?" Stella looked back at Beau with hope. "I mean, it's worth a try."

"I don't know at this point. Look at me! I'm stuck in this bed and will be for a while. It's not like I can drive over and do it. And...apparently, she doesn't want to see me...maybe we're over?"

Whitney leaned back closer to him and squeezed his hand. "She probably just doesn't know what to say."

Reluctant to tell him, she knew he needed to know. "Beau, I can't keep this from you. I think the reason Charlotte didn't want to see you is that...well...she feels guilty – she feels like she's the reason you're in here."

"What!? No, this isn't her fault!" he shouted. "This is all on me. I ran off the road. I should have been going slower around the curve."

***

Jackson and Blaine stopped by the law firm after conditioning practice. AELs had catered a luncheon and Allison told Jackson and his friends to come by to get the leftovers.

"Jackson...Blaine...fellas," Tucker nodded walking past the guys in the hallway.

"Hey, Mr. Corbin," feeling obligated to ask about Beau he continued, "how's Beau doing?" Jackson hadn't been by the hospital since the night of the accident. He didn't know what he would say to Beau, and there was a small ounce of guilt residing in him for not speaking up about seeing Isabella in Tucker's office. So, he chose to avoid him.

"He's awake now...doesn't remember anything...so we're giving him time to absorb it all. I'm sure he would enjoy a visit soon. The team should go by there." Dad looked at both Jackson and Blaine and continued, "You know, Beau is lucky to have both of you as friends. Damn lucky."

Blaine stared at the floor as Dad patted each of their shoulders. "He's going to need both of you to get him through the upcoming fall season. Not being able to play on that field is going to kill him. Ya'll will help support him, right?"

"Oh, yes sir!" Jackson nodded and Blaine followed suit.

Both felt a weight come over them knowing the secrets they were keeping would dramatically impact their friendship with Beau if he were to find out.

Blaine kept replaying Dad's words, 'not being able to play on that field', and he had to leave.

As they passed Dad's office the image of Isabella shutting the cabinet door flooded Jackson's mind. He tried to block it out.

As Jackson walked past Allison's office, she stopped him. "Jackson, do you have a minute?"

"Sure, Mom, what's up?" he said as he plopped down in the chair.

"I'm out dude. I'll wait for you outside the pharmacy." Blaine waved to Allison as he passed her office.

"Alright, ya'll wait for me. Oh, that's right...ya'll have to because I drove!" Jackson said laughing as Blaine was already halfway down the hall.

Allison closed the door to her office and sat on the edge of her desk in front of him.

"I need you to be honest with me, Jackson. And, I'll know if you're lying." Allison was pointed and Jackson knew where this was going.

He leaned forward in the chair and clasped his hands.

In a desperate attempt to deflect, he quickly responded. "I know I haven't been by the hospital, Mom. It's just...hard to see Beau that way."

She crossed her arms on her chest. "You haven't been by to see Beau? That's surprising to me. You're one of his best friends."

"I'm going to try to go by there tomorrow. I know...I should've gone by now." He attempted to get up from the chair. She put her hand out to stop him.

"Stay put, son. That's not why I asked you to come see me. But, you best get your butt over to see Beau in the next few days. I mean it." Jackson knew by her stare that she was serious.

"Mom, am I in trouble or something?" He was afraid to ask.

"It depends. If you're honest with me and tell me everything, you won't be." Allison continued.

"I need to know what happened the night you saw Isabella here at the firm. I know she was up to something so tell me what you saw." She watched as he breathed in deeply and his eyes wandered to the walls.

"Jackson...I need you to tell me what you saw." Allison's eyes narrowed and her lips tightened.

Jackson rubbed the nape of his neck and closed his eyes. With a bowed head, he reluctantly responded. "Okay, Mom, *maybe* I did see something."

"What did you *maybe* see?" She leaned in closer to him.

"I saw her by the filing cabinet. I didn't see what she was doing...I swear...she turned around really quick." Jackson paused, ashamed he'd lied to his mom.

"Jackson, why didn't you tell me this sooner? I asked you over a month ago about this and you lied to me...said you didn't see anything. Why would you do that?" Allison sat down in the chair next to him.

"I don't even know if I saw anything. That's why I didn't feel comfortable saying anything. I knew I surprised her." Jackson felt ashamed for keeping the secret.

Allison reached over and grabbed his hand. "I'm proud of you for telling me the truth. I'm not happy about you lying when I first asked you, but I'm glad you shared this with me."

"Mom, there's one more thing. I like Charlotte. I didn't say anything because...well...I was afraid I'd lose my chance at being with her if the paternity test was false." Jackson gripped the side of the chair. "Before you say anything...I know it's wrong. But, I've sat on the sidelines to Beau in football and now it's affecting my personal life – someone that I like...Charlotte. I'm tired of putting myself second."

Allison was shocked and speechless. She composed herself before responding. "Honey, I think you know the right thing to do here. Beau is your friend, and he's been through so much. Taking advantage of the situation for your own gain...that's selfish...and not like you."

Jackson stood up from the chair. "I knew you wouldn't understand, which is why I didn't tell you.! Charlotte realizes it's over between them anyway. Whitney and Beau apparently are talking. He's moved on too. So, I'm not taking advantage of anyone."

Allison watched as Jackson stormed out of her office.

I'm not so sure Jackson. Isabella was definitely up to something that night. I can't promise that I'll keep this to myself – for all of our sake.

***

"I think it's on aisle two...on the top shelf." Charlotte pointed toward the aisle directing the customer who was searching for antacids. Occasionally, she would run the register while Melissa stocked inventory. "And...three dollars and fifty cents is your change," Charlotte said politely as she watched the customer leave through the glass doors.

As the customer exited, her eyes became focused on the crowd of football jerseys standing on the sidewalk outside the pharmacy.

The football team. Uh...just what I want to deal with today.

Jackson led a few of the guys into the pharmacy, and she watched them head to the coolers. "Get me a Gatorade, man," one teammate said as Jackson scanned the cooler.

"Heads up!" Jackson yelled as he pitched one over the aisle.

Jackson casually placed a few items down by the register and slowly leaned across the counter toward Charlotte.

"Hey, how's it going?" He asked smoothly as the rest of the team mumbled behind him.

"It's going okay…I guess." She replied as she quickly began scanning the items.

Jackson struggled to find the right words and fought the urge to flirt with her. It wasn't the right time for that.

The annoying beep from the scan gun filled the awkward silence as he heard her say, "Fifteen dollars and sixty-two cents."

"Thanks…and ugh…maybe I'll see you later?" Jackson mumbled with a smirk.

"Yeah, maybe so. I'm working here for a few days this week. Maybe I'll see you around." Charlotte's half grin and flat demeanor were not what he'd hoped for as a response, however, he wasn't giving up that easily.

"Okay, then…maybe I'll stop by tomorrow." Jackson smiled back at her, but she quickly looked away with no response.

As he left the store, she watched the guys push each other around jokingly with their macho football antics and sighed – this made her think of Beau even more. Her emotions ran rampant, and she became irritated that Beau was ignoring her.

Beau, why don't you want to talk to me…you shut me out. He must be blaming me for all of this. That is the only logical reason.

She continued watching the football team as they lingered on the sidewalk…which made her miss Beau even more.

I'm not giving up on him. He at least needs to hear from me that I'm sorry.

Charlotte mustered up the nerve to call the hospital hoping maybe Beau had changed his mind. "Beau Corbin's room please."

To her dismay, the nurse quickly replied, "Ma'am I'm sorry, but he's not accepting any phone calls or visitors. I'm unable to put you through."

Charlotte slammed the phone down. "Dammit! Why doesn't he want to talk to me?"

***

"Can you check me out here? The line is extremely long at the pharmacy window." Charlotte heard *her* cold voice and wanted to crawl under the counter.

She attempted to avoid eye contact with Isabella as she stood with her arms crossed glaring at her. "Here...this should cover it all." Isabella handed a twenty-dollar bill to Charlotte and stepped back from the counter.

As she placed the cash into the drawer, Charlotte felt Isabella's continued stare. Her vindictive nature could never be tamed.

"Beau just doesn't know what to think about everything. He's going to be in that hospital bed for a while...and...then with therapy...well, football is out for him. His life has changed, unfortunately...and to be honest, I can't help but blame *you* for all of it. Honestly, I don't know how he would ever be able to forgive you."

Isabella grabbed her things from the counter and started to walk away. She struggled with the fact that Beau was lying helpless in the hospital bed while Charlotte was living a normal life. "You know, Charlotte, that pink rose you left for Beau was severely faded. It sort of resembles the relationship between the two of you now – faded and withered."

Charlotte stared blankly back at Isabella...not shocked by her crudeness. She was numb to Isabella's hatred of her at this point. She was most worried that her words, 'ever forgive you', might be true.

Beau may never forgive me for this.

Chapter Forty

Raging Emotions

The library was typically empty during summer...and I liked it that way. The occasional sound of the librarian stamping the back covers of books reminded me that I wasn't alone. I escaped to my usual table and buried myself in the text. The quiet was my solace.

The words on the page became blurred as my mind wandered to Beau, then to Dad, and last, Tennie. *Tennie...of all people.*

My mind drifted back to the night of Tennie's party. Besides the fact that I drank too much, it was a defining moment for me. For the first time, I felt rebellious. I didn't overthink my next step – I simply responded to how I felt at that moment. My actions were fierce and untamed...so unlike me.

My mind quickly shifted to the moment Brice grabbed my hand refusing to let me drive home. The warm yet rough touch of his hand mesmerized me, and I longed to feel it again.

My daydream continued with him holding me close and pressing his lips on mine. As I kissed him back, I felt a tap on my shoulder that brought me back to reality.

To my dismay, it was Owen.

"Hey, Nessie. Can I sit?" Owen stared blankly toward the floor as he awkwardly awaited my response.

I looked back at him intently and replied, "No. I came here to be alone." I quickly stared at the pages of my book. He didn't get it. His family was the reason mine was falling apart. I couldn't be friends with him. I needed space.

I could feel his continued stare. He wasn't leaving. "Nessie, what's wrong with you? You're acting weird...always wanting to be alone...not talking to anyone anymore...well...except..."

"Except *who*, Owen?" I snapped back at him.

"Nothing. Just forget about it." Placing both hands in his pockets he began to back away from the table.

"Oh, no, you don't get to just say that and then walk away. Get it off your chest!" I'd become annoyed with him easily. Shrugging his shoulders, he continued to look down at the floor in defeat.

I never was this rude to Owen before – he was my best friend. But he obviously had something to get off his chest. Nonetheless, he was going to share whatever he was hiding from me.

"I'm waiting, Owen!" My voice had become stern.

"It's Tennie! Tennie Adams. Everyone in town knows about it." Owen, while trying to remain calm, was becoming more agitated. "You got drunk at her trailer-real drunk-what's gotten into you?"

At this point, I was fuming inside. There was a rage burning inside of me that wanted to take him down from across the table. I took a deep breath before replying, "Why do you care? So, I had a little fun for once."

"It's just not like you at all, Nessie." Owen's eyes narrowed as he grabbed his book from the table and walked away.

Ugh! What's wrong with him? Maybe I'm exhausted from always being the level-headed one...the one that just makes everything work. My permissive demeanor had gotten the best of me.

I couldn't read anymore after being distracted by Owen. I gathered my things from the table and stood up while placing them in my book sack.

That's when I noticed Brice entering the library. The lady at the front desk pointed him toward the back of the building.

What's he doing here? He's definitely not the library 'type'.

I sat back down in my chair and quickly pulled out my book. Pretending to be deeply engaged in the pages, I heard his voice.

"Nessie...hey...?" I immediately felt a wave of emotions flood me as he pulled a chair back to sit down across from me.

"Hey," I weakly replied." I adjusted my frames and stared back at the pages in my book.

Brice leaned closer to me across the table with his hands clasped.

"What are you reading?" He casually grabbed the corner of my book and pulled it to him across the table.

"Nothing you would be interested in." Realizing quickly that I probably sounded rude I tried to overcome.

"I...I didn't mean anything by that...sorry!"

"Yeah, I don't get all this reading stuff. It's not really my thing." He slid the book back to me, pushed away from the table and stood up. His eyes locked with mine. His face remained expressionless.

"Guess I'm going to head out. I had to drop something off to my Aunt. This library thing really isn't for me." His eyes locked on mine for a split second.

"I've got to go by The Dixie and get something from Tennie. Guess I'll catch ya' later?" Continuing to stare at me, he slowly turned and began walking away.

As I struggled what to do next, his casual, yet confident demeanor was charming, and it drew me in.

"Wait! I'll ride with you." I blurted before thinking it through.

He stopped, glanced back at me, and smiled. "Yeah...sure."

Maybe I was lying to Owen and to myself. I didn't want to be left alone completely. For some reason, I was intrigued by Brice's soft, yet confident approach, and the fact that he was oblivious to how dysfunctional my family truly was.

As we walked out the library, I caught a glimpse of Owen sitting alone. He looked up from his book, shook his head, and went back to reading.

***

Whitney and Stella finally convinced Charlotte to meet them at AEL's for a late lunch. While Charlotte had been busy helping Melissa at the store most weekdays, she'd purposely avoided her friends.

"Girl, you've completely blocked us out. What's been up?" Stella stared at Charlotte demanding an answer.

"I know, and I'm sorry. I just needed some time to think through everything. I'm not sure I made much progress. Beau still won't talk to me." Charlotte fidgeted with the paper napkin that surrounded her utensils.

"What can I get for you ladies today?" the waitress kindly placed menus on the table.

"Three waters and the special for today, please." Whitney handed the menus back to the waitress noticing Charlotte staring out the window.

"Char, have you tried calling him?" Whitney paused to let Charlotte respond.

"Yes, I did the other day, and they keep telling me he wasn't accepting calls. I don't understand why he doesn't want to talk to me." Whitney and Stella grabbed her hands as she continued. "Then, his Mom came into the pharmacy and blatantly blamed me for the accident. He may never forgive me ya'll. I don't know if my heart can take much more." Charlotte began to cry softly and leaned into Whitney's shoulder.

The waitress kindly smiled at Charlotte and patted her hand as she set three baked ham plates on their table.

"I realize we can't be together, but I need to see him and talk to him. I want to make things right and hope he doesn't blame me for the accident." Charlotte's cry became louder and several guests dining at other tables began to look at them.

"Char, he doesn't blame you. He wants to see you." Whitney consoled her and continued. "We decided to visit him the other day and he was asking us the same thing – why haven't you come by or called."

Charlotte quickly wiped her tears. "What? Ya'll went by there without me? Why would you do that?"

"You wouldn't return our calls, Char. He's our friend too, and we wanted to check on him." Stella could tell Charlotte was frustrated. "We didn't mean anything by it. We didn't want to pressure you – and we hadn't heard from you – so we just went by there."

"He was doing okay, by the way. He was hoping you were with us." Whitney nudged Charlotte's shoulder and smiled. "He's been hoping you would come by this entire time."

Charlotte wiped her tears and smiled. "Oh, that makes me feel so much better. But, how did ya'll get in to see him? And why would he tell the nurses he didn't want any visitors or calls? That doesn't make sense."

Charlotte stirred the buttered carrots on her plate and noticed Stella's pursed lips. "I have one word for you...Isabella. If I had to take a guess, I bet she told those nurses he couldn't have visitors. Beau told us she doesn't want him to have visitors – he needs to rest." Stella continued, "Beau saw us through the door and let us in. I don't think it's him who doesn't want visitors."

Whitney attempted to defend Isabella. After all, she had a closer relationship with her and was slightly offended that Stella easily accused her. "Look, I know Mrs. Issie isn't the nicest person in town, but I know she would never do something like that – especially if she knew it would hurt Beau."

Charlotte glared at Whitney, shocked she was defending her. "Whit, what planet do you live on? That woman is every bit of ruthless." Taking a bite of her ham, Charlotte motioned for the waitress. "I can't focus on eating. Can we get some boxes to go and maybe a few slices of the pecan pie?"

"Sure thing!" The waitress quickly packed up their lunch.

"Sorry to cut lunch short, but Isabella isn't going to stop me from seeing him. It's time Beau knows exactly what she's capable of." Charlotte was determined to tell Beau everything.

***

Brice didn't say much on our way over to The Dixie. While it was an awkward silence, I still felt comfortable. When we pulled into the parking lot, Tennie leaned out the order window and smiled seeing me in the front seat next to her brother.

"You can wait here. I'll just be a minute." Brice opened the door and quickly noticed I was almost at the order window. "*Okay*...or you can just come." He laughed quietly to himself as he shut the car door.

"Well, well, if it isn't Miss Per...damn...it's gonna' be hard to not call you that anymore," Tennie said as she leaned out the order window with her hands clasped.

"What brings you two here – together?" Her eyebrow raised.

"I just need to get Mom's key to the storage unit. She said you had them last, and they weren't at the house." Brice casually leaned against one of the poles outside the order window.

"It's in my purse. I'll go grab it. Be right back." Tennie smiled slyly toward me and smirked.

I looked at Brice leaning on the pole hoping he would say something...*anything*.

I glanced back through the window hoping Tennie would take her time finding the key to give us more time alone.

Just as I was about to speak, Blaine walked up to the window. "Hey, Nessie. What's up?"

"Not much, Blaine." I continued staring at Brice as Blaine leaned through the order window. "Yo! Anybody working this window?" He slapped the metal counter a few times with no response.

"She's in the back, Blaine. Just chill out." Brice continued leaning against the pole.

As Tennie approached the window, Blaine began to antagonize her to take his order. "Girl, what you doin'? You're supposed to be working the window. Can't keep me waiting. I'm starving!"

"Whatever Blaine. What can I spit on for you today?" Tennie grabbed her order tablet and brushed her red curls out of her face.

I gave up on Brice talking to me and started walking back to his car. As I got close to the curb, I felt someone grab my arm.

Oh great...here he goes thinking I'll fall.

But it wasn't him. It was Blaine.

"Hey, Nessie, how's Beau?" Blaine wasn't as cocky around me...I guess since I was Beau's sister.

"I guess okay. He doesn't want to see anyone. He told me to leave his room. I haven't been back."

"You ready," Brice asked as he walked close to the side of Blaine, staring him down, and opened my door.

"Yeah, I guess." I caught Brice's eyes lock with mine and he smirked.

"All right, then. I guess I'll see ya'll later." Blaine went back to the window to harass Tennie.

***

As we drove down Main Street, Brice propped his right arm on his console. Every move he made was smooth. My breathing became heavier as silence filled the car. For a moment, I imagined him pulling over and kissing me sweetly. I remained lost in this moment when I heard, "Nessie...do you mind?"

"What? Do I mind what?" I couldn't believe that I'd faded into some stupid fascination moment...again.

What was wrong with me?

Brice softly laughed, "Going by the storage unit."

I completely missed the conversation; however, it didn't matter. I would go anywhere with him.

"I need to stop by and grab a few baseball things. I'm thinking about trying out again next school year." Brice turned into the storage parking area.

I didn't want to press him about it but was curious why he'd quit something he seemed to love.

What the hell. Just ask him Nessie.

"You seem to really miss playing...why'd you quit?" Silence filled the car as he hesitated to respond. "That story is for another day."

When he got back into the car, we sat for a moment. He looked toward me and grabbed my hand.

My heart began to beat faster. I'd waited for this moment forever...to feel needed and wanted. I wasn't sure who it would be with...and I never thought it would be with someone like Brice Adams...but his cool, yet humble demeanor captivated me.

"Wanna go to a party tonight with me?" The warmth of his eyes penetrated me.

He wants to go to a party...with me?

"Sure...what time and where?" I tried to compose myself but I wanted to scream.

"I'll get you around eight o'clock. We're all going to the Abyss." He removed his hand from mine and cranked the car. "Tennie is going to be there but promise you will stay by me."

"Okay...but she's my..." I attempted to respond.

"Your what? Friend?" Brice laughed as he sped out of the parking lot. "Tennie doesn't have friends. No one hangs around long enough to be her friend. Trust me."

I was overwhelmed with excitement, nervousness, confusion, guilt...you name it.

I was going on a date with Brice Adams!

Chapter Forty-One

A Different Perspective

Trisha flaunted around Charlee's Bar in a tight, blue jean miniskirt paired with a top that resembled a bra. She played the bartender role during the day and waitressed at night. She'd worked for Charlee Jr., the owner of the bar, since graduating from high school.

"Here you go guys...that'll be twenty-five dollars for the bucket of beer. Going on your tab?" Trisha playfully set the bucket on the table. One of the guys pulled her close and carefully placed a twenty-dollar bill in the waistband of her miniskirt. "You keep that...and put the beers on the tab. And keep our bucket fresh."

"I'll be watching you boys," Trisha leaned over and blew a kiss making eye contact with them.

The night tips were much better considering the majority of the clientele were men. Trisha never was the settling down type – marriage wasn't in her vocabulary. After all, she'd succeeded in having two children with different men and neither were 'dad' material.

She made her way back to the front bar when she heard, "You going to let me sit at this bar all night and drink by myself?"

Trisha was startled by the comment.

It can't be her. It's been years since she's been here.

Trisha turned around slowly, and her speculation became reality.

"Charlene! What in the hell are you doing here?" Trisha ran over to her high school friend and almost knocked her off the barstool.

"Surprised to see me?" Charlene set her beer on the bar top.

"Look at you! My gosh, it's been too long!" Trisha stepped away from Charlene for a moment and quickly reached for her friend's hands. "You shouldn't have been a stranger. I've missed you so much!"

Charlene looked around the bar and smiled. "I sure do miss this place. You won't find a place like this in the city." Charlene watched as a couple two-stepped across the make-shift dance floor.

"It's amazing how so much time has passed, and it all still looks the same." Charlene admired the sticky parquet floors and the walls adorned with various signage.

"I'm just happy you're here! I mean...are you back for good...or just visiting?" Trisha leaned closer.

"Well, I'm not sure honestly. I'm here..." Charlene struggled to continue.

Trisha noticed the hesitation in Charlene's voice and softly touched her friend's hand. "Hey, what's going on? You know you can tell me anything."

Looking down at the bar top and then at Trisha, Charlene continued, "It's time I tell her, Trisha. She needs to know. I'm sick, and I don't have much longer to live. I need to tell my daughter that I love her...I've always loved her."

***

Brice parked on the main road, so it was a long walk to get to the party. "Are there always this many people here?" I'd never been to parties before...it really wasn't my thing...until Tennie 'invited' me to hers.

"It depends." Brice casually grabbed my hand and pulled me closer by his side.

As we continued walking, his pace began to slow, and he turned toward me. His green eyes penetrated my soul, and my heart began to beat rapidly.

Is he going to kiss me? What if I mess this up?

His hands softly cupped my face as he leaned in closer and softly kissed my lips. My body became weak as his mouth touched mine. My breathing had become shallow hoping he would not stop.

He pulled away for a moment and stared at me and smiled. "You're so beautiful. I never thought in a million years I would be kissing Nessie Corbin."

I was completely mesmerized by his kiss and brought my fingers up to my lips. "You...you've been waiting to kiss *me*?"

"Don't sound so surprised!" He secured both of my hands in his and brought them to his lips. "Let's just say I wanted to get to know you better over the last year. There's something about you that intrigued me. I don't know what it is, but you're all I think about."

I felt like I needed to pinch myself to wake up from this dream that I knew could never be true. Brice Adams...the baseball superstar...was interested in bland and direct me.

"You know, normally when someone says they like someone, the other person either says that back or tells them to leave them alone!" Brice laughed. His coolness was effortless and sweet. With his hands still intertwined in mine, he pulled me closer to him.

"Being that you seemed to kiss me back and your grasp on my hand is pretty solid, I want to think you're interested?" Brice whispered in my ear.

I swallowed deeply and attempted to respond, *yes,* but my nerves got the best of me. Everything about Brice shattered the one thing that defined me – the ability to say what I thought without hesitation.

My lips quickly found his neck as my arms pulled him in closer. "I am interested," I softly responded.

His lips found mine and everything faded around us. His kiss was light and sweet, innocent, and playful – everything I imagined my first kiss would be. I didn't want it to end.

Brice pulled away and smiled. "As much as I don't want to stop, maybe we should go check out the party for a little while?" Brice continued smiling as he secured his hand with mine.

As we walked up to the rest of the group, I heard Tennie's voice across the music.

"What's up Nes…sie!!!" Tennie yelled while struggling to walk toward us.

"Figures…she's wasted already. Nessie, just don't…" Brice turned to me and softly touched my side.

"I'll be fine Brice. Trust me, I can handle her." My 'inner' Nessie I'd suppressed wouldn't have shown up at the party with Brice let alone stand up to Tennie.

"Hey, ya'll, where've ya been? I've been here for like, hours." Tennie stumbled around and almost fell before Brice caught her.

"Tennie, c'mon. You've had way too much to drink. I can take you home." Brice knew Tennie was not going to be easy to persuade.

"Little brother to the rescue, huh, in front of your pretty, little, perfect girlfriend." Tennie reached for a cigarette and attempted to light it. With her eyes half shut, she struggled with the lighter.

I wasn't sure what to say, but I saw the tension building on Brice's face. "Tennie, you're such a joke. I'm done with you."

Brice extended his hand to mine. "C'mon, Nessie, I'm not feeling the party tonight. I'll take you home."

I stood motionless, my hand now clasped with his...but I couldn't move. I stared at Tennie struggling to make sense of what Brice had just said. I watched as each draw of the cigarette she breathed in affected her balance and she became more unstable.

Images from the night of Tennie's party flooded my mind again, and I honed into how I felt just like Tennie in that moment - weightless and free - before the sick part. A strong urge suddenly came over me like a pit in my stomach, and I released my hand from Brice's. "You have any more of those cigarettes? I'll take a beer too."

"Nessie, c'mon, this isn't like you." Brice moved closer to me. "C'mon, I'll take you home, or to The Dixie."

I fought the urge to nuzzle my head in his chest and for him to hold me close and kiss me, but I resisted.

His comment annoyed me. "What does 'like me' mean exactly? You hardly even know me! I'm so tired of everyone thinking they know me!"

Tennie smirked slyly at Brice and handed me a cigarette. "Let the girl live, Brice. Come hang out for a while with us. Geez...relax a little bit!"

I did it again. What was wrong with me? Brice was finally opening up to me and kissed me...and I pushed him away...for Tennie.

Realizing that I was not going to back down he replied, "I'll be in the car waiting for you then." Brice's face was long as he turned around and walked away.

"You think I should stop him and make him come with us?" I whispered to Tennie as we continued walking to the party.

"Nah. He's stubborn, Nessie. The more you hang out with him you will see it. You came here to have fun, didn't you? I'm much more fun than my brother." Tennie handed me a drink as we watched Brice escape into the darkness.

***

"Yo, Jackson, come give me a hand with this ice chest," Blaine yelled across the music making his presence known. "And...free beer for the ladies!"

Jackson shook his head and laughed at Blaine – always trying to be the center of attention.

Leaning against the tailgate, Jackson scanned the party. He hadn't been able to catch Charlotte alone and hoped tonight would give him the opportunity.

"You haven't gone by to see Beau lately, have you?" Blaine chugged one of his beers and reached into the ice chest for another.

"No, man, I haven't. Besides, I heard he doesn't want visitors – so I'm respecting that." Jackson wasn't eager to talk about Beau or go see him in the hospital. He'd tried to block out that night, seeing Isabella, and had been successful until someone brought up Beau in conversation.

But, with every slight mention of Beau, Jackson felt the weight of keeping a secret that might destroy his chances with Charlotte.

***

"Char, girl, c'mon, you'd be late for your own wedding!" Stella was anxious to get to the party.

"I'm not gonna go. It feels weird having fun while Beau is stuck in that hospital bed – because of me." Charlotte sat on the bed next to Stella.

"Oh, no...we aren't going to do this tonight. Get yourself together! We're past the whole 'blame' part of this. Get your butt dressed, and we're going to this party!" Stella's persistence was more than Charlotte felt like dealing with. She knew Stella wouldn't back down.

"Fine, but we aren't staying long. I mean it. We can go for a few hours. I want to get back early so I can go to the hospital in the morning to see Beau. Isabella isn't going to stop us from talking." Charlotte smiled at the thought of getting to see him and telling him she was sorry for what happened.

***

Jackson sat by himself most of the night. Blaine was too busy flirting with all of the girls. Typically, Beau stood beside him watching everyone else make fools of themselves. Now, he stood alone.

The only reason he came to the party was to see Charlotte. He decided to leave.

But, as he walked to his Jeep, he saw her.

Damn...she's so beautiful.

"Hey...Charlotte...ya'll want a drink?" Jackson smiled staring at Charlotte while Stella rolled her eyes.

"No, Jackson, we don't want anything. Besides, we aren't staying long." Stella was quick to interject. A small part of her heart still longed for Jackson to want her, but seeing his continued persistence to get Charlotte, it was becoming easier for her to move on.

"I'll take one! Stella's driving tonight." Charlotte nudged Stella with a sarcastic grin on her face.

"Here you go," Jackson handed a drink to Charlotte and took it upon himself to follow them.

Stella rolled her eyes. *Great, now we have to babysit him all night.*

"Where are the rest of the guys?" Stella pointedly asked Jackson.

"It's just Blaine...and ya'll know where he's at." Jackson laughed while staring at Charlotte hoping she would let him hang out with them.

"Stella, what's going on with you," Charlotte whispered as she leaned in closer so Jackson wouldn't hear.

"Nothing, I just don't know why he's following us around." Stella glared at Jackson as they sat on the tailgate of a truck.

He leaned up against the back end of the truck close to where Charlotte was sitting.

"It feels weird not seeing Beau here. Last time I was here..." Charlotte took a sip of her drink and looked at the ground.

"Uh, no...we aren't gonna' do that tonight. We're here to have a good time." Stella sighed knowing it was going to be impossible to get Beau out of her mind. Maybe Jackson being here was a good thing – at least to take her mind off Beau.

Charlotte finished her drink and lay in the truck looking up at the stars. Jackson turned to face her. "You want another drink?"

"Nah, I'm good." She continued staring at the sky.

He fought the urge to grab her hand and tell her how much he'd longed for her to be his girlfriend. As he leaned over the side of the truck, he watched her stare toward the stars.

"It's absolutely beautiful, isn't it?" She closed her eyes and imagined Beau lying beside her and the sweet smell of his cologne. His fingers followed the curves of her body up to her lips as he turned her face to kiss him. She smiled embracing his kiss and touch. She didn't want to leave the moment but was interrupted by the touch of Jackson's hand.

"Hey, what are you thinking about?" Jackson lightly grabbed her hand, but she quickly pulled it away.

"Nothing...I'm not thinking about anything - just taking in the night sky." She looked at him and noticed him staring which made her uncomfortable. She sat up next to Stella.

He remained leaning up against the side of the truck while she leaned her head on Stella's shoulder.

Jackson wasn't giving up that easily. He decided to switch the conversation to something he knew she would be interested in—cheering.

"Charlotte, Coach is having a scrimmage this coming weekend. Has he talked about the cheerleaders coming to support us?"

"Yeah, he did, and we plan to be there. There are a few girls that won't be able to make it, but we should have a good turnout." Charlotte smiled at Jackson thinking about the next football season.

Her smile quickly faded remembering Beau would not be on the field.

"Let's go, Stella. I have cheer practice in the morning and want to go by the hospital." Charlotte scooted off the tailgate.

Jackson became frustrated that Charlotte wasn't moving past Beau – her half-brother. "I don't think you can see him. The last I heard he didn't want visitors."

Jackson hoped she would change her mind and stay at the party longer giving him more time alone with her.

"Yeah, I know. But, I don't care anymore. I'm going to see him and will get into his room somehow. I'm not leaving until I can talk to him." Charlotte stared at Jackson. "I guess we'll see you later."

"Alright, well, hopefully I'll see you around soon." Jackson sighed as the girls latched arms and walked away. He mumbled under his breath, "I have to get close to her again. Maybe she won't be able to see Beau tomorrow."

***

"I feel so bad. I really do! But, everything lately has crumbled around me--this feels like a good escape." I sat on the tailgate looking up at the moon overwhelmed with a sense of happiness.

Every ounce of my existence wanted to scream as loud as I could into the night air.

I kept drinking and smoking...hoping the frustration and worry would leave me.

I could hear Tennie's laugh in the background echoing over the music that was playing.

I became dizzy and fainted.

***

"Get up Nessie. C'mon, you passed out." The voice was muffled and between the alcohol I'd consumed and the loud music, I wasn't sure who was talking to me.

"Brice," softly left my lips, and I smiled as I felt someone pick me up from the tailgate of the truck.

"No, Nessie, it's Blaine. Girl, your Mamma and Daddy are going to be pissed when they see you like this!" Blaine continued walking to his truck carrying me through the remnants of the party.

"Put her down!" Brice stood fiercely in front of Blaine not allowing him to pass. "You aren't taking her anywhere. Just put her down."

Blaine laughed as he repositioned his hold on me. "Dude, chill out. She's like a sister to me. Besides, she was alone over there on that tailgate passed out. Where the hell were you if you care so much?"

Brice clenched his fist and stepped closer to Blaine.

I clearly felt the tension between both of them, however, I was not capable of interjecting.

"Put her down. I'll take her home." Brice clenched his fist tighter, and I felt his other hand touch my arm. "She's with me."

"Dude, calm down. I'm not gonna fight over her. Besides, I was just gonna put her in my truck to sleep it off. I'm not leaving the party this early." Blaine released his hold on me.

Brice took me in his arms and packed me to his car.

I wrapped my arms around his neck and pressed my cheek up against his chest. "Thank you. This feels nice--being close to you." I looked up at him, hoping he would respond, but there was only silence.

Brice dropped me at home without speaking a word. As I stumbled to the porch my mind was whirling.

Was this newfound freedom from my 'inner' Nessie worth losing the one guy that my entire world was beginning to revolve around?

Nothing was clear anymore. I'd longed to feel needed and wanted by something – and Brice gave me that.

Why was I so adamant on ruining it by hanging around Tennie?

Chapter Forty-Two

Ready or Not

Beau's room was filled with numerous doctors and nurses as they prepared him for surgery.

Dad went home before daylight to check on things at the lake house. When he returned a few hours later, he was met with the madness inside Beau's room.

"What's all the commotion about? Did something happen?" Dad questioned one of the nurses.

"Mr. Corbin, Dr. Carlton, who was scheduled to perform Beau's back surgery had an opening in his schedule. His attending physician indicated he's stable and can withstand surgery now. We're getting him prepped now. I'll need the parents to complete the necessary paperwork."

Dad was caught off guard and took a seat in one of the chairs near the waiting area. Isabella approached him from Beau's room. "We need Mason here for his signature. They won't perform surgery until he signs as guardian."

Dad ran his fingers through his hair while staring at the hospital floor. "Why didn't you call me...or Mason...before making this decision?"

"There was no time to wait for you and Mason to opine. I made the call." Isabella continued staring at Dad.

"Are you really mad that I didn't call you? I made a professional opinion. I think I have the credentials to make medical decisions for my son. Dr. Carlton is the best surgeon, and he's available now." Isabella crossed her arms.

"You're something else, Isabella." Dad stood up while shaking his head and laughed, "You're a real piece of work."

***

Mason had planned to drop by the hospital on his way into the pharmacy to check on Beau.

Dad met him in the hall.

"Mason, hey, some things have changed from the original plan. I'll fill you in." Dad walked down the hall with Mason.

"Does Beau want this?" Mason asked as Isabella met them at the door.

"It doesn't matter what Beau wants honestly. I'm his mother, a physician, and I know what's best for him. As I told Tucker, Dr. Carlton is a phenomenal physician. I don't want anyone else working on him. He isn't available next week when the surgery was originally scheduled." Isabella glared at Mason expecting him to stand down.

Mason felt defeated…did he even have a hand in this game? "Well, it appears the decision has been made already; however, I would like to have a minute with my son to make sure he's okay with it."

"Whatever. That's fine. I just need you to sign this paper." Isabella handed him the paper with a pen and turned away.

Dad and Mason entered Beau's room. Most of the medical staff had left, and Beau was staring up at the ceiling.

"Hey, Beau, so it sounds like the surgery came a bit quicker than expected. I wanted to be sure you were okay with it." Mason stood at the foot of his bed as Dad remained close to the door.

Beau looked over to Dad and then to Mason. "I guess so. Mom said Dr. Carlton is the best around...so we have to do it when he's available. Honestly, I just want this to be over and get out of this bed."

"I know you're ready for it all to be over, son. I get it." Mason knew it wouldn't be that easy with therapy, but he focused on being supportive.

"Dad...well...Tuck...," Beau became easily frustrated as both Mason and Dad walked closer. It was an awkward moment. Mason could see the desperation in Beau's face and backed off allowing Dad to get closer.

"You're going to be just fine. You're in good hands, and we'll be right here waiting when you get out." Dad patted Beau's arm and smiled. "It's going to be okay."

Dad placed his hand on Mason's shoulder as he passed by and whispered, "Thank you for that. This whole thing has been extremely tough."

Mason nodded in agreement.

Maybe Mason wasn't as bad as Isabella made him out to be. This ordeal had certainly brought Dad and Mason closer than anyone could have imagined. Maybe it was forced, but they embraced the tiny fraction of positive in light of all the negative.

***

"Who in the world is knocking this early in the morning?" Whitney's mom, Barbara, approached the front door of their home. "What...what are you doing here?"

"Hi, I know it's been a long time. I'm really sorry for the unexpected visit. Could I...come in?" Charlene had dreamt of this moment for a long time and hoped her Aunt Barbara would oblige.

"Whitney's here. I'm not sure if this is the best time. You should have called." Reluctantly, Barbara opened the door.

"Where's Uncle Carl?" Charlene searched the room hoping he would be home.

"He's gone to the store. He won't be back for an hour or so." Barbara fought the urge to be hospitable, however, her Southern nature couldn't help it. "I'll get you some coffee."

"That'd be great, Aunt Barbara. Thank you!" Charlene looked around the living room and her eyes stopped on a picture of Whitney.

"That one was taken last year at the high school – her freshman year. Can you believe it? She's growing up too fast on us." Barbara placed the coffee on the table in front of Charlene.

"I don't mean to be direct or ugly...but what in the world are you doing here?" Barbara's Southern hospitality was deeply rooted; however, it was negated by her strong and direct approach.

"I know I should have called you first. Things just happened so fast. I didn't put much thought into it. Maybe I should just go." Charlene took a small sip of coffee and attempted to stand up.

"No, you just sit down. You're already here so it's foolish if you up and leave. Tell me, what brought you back to Sedipar after all these years?" Barbara rocked slowly in her chair as she listened to Charlene's story.

"Things got really bad for me after I left. I was really messed up...you know that. After Whitney was born, and I realized I couldn't keep her, I felt lost. I moved to East Texas hoping to remain close enough to visit and watch her grow."

Charlene took a long sip of her coffee and continued. "Things didn't go the way I planned them. It's all my fault. I've made many poor choices in my life, and not being able to raise Whitney was one of them. I regret it every day."

Barbara continued rocking and listened intently.

"A lot has happened in the last six months. It's not good...I was diagnosed with stage four lung cancer. I don't have much longer to live." Charlene wiped a tear from her eye and continued.

"My entire life I've been so selfish. I know I did wrong by not raising Whitney. I wasn't in a good place then, and I'm so grateful you and Uncle Carl were willing to help me." Charlene's words were choked.

"I'm alone, Aunt Barbara, and I'm dying. I need..." Barbara quickly interrupted.

"No, not even up for discussion. I know where this is going, and I don't like it one bit." Barbara stood up from her rocking chair and walked into the kitchen.

Charlene followed.

"It's not what you think. I just want to meet her...see how it goes...and maybe...tell her the truth...before I'm gone? Is that too much to ask?" Charlene could tell Barbara was getting frustrated.

"Yes, to be honest, it is. You asked Carl and me to adopt Whitney after she was born. Then, you don't call, you don't stop by – nothing – for years! I'm so sorry to hear that you're sick, Charlene. I really am. But I don't think anything good is going to come out of Whitney knowing the truth. It's too late for that."

"Too late for what?" Whitney asked as she rounded the staircase near the kitchen.

Barbara froze with her back turned to Whitney. Hearing Whitney's sweet voice made Charlene smile.

"Oh nothing, Whitney, it's nothing you need to be bothered with. One of the ladies from the church stopped by about an event we missed on the calendar." Attempting to change the subject she asked, "Where are you off to?"

"Me and Stella are headed to Charlotte's house. She's adamant on talking to Beau today after practice so we're going to be her support." Whitney hugged Barbara's neck and grabbed her purse.

Charlene turned around facing both of them and said, "It's so wonderful to have such good friends!"

Whitney, with a half-smile, said, "Yes, it is. Do you go to our church? I don't think we've ever met."

Barbara became anxious as Charlene moved closer and responded. "No, honey, I used to a long time ago. I haven't been to church in quite some time."

Barbara fumed inside; her eyes fixated on Charlene.

"Well, Whitney, you better get going or your friends are going to leave without you!" Barbara's eyes focused on Charlene coldly.

"Yes, ma'am. I'm going. I'll be back later this afternoon." Looking at Charlene, Whitney continued, "It was nice to meet you!" and shut the door behind her.

***

Charlotte had been waiting for this moment since the accident...the chance to tell Beau how she truly felt...and that she was sorry.

"What if he doesn't want to talk to me? Maybe this was a bad idea." Charlotte changed out of her cheer clothes from practice. "I can't do this, Stella!" Charlotte said frantically as her emotions ran wild.

"Uh, no, girl, we're taking you to the hospital to talk to Beau so ya'll can work this out," Stella replied as she pulled out of the school parking lot.

"I know, it's just, I can't get it out of my head that he's going to blame me. The worst part is, we may never be able to be together—with the paternity test results—I don't know what to think." Charlotte stared out the window thinking about how great things used to be and wished she could turn back time.

Charlotte was reluctant to make a jab at Isabella since Whitney seemed to always defend her. But she was over being nice. "Besides, his mother will never approve of me anyway. I'm probably just wasting my time. For some reason she hates me...I may never understand why."

"Char, she doesn't hate you. Mrs. Issie doesn't hate anyone. She's just going through a lot right now that's all." Any attempt Whitney made to defend Isabella fell on deaf ears with Charlotte. Even if Beau was able to get the second paternity test and they could be together, Isabella wasn't going to accept her.

***

"Ugh...there isn't anything to eat in this house!" I slammed the refrigerator door.

My head throbbed and the nausea hadn't completely escaped me.

The beeping noise from the answering machine indicated someone had left several messages which annoyed me, so I unplugged it and went back to bed.

I can't deal with anything else right now.

I woke up around noon still feeling miserable.

Immediately images of Brice flooded my mind. I smiled thinking how he held me close and kissed me. He'd finally let his guard down and wanted to spend time with me. But the nagging of my headache quickly reminded me that I drank too much. Images of Brice were suddenly replaced with Tennie.

I hope you enjoyed that one night with him...you really blew it this time. Maybe I should call him.

Once again, I let myself fade into a place where I seemed to fit in...a place I'd never let myself go before...and it was refreshing...until the aftereffects showed up. But in the moment, it felt right. I was impulsive and carefree. It was invigorating. Now I was paying for it. And, I might have lost Brice.

I tried calling him to apologize leaving several messages. He didn't return my call.

I fell back asleep hoping my headache would subside. That afternoon, I called the hospital and was shocked to hear that Beau was in surgery to repair his back.

Dammit!

I wasn't there when Beau woke up after the accident. Now, I wasn't there when he went into his second surgery. Both times were one-hundred percent my fault, and I owned it. I finally did something that I wanted to do. It's not like anyone was worried about me.

Regardless, I knew I wasn't going to hear the end of it.

***

"Why isn't he in his room? Where is he?" Charlotte questioned the nurse as she walked out of Beau's room.

Stella and Whitney waited for Charlotte in the waiting area.

"Ma'am, he was moved. That is all I can tell you. Are you family? Maybe there's someone you can call to get an update?" The nurse tried to be compassionate but rules were rules.

"I don't understand. I know he wasn't ready to be discharged. I'm his girl..." Charlotte felt defeated. She longed to see Beau and talk to him, but that was becoming impossible. "I'm just a friend of the family."

Stella and Whitney came up behind her. Charlotte turned and saw Isabella standing near the nurse's station.

Ugh, I could have gone all day without seeing her.

"Whitney, sweet girl, so nice of you to come by and check on Beau." Isabella eyed Charlotte as she walked toward them.

"Hey, Mrs. Issie. Yeah, we brought Charlotte up here to check on Beau."

"He's not in his room. Where is he?" Charlotte demanded.

Isabella rolled her eyes. "Excuse me! I don't owe you anything. In fact, you shouldn't be here. Haven't I expressed that you're the reason my Beau is in this mess?"

Charlotte was exhausted from backing down.

"You might not owe *me* anything, but we're his friends. We just came to check on him. And...by the way...I take responsibility for this. I'm not hiding from it." Charlotte stared her down.

Isabella smirked. "Oh, that's perfect, you take responsibility for this. That doesn't mean anything! He's in surgery again because of you. He doesn't want to see you." Isabella leaned into Whitney and whispered, "Honey, you really need to find better friends."

Whitney's jaw dropped open, and a few minutes of awkward silence felt like hours. Isabella continued glaring at Charlotte.

When Mason and Melissa rounded the corner, Charlotte made her escape. "Mom...Dad...he's in surgery again!"

"Yeah, they just took him back." Melissa hugged Charlotte and immediately knew something was wrong.

"I'll go get the car," Mason said as he walked toward the entrance.

"What's going on Charlotte? You seem flustered." Melissa knew it had to be Isabella; however, she wasn't going to pry.

"It's nothing. I really don't want to talk about it." Charlotte felt as if a weight was dropped on her chest, her breaths were shallow, her heart was broken, and her strength diminished.

Leaning on Melissa, Charlotte continued. "Mom, I came here to tell Beau I was sorry, and that the accident was all my fault. I missed my chance again to tell him."

"Honey, I'm sure you will have a chance once he gets out of surgery...maybe in the next few days." Melissa hugged Charlotte as Isabella stared at them from the nurse's station.

"Whitney, would you mind grabbing a few things for Beau's room? I want him to have a few things when he gets out of surgery. I've got to head back to the clinic and don't have time to stop." Isabella handed Whitney a list of items. "I know he would love to visit with someone other than myself when he gets out of surgery. Maybe you can hang out with him?"

Whitney wasn't sure how to respond. She felt the pressure of Charlotte's stare coupled with the weight of Isabella's request.

"You can do that for me...and for Beau...right?" Isabella demanded an answer from Whitney as she shook her head 'yes' and walked away.

"You coming with us, Char?" Stella asked.

"No, I'm going to ride home with Mom. But thanks. I need some time alone." Charlotte stared at the floor – saddened that she hadn't been able to talk to Beau and distraught by Isabella's blatant pull toward Whitney.

"Char, you need anything?" Whitney asked hoping she would respond.

Charlotte looked up and focused on Whitney. "There's one thing you can do for me, Whit."

"Anything, Char...anything!" Whitney felt relieved Charlotte was talking to her.

"Tell me how you won Dr. Corbin over? It sure seems she's very fond of you." Charlotte grabbed her purse and walked past Whitney.

Whitney attempted to respond as Charlotte raised her hand in the air insinuating she didn't expect an answer.

***

I'm so sick of these hospital walls...the annoying beeps from the various medical machines...the squeaky shoes on the extremely well-polished hall floors, and most of all Isabella.

"Nice of you to stop by to check on your brother so late in the day. He's almost finished with surgery, and you finally show up." Isabella's cold eyes rolled as I ignored her comment and walked past her to meet Dad.

Between the impromptu decision on Beau's surgery coupled with Charlotte's appearance at the hospital earlier that morning, Isabella was ready to tear down everything and anyone in her path.

I wasn't in the mood for her shenanigans today.

"Nessie, where on earth have you been? I left multiple messages for you at home!" Dad was worried and angry – mainly that I wasn't there to support Beau.

"Dad, you okay?" I was reluctant to ask.

"Yes, I'm fine, Nessie. Seems like I should be asking you that question. Where were you?" Dad's eyebrows raised as he questioned my whereabouts.

"I...I was at the library last night with Owen and just slept in. I got your messages as soon as I woke up though...and came straight here." I hated lying to Dad, but now was not the time to reveal to him my new friends, party habits, and potentially new boyfriend."

It's not like he cared much anyway. He didn't really want me around.

"So that's it, huh? Late night at the library. You sure you're okay? You never sleep in like that." Dad was good at reading people...it's what he did for a living...so I knew I needed to change the subject, or he would keep digging for more clarity.

"So, tell me why Beau is in surgery. I thought it was scheduled for next week?" I figured Isabella had something to do with it. And I was right.

"Your mother wanted Dr. Carlton to perform the surgery, and he wasn't available next week as scheduled. The spot opened up today, and we grabbed it. Or should I say *your mother* grabbed it...and here we are." Dad looked defeated...beaten down again by his scornful wife. "It was the right decision; I just wish we had more time to discuss it."

"Me too, Dad. Me too." I didn't want to be there. I'm sure he really didn't want me 'bothering' him.

"I need Beau to get through all of this, so our life gets back to normal. I need my son to get better." Dad slouched in the chair.

We sat in silence.

Chapter Forty-Three

Secrets That Surface

"I can't believe she showed up here unannounced expecting to tell Whitney everything. What on earth is wrong with her!?" Barbara scraped the brownie batter from the bowl into the baking dish.

Carl sat at the table reading the newspaper halfway engaged in the conversation.

"Carl! Are you listening to me!?" Barbara yelled as she turned toward him awaiting a response.

"Yes, I'm listening. Honey, you had to have known one day Charlene was going to return. I figured she would turn up eventually and want to meet her daughter. And she's dying. I guess I can't blame her." Carl hid behind the newspaper knowing what was coming next.

"Well, if I haven't heard enough. Carl Taylor! Why on earth would you take her side? After all that girl...and I mean *girl not woman*...put us through when Whitney was born. She ought to be ashamed coming here." Barbara put the brownies in the oven shaking her head back at him.

"That must be Stella," Barbara said as she heard a car drive up in the driveway. "Whitney said she was coming over this morning."

"I'll get it!" Whitney yelled as she ran down the stairs expecting it to be Stella. As she opened the front screen door, she was surprised to see the lady that had visited the other day.

"Hi Whitney," Charlene smiled as she continued, "Can I come in?"

"Stella, dear, the brownies are almost rea--" Barbara stopped at the sight of Charlene standing in her living room...next to Whitney.

"Oh, I thought you were one of Whitney's friends. Whitney, where's Stella?" Barbara glared at Charlene infuriated that she'd just stopped by again unannounced.

"She should be here any minute, Mom." Whitney immediately felt the tension between her Mom and Charlene.

Before Barbara could speak, Carl walked into the living room and broke the silence. "Well, I'll be damned. If it isn't Charlene standing in my living room...after all these years."

"Hey, Uncle Carl," Charlene made her way past Barbara to give him a hug.

Whitney became confused hearing Charlene call her Dad, 'Uncle'.

"You haven't changed a bit," Charlene continued as she felt Barbara cutting both of them with her eyes.

"Barbara said you came by the other day. I was gone up to the store for a few things. Sure is good to see you...like I said...it's been a while." Carl sat back in his recliner and opened the newspaper.

"Well, it's good you two have caught up. Charlene, nice of you to stop by, but we have a few things going on this afternoon so we can't entertain company." Barbara watched Whitney walk back to the front door as she saw Stella pull into the driveway.

"I've got to grab my purse. Tell Stella I'll be right down." Whitney hurried up the staircase.

Once Whitney was out of sight, Barbara stepped closer to Charlene. "You've got some nerve showing up here again. You might have some cute little reunion with Whitney planned out in your head...but it ain't gonna happen! So, it's best you just carry yourself on out of here and leave Sedipar."

Charlene understood why Barbara wanted her to leave. She owned everything that happened since Whitney was born. She was young and fell for a random guy she met at the local bar right after graduation. He hung around in town for a few days, and then she never saw him again. A few weeks later she found out she was pregnant. At the young age of eighteen, she was alone, jobless, and pregnant; she pleaded with her Aunt Barbara and Uncle Carl to adopt her baby. She left town and never looked back. Years of drinking and abusing drugs plagued her and now had caused her health to deteriorate quicker than she expected.

"I just want Whitney to know me. Honestly, that's all I want. When I gave her up all those years ago it broke my heart. I didn't want to give her away. I didn't have a choice. She wouldn't have had the life she has today if it weren't for both of you, and I'm grateful for that." Charlene sat down on the sofa and wiped away the tears from her face. "I promise I'm not trying to take your place as her mother. You've earned that. I just want her to know who I was and why I did it. That's all."

Barbara shifted her stance and remained silent. Charlene's presence brought back memories of the day she walked into their living room with Whitney cradled in her arms. She was young and scared, but most of all she was selfish. It was difficult for Barbara to forget that day.

"I'm sorry, Charlene. I know you probably think I'm being heartless, but my answer is still 'no'. Years have passed with no call to check on her - see how she's doing in school - nothing. *Zilch*! Just like the day you left here, without your newborn baby, you were young, selfish, and foolish. And today you're going to stand here and reveal to Whitney that you're her birth mother and top it off with the fact that you're dying!?" Barbara stared intently at Charlene refusing to back down. "I have to put Whitney first."

"We had to pick up the pieces from your mistake all those years ago, and Whitney has a good life. I would've loved to have had you in her life. In fact, I longed for you to make contact, but you never did. Now, you expect me to allow you to slam this news on her and then break her heart that you're dying? Too much time has passed for that."

Charlene sat motionless as she noticed Whitney standing near the threshold of the living room and kitchen. She'd used the back stairs into the kitchen area, and they were unaware she'd been listening.

Carl closed his newspaper and sat up in his recliner.

"*What...in...the...hell,*" Whitney leaned up against the wall confused, "did you just say...no...you didn't say..."

Barbara closed her eyes with disgust and sighed deeply.

"Whitney, no, I can explain." Barbara turned immediately.

"Knock knock Taylors!" Stella sang as she typically did when she visited. She immediately noticed the tension in the room and Whitney's blank stare. "*Okayyyy...*" she said as she slowly backed toward the door.

"Stella, no, you can stay. There's just a little confusion we need to straighten out that's all." Barbara helped Whitney to the living room and sat down next to her on the sofa across from Charlene.

"What's going on, Mom? I heard what you said, and I have *so* many questions." Whitney's emotions were running rampant as she looked at Charlene and then back at Barbara.

"Well, someone better start talking and tell me something!" Whitney stood up from the sofa.

"Honey, sit down. I'll explain everything," Charlene said in a soft voice.

Barbara took Whitney's hand and encouraged her to sit back down. Looking directly at Charlene she dryly said, "I think you have overstayed your welcome. It's best you leave."

"I don't think that I can.." Charlene was immediately cut off by Barbara.

"I don't give a damn what you want. I'm asking you to leave my house." Barbara stood up and pointed toward the front door.

Stella moved away from the door and sat on the first step of the living room staircase.

"I'm sorry, Barbara, but I'm not leaving. I can't do this again. I can't leave this life not telling my sweet daughter how much I truly loved her and why I left." Charlene reached her hands across to Whitney's.

"I'm your mamma, honey. I gave you up when you were born because I was young and foolish and couldn't take care of you. I've regretted that every day of my life." Charlene placed her hands on Whitney's and continued. "I just wanted you to know that I love you so much, and I'm so proud of you."

Stella's eyes widened as Charlene kept talking.

"Stop! That's enough! I mean it! You've already done enough damage here. Get out!" Barbara attempted to push Charlene's hands from Whitney's, but Charlene fastened her hold.

"I'm not leaving Aunt Barbara. She needs to know the truth. Just let me explain everything to her." Charlene attempted to continue as Barbara sat back down next to Whitney.

Whitney stared blankly into the distance looking past Charlene's half-smile and through the living room window. Her heart raced as her mind was flooded with questions.

"What...you're my...my mom?" Whitney struggled to get the words to leave her mouth.

"Yes, Whitney. I'm your Mom." Charlene attempted to lean in closer, but Whitney stood up.

Looking at both Barbara and Charlene she continued. "How...and why didn't anyone tell me sooner?"

"It's a long, complicated story. That part doesn't matter. Charlene is here now." Barbara suppressed the desire to expose Charlene's selfish nature.

"Complicated!? I just found out who my birth mom is, and you assume it's not important to know the story? Mom, that's not fair." Whitney became irritated as the word 'Mom' rolled off her tongue.

Whitney noticed Stella was hiding on the staircase and motioned her to come to sit by her on the sofa. "I need you. You're family to me."

Once Stella sat down next to her, Whitney looked at Barbara and Charlene directly and said, "I'm ready. I can take whatever it is – complicated or not. I'm ready."

Barbara stood up and walked closer to Carl. "Well, you started this mess, Charlene. Go ahead and tell her."

Charlene explained how she couldn't take care of Whitney soon after she was delivered. Charlene's mom was a single parent and moved away from Sedipar the minute Charlene turned eighteen. She was alone, jobless, and afraid. Barbara and Carl were anxious to adopt since they were unable to have children and she was grateful that someone in the family would raise her baby.

Whitney sat motionless and quiet as Charlene continued.

"I wanted to come and see you, Whitney. I promise I did. I made many terrible mistakes...the first mistake was leaving you and not coming home or calling to check on you. I was embarrassed and young and honestly probably wouldn't have been a good parent. As years passed, I missed you so much and longed to reach out, but life got in the way."

"I don't understand. How could you just leave me and never come back...never call...never want to see me?" Whitney leaned away from Charlene wiping tears from her face.

"You wouldn't understand. It was a difficult time in my life. As I said earlier, I made many poor decisions, and I have to live with that. But I wanted you to know I never stopped thinking about you and loving you." Charlene tried to grab Whitney's hand, and she quickly pulled it away.

"No, you don't get to do that. You don't get to just come here out of the blue and tell me you've missed me and love me. No...I can't!" Whitney stood up and grabbed Stella's hand. "C'mon, I've got to get out of here."

Barbara rushed over to Whitney to console her hoping she would stay. "I can't Mom...I just can't be around her right now."

Looking back toward Charlene with her head hung in despair, Barbara hugged Whitney and whispered, "Look, I know this is hard to swallow. I knew in my heart this was a bad idea, but unfortunately, there's more I think you should know."

Charlene breathed in slowly looking at the floor.

"Well, c'mon now, Charlene. You've gone this far—don't stop now." Barbara was fuming about how this was going but knew Whitney needed to hear the rest of the story.

"You owe it to her to share the rest of it. I know it's hard, but it's the right thing to do." Barbara stood with her arm around Whitney.

Charlene assumed it would be easier to share the news about her health with Whitney, but it wasn't. "I came back to Sedipar to meet you, and to tell you that...well, gosh this is difficult..."

Whitney could see that Charlene was struggling to get the words out. "Just tell me...I need to know everything."

"Whitney, I'm dying." Charlene looked up; tears welled in her eyes.

Whitney felt weak and leaned against Stella and Barbara to hold her up. "You're...*dying*? I don't understand...you seem okay."

"Yes, I'm dying. I have stage four lung cancer with only a few short months to live. I didn't choose treatment. I want to live out the rest of my days as comfortable as possible — hopefully with you." Charlene was afraid to look at Barbara fearing her attack for the last comment.

"I can't...this is too much to digest. I need some space." Whitney turned to grab her keys and Stella stopped her. "Let me drive, Whit." Whitney released her keys as she walked toward the front door.

Stella hugged Barbara and whispered, "We'll be back shortly."

As Whitney opened the door, Charlene blurted out, "Will you move with me back to Texas to live out my last few months? I need my daughter close by."

Whitney turned slowly and wasn't sure how to respond. She placed her hand on the doorframe and glanced at Barbara who was breaking Charlene apart with her stare.

Whitney turned and walked out of the house.

Stella cranked the car and sighed. "I'm so sorry. I don't know what to even say."

"Just drive. I need to get far away from here." Whitney stared out of the window as Stella sped down the driveway.

"Take me to see Mrs. Issie. She will know what to do."

Chapter Forty-Four

Confrontation

"Jackson, what brings you to the clinic today?" Isabella asked as she sat on the stool across the room.

"Coach wanted me to check out my arm. It's been bothering me a little in my elbow, so he asked me to come by." Jackson sat staring back at Isabella.

"Okay, well, let's check your vitals first to update our records, and we'll go from there." Isabella smiled and grabbed her stethoscope.

"Well, everything looks good. Your blood pressure is normal, no fever...let's take a look at this arm and see what's going on. Does it hurt anywhere when you bend it?" Isabella attempted to extend Jackson's arm, and he pulled it away.

"Dr. Corbin...I'm, um, not actually here for my arm." Jackson turned his head away from her confused stare.

"Okay...well...then tell me what's going on?" Isabella placed his chart down on the examination bed, crossed her arms, and waited. Seeing he was reluctant to continue, Isabella pressed him. "Well, why are you here?"

Jackson immediately regretted coming to the clinic. "I should go. Never mind."

As he stood up from the examination table, she stopped him. "Look, just tell me why you're here. Obviously, it was important to you. Just tell me."

"Is it Beau...did something happen? I just left the hospital a few hours ago, and things were okay." Isabella began to worry.

"No, Dr. Corbin. It isn't Beau." Jackson knew he couldn't maneuver his way out of this.

Just ask her. Get it over with so you can move on.

"It might have something to do with Beau...like the paternity test." As the word 'test' left his mouth, he noticed Isabella's stance stiffen.

Isabella clenched her teeth upon hearing those dreaded words--paternity test.

She'd been waiting for Jackson to confront her since that night and had hoped that he'd possibly forgotten. Apparently, he hadn't.

"So, you have questions about the paternity test? How can I help?" Isabella attempted to deflect.

Jackson didn't respond as he wasn't sure what to say at this point.

"Jackson. What do you have questions about? You need to tell me so that I can help you." She adjusted her tone to be less stern and demanding hoping to encourage him to speak up.

"It's...well...it's probably nothing really. I should have just let it go, but it keeps popping up in my mind." Jackson placed his hands in his pocket and bit his lip regretting he was there.

"Okay, well, what keeps popping into your mind that you want to talk to me about? I want to help you, but I have other patients to attend to. I can't keep them waiting!" Isabella's voice had reverted back to its normal tone, but she was becoming impatient.

What the hell, Jackson? Just spit it out!

"The night I picked Mom up from the office...you were in Mr. Corbin's office. I saw you by the filing cabinet." Jackson swallowed deeply as he looked down at the floor.

"Yes, I was there taking care of your mom. Remember, she passed out from drinking too much." Isabella remained poised.

"Well, at the time, I didn't think anything of it really until I overheard Mom and Mr. Corbin talking about the paternity test and where they were stored." Jackson paused as he struggled to continue. "I'm probably mistaken, Dr. Corbin, but you seemed surprised when I picked Mom up."

"Well, yes, Jackson, I was startled. It was late in the night, and I was practically alone in the office since your Mother was inebriated. You could have spoken when you entered the office!" Isabella cunningly replied. "I was picking up a few things that had fallen on the floor that's all. Is that it? I really need to see my next patient."

"No...no ma'am...that isn't it." Jackson stuttered wanting the conversation to end, however, he was too far in to not get the answer he needed.

"Why were you standing near the cabinet where the tests were stored? You...well...kinda seemed surprised when I was standing in the doorway." Jackson breathed shallowly waiting for her response.

Her eyes became cold as they focused on him. "Young man. I'm not sure what you're insinuating or how any of this is your business. I just told you what I was doing. I had every right to be in that office and can do whatever I damn well please while in there."

He moved closer to the door as she ranted.

"I'm not sure why I'm wasting my breath on a sixteen-year-old inquisitive boy. I don't owe you an explanation. Now, get out of my clinic!" She forcefully opened the door and nodded for him to leave.

Leaning against the door she mumbled, "I knew that boy might be a problem."

***

"They finally came in," Allison said as she handed Dad a sealed envelope.

"Divorce papers...all signed?" he grinned as he sat in his office chair.

"I assume so," she replied while shutting his office door behind her.

He knew divorcing Isabella was the right thing to do. Her manipulative and deceitful behavior was not something he desired. She'd put him through hell, and he was ready to move on.

As he pulled the papers out of the envelope, he noticed his name written in red on a sticky note on one of the pages.

"Dammitt!" he slammed his hands down on his desk.

Allison heard the commotion and bolted into his office. "You okay!?"

"No, she's relentless. She won't let go." He paced around his office. "She doesn't want to give me *my* house! We talked about it several times and agreed she could stay in the house until Nessie graduated. Now, she wants the house indefinitely."

"There's no way in hell she's going to win this. That property and house have been in my family for years! She's lost her mind!" He grabbed his blazer from the coat rack. "She's not heard the end of this! Beau should be out of surgery, so I need to get back anyway."

***

I patiently awaited my turn to visit Beau. After the nurses finished getting him settled, Isabella took the room first and shut the door behind her.

Figures! She always assumes she's better than everyone else.

Mason appeared shortly after. "He's out of recovery?"

"Yeah, they just got him back in the room. Isabella's in there now." I could tell he was reluctant to go in.

"I'll just give them a moment." Mason took a seat next to me.

Just when I thought things couldn't get much worse between Dad and Isabella, a bomb went off.

Dad plowed through the nurses in the hall, ignoring anything and everything in sight. As he approached Beau's room, he collected himself before entering.

"Hold these, Nessie, for a moment." Dad threw a manila envelope at me.

There was complete silence for a moment. Minutes later Isabella followed Dad out of Beau's room infuriated by his 'attack'.

"You're ridiculous! Beau just got out of surgery, and we need to be there for him. All you can think about is the house and these stupid papers!?" Isabella was oblivious to the crowd that had gathered due to the commotion.

"Damn right, I am! You've taken everything from me! You've destroyed our marriage. I've lost my son...who was never my son! Our family is shattered!" Pointing his finger angrily at her he continued, "*You* did this! *You* did *all* of this!"

Dad was caught up in the moment. I knew he would be embarrassed by the crowd, so I approached him.

"Dad, c'mon. Just leave it alone. She's never going to accept that she did something wrong." I put my arm around him, but he didn't budge.

Isabella wanted to scream as the fury inside her raged, however, she remained poised once she noticed her colleagues and other staff were entertained by the 'show'.

"Nothing to see here...get back to work!" Isabella turned toward the nurse's station attempting to refrain from responding to Dad.

"We're going to discuss this, Isabella. It's not over. That house is mine! It's been in my family for years. To think that you would stoop so low as to take it from me!" Dad shook his head and laughed with disgust.

"Let's take this discussion somewhere else, Tucker. I've got work to do." She grabbed a patient's chart and walked away.

***

Beau was relieved to be free of the arm constraints. Lying in bed, now able to move around more freely, he reached for the phone on the side table near him to call Charlotte.

Just as he took the handset off to dial her number, Dad interrupted him. "Hey, I'm so glad to see you sitting up!".

Beau set the handset down as Dad reached out to him for their odd and rambunctious handshake. "What was all that about with Mom?" Beau was curious after watching Isabella storm out of his room.

"Nothing you need to be bothered with right now. I'm handling it." Dad smiled and tried to change the subject.

A sigh of relief came over me as I watched from a distance by the door.

Things were slowly getting back to normal...even though their handshake always seemed obnoxious to me. I welcomed it considering what we had all been through -especially Beau.

"Nessie, you just gonna hide over in the corner or come in?" Beau motioned for me to come closer, and I hesitated.

"Well, the last time I was here..." I felt Dad's eyes cut me in half and I started over. "Yeah, hey, Beau. How are you feeling?"

"Glad the surgery is over. I'm in a lot of pain, but I know I'm on the road to recovery now. Mom said it's going to be several weeks of therapy." Beau fidgeted with the TV remote and continued. "And ya'll don't have to dance around it. I know I can't play football this season, which sucks, but I'm trying to look at the bright side."

"That's a wonderful way to think about it, Beau." Dad smiled and turned my way. "Nessie spent a lot of time up here at the hospital with us. I know you two don't see eye to eye most days, but I think it's worth noting that we come together as a family when we need to."

I looked away unsure of how to respond. The last time I was in Beau's room he ordered me to leave. Dad was right though, we weren't close, but I still considered him family and that meant something.

"Thanks, Nessie – maybe you aren't the brat sister I always thought you were!" Beau said laughing.

I hadn't heard him laugh like that in a long time. Dad smiled. "Good to see you back to yourself again."

"I gotta go meet some frie--I mean Owen...so I'm heading out. See you tomorrow though?" I cringed as I waited for Dad to catch me in my lie.

"Have fun...I guess," Beau said shaking his head assuming I was headed to the library. Boy was he wrong.

"I'm staying here for a bit longer. See you later on at the lake house?" Dad was probing...I was not off the hook yet.

"Yeah, I'll be late, but I'll be there." I swiftly made my exit.

***

"What in the hell!? Charlene is your mother!? Whitney, I'm so confused!" Isabella listened intently. "Yeah, she's my birth mom apparently...and she's dying. Mom is going nuts right now. She's so mad that Charlene showed back up after all this time has passed. I guess I can't blame her."

"Honey, this is great news that you finally know who your birth mother is...but in the same breath...she's terminal. I'm so sorry." Isabella wasn't sure what else to say, and she was reluctant to let on that she knew about Charlene and the adoption. Emotional support wasn't her strong point – everyone knew that – but she was different with Whitney.

"Come here," Isabella said as she wrapped her arms around her. "You will figure this out."

Whitney's emotions ranged from feeling outraged that Charlene showed up unexpectedly at her home, dropped the bomb that she was dying -- to excitement and closure that she had the chance to meet her birth mom. Over time, she didn't give her birth mom much thought – she was happy with the Taylors.

"There's more, Mrs. Issie." Whitney sighed. "She wants me to move to Texas with her and spend time with her before she..." She began crying.

Isabella quickly became more uncomfortable as she was friends with the Taylors and didn't want to overstep...something that generally came easy to her...but she actually liked the Taylors.

Attempting to deflect and hoping Whitney would oblige she suggested, "I've got the perfect idea. Why don't we go and see Beau?" Isabella had hoped she could get them together and not seem forced.

"I don't know if I'm up to it, Mrs. Issie. I'm not going to be good company. I'm a mess. Besides, Stella should be here any minute to pick me up." Whitney grabbed Isabella's hand and smiled. "I appreciate you always being there for me when I need you. You were there for me with the baby and miscarriage, and I appreciate you so much."

"You're like family to me Whitney. You know...I always hoped you and Beau would become an 'item'." Isabella still desperately hoped Beau would see Whitney as more than a friend.

"Oh, Mrs. Issie, that's silly. I mean, we're great friends, but his heart belongs to Charlotte." Whitney grabbed her purse and stood up from the sofa.

"Excuse me! His heart doesn't belong to anyone! He's a sixteen-year-old boy with his entire life ahead of him." Isabella realized her tone was harsh and quickly softened it. "I know he thinks Charlotte is the one, but honey, they can't be together regardless. It's time they both move on."

Whitney had suppressed her feelings for Beau – what girl didn't!? She had always been mesmerized by him; however, he was never interested in being more than friends.

"Just come with me to the hospital. It will be good to get your mind off of Charlene for a while." Isabella grabbed her purse and took Whitney's arm. "You're coming with me!"

As they walked to Isabella's car, Stella drove up.

"Where are ya'll off to? I'm back with all the things you wanted for Beau." Stella stood by her car agitated they were about to leave her. "I didn't get all of these things for nothing...so where ya'll going?"

"Oh, that's wonderful. You picked up everything! I've gathered some things from home. Follow us to the hospital then," Isabella said as she opened her car door.

***

Blaine reluctantly walked toward Beau's room and almost turned around several times before reaching it.

Why am I here? This is a mistake.

"Blaine, dude, you just gonna stay out there in the hall? What's up!?" Beau caught a glimpse of Blaine from his room.

"Hey, bro, yeah, hospitals just aren't my thing." Blaine shrugged.

"Try being in this bed for about a month! I'm over it. I'm ready to do therapy and get out of here." Beau could tell something was wrong.

"You okay?" Beau asked as Blaine leaned against the ledge by the window.

"Yeah, man, I'm good. I just hate seeing you in that bed." Blaine stared at the floor unsure of what to say next.

"I've got therapy for several weeks and then I'm not sure what's next. Football is out...which sucks. It hasn't really hit me yet. But I know when fall gets here I'm going to struggle." Beau threw the football Dad had brought him to Blaine. "Heads up!"

Blaine was caught off guard but caught it. "Man, we miss you on that field. Practices haven't been the same. Jackson's good and all...but he ain't you."

"I want more than anything to be out on that field but look at me." Beau threw his hands up in the air near his sides. "I'm not even sure if I'll ever be able to play football again."

Blaine swallowed deeply recalling the events from the night of the accident.

"Blaine...well...have you talked to her?" Beau's eyes were fixed on Blaine awaiting his response.

"Have I talked to who?" Blaine finally responded.

"Charlotte. Dude, you faded on me for a minute. What's going on?" Beau had never seen Blaine this distracted.

"Oh, no, man, I haven't talked to her. I saw her at the Abyss the other night, but she stayed by Stella and Whitney." Blaine tossed the football up in the air watching each spin as it spiraled back into his hands.

"I haven't seen her since the accident. I was hoping she would come by. I was told she thinks this is her fault. It's not, man. I should've been driving slower around that curve."

"It's not your fault either. Accidents happen. It was nasty that night. When I drove home...man...I could hardly see the road." Blaine felt a lump in his throat. He hated lying to Beau. Blaine tossed the football back to Beau.

Realizing that Blaine said he saw her, he questioned, "So, you didn't talk to her?" Beau closed his eyes as an image of Charlotte's car flying off the road and into the air flashed from his memory.

"No, I didn't. I was too busy chasing other girls...oh...and helping your drunk sister." Blaine laughed remembering how jealous Brice had become as he carried Nessie to his truck.

"What!? My drunk sister?" Beau laughed out loud. "No way Nessie Corbin was drinking!"

"I know, dude, I was surprised to see her at the Abyss. She was wasted and passed out in the back of a truck. The crazy part is she was hanging around Tennie Adams!" Blaine laughed as he continued tossing the football in the air.

"You're crazy! Quit with the jokes man! Nessie has never been to a party, nor would she want to go to one." Beau shook his head laughing.

"I thought it odd too, but she was there. I picked her up after seeing her passed out in the back of a truck...Brice almost fought me when he saw me packing her." Blaine laughed. "Like that little punk could take me on."

"I don't know. This is all crazy. I've missed a lot being stuck in this hospital bed. Why's Nessie with Brice—and she's partying with Tennie!" Beau stared up at the ceiling.

Blaine continued reliving that night. "That's not the only thing that's crazy. Jackson seems to be trying to talk to Charlotte. He was chasing her around the party all night. I don't think she noticed him much."

"What!? No, that can't be. Jackson?" Beau became perturbed. "I don't believe it. Jackson knows how I feel about Charlotte. He's probably just trying to keep watch on her since I'm not there...being a good friend."

Blaine smirked. "Whatever you say, man. If you call leaning over the back of the truck bed and holding her hand 'watching out for her' then I'm sure it was nothing."

Beau quickly became enraged. "Jackson hasn't been here to visit. I thought that was odd. But, I swear if he's trying to get close to Charlotte—there's know way that'll happen!"

Chapter Forty-Five

Tug of War

"Hey! Brice! You have a minute?" I yelled across the shop floor.

Brice didn't look up. The dilapidated shop fan churned and squeaked overpowering my attempt to get his attention.

I yelled louder. "Brice! You got a minute!?"

Mr. Beale appeared from the office door. "Nessie? What brings you to the shop today?"

"Oh, hey Mr. Beale. I came by to see Brice. He's either ignoring me or doesn't hear me." I wasn't in the mood to play games.

"Well, I can help you with that!"

Kent grabbed the intercom and yelled, "Brice! You've got a visitor."

Brice reluctantly dropped his tools on the concrete and walked over.

Mr. Beale stepped back into his office smiling.

Brice didn't realize how perfect he was. His shop uniform left more to be desired. It was unbuttoned exposing his white 'wife beater' tank. His abs, hidden underneath, were screaming to explode. He wiped the sweat from his forehead and stopped a foot or so from me.

"What's up?" he casually asked as if he didn't know why I was there.

He hadn't called me since the party at the Abyss. I missed his touch. I missed him.

"You haven't called me. I've missed you." I'd become blunt. No more hiding and waiting for things to happen. I wanted to be with him more than anything. And I knew he wanted to be with me.

"I've been busy. Some people have to work, ya know." His eyes darted in every direction but on me.

"You mad or something? You know...you can tell me." I was tired of playing games.

"Maybe. I might be." He leaned against the wall near the shop office and crossed his arms.

"Look, I know the other night didn't end how you planned. I'm sorry for that." I wanted to get closer to him, but I kept my distance.

"Oh really? And just how did I want the night to end?" Brice seemed unnerved by my comment.

"Not with Tennie. That's all I meant." I wanted to tell him how I wanted it to end with him staying with me at the party, but I knew that would drive more of a wedge between us.

"It's just that...well...when I'm around Tennie I feel like the world isn't closing in on me...like I'm not the one having to hold it up. All my life I've been the one everyone turns to when they need something. I'm the one that holds it all together. I'm tired Brice. I need more than that. And, Tennie has opened that door for me." I knew what his response would be, but I wanted to be honest with him. I wasn't ready to dismiss her friendship.

I waited for him to respond. It seemed like minutes passed by before I felt his soft touch. He leaned in closer, and whispered, "I want to be with you and there for you. I do. Nessie, you make me feel different. I can't explain it."

I smiled back at him relieved that he didn't hate me since I'd pushed him away at the party.

"But, you have to choose between Tennie and me. She's trouble Nessie. She's not good for you or anybody. She'll drag you into her messy life, and you will not come back from it." Brice softly caressed my hands and then guided them around his waist. He pulled me closer as his lips softly touched mine. "I need you Nessie. You're one of the best things that has happened to me in a long time. I'm not going to sit back while Tennie tries to destroy it."

I didn't know what to think or feel. His touch and kiss mesmerized me. I wanted to live in this moment forever.

"I need you too, Brice, but being friends with Tennie has awakened something in me. And you're a big part of that too. I've longed to feel needed...and loved. I've never felt like this before." I attempted to wipe the smudge of dirt from his forehead, but he stopped me.

"I get it. You've uncovered some sort of freedom by hanging out with Tennie – but she's bad news. I can't sit back and watch you fall into her trap." Brice released my hands and turned away from me.

My emotions got the best of me as I quickly wrapped my arms around his waist. Through the sweat and dirt covering his uniform, I could faintly smell his cologne. My lips found his ear and I whispered, "I can't lose you either...and...I won't."

Brice stood still and silent as my hold on him tightened. My face rested snugly against his back embracing every moment of being close to him.

"I've got to get back to work. I'm sorry." Brice broke free from my hold and faced me. "I can't do this right now. I'll maybe see you later..."

***

"Hey, what's all of this?" Beau was surprised as Isabella, Stella, and Whitney paraded into his room.

"Well, son, we got you some things for your room since you'll likely be here another week." As soon as Isabella set the bag on the sofa, her pager went off.

"I need to go...I'm sorry...the clinic is paging me. Dr. Dawson has been battling a severe cold which has left me running the clinic alone." Isabella was disappointed but smiled knowing Beau and Whitney might have some time alone.

"So, you got those 'cuffs' off your arms I see," Stella laughed as she organized the snacks they had brought in.

"Yeah, real funny, Stella. You would've been over this a long time ago...being restrained in a bed." Beau laughed at the thought of Stella being told she had to do something she didn't want to do.

"Shut up!" Stella threw a bag of chips at him.

"My favorite, how'd you know?" Beau responded sarcastically as he opened them.

"You two cut it out. Geez! It's always a joke with ya'll." Whitney found a blanket and snuggled up in a chair next to Beau's bed.

"Relax Miss Uptight!" Stella said as she finished unloading the bag and noticed the time. "Oh, shoot, I've got to get home before dinner. Mom is having a few friends over to play Pokeno which means I have to grab dinner before her friends get there."

"That's fine, Mrs. Issie can bring me home." Whitney sank deeper into the chair.

"Muah," Stella blew a kiss toward Whitney and waved at Beau as she left the room.

Once the door closed, he stared at Whitney and asked, "What's up with you, Whitney?" Beau could tell that something was bothering her.

"Oh, nothing, I'm just exhausted. It's been a long day." She was not ready to talk about Charlene openly.

"Yeah, right. Lie to someone else. I've known you forever. You can't lie to me. What's going on?" He threw an extra pillow from his bed at her, and she cracked a smile.

"The last thing you want to hear is my problems after all you've been through." She resisted the urge to burst into tears respecting that Beau had already been through so much himself.

"Honestly, I'm tired of talking about the accident, thinking about the accident, my surgery, the second surgery...and on and on and on...I just want to concentrate on getting out of here, completing my therapy, and going home." He waited for her to respond. "I'm not going anywhere, so you might as well tell me," Beau said laughing.

She smiled. "You asked for it then."

He listened as the story unfolded about Charlene.

"She wants me to live with her in Texas. Beau, I don't know what to do." She couldn't resist the tears at this point and her hands cradled her face.

"Whitney, I'm sorry." He didn't know what to say or how to respond.

"I know you have a lot going on right now. You've been through so much. You don't need all of my drama. But, I just don't know what to do. I feel so lost." She leaned forward in the chair and clasped her hands.

Beau reached over and lightly caressed her hands. "Look, I know what you're feeling. It was a huge blow when I found out Mason was my Dad. It took me a while to come to terms with it...and honestly, I still haven't."

His touch was soft and warm.

"Hey, I'm sure Charlene doesn't expect you to decide soon. That's a lot to take in...meeting your birth mom and finding out she's dying. I'm sorry Whitney." He understood her feeling of defeat.

She pulled her hands back from his and sank back into the chair.

"I've no idea what to do next. I have so many questions for Charlene. I want to get closer to her, but I also resent her for keeping distance from me for so long. I can't hurt Mom and Dad either. Ugh...I'm not sure what the right answer is." Whitney closed her eyes hoping all of this was a bad dream.

***

A couple of hours passed, and Isabella returned to Beau's room. "Stella left? So, you two have been catching up?"

"Yeah, she had to get home. I probably need to get home too...not that I want to." Whitney sat up in the chair.

"Well, I'm sorry. I can't leave just yet. I've been asked to fill in as co-surgeon in the operating room. It should only be a few more hours. You can stay here and hang out with Beau and keep him company." Isabella didn't give either Whitney or Beau time to reply as she quickly left the room.

"Ugh...I'm so tired. I just want to crawl into my own bed, but I don't want to face Mom or Charlene!" Whitney fell back into the chair and snuggled into the blanket.

"Sorry, I know you didn't plan to get stuck here in this hospital room. It sucks. I'll be honest!" Beau laughed softly. "It's been my 'home' for a month now, unfortunately."

"It's ok. I'm so tired I'll probably pass out from exhaustion." Whitney yawned and tried to get comfortable in the chair.

He flipped through the channels on the TV and couldn't find anything that piqued his interest.

"I guess you haven't talked to Charlotte, have you?" Beau was curious if what Blaine said about Jackson was true. He hoped Whitney might know.

Whitney didn't respond.

As Beau looked over toward her, she'd fallen asleep.

***

Conditioning practice was brutal – the middle of summer in Louisiana – being outside was no joke. Jackson and Blaine finished up their three-mile run and headed to the field to practice a few plays.

Jackson noticed Charlotte on the sidelines practicing with the cheer team.

As she collected her things from the bleachers, Blaine saw Jackson approach her and thought, *Man, you're messing with fire.*

"Hey...Charlotte. What's up?" Jackson said casually.

"Oh, hey Jackson. We're just wrapping up practice." Charlotte continued packing her bag.

Jackson didn't waste much time and asked, "I was wondering if you wanted to have lunch at AELs today after practice?"

Charlotte was caught off guard and hesitated to respond. She grabbed her water thermos and bag and turned to Jackson. "I'm not sure. A few of the girls were planning to go to the beach at Lake Danik today."

"Oh, yeah, I get it. No big deal. Maybe some other time." Jackson wanted Charlotte to say 'yes' more than anything.

If she would just give me a chance, I know she would like me.

Stella appeared from behind the bleachers. "You ready, Char?" She glared at Jackson irritated that he wouldn't let go of his infatuation with Charlotte. She couldn't help herself. "You ready to go see Beau?" She made sure Jackson heard her say Beau's name.

"Oh, you're going by the hospital?" Jackson questioned.

"Yeah, that was the plan. I haven't seen Beau since the accident. It's weird. Every time I go to see him something always seems to get in the way of us talking. I miss him." Charlotte threw her bag on her shoulder and glared back at Whitney. "Thanks, Jackson, for the offer on lunch. Maybe some other time!"

"Yeah, some other time," Jackson muttered as he walked back onto the field.

"Heads up bro!" Blaine shouted as he hurled the football to Jackson.

"Let's run a couple of plays and get the hell out of this heat." Blaine waited for Jackson to get in position.

"Man, what you up to with Charlotte?" Blaine couldn't resist asking.

"I'm not up to nothing with her. I just asked if she wanted to have lunch, that's all. Just get in position man. Let's get this over with." Jackson was not in the mood to answer Blaine's questions.

"Okay, okay, I get it. None of my business. I'd just be careful man. If Beau finds out…" Blaine knew Beau would never forgive Jackson.

Jackson stood with the football resting on his side agitated by Blaine's comment. "If Beau finds out what? Not that anything is going on between us…but they're over…remember, the paternity test?"

"Look, forget I said anything. Let's get these plays over with so I can go home. I have stuff to do at the farm."

Blaine laughed to himself knowing that Beau would never be 'over' Charlotte.

***

"Where was Whit? I didn't see her car in the parking lot." Stella always asked loaded questions.

"She didn't show up to practice. I haven't talked to her nor do I want to. After the other day at the hospital with Isabella...it's like she can't tell that woman 'no'." Charlotte stared out the car window.

Stella changed the subject. "Jackson...what did *he* want?" Stella asked as she drove out of the school parking lot.

"Nothing," Charlotte replied dryly.

"Whatever, Char. It's so obvious he's 'into' you! What'd he say?" Stella was never afraid to pry.

"Jackson!? Into me!? No way." Charlotte had a feeling he liked her, but she wasn't going to give Stella the satisfaction of being right.

"Oh, okay, then. He's *not* 'into' you. Yeah, right. Char, every boy in this school is 'into' you!" Stella pulled into AELs parking lot. "I'm starving."

There was some truth to what Stella said about every boy wanting her, but Charlotte only cared about Beau. "I hope I don't see Jackson here. He asked me to eat lunch with him. I told him we were going to the lake."

"Girl, you don't owe him anything. Now get your butt out of the car so we can get some lunch."

As they got closer to the entrance, Stella noticed Whitney sitting in the front seat of Isabella's car.

"Oh, look, they have pot roast on the menu today! My favorite!" Stella attempted to steer Charlotte's attention to AELs window.

But her attempt to distract Charlotte was a lost cause. Charlotte froze when she entered AELs...Isabella was at the checkout counter.

Isabella stared Charlotte down locking eyes as she entered the restaurant.

She turned back to the cashier, paid for her order, and walked toward the girls.

"Hey, Dr. Corbin!" Stella said politely hoping to deflect the attention from Charlotte.

"Hi, Stella." Isabella stared coldly at Charlotte.

"We're going to grab something to eat and then head by the hospital to see Beau." Stella knew once it rolled out of her mouth she shouldn't have said anything.

Charlotte nudged her side.

"Ah, I see." Isabella continued staring directly at Charlotte. "I've been very clear that I don't want *you* around Beau. *You're* the reason he's stuck in that bed."

Charlotte rolled her eyes. She'd heard this so many times that she'd become numb to it.

Before she could respond, Isabella continued. "Besides. Beau is moving on. Whitney spent the night with him at the hospital." Her eyebrow raised as she watched Charlotte's face lose its color. "They seem to be getting close. It's not a surprise to me. They've been such close friends since childhood. I knew it would be only a matter of time they'd become more than just friends."

Isabella walked past the girls smiling to herself. "So, it's pointless to go see him, Charlotte. He's moved on...with Whitney."

Charlotte breathed deeply and leaned against the counter. Stella moved closer to her.

"Char, I'm sorry. Let's go." Stella grabbed Charlotte's arm and she pulled it away.

"What a horrible person. I can't even..." Charlotte muttered as tears rolled down her cheeks. "Whitney...one of my best friends...how could she do this to me!?"

Stella was having a difficult time processing what Isabella had just shared. "There must be an explanation. You know how Mrs. Issie feels about you. I'm sure she has this all wrong."

"No...it was different this time. Her glare and smile. She's happy for them. She's been wanting this all along and it was right in my face – I didn't see it. I've lost him Stella." Charlotte wiped her tears and bolted for the door. "Maybe I don't need to be a part of that crazy family. It's been nothing but drama since we got together. Maybe it's for the best."

***

"Well, I'm glad you decided to come home!" Barbara was infuriated that Whitney hadn't called.

"I'm sorry, Mom. I was just so exhausted. Mrs. Issie had to work late, and Stella left me. I didn't have a choice." Whitney started up the stairs when Barbara grabbed her hand.

"We still need to talk, you know. I want to discuss this whole 'Charlene' thing with you." Barbara was always blunt. It came naturally to her.

"Really, Mom, that's what you call it? A *thing*? It's my birth mom!" Whitney stopped on the staircase and glared down at Barbara.

"Honey, I didn't mean it that way. Honestly, it's been a lot for me to take in as well. I'm sorry." Barbara wasn't sorry...she was furious that Charlene had just popped in and dropped a bomb on her family. And hearing Whitney call Charlene 'Mom' made her heart hurt.

"It's fine. I get it. You don't want her around. But...I do! I hate the way she just popped back into my life, but at least she did before she...well...you know..." Whitney looked away fighting back the tears that had welled in her eyes.

"Honey, we'll figure this out." Barbara lightly touched Whitney's hand and she pulled it away.

"Thanks...but...I just need some sleep. I'll figure all of this out myself. I feel like everyone is pressuring me – like a horrible game of tug of war – I want it to stop. I need to make this decision on my own." Whitney turned and headed up the staircase thinking, *It seems like the only person who gets me is Mrs. Issie. She's the only one that truly cares about what's good for me.*

Chapter Forty-Six

Defeat

"I'll sign over all rights to the clinic. I don't want any part of it. You can have it – no strings attached. Just give me the house." Dad rotated the stem of his wine glass awaiting Isabella's response.

"I'm not sure, Tucker. This house is all I have. The memories...that's all I have to hold on to." Isabella walked to the living room hoping Dad would follow.

"This isn't up for debate, dammit. I've had enough of this. You manipulate everything in your path and always seem to win." The rage inside Dad was obvious as he threw his wine glass into the sink.

"As if, Tucker. I didn't want to leave you. You insisted on the divorce. We could have worked things out." Isabella knew that comment would strike a nerve and didn't make eye contact.

"That's *never* going to happen! You hear me! You've turned into someone I don't even recognize. Our daughter despises you. Our son, who's not *our* son needs his mother and all you seem to care about is destroying the one thing that means the most to him...Charlotte." Dad grabbed his keys and headed for the carport door. "I'm done here. The house is mine. I'll get Allison to draw up the papers giving you the clinic."

Isabella stood with her empty wine glass waiting for her opportunity to defend herself. "You wait just a damn minute, Tucker. Nessie despises me? Did she tell you that? And Beau, I'm doing what's best for my son. Charlotte is nothing but bad news. He will see that one day. Besides, Whitney and Beau are getting closer. He asked her to stay with him the other night when I worked late. You know, they've always been friends, but they definitely have a connection."

Dad shook his head and remained silent. He knew anything he said at this point was useless.

"You can't say mean things and not explain. I love Nessie. We may not see eye to eye on everything, but she knows that I love her. And Beau, well, he just doesn't realize what's best for him. It's *my* job to protect him." Isabella stood facing Dad blocking his attempt to leave.

"Isabella, honestly, I don't have enough breaths in me to debate this with you. I'm sorry that you can't see through your selfish nature that your daughter yearns to mean something to you and get an ounce of your attention. She's fading Isabella, and before too long, she won't care anymore." Dad reached out his hand and pushed Isabella aside. "And Beau, he's a smart boy. He loves Charlotte, and they seem happy together. Sometimes love makes you do crazy things. I'll have those papers drawn up by tomorrow. This house is mine."

Tucker slammed the door and Isabella jumped from the rattle it caused.

***

Brice picked me up from Dad's lake house around nine-thirty. Luckily, Dad had to work late so I didn't have to make introductions – even though Dad knew exactly who Brice was.

I wasn't ready for the whole 'let's meet the boyfriend' thing.

Was he even my boyfriend?

Thinking back over the last couple of weeks, when he held me close and kissed me, told me he needed me more than anything, that I made him feel important...it all felt so right. But I couldn't let Tennie's newfound friendship go that easily either. Even in the freedom and clarity I felt while hanging out with her was close to destroying any chance I might have with Brice.

"Nessie? You with me?" Brice stared at me as we made it to the fork in the back road outside of town. He put the car in park — there's never much traffic on the back roads at night.

"Oh, sorry, I was just making sure I turned everything off inside. Dad might be late tonight. Were you asking me something?" *Whew! I played that one off.*

"Yeah, I wanted to know if you felt like going to the theatre tonight in Glena. I went today and bought us tickets for *Ghost*. It's supposed to be some sappy romance movie...figured you might like it?" Brice reached his hand toward mine and brought them to his lips.

"Awe, so sweet to think of me...but I'm not into that sappy stuff. What else was playing?" After the words came out of my mouth, I regretted every word.

He laughed. "I don't get you at all."

Turning toward him in my seat I nudged him, "Well that was mean!"

"No, I'm sorry. I didn't mean anything by that. It's just... you're different from other gir..." He stopped realizing that wasn't the best response.

"Oh, so I see...other girls huh!?" I leaned on the console that was wedged between us.

He looked surprised. "I didn't mean it like that, Nessie. I just question myself a lot when I'm with you...you aren't like most teenage girls...in a good way!"

"I'm not sure what that really means...but I'll take the compliment...*I guess?*" The smell of his cologne penetrated through me as I nestled my face in the nape of his neck.

"This feels nice," I savored every moment near him.

"*Ghost* is fine, really. I think it's sweet you went early and got our tickets." He pulled my chin up to meet his lips and we kissed.

"All I want is to spend time with you, Nessie, and get to know you better." His green eyes were mesmerizing, and I couldn't help but kiss him again...this time more deeply. His hands found their way up the back of my shirt as my hands cradled his face.

My body felt weightless. Everything that plagued me suddenly disappeared. Kissing him was effortless, and I found myself falling for him.

He suddenly pulled away as headlights appeared in his rearview mirror.

He kissed me once more quickly as the impatient truck behind us laid on the horn.

"Alright...alright...I'm going!" Brice yelled as he waved out the window.

The honking didn't stop as we drove toward Main Street.

"Who in the world is that?!" Brice adjusted the rear-view mirror so he could see.

"I have no idea, but they're following us." I watched the lights as they approached the side of Brice's car...attempting to pass us.

"OMG...it's Tennie!" I shouted as I saw her hanging out the back window of the truck.

"What's up ya'll!" Tennie shouted, holding a cigarette in one hand and bottle of whiskey in the other.

Brice slammed on the brakes. "I'm not down for this. I'm turning around."

As he put his car in reverse, I watched the truck stop up ahead and Tennie jumped out.

"Great...here she comes." Brice shifted the car into drive and revved it up. "I don't have time for this Tennie."

"Oh, little brother, just stop with all the "good boy" shit. You know your ass wants a taste of this whiskey!" Tennie taunted Brice with the bottle as she leaned over through my window.

"Hey, my friend," her eyes wandered as she held her balance, "Nessie...right...yeah...Nessie." She took a long drag of her cigarette and exhaled in my face.

"Tennie, get out of here. You're drunk. Go hang out with your loser friends." Brice pressed the gas and Tennie lost her balance.

"Shit, Brice, you trying to run me over!?" Tennie laughed hysterically as she reached both arms up to the sky and yelled from the top of her lungs, "Nothing will stop me! I'm invincible!"

Just as she finished those words the driver of the truck yelled, "We gotta go Tennie...I see blue lights ahead."

Tennie flicked her cigarette into the ditch and watched the flashing blue lights. "I'm not scared of them."

Tennie attempted to climb back into the truck, but she lost her balance and fell back on the pavement.

"Tennie...OMG...!" I screamed as my instincts kicked in and ran over to help her.

The truck sped away. *Good friends, huh?*

"Nessie, c'mon. The police are coming. I don't want to be involved in this. Let's go!" Brice yelled at me hoping I'd leave Tennie.

"I'm not leaving her here, Brice. She's bleeding!" I yelled hoping he would come help me.

Tennie laughed as she raised her whiskey bottle to the sky.

"C'mon, Tennie, you have to get up. We can't get caught here." I tried to pick her up but she resisted.

"I'm not scared Nessie. I didn't do anything wrong. I'm just sitting here looking up at the sky." Tennie faded in and out as the police got closer.

"Nessie! Get in the car, now!" Brice yelled as I stared back at Tennie laying happily on the pavement.

"We can't leave her, Brice! She's drunk and she's in the middle of the road!" I screamed back to him.

"I don't care about her, Nessie. I need you to get back in the car. Nothing good is going to come out of this! We can't be here!" Brice shouted again...in a demanding tone.

I froze.

It was just like Isabella ranting and raving to me about everything I did wrong. Or...what I need to do better or *her* way.

I sat down next to Tennie and helped her sit up. I looked back toward Brice as he sped away.

It was dark...and humid...and for a split second...quiet...until I heard music blaring as it approached us.

It was Blaine.

"You two stupid or something? Ya'll gonna get yourselves run over! Hop in!" Blaine laughed as he helped us into his truck.

"Nessie? What in the hell are you doing out here?" I was the last person Blaine expected to see.

"I...was with...Brice...and we..." I struggled to tell him. I felt overwhelmed. Brice had left me. Tennie was drunk.

"Brice left her here with me. He says I'm not a good person for her to hang around." Tennie's words were slurred, but Blaine didn't care. He thought it was funny.

"Just take me home, Blaine," I said as he turned in the opposite direction of the police lights.

"Oh, no, little Miss Per...I mean Nessie, you aren't going home. The night is still young! Right, Blaine!" Tennie said laughing.

"I'm not getting in trouble with her parents...or Beau. Nessie, you want me to take you home?" Blaine looked at me as he threw a beer can out the window. I watched as it landed in the bed of his truck.

I've really messed up again. You're so stupid, Nessie!

That feeling had come over me again. The feeling that someone needed me for something other than making things right was replaced by a burning rage to do something irresponsible and stupid.

"No, I don't want to go home. Where're we going?" I asked.

"The Abyss. Where else?" Blaine laughed as he opened another beer.

Dad would kill me right now if he knew I was riding around with Blaine – drinking.

"Blaine, maybe you shouldn't be drinking and driving." I hesitated knowing Blaine would just laugh it off.

"Girl, lighten up...and have a drink." Tennie opened the ice chest on the floorboard and handed me a beer.

I downed it.

What had come over me? I had a sweet guy who seemed to care a lot about me. He planned a date night at the movies...and I completely ruined it.

But, after a few more beers, Brice was a distant memory. I was still mad that he left me in the middle of the road.

I drank a few more beers on the ride out to the Abyss. Tennie shared her cigarette with me and Blaine as we laughed, sang songs over the radio, and drank to good times.

As we neared the Abyss, I rolled down the window with my arms flailing out the window. The night air was thick, and I embraced the occasional gusts of air provided by the movement of Blaine's truck. I felt free and wild...like nothing was holding me down...it felt good to let go of everything that had weighed me down.

Blaine and Tennie laughed as I sang out the window. I clearly had too much to drink.

Once we got to the party, Blaine immediately left us and found his circle of friends.

"Figures!" Tennie said under her breath.

"C'mon...we didn't come out here to stand by the truck!" I locked my arm into Tennie's as we approached the party.

I found myself in the middle of Tennie's friends. They were all older than me...drinking and smoking...partying like they did every night of the week.

"Hey, I remember you from Tennie's party a few weekends ago." He laughed as he finished his beer. "You came back for more I see?"

"Yeah, I came with Tennie." My eyes followed the swirls of tattoos on his forearm, up to his exposed bicep.

"You like them?" He pulled me closer into his chest.

"Like what?" I pretended to not understand. He'd caught me staring, and I felt a little embarrassed, but I wasn't going to show it.

"My tattoos...you tryin' to figure them out?" One hand had reached around my left side while his other cradled his drink.

His hold was strong and powerful, and he leaned in to kiss me.

I backed away. "No, I can't."

"Why the hell not?" He laughed and took another long sip of his beer. "You got someone here with you?"

"No...well...I...I just met you. I'm not like that." I felt a burning inside me to just kiss him. He was nothing like Brice – way too forward – but it intrigued me.

"You have any more of those beers?" I asked.

He smiled and responded, "I sure do!" as we walked over to his truck.

We sat for a few hours talking about nothing. He was too old for me, but he filled the empty pit in my stomach. The conversation meant nothing to me as he rambled on about his job and how much he parties.

He let me take a few drags from his cigarette and kept feeding me alcohol.

My head started to spin. I tried to close my eyes but that made the spinning worse. I could hear laughing in the background and people talking but everything was muffled. I couldn't make out the conversation – it was all just a lot of noise – just like my family life.

***

Dad pulled up to the lake house around eleven o'clock and noticed a car parked in the driveway.

Who in the world is this?

Brice got out of the car the minute Dad shut off his car.

"Mr. Corbin, hey, I'm a friend of Nessie's. I'm sorry to just show up like this here on your property." Brice was nervous and began to second-guess his decision to wait for Nessie at her house.

Dad grabbed his briefcase from the front seat and walked closer to Brice.

"Brice Adams, sir. I live across the…" Brice's hands were sweating as he reached out to shake Dad's hand.

"I know who you are, son. The question is what are you doing in my driveway this late at night?" Dad searched for his house keys in his pocket keeping his eye on Brice. "And, you mentioned my daughter, Nessie. Is she okay?"

"Well, that's why I'm here, sir. You see, I picked her up earlier from here and she…" Brice attempted to share with Dad, but Dad quickly interrupted him.

"*You* were with Nessie this evening? Where in the hell is she then? I thought she was going to the library with Owen?" Dad was beginning to get worried.

"Yes sir, I can explain. I'd planned for us to go to the movies, and well…we ran into my sister…" Brice knew the more he talked the more distance he was putting between us.

"So…where is she now?" Dad's eyes widened as he stared at Brice waiting for his response.

"I…I honestly don't know. That's why I'm here. I'm hoping someone will bring her home." Brice looked down at the ground knowing what he just said sounded awful.

"So, let me get this straight, son. You took my daughter out with intentions of taking her to a movie – which I had no idea she was going on a 'date' – you ran into your sister – and now Nessie is missing!? Nessie doesn't hang around with Tennie. That girl is nothing but trouble. You must have something wrong." Dad had become agitated.

"I wish I was wrong sir. I've tried to ask Nessie to stay away from Tennie. She's my sister, but I know she's nothing but trouble." Brice stuffed his hands in his blue jean pockets and stood waiting for Dad to respond.

"C'mon inside, son. We can talk more about it in the house where it's cooler." Dad knew Brice had more to offer to the story.

Brice told Dad *everything. Yep...everything.*

There was a huge piece of Dad that wanted to deny every bit of it, but he believed Brice.

"Don't you work at Kent's shop?" Dad remembered seeing Brice there before.

"Yes sir, I've been working there for almost two years." Brice looked down at the ground.

"That's good son. Kent's a good friend. If he trusts you in his shop, that says a lot." Dad continued. "Do you know where Nessie might have gone?" Dad asked as he saw headlights pull into the driveway.

"Who the hell is this?" Dad opened the blinds to get a better look. "Blaine...what the hell is Blaine doing here?"

Brice's hands fell into his face as he sat in the living room chair wishing that he hadn't come by.

"Mr. Corbin...hey...I brought Nessie home." Blaine walked around the front of his truck and opened the door.

And...there I was...passed out across Blaine's seat... one hundred percent unaware of my audience.

"What the hell, Blaine!? Is she okay?" Dad attempted to pick me up from the seat.

"Honestly, Mr. Corbin, I'm not sure. She was at the Abyss with Tennie Adams...I saw her drinking with Tennie's friends, but I'm not sure how much she drank. But...apparently she drank a lot...I found her passed out in the back bed of one of the trucks." Blaine offered to help pick me up from the seat and bring me inside.

"Just bring her to her room, please." Dad watched as Blaine carried me to my room. The news had broken him.

"I should go now, I'm sorry for all this. I shouldn't have let her leave with Tennie." Brice got up from the chair and Dad stopped him.

"No, son, you shouldn't have, but Nessie has her own mind. She chose to leave with Tennie and go to that party. She made those decisions on her own."

When Blaine came back into the living room, Brice looked away.

"Blaine, you took Nessie to that party with Tennie?" Dad stood in front of Blaine demanding a response.

"Yes sir, I did. I'm sorry Mr. Corbin. I really am." Blaine stared down at the floor and then looked over at Brice. "But I couldn't just leave them in the middle of the road. He sure took off and..."

Brice's jaw clenched and his fist tightened. Before he could defend himself, Dad interjected.

"Okay, guys, it's been a long night. I think everyone just needs some rest. Thanks for bringing her home, Blaine. And Brice, thank you for checking up on her." Dad walked them to the door and shut it behind them.

As he leaned against the door he sighed.

As he leaned against the door he sighed and said, "Our family keeps crumbling...one by one...something has to change."

Chapter Forty-Seven

Caught Up in the Moment

Charlotte left cheer practice early to help her Mom at the pharmacy. While she wasn't overly excited about working today, she was glad to get away from Whitney.

Whitney tried multiple times to talk to her during cheer practice, and each time Charlotte purposefully avoided her.

"I'm just not ready to talk to her, Mom. I mean, I know Whitney and Beau have been close friends for a long time, but she knows how much Beau means to me. For her to do this-be close to him-when I want to be there for him. It's just wrong." Charlotte threw her purse down on the counter as Melissa made her way down the aisle to the pharmacy window.

"Just remember ya'll have been friends for a very long time. Don't let this hiccup crush your friendship. I'd hate for that to come in the way of..." Charlotte interrupted her mom.

"Hiccup! Mom! I'd call stealing your best friend's boyfriend more than a *hiccup*!" Charlotte yelled as Melissa kept walking to the back of the store. "Everyone seems to be worried about Whitney's feelings—what about mine!?"

Just as she finished her thought, Jackson walked through the door.

He smiled and casually walked over to her.

"Hey, you snuck outta practice early this morning, huh?" Jackson casually leaned over the counter.

"You watching my every move or something?" Charlotte playfully responded.

"Maybe!" Jackson's eyebrow raised, and he smirked.

"Well, you should reconsider. I'm not that interesting." Charlotte pretended to organize some items under the counter.

"Look, a few of us were going out to the lake today...I wanted to see if you could come with us?" Jackson waited for the rejection.

"Well, I've got to work today. It does sound like fun though!" Charlotte put change into the register and closed the drawer.

"What sounds like fun?" Melissa asked as she approached the front of the store. "Hey Jackson!"

"Hi, Mrs. Callaway." Jackson stood upright still facing Charlotte.

"Nothing, Mom! Just a few friends are going to the lake today, that's all." Charlotte rolled her eyes and smiled back at Jackson mouthing quietly, "She's so nosy!"

"I heard that! And I think you should go. I can handle the counter. Dad has the back covered for now. We should be fine."

"You sure...I mean...I planned on helping today here."

"Nope, we can take care of it. Go have fun with your friends!" Melissa nudged Charlotte to move from behind the counter.

"Well, Jackson, I guess I'm going to the lake then." Charlotte glared at Melissa as she followed Jackson through the doors.

"You can ride with me if you want. I'll bring you back this afternoon." Jackson opened the door not giving Charlotte time to reconsider.

"Okay, well, then I guess I'm riding with you." She hopped into his jeep.

Backing out of the parking space, Charlotte's eyes met Whitney's as she opened the door to the pharmacy.

Charlotte quickly looked away hoping Whitney wouldn't stop to talk.

***

Later that day, Beau was released from the hospital to the therapy center.

"This room is so much better than that hospital. The walls were closing in on me." Beau stood up from the wheelchair and sat down on the bed. "I'm ready for that thing to go away too," he said pointing to the wheelchair.

"You're almost to the finish line, Beau. A few weeks of therapy, and you'll be home before you know it!" Mason stood looking out the window. "Nice view you got here too!"

"Anything for my sweet boy," Isabella said as she entered the room. "I expect nothing but expert care for my son. Therapy in the morning and light therapy in the evening. Dr. Carlton said he should also utilize the therapy pool as much as possible."

The therapist nodded and rolled her eyes as she walked away. Mason noticed it and laughed quietly.

"What's that about?" Isabella glared at Mason.

"What, I didn't say anything." Mason grinned.

"You were laughing at something. What was it?" Isabella stood with her hands on her hips facing Mason.

"Mom, he wasn't laughing at you. Cut it out. Geez, you're so high-strung these days. He was laughing at me." Beau tried to diffuse the tension in the room.

"Oh, well, I've got to get back to the clinic. Call me later okay? Maybe we can do dinner here?" Isabella kissed the top of Beau's head. Looking over at Mason, she said pointedly, "And...you're not invited."

Mason replied sarcastically, "Well, I would love to have dinner, Isabella. Thanks for the invite!"

"Cut it out you two. Can you get along for five minutes?" Beau rested his head back against the pillow on the bed.

Isabella seized the moment with Mason in the room to bring up Whitney. It was the perfect opportunity. "Speaking of invites, I'll bring Whitney back here when I finish at the clinic. She's got a lot going on you know, and she enjoyed your company the other night." Isabella glared at Mason and turned back toward Beau smiling.

"Mom, she told me what's going on. She knows she can come by anytime. I feel sorry for her, ya know, she's been hit with a lot...all at one time." Beau stood up to stretch his legs.

"What's going on with Whitney? Everything okay?" Mason moved closer to Isabella.

"Nothing. It's personal. Family business. She's confiding in Beau, and she needs him." Isabella watched as Beau slowly walked into the hall. "By the way, I told your daughter she needs to move on. Beau is moving on, and Whitney has been there for him. More than I can say for Charlotte. See...he's not even asking about her anymore."

Mason's eyes narrowed. "You leave my daughter out of this. She's just as much a victim in this as Beau. Don't you think they both have been through enough? She knows she needs to move on based on the paternity test results, but I'm giving her time. Love doesn't cease automatically." Mason laughed to himself thinking Isabella wouldn't be able to relate to any of this.

"Is that supposed to be aimed at me?" Isabella asked. "I know love doesn't cease automatically, but it certainly has to in this case. They're half-brother/half-sister!"

Isabella noticed Beau coming back into the room and motioned Mason to stop talking.

"Well, I have to get back and Mason does as well. I'll see you later this evening. Get some rest." She watched as Mason headed to the door.

"I'll be back to check on you tomorrow and see how therapy is going." Mason said as he reluctantly left the room.

He watched as she guarded the door making sure he wasn't going to try to sneak back in. He muttered under his breath, "Charlotte needs to keep her distance. I know Isabella is behind all of this Whitney stuff, but it's in Charlotte's best interest to stay away from Beau. Isabella is evil. I have to protect my daughter."

***

The lake felt perfect. Jackson pulled Kent's boat up onto the shore as Charlotte laid a towel out on the beach. His friends took it back out on the water.

"This isn't like Florida sand, is it!?" Charlotte laughed as she sat down next to the water's edge.

"No, it's not like powder at all," Jackson replied as he sat down next to her.

Charlotte laid back on her towel to tan.

Jackson struggled not to stare. Her body was perfect – especially in her hot pink bikini.

"Girl, I thought you were working today at the pharmacy?" Charlotte heard Stella yell from the other side of the beach.

"I came with Jackson. He picked me up from the store. Mom covered for me. Come over here and lay out with me!" Charlotte began to feel odd sitting alone with Jackson.

Stella appeared minutes later and plopped down on the other side of Charlotte.

"Ya'll not going on the boat?" Stella looked at Jackson hoping he would take the hint to leave them alone. "Don't ya'll like to slalom and stuff when ya'll come out here?"

Jackson shrugged and laughed. "Yeah, I guess we do, Stella. But, we just got out here. I was just sitting here talking to Charlotte."

As mad as Jackson made her, she still longed for him to show her attention. His muscular arms rested beautifully on his knees and his skin glistened in the sun.

"Stella! Watch out!" Charlotte yelled as a football bounced off Stella's head.

"Ouch!" Stella said as she nurtured the burning sensation on the side of her cheek.

Jackson laughed but quickly stopped upon realizing Stella was embarrassed. "I'm sorry, Stella. It's just...funny!"

Charlotte slapped Jackson's side. "That's so mean, Jackson. It's not funny. That hurts so bad. I've been hit several times by one on the sidelines." Charlotte reached out to Stella and she pushed her hand away. "I'm fine, really. It just stings a good bit. I'll be fine."

Stella looked up and caught Jackson staring at Charlotte. He quickly looked away.

"Enough of this! I'm going on the boat. Ya'll wanna come?" Stella jumped up from the sand and waded in the shallow water. "It'll be fun!"

"Nah, I'm going to stay here and tan. You sure you're okay?" Charlotte questioned Stella knowing she didn't like being pampered.

"*Yes*, I'm fine," Stella said rolling her eyes. "Jackson, you wanna come?"

"Nah, I'm gonna hang here with Charlotte." Jackson glanced over his shoulder and smiled at Charlotte.

"Whatever! Be losers then!" Stella waved for the boat to come pick her up.

***

They watched as their friends made several loops around the cove.

Charlotte flipped over on her stomach to tan her back. Jackson laid on his side facing her hoping to get closer.

"Thanks for inviting me," Charlotte said as her eyes fixed on Jackson.

"I was hoping we could have some time alone." Jackson couldn't resist knowing his time alone with her was limited.

Charlotte imagined herself lying next to Beau...him holding her close...caressing every inch of her body and kissing her softly. She missed him more than anything. As she imagined his lips touching hers, Whitney appeared and took Beau's hand — leading him away. Isabella's ridiculous laugh penetrated her soul and the dream faded.

"Charlotte! Do you want to?" Jackson had moved closer and was inches away from her face.

"I'm...sorry...do I want to what?" Charlotte asked.

"Go to dinner tonight…with me?" Jackson took a deep breath and waited for her response.

"I don't know if it's the right time, Jackson. I'm confused. A lot has happened the past few days and I'm not sure where Beau and I stand. I mean, I know we can't date anymore since…well…the paternity test and all. But he was so sure that it was a false result and I believed him. But since the accident, I haven't been able to see him. And now Whitney and him are a thing, and…" Charlotte rambled on until Jackson stopped her.

"Whoa, what? Whitney and Beau? No way, c'mon! Who told you that?" Jackson swallowed deeply thinking this could be his chance to have Charlotte.

"I just know, okay. I don't feel like getting into it. I thought Whitney was my friend. She turned out to be the opposite. I'm done with her." Charlotte played with the frayed ends of her towel. She felt Jackson's hand slide up her back in a slow caress that made her heart beat wildly.

He pulled his body closer to hers as she turned on her side facing him.

His hands cupped her chin as his lips found hers.

She stopped him. "I'm not sure if I'm ready for this, Jackson."

Charlotte fought the urge to kiss him back. She longed to be held again. Jackson's touch was soft and gentle, and she wanted more…but Beau's face kept popping up when she closed her eyes. She wanted so badly for Beau to hold her again…for things to be like they were before their world was shattered.

She felt Jackson's lips touch hers again. And she kissed him back.

She felt weightless as his muscular arms wrapped around her body pulling her even closer. His kiss remained gentle, but his arms tightly held her close to him.

For a moment she let her body react. She kissed him back as her hands found their way across his muscular back.

His fingers carefully played along the outline of her body as he slowly pulled away and stared into her eyes. "You're gorgeous."

Charlotte smiled and bit her lip.

He leaned in to kiss her once again but was interrupted by Stella.

"What in the hell!?" Stella said sarcastically as she walked onto the beach.

Charlotte quickly sat up and grabbed her bag. Stella knew she was embarrassed.

"It's none of my business and all...but everyone saw ya'll. It's not like the lake is that big." Stella laughed out loud, but she really wanted to cry inside. She longed for Jackson to kiss her like that. She wouldn't be embarrassed like Charlotte.

"I need to get home. Jackson, can you take me?" Charlotte tried to avoid Stella as much as possible.

"Yeah, sure. I'll bring you back to town. You wanna grab dinner first?" Jackson hoped the answer would be 'yes'.

"Maybe some other time." Charlotte grabbed her things and headed up the embankment to Jackson's Jeep.

Stella watched as he grabbed his things.

"You know she's on the rebound...she still loves Beau. He's all she talks about. She's holding onto a thread of hope they might be able to get back together." Stella walked closer to him.

He backed away and started heading up the embankment to his Jeep.

He turned halfway and said, "We'll see about that."

***

"Whitney, good to see you here! Glad I ran into you!" Charlene rounded the aisle in the pharmacy catching Whitney off guard.

"Hi," Whitney responded as Charlene pulled her in for a hug.

"Look, I know you have a lot on your mind, and I don't mean to keep showing up unannounced, but I really want to talk to you. I felt so terrible the other night leaving things the way they were. I know it was a huge shock to learn I was your Mamma and then to hear I was sick. I'm so sorry for that." Charlene wanted to continue when Whitney stopped her.

"Look, I do want to talk, but this isn't the time nor the place. I still need some time to think it through." Whitney walked past Charlene toward the cashier.

"Hey, Whitney. How's your summer going, sweetie?" Melissa asked as she noticed her talking to Charlene. "Is that lady bothering you?"

"Oh, no, ma'am, I'm fine." Whitney responded nonchalantly as she put her money on the counter. "That should do it. Thanks!"

"Oh, sweetie, I owe you a dollar and…" Melissa tried to catch Whitney, but she'd already ran out the door.

Charlene stood at the counter smiling and said, "She just learned I'm her Mamma and I'm dying. I've asked her to come live with me for a little while so we can spend my last few months together."

Melissa stood in silence. She didn't know how to respond.

***

"What in the hell were you thinking Nessie!" Dad's yelling made my head pound more.

"I…don't know…I guess…I just," I didn't want to tell him the truth. I didn't want him to know that Tennie had become my escape. She was my only 'out' – an avenue I'd found to let go of everything that weighted me down. The reality of my life that no one had ever bothered to dive into. My unhappiness.

"Well, you may not know...but I know one thing. You will *not* be hanging around Tennie Adams as long as you're under my roof!" Dad slammed his hands down on the granite countertop. "Do you hear me, Nessie? She's nothing but bad news."

I remained silent. My head pounded, and I was extremely thirsty yet knew it wouldn't take much before my nausea won over my dry mouth.

"You're going to sit there silent...not a word, huh?" Dad stared me down. "I do this interrogation thing for a living, you know. I could be here all day waiting on your response."

I knew he wasn't going to let this go.

"I know I shouldn't drink that much. And I get it. Tennie isn't one of 'us'. She likes to party and have fun – laugh and make jokes – what's wrong with that? That's really why you have a problem with it. Just be honest. You don't want me hanging around *her* – because of who her family and and where she lives." He wanted to know how I felt – so I told him.

"What has gotten into you lately? You aren't yourself at all and the sad part is you don't see it." Dad sighed as he walked into the living room. "I can't let you behave like this. It's one thing to drink casually, supervised of course at your age, but getting so drunk that your brother's best friend has to pick you off of a tailgate and..." I didn't allow Dad to finish his sentence.

"What? Blaine brought me home? No, I was with Tennie. We were hanging out at the Abyss with a group of her friends and..." I struggled to remember all the details but didn't remember seeing Blaine again after we drove up to the party earlier that night.

"See, that's what I'm trying to tell you. And Brice saw it too. He came here and…" Dad saw the expression on my face and knew he'd hit a nerve.

"What!? Brice came here…to the house? When?" I quickly became enraged that Brice would show up at my house.

"Yes, he was looking for you. He said he left you near town when you got out to help Tennie. He was worried about you, Nessie." Dad waited for my response.

I didn't know what to say. He didn't know me and Brice were even a 'thing'.

"Well, why was Brice Adams in my driveway waiting on you to get home, Nessie?" Dad's eyes pierced through me like I was someone on the stand in court.

"I…well…ughhhh," I ran my fingers through my hair and sat back in the chair. "Okay…we have become close friends …that's all." I hoped he wouldn't ask any more questions.

"Well, he seemed pretty interested in finding you to be just 'close friends'. Sounds much deeper than how you're explaining it." Dad got up from his chair and walked to the kitchen to refill his wine glass. "I might get comfortable with Brice, but Tennie is a definite 'no'. You're not to hang around her anymore.

I wasn't ready to give up my new friendship with Tennie. I wasn't naïve. I knew she was not a 'true friend', but that's what I'd longed for – something spontaneous, new, and dangerous.

Chapter Forty-Eight

Off the Deep End

"I'm leaving, Tennie!" Brice yelled as he gathered his things and closed the door. He was going to Texas with Kent to deliver several cars they'd repaired.

Later that morning, Tennie rolled over in her bed shielding the sun coming through her bedroom window. She tried closing her eyes tighter hoping it would fade behind the clouds, but it didn't.

One last attempt to get a few more hours of sleep in, she pulled her pillow over her face to find refuge.

Just as she began to fall back to sleep, she heard knocks that turned quickly into 'bangs' at the front door.

"Okay...okay...geez...give me a minute!" Tennie put on her oversized sweatshirt as she walked down the hall.

"Whatever this is about it better be important...waking me up earlier than I need to." When she opened the door, Tennie was surprised to see me on her doorstep.

"Just perfect...what are *you* doing here?" Tennie rubbed her eyes thinking they were playing jokes on her.

I shrugged my shoulders holding two overnight bags in my hands. "I need a place to stay. You're the first person I thought of."

A part of me was relieved that Brice wasn't home...at least his car wasn't in the driveway.

"Here...no...I mean...you can but...you sure you don't have anywhere else to stay?" I was surprised by Tennie's response.

Tennie seemed agitated. I liked her better when she was drinking.

"Just throw your stuff over there for now. You can stay in Brice's room. He's gone for a few days." Tennie lit a cigarette and plopped down into the recliner.

The living room was much smaller than I recalled.

"Welcome to my home, Nessie! Our little paradise." Tennie laughed.

"Look, I just need somewhere to crash for a few days. Thanks for letting me stay here. I didn't know where else to go." It was different being around Tennie sober. I was timid and shy – the old Nessie – and she was dry and direct.

"I don't get you...at all. I mean, at first, I didn't like you. I'm just being honest. You Corbins parade around this town pretending to be so perfect. I gave you a chance and well – you're okay – but you're still not 'one of us'." Tennie took the last drag off her cigarette and put it out in the ashtray.

"Where's Brice at?" I was curious where he'd gone.

"He had to bring some cars with Kent to Texas or something. He'd shit if he knew you were here. He's mad at you!" Tennie laughed.

"I really screwed things up with him." I looked down at the floor as Tennie continued.

"Yeah, I'd say you did. It's not all your fault though." Tennie lit another cigarette. "He's my brother, but he can be a complete ass." Tennie exhaled the smoke in my direction.

"I shouldn't have left him the other night at the Abyss. I should have stayed with him. He got us tickets to go see a movie in Glena. He was sweet about it. I'm the ass! I screwed that up." I sighed.

"I think you made the better choice. Who wants to watch a lame movie? He's uptight *all* the time. I tell him he needs to loosen up and enjoy high school." Tennie was on her soap box.

"Well, he certainly doesn't like me hanging out with you." I cringed as the words left my mouth waiting for her to kick me out.

"Baaahhhhhaaaa," Tennie laughed uncontrollably, "that's hilarious!" She continued, "Is he like your *dad* or something!" Tennie had fun mocking him.

I stared silently back at her – afraid of what she might say next.

"I don't agree with him often, but he's right this time. I'm a terrible influence, and you probably shouldn't hang out with me." Tennie got up from the chair and walked into the kitchen.

"Speaking of bad influence...you want a drink?" Tennie grabbed a beer from the fridge.

I wanted to barf just at the thought of alcohol. "No, I'm good. My stomach is still turning from last night."

Tennie shrugged and sat down next to me on the sofa. "Hair of the dog!"

"Hair of the *what*...?" I was confused.

Tennie laughed, "Never mind."

"I know you like Brice. I get it. He's not right for you. I think this is just some type of fling though- a chase - he should know you're too good for him." Tennie became more serious. "I think you're pretty cool showing up here uninvited...twice...I do admire that."

I wanted to ask her why she thought I'm too good for him—but I knew the answer and didn't feel like defending it.

She continued. "Brice isn't good for you either. He's tried to change since he went to that detention center last year, but he'll get tired of the straight and narrow and fall back into his ways again."

My mouthed dropped. *Detention center?*

"What? You surprised or something!? He didn't tell you? That's the reason he got kicked off of the baseball team his freshman year." Tennie smirked. "Based off of the look on your face – my brother didn't bother letting you in on his secret, did he?"

"No, um, he didn't. He mentioned thinking about playing baseball again. I asked him why he quit, and he avoided answering me. Now I understand why."

Tennie laughed shaking her head. "That's what I've been trying to tell you. People like me and Brice don't mix easily with you rich people. He didn't tell you because he was afraid you'd judge him."

I didn't know how to respond. The one thing that drove me crazy – being judged by my last name – kept surfacing, destroying every ounce of happiness I'd longed for.

"I guess I hit a nerve." Tennie stared at me waiting for my reply. "You can hang with the best of us – a little party maniac – that surprised me most." Tennie lit another cigarette.

I remained silent.

She continued talking after taking a long drag of her third cigarette. "You can stay here...like I said...Brice will be gone for a few days...but I'm not responsible for this. You're here because you chose to be here. Don't drag me into your family mess. You got that?" Her eyes fixed on me like I was her child.

"Yeah...I get it. No one knows where I am." I grabbed my bag and stood from the sofa.

"Where's his room?" I asked.

Tennie pointed toward the hall. "This isn't a mansion. Kinda hard to get lost. One way in and one way out – down that hall. Not like your place." She grinned.

"Thanks," I replied and walked down the hall to find Brice's room.

What are you doing here, Nessie? Dad would kill you if he knew where you were. You're with the one person he told you not to hang around.

***

Cheer practice ended early. Charlotte gathered her things from the bleachers.

Coach had the team run several laps around the track to finish up practice. As Jackson made his second lap on the track, he couldn't resist stopping to talk to Charlotte. Maybe Coach wouldn't see him.

"Hey, ya'll finished practice early?" Jackson asked as he tried to hide from Coach.

"Yep, it was a good practice. And it's so hot. I just wanna find some A/C!" Charlotte threw her cheer bag over her shoulder and faced him.

As he stood in front of her, shirtless, his sweat glistened over his muscular abdomen.

"Whatcha doing later today?" he quickly asked seeing Coach heading his way across the field.

"I don't have any plans." Charlotte noticed Coach heading toward Jackson and smiled, "I think you're about to be in trouble."

"Oh yeah, I better get back to running," Jackson said while jogging backward. "Can I call you later?"

"Sure, I'd like that." She smiled back at him as he sprinted away.

I might as well give him a chance. Beau seems to have moved on with Whitney.

***

Whitney watched through the window of the door as Beau tossed his football up into the air.

Sadly, Whitney didn't have anyone else to turn to. She felt lost without Charlotte. She needed her now more than ever.

Whitney was lost in thought as she was startled by Isabella who had snuck up behind her.

"Whitney, honey, so glad to see you!" Isabella hugged Whitney. "Are you just going to stand out here in the hall or go on in there to see Beau?"

I was actually about to leave before anyone saw me.

"Oh, hey Mrs. Issie...yeah...I was about to go in." Whitney forced a smile.

"Hey Mom, Whitney, what's up?" Beau put the football by his side.

"Just checking on you during one of my breaks. I found her lurking outside your door. She came by to spend time with you." Isabella nudged her and smiled.

"Actually, I just came by to chat with Beau about Charlene. She confronted me again about going to live with her." Whitney blurted out hoping to draw attention away from Isabella's comment – 'she came by to spend time with you'.

Maybe there's something to what Stella and Charlotte have been saying.

"Well, I've got to get back to the clinic. I'm so glad you're spending more time together." Isabella kissed his cheek, hugged Whitney, and stared at both of them with a sly smile as she left the room.

"What's up with her lately?" Beau watched as Whitney plopped into the chair next to his bed.

"I don't know…she seems the same to me." Whitney shrugged.

"She's just acting weird and all…talking about me and you spending time together. What's all that about?" Beau noticed Isabella's odd gaze at both of them when she left the room.

Whitney didn't respond while she played with her hair hoping to avoid answering. She'd defended Isabella time and time again, but she felt uncomfortable this time for some reason.

"Whitney…hello over there. What's on your mind?"

"Everything is on my mind, Beau. But, you have enough on your plate. I just came because I needed a friend, and honestly, I had decided to leave before your mom caught me at the door and practically pushed me in here." Whitney knew the conversation would eventually lead to Charlotte, and she didn't want to be the one to tell Beau about her and Jackson.

"Well, I'm your friend. Give it to me! Besides, you're the only one who has been coming to see me since my back surgery, besides Blaine." Beau's mind immediately drifted to Charlotte.

"Is Charlotte mad at me or something? She hasn't been here to see me. I know ya'll told me she wanted to see me, but she still hasn't come by." Beau stared at Whitney waiting for an answer.

"She hasn't been talking to me either." Whitney continued playing with the ends of her hair, avoiding making eye contact with him.

"No way! Ya'll are inseparable most days. What's going on?" Beau sat on the edge of the bed facing her.

"Nothing, just girl stuff. She'll get over it." Whitney attempted to change the subject. "Charlene confronted me the other day again...asking me to move in with her."

Beau cared about Whitney as a friend and knew she was there for support, but he was more interested in finishing the conversation about Charlotte. He was still pissed at what Blaine said about Jackson getting closer to Charlotte at the Abyss and holding her hand. He was determined to find out more.

"Look, I want to talk about your birth mom...I do...but can we please finish talking about Charlotte? It's killing me being in this room. I've tried calling her house a few times and no one has answered. Ya'll said she wanted to see me – I don't understand why she hasn't. It's like she's avoiding me." Beau stood up from the bed and paced the room. "And I heard Jackson is trying to get closer to her...is that true?"

Whitney sighed. "She's not avoiding you, Beau. She did want to see you. She came by the morning of your back surgery, but you were already in surgery." Whitney dreaded where this conversation was going.

"So, why didn't she hang around? You came back that evening with Stella." Things weren't adding up.

"Blaine visited earlier in the day and mentioned something about Jackson holding her hand at the party. Did you see that?" Just saying the words out loud made his blood boil.

Whitney closed her eyes tightly.

"Whitney, look, I know you'll be honest with me. What's going on?" Beau sat back on the bed in front of her.

"I wasn't at the party, Blaine. Charlotte is mad at me because...well...she thinks I'm trying to get closer to you." Whitney looked up at the ceiling with her hands gripping the chair. "Ughhh ....why is my life such a mess!?"

Beau sat confused. "She...thinks that me...and you...are getting closer? That's ridiculous." Beau laughed.

Whitney's hands clenched the chair even harder. A small piece of her imagined Beau would lean closer to her, kiss her and tell her everything was going to work out the way it should. In that brief moment of time, Whitney smiled. But, the reality was that Beau loved Charlotte, and Whitney knew that in her heart. She was okay with it. They were meant for each other.

"Yeah, it's ridiculous. I agree." Whitney's lips pressed together as she folded her arms across her chest.

"Why does she think that about us? What would make her think that?" Beau shrugged.

Whitney remained silent with her eyes closed. She wanted the conversation to be over.

"Whitney, what are you keeping from me? I know you're hiding something." The tone in his voice became deeper.

Whitney had enough drama surrounding her. She had avoided sharing with Beau she'd seen Jackson and Charlotte together. But she knew Beau was not going to let her remain quiet.

"I wasn't at the party. Charlotte was avoiding me...like I said earlier. But I did see them in town the other day...in Jackson's Jeep." Whitney stared at the wall afraid to see Beau's response.

"What!? She was with him? Where were they going?" Beau stood up and paced the floor again.

"I think everyone was going to the lake to hang out. That's all I know, Beau. I'm sorry."

"Does she think that I don't want to see her? Ya'll told her I did want to see her right?" Beau continued pressing her for answers.

"Yes, we told her. But like I said, she came by, and you were in surgery, so she left." Whitney didn't want to relive that day when Charlotte blew her off.

"So...why hasn't she come back? That doesn't make sense to me. She was here, so she apparently wanted to see me, and then she didn't come back. And now she's with Jackson!? Something isn't adding up, Whitney." Beau became out of breath from pacing and had to sit back on the bed.

"I don't know. I can't explain it." Whitney refused to tell Beau the truth, that Charlotte was mad at Isabella for meddling and always including her, and being ruthless to Charlotte. It wasn't her place to tell him.

"Well, I've had enough of this! I'm going to call her and tell her we need to talk. I know we aren't together anymore – and may never be – but I need to clear the air. Maybe she's already moved past me and doesn't need to clear anything, but I do. I was planning to get the paternity test once I get released from therapy." Beau ran his fingers through his hair. "I'm sorry Whitney. You're stuck in the middle of this, and I hit you with all my questions. I'm glad you're here."

She smiled back at him and released her hold on the armrests. "I don't like being in the middle of it. Charlotte is my best friend, and I just want her to be happy. I want you to be happy, too."

"Changing the subject...so what about Charlene?" Beau knew Whitney had a tough decision to make as well. "What are you going to do?"

***

Three-thirty in the afternoon and I found myself wasted...again. Tennie had invited a few friends over and the day had quickly turned into a party. My legs were extended out on the sofa across two guys I'd never met.

"You passed out for a minute there," one of the guys said as he offered his cigarette to me.

"No thanks, I'm good for now," I said as I pulled myself up from the edge of the sofa.

"We didn't want to wake you up, but we needed somewhere to sit and roll this." I wiped my eyes and recognized the older guy from the party the other night at the Abyss.

"What's that?" I wiped my eyes to gain more clarity.

"Grass...and not like the kind in the yard," the guy laughed as he licked the paper to seal the drugs inside.

Great...my legs were the cutting table for drugs...while I was passed out.

I stood up...well, attempted to stand up, and fell back down on the sofa.

My eyes danced around the room until I passed out again.

***

Jackson picked Charlotte up that evening. Owen met him at the door.

"Hey, Jackson, I haven't seen you around much," Owen tried to be cool around Jackson, but it was awkward. Jackson and Owen weren't necessarily friends, however, Jackson was always nice to him – after all he was Charlotte's twin – everyone was probably nice to him because of her.

"Yeah, I know. Football conditioning has me busy most weekends. Is Charlotte ready?" Jackson wasn't really in the mood for small talk.

"I'm ready...just give me a few minutes!" Charlotte yelled from upstairs.

Jackson placed his hands in his pockets as he waited in the awkward silence with Owen.

Several minutes later, Charlotte met him at the bottom of the staircase. "Let's go!"

"Owen, just tell Mom I'll be home later...definitely by curfew...but I'll miss dinner." Charlotte didn't give Owen time to respond.

On the steps of the front porch, Charlotte asked, "So where are we going?"

"Dinner...and then whatever you feel like." Jackson's hand brazed hers, but he decided not to rush it.

Charlotte felt his light touch and secured his hand in hers. She turned to face him as he opened the Jeep door. "Look, this is all kinda weird to me...being that me and Beau...well...and then me and you kinda..."

Jackson cut her off.

"I get it. No need to explain. We'll just take things slow...see where it goes." Jackson leaned in and sweetly kissed her cheek.

Her breaths became shallow as his lips teased hers and he pulled away.

Something came over her – and she moved her lips to his – and they kissed.

She pulled away and smiled, "I didn't say we had to take things that slow. I just said it feels weird." Charlotte smiled, eyebrow's raised and continued, "But, it feels nice when you kiss and hold me."

His hold on her became stronger and his kiss became deeper. She felt needed and wanted again – and it felt perfect. She closed her eyes as her fingers ran through his hair. Beau's face popped into her mind. Her eyes immediately opened, and she backed away.

"What's...wrong?" Jackson asked still holding her hands.

"Oh, nothing, just...we don't want to be late for dinner!" Charlotte smiled and hopped into the front seat of the Jeep.

***

I couldn't see anything – it was pitch black – and quiet.

I faintly smelled his cologne, and my pulse began to race – then I remembered I was in his bed.

I searched for the lamp on the bedside table then struggled to find the knob to turn it on. My head pounded. My body ached. My mouth was dry.

I finally secured my fingers around the knob on the lamp and the light blinded me.

My vision was blurry, and I squinted to shield the light. I tried to make out who was sitting in the corner of the room.

I reached for the nightstand and found my glasses.

As I put them on, it became clear to me he'd been watching me – who knew for how long.

Brice.

"What...what are you doing here?" I struggled to get the words out as I covered myself with his comforter.

"I guess I should ask you that question being that you're in my house, in my bedroom, passed out in my bed." Brice's tone was harsh.

"Yeah, I guess so. I'm sorry." I wasn't sure what to say. "I needed a place to stay – to get away from everything. Tennie said I could crash here a few days." I wanted him to come closer and hold me. Instead, he sat back in the chair staring at me coldly.

"I thought you were going to be gone a few days. At least that's what Tennie said." Brice shook his head with distaste. "Yeah, that was the plan."

"Oh, well, you came back early, then?" I attempted to deflect why I was in his room.

"What day do you think it is, Nessie?" Brice asked me directly.

"Friday...I think...yeah...it's Friday. I came over this morning to ask Tennie if I could crash with her a few days." I was confused why he was asking. Based on his stare I began to question myself.

Is today Friday?

"It's Sunday, Nessie. You've been passed out – in and out – for a day and a half. Tennie said you got wasted Friday and didn't stop. I got home late last night and found you passed out in my bed." Brice continued staring directly at me.

My head pounded, and I laid back down on his pillow closing my eyes.

He stood up and walked over to the bed. "You gotta leave, Nessie. You can't stay here. It was wrong for you to come here."

I placed my hands over my eyes as the throbbing became worse. "I'm so thirsty. Could you maybe get me a glass of water?"

Brice laughed to himself. "Sure, anything else I can do for you?"

As he walked to the door of his room, he turned to me and said, "I just need you to leave."

"Fine! I'll get my things." I sat up too quickly and my head spun. I laid back down. "I just need a minute."

Brice came back with a glass of water and set it on the nightstand.

"Thank you. My mouth is so dry. I don't think I've eaten much either. My stomach is growling, but I'm so nauseated." I told myself to quit talking.

"I don't feel sorry for you. You're better than this, you know. I asked you to stay away from Tennie, and you keep finding your way back to her. I told you I can't do this anymore, and I meant it. You need to leave." Brice sat on the edge of the bed facing away from me.

I longed for him to hold me, wrap his arms around me and kiss me.

I sat up on the bed and positioned my body behind him. I attempted to wrap my arms around him, but he pushed them away. "I can't...I want to...I want you to...but I can't." Brice stood up from the bed and turned toward me.

"You need help, Nessie. You're on a road to disaster. You may think you have found this great freedom and it's attractive and wild – but it's dangerous – and you're going to hit rock bottom if you keep it up." Brice squatted in front of me and grabbed my hands.

"Tennie said you...well...you took some drugs from a few of her friends. Ya'll partied all weekend and you passed out in the living room. She got one of the guys to carry you to my room. That's about the only responsible thing she did while I was gone." Brice's touch felt amazing...I missed him and needed him now more than ever.

I didn't take any drugs. I sat for a moment and remembered, *Ugh, that stupid guy I met at the Abyss with the tattoos—used my legs as a place to cut it up. I must have smoked it with them.*

I drank another sip of water, deciding not to comment, as he continued.

His mood began to soften as he kept talking.

"The other night when I met your dad...I was so nervous. I didn't know where else to go. You scared me, Nessie. So, I just showed up hoping you would be there. When I saw your dad, I knew I'd messed up going there, but all I wanted was for you to be safe."

My hands softly cradled his face. His eyes met mine as he leaned in closer to me. His head fell into my chest.

"I don't want to lose you, Nessie. I can't lose you." Brice attempted to pull away from my hold, but my arms wrapped around him and pulled him back closer to me.

"You haven't lost me, Brice. I'm here." I whispered softly to him.

His hand found my face as his fingers lightly traced my cheek and found my lips. He gazed directly into my eyes and kissed me – then backed away.

"I can't be with you like this. I've told you how I feel. You need help, Nessie. You get the help – and we can be together. It's that simple." His tone quickly reverted to being sharp and cold. His eyes darted around the room.

"I need *help*. Excuse me!? You're an asshole. *You* need help! I know about the detention center!" I covered my mouth realizing I'd let it slip.

"What did you just say?" he asked as his eyes narrowed.

"Nothing. You shouldn't be accusing me of needing help – that's all." He'd turned a wonderful moment into a disaster within five minutes.

"No, you said detention center. How'd you know that?" Brice knew the answer to his question, but he wanted me to confess.

"I'm sure you'll figure it out. I don't have any answers for you. Apparently, I need help!" I gathered my bag and ran out of his room. He didn't follow.

"You leaving so soon?" Tennie said laughing.

"Shut up, Tennie," I replied as I bolted through the front door.

Chapter Forty-Nine

Moments of Truth

"Can I talk to Charlotte? Is she home?" Beau's voice cracked, nervous that she might not want to talk to him.

"Hey, Beau! It is so good to hear your voice. How are things going with therapy?" Melissa was glad he was reaching out to Charlotte. "Give me a minute. She's upstairs."

Beau smiled. His mind and heart were focused on one thing only – Charlotte. "It's going good. I'm just ready to get out of here!"

Melissa tried to hand Charlotte the phone.

"*Mom*, no! I don't want to talk to him!" Charlotte shut her bedroom door.

Melissa persisted. "Charlotte, honey, just give him a chance to explain himself. Neither of you have spoken since the accident. Don't you want to know if he's okay? You know – even if it's closure – that's the right thing to do."

Charlotte rolled her eyes. "Mom, if I didn't know any better I'd think you were taking his side. Why are you so adamant that I talk to him? He obviously moved on with Whitney and doesn't care about me. I'm not talking to him."

Melissa sighed and tried one more time. "Just give him five minutes honey. I think you both deserve it after all you have both been through."

Charlotte rolled her eyes. "Fine. Give me the phone."

She took a deep breath in and answered, "Hey, it's Charlotte. I'll give you five minutes."

There was silence on the other end of the line.

"Hello!? *Hello...Beau...you there?*" Charlotte questioned repeatedly with no reply.

"Mom! He's not even on the line." Charlotte yelled as her finger went to press the end call button.

"Charlotte, wait...I'm here. Don't hang up!" His voice sounded so sweet.

"Yeah, okay, well now you have only four minutes." She wasn't giving him any slack.

"I think we need more than four minutes, Charlotte. I wanted to see if you could maybe come by and visit...at the therapy center?" Beau waited for her response.

"I can't, Beau. I can't come by." Her tone had become softer.

"You can't come by, or you won't?" He became irritated at the thought of Jackson holding her back.

"Well, I don't see why it matters. It's not like you have wanted to see me since the accident. And now...it seems...well you have got someone to keep you company. You don't need me." The words flew out of her mouth before she could stop them.

"What in the world are you talking about? All I've wanted since I got out of surgery was to see you. I've waited for you Charlotte and you never showed up." He held off bringing up Jackson.

"I...I don't understand. You...you did want to see me?" Charlotte's heart began to beat wildly.

"Yes! We need to talk, in person, Charlotte. I miss you." He waited for her to say 'yes'. He wasn't taking 'no' for an answer.

She was torn. Was he playing some kind of game with her heart, or did he really miss her?

"I'll be up there in a few hours." Charlotte hung up the phone.

She laid back in her bed and cried.

***

"He saw what? Why did he keep that from you?" Kent was frustrated that Jackson had lied to Allison.

"Keep your voice down! I wanted you to know first before I shared it with Tucker. Do you think it's the right thing to step in the middle of all of this?" Allison sat at the kitchen table.

"Yes, the question is not should you tell him – it's *when* are you going to tell him? I told you not to trust Isabella." Kent finished loading the dishwasher and sat next to her at the table.

"I know it's the right thing to do...it's just that...he didn't *see* her do anything with the tests. She was very startled when he saw her, and she was standing in front of the same filing cabinet that I locked the results in. It makes sense...but we don't really have any proof." Allison grabbed Kent's hand. "I just hate being in the middle of this. And dragging Jackson in it."

"I get it. But this affects people's lives. Look at what poor Mason and Tucker have been through – not to mention Beau – and for what? I think we owe it to Tucker at least." Kent knew this was going to be hard on Allison. "I'll go with you to tell Tucker."

Allison leaned closer to Kent and kissed him. "I'm so lucky to have you."

***

"I've given it a lot of thought and I think...well, I know, it's best for me to go and live with Charlene – at least until she, you know...I can't say it." Whitney sat across the dinner table from her mom and dad.

Barbara threw her napkin on the table. "Whitney, you don't know what you're doing! I can't let you mess up what you have going here. With cheer, school clubs, your friends...what about all of that?"

"Mom, I've thought it over--a lot. Cheer is probably the hardest thing for me to leave. It was much better when Charlotte actually talked to me – but that's over." Whitney stirred the peas on her plate.

"What on earth do you mean? You girls aren't friends anymore?" Barbara had lost her appetite and stared at Whitney for answers.

"No, we're not. She's mad at me for something I had zero control over. I don't feel like getting into it." Whitney sat back in the dining chair and pushed away from the table. "Can I be excused? I don't feel like talking anymore. I just want to be left alone."

Barbara walked over to sit near Whitney. "Honey, I know there has been so much flooding your mind lately...decisions that I didn't want you to be faced with at sixteen. I want to help you...but you need to tell me what's going on."

"It's nothing, Mom. I promise." Whitney looked around the room and noticed her dad finishing his dinner avoiding the conversation.

"I'm moving in with Charlene. I've made that decision. She has room for me, and I think it's best for me to get out of this town for a while and see something different. Can you support me on this decision?" Whitney grabbed Barbara's hands and continued. "Just give me this, please. I'll call ya'll and visit on weekends. I love ya'll so much, but I need to do this for her...and for me."

Barbara pulled her hands away and walked into the kitchen. Her emotions ran wild at the thought of Whitney moving in with Charlene and leaving them – alone.

Whitney followed Barbara into the kitchen and hugged her. "I don't like it one bit, Whitney. You're in high school. You barely know her. You need to concentrate on your work and being a kid – not assuming the role of a caregiver. Who is going to support you?"

"I haven't gotten that far, but hopefully Charlene has that figured out." Whitney knew it was best for her to leave Sedipar for a while. This was her opportunity – and hopefully, the rest would fall into place.

"I love you Whitney, and this may seem crude, but I'm not giving Charlene a dime. She brought this so-called 'opportunity' to you and unfortunately, we have seen the mess she causes – always unable to clean it up." Barbara was angry and saddened that Whitney had made this decision alone. She knew she could make her stay, but she thought, *Do I want to live with this the rest of my life...being the one that kept Whitney from being with Charlene during the last few months of her life?*

***

Charlotte was nervous to enter the hospital – dreading running into Isabella.

She breathed a sigh of relief seeing Tucker leaving Beau's room.

"Hey, Charlotte, so good to see you!" Tucker hugged her as she scanned the hall for Isabella.

"Beau said you were coming by today. He's been smiling all morning -- probably the most he's smiled since the accident." Tucker stepped out of the way and opened the door. "He's all yours!"

When she entered the room, Beau's eyes fixed on her and watched her set her things on the table.

"Hey...um...just saw your Dad leaving." Charlotte felt awkward and didn't know what to say.

"Yeah, he brought me some things from home I asked for." Beau stopped her from sitting in the chair. "Please sit here by me. I've missed you so much." Beau motioned for her to sit on the bed next to him.

"Beau, I don't think that's a good idea." Charlotte swallowed deeply resisting the urge to fall into his chest and hug him.

"I get it. I'm sorry. It's just so hard to see you and not have you close to me...I just..." This was harder on him than he realized it would be.

"Maybe I should just go?" Charlotte attempted to grab her things.

"No! No, please don't leave." Beau's voice was soft and sweet.

Charlotte sat in the chair next to his bed. "So, what did you want to tell me?" Charlotte hoped Jackson's name wouldn't surface.

"I think we need to catch up and all. I haven't seen you since the night of the accident." Beau stared intently waiting for her reply.

"Yeah, well, that's not my fault!" Charlotte snapped back.

"Ouch...well, I get it. I didn't say it was your fault. I've just missed you." Beau realized he hit a nerve.

"I'm sorry...I've just got a lot on my mind." Charlotte wanted to tell him how sorry she was for getting drunk that night and him having to drive her home.

"As I said on the phone, I've waited for you to come by. I told Stella and Whitney, and they said you tried to see me, but things kept getting in the way." Beau kept his composure. He didn't want to upset her any more than she already appeared to be.

Charlotte delayed her response unsure if it was the right time to dump her feelings about Isabella on Beau. After all, he'd been through so much, and she hadn't been there. She still felt guilty for the accident – but Isabella wasn't going to win.

"Beau, I've wanted to come by to tell you that I'm sorry." Charlotte struggled to make eye contact with him.

"Sorry for what? You don't have to be sorry for anything!" Beau knew where she was going based on what Whitney and Stella had shared with him, but he let her finish.

"Yeah, I do. You wouldn't be in here if it weren't for me. You had to drive me home because I drank too much – I did this!" A tear rolled down her cheek as she felt some relief apologizing.

"You're *not* the reason I'm in here, Charlotte. Quit blaming yourself! You don't owe me an apology. This is on me." Beau looked up at the ceiling frustrated that Charlotte was taking the blame.

She continued. "Well, regardless what you think or feel…I just wanted you to know that I'm sorry. And I tried to come by several times to tell you that. I even brought you a dried rose from my homecoming corsage. I wanted to tell you that I'd wait for you to get the paternity test…and that I was sorry."

"So, what stopped you? You said you tried several times. What happened?" Beau was confused.

"I don't know how to tell you this. I've tried so many times to explain it to you in a way that I felt wasn't 'calling her out' – there's no easy way – but just to tell you." Charlotte's eyes danced around the room unable to make eye contact with Beau.

"What is it? You know you can tell me anything." Beau was sincere.

"The reason I wasn't able to...what kept me from seeing you...wasn't me not wanting to see you...it was...*your*...*Mom*."

"My *Mom*!? What!? How could she keep you or would keep you from seeing me? She knows how I feel about you, Charlotte. She would never be so cruel!" Beau shook his head in disbelief.

"I figured that would be your response – which is why I need to leave." Charlotte stood up and attempted to walk back to the table to grab her purse.

"No, don't leave. I'm sorry. Please sit back down." Beau grabbed her hand. His soft touch melted her.

She closed her eyes tightly and turned toward him. She pulled her hand away softly and said, "Beau, if you're not going to believe me then there's no point in me staying."

"I get it...I'm sorry. That's just a lot to absorb – my Mom is the wedge that kept us apart? It just sounds bizarre--that's all." Beau grinned as Charlotte sat on the bed next to him.

"I need you to listen, and believe me, Beau. She's ruthless. She's hated me since the beginning. I have so many stories to tell you...*gosh*...I don't know why I kept it from you. I thought I was doing the right thing keeping it to myself."

"Tell me now. I want to know. If my Mom has been the source of all of this...I need to know." Beau reached out and grabbed Charlotte's hand again. He grabbed it tightly securing her hand in his.

She didn't resist. She missed his touch.

Her heart began to beat wildly as his hand cradled hers.

With her eyes fixed on his, she went back to the day she asked for birth control. Beau's eyes widened and fury built within him as she unraveled the chaos Isabella had put her through since they started dating.

"Mom told me you left that day...so I assumed you didn't want to see me." Beau stared intently at Charlotte.

"Yeah, it's because she told me and everyone else that you didn't want any visitors." Charlotte rolled her eyes. "See, Beau, she's been manipulating everyone. And she hates me."

"She doesn't hate you. But I don't know why she's been so cold toward you." Beau was still confused. The news of his ruthless mother weighed him down. The one person he loved more than anything, Charlotte, his mother despised.

"Oh, yeah she does hate me. It's obvious." Charlotte continued sharing the snide comments Isabella made about Beau never forgiving her which ended up leading to, Whitney. Charlotte released her hand from his hold. "The next part...well, I'm still not over."

"There's more?!" Beau ran his fingers through his hair. "Let me have it, then. I'm ready."

"Whitney." Charlotte stared blankly into his eyes.

"What about Whitney?" Beau asked.

"I think...well, I know because your mother made a point to tell me, that you and Whitney are getting closer and are a 'thing'." Charlotte stood up from the bed.

"What in the hell? No! No way!" Beau laughed and quickly stopped once he saw the despair in Charlotte's eyes.

"It's not funny Beau. She's been coming by here and spending time with you when *I* should have been the one here with you. Your mother forced me away every opportunity I had while opening the door for Whitney to get close to you. I can't compete anymore. I've lost a friend and a boyfriend who both meant so much to me. I'm done." Charlotte stood facing him with her arms crossed on her chest.

"Babe...look, there's *nothing* and *I mean nothing* going on between me and Whitney. I promise. She has been a family friend for a long time, but I have zero feelings for her *like that*. I told you that before. As for my mom, well, some things are beginning to make sense." Beau began to realize that the questions he had about Isabella acting strange were warranted.

Curious, Charlotte sat back down at the end of the bed. "What do you mean?"

"Mom's just been acting weird lately...around Whitney. I asked Whitney if she noticed it, but she said she didn't. I get it now. Mom has always hoped we would be a 'thing'. I've told her over and over again that I'll never see Whitney 'like that'." Beau moved to the end of the bed to sit beside her.

"I'll never see anyone the way that I see you..." Beau ran his fingers through her hair, and she turned away from him.

"I can't do this. We can't fall back into this." Charlotte turned back toward him.

"I know...but it feels right. We belong together, Charlotte." Beau smiled and leaned in closer to kiss her.

She pulled back. "I can't...I can't do this."

He sat back with despair.

"When I get outta here in two weeks, Dad and I plan to take the paternity test – like I planned to do before the accident." Beau waited for her response.

"That's good. But, Beau, honestly, nothing is going to be different. That test could come back the same as before – we can't be together now, and the second test won't change anything." Charlotte stared at the floor. "Besides, your mom hates me and will never allow us to be together."

"Mom doesn't get to decide who I choose to be with! Once the results come back and prove the first one was wrong, we can be together. And...I'll take care of my mom. She's not going to bother you anymore. I'll be damn sure she doesn't come between us again."

***

"Tucker, hey, I didn't think you would be in the office today. I figured you were at the therapy center with Beau." Allison dropped her purse on her desk and turned to where Kent waited in the hall.

"Yeah, I decided to come back and take care of a few things. Besides, Charlotte visited Beau this morning." Dad smiled. "I was happy to see her. I gave them some time to catch up."

Allison smiled at the thought of something positive. "That's so good to hear. It sounds like Beau is on a good recovery path."

"Yeah, he is. Speaking of a recovery path, Beau and I discussed the paternity test, and we plan to make appointments once he gets finished with inpatient therapy." Dad fumbled with several papers on his desk. "There they are."

Dad looked up and realized that Kent was standing near Allison in the doorway. "Oh, hey Kent! I didn't know you were here. What's been going on, man?" He reached out to shake Kent's hand.

"Hey, nothing much. Just coming back from lunch." Kent stepped back behind Allison.

"Tucker, we...have something to tell you if you can spare us a minute or two?" She sat down in one of the chairs facing his desk.

"Sure, yeah, what's up?" Dad continued shuffling through more paper and mumbled to himself, "And that one...I needed it as well." He looked up as he sat down in his chair and saw Allison and Kent staring blankly back at him.

"Okay, so...you have something to tell me? What is it?" He loosened his tie and leaned back in his chair.

"I don't know how to say this, or if it will mean anything. I'm not sure if it--" Allison was cut off midsentence by him.

"Well obviously it's important or you both wouldn't be here. Now, I'm getting a little nervous to be honest! You're not quitting the firm are you!?" He cringed at the thought of her leaving.

"Oh, no way, Tucker! You aren't getting rid of me that easy!" She laughed.

"Well, the suspense is killing me!" Dad smiled back at both of them.

"Here goes!" Her pulse raced...unsure how he would respond.

"Do you remember the night Isabella came by the firm...while you were out of town? I had a little too much *fun* and – Jackson had to pick me up?" She knew he would remember the night.

"Yes, of course, I remember it well. What about it?" Dad clasped his hands together and leaned forward interested to hear more.

Allison proceeded to share what Jackson saw and how he had been afraid to say anything since he wasn't sure if he'd seen anything of importance.

"Well, I be damned! I can't believe she would stoop that low. How dare her!" Dad jabbed his finger down on the desk. "I should have known she was up to something!"

"Well, we don't really know if anything happened. Jackson didn't actually *see* her doing anything. He said she seemed very startled and was standing by the same cabinet where I stored the tests." Allison wanted to be sure Tucker heard her correctly.

"Yeah, I hear what you're saying...but it's too coincidental. She didn't *hang* around that day to befriend you, Allison. She doesn't have any friends, nor does she want them. She's all about herself. Period."

Dad grabbed his coat. "I'm going to get to the bottom of this. Her wrath on this town ends...today."

Chapter Fifty

Nowhere to Hide

I bounced between the lake house and Isabella's attempting to avoid everyone. She had worked late nights at the local hospital filling in for other physicians who were on vacation. Therefore, she wasn't home much.

I had the place to myself - no one to tell me how I was doing everything wrong – no one confiding in me or asking me for help – no one but myself to worry about - and it felt good.

I stole a pack of cigarettes from Tennie's house while she was preoccupied, and I found Dad's bottle of whiskey he 'secretly' stored under the cabinet for 'special events'.

I think this certainly calls for a celebration.

I turned the crank on my bay window inviting the hot summer night air to infiltrate my room. It had been a while since I sat here and wrote in my journal. But, I wasn't writing tonight. I had other plans.

I wanted to drown out everything. My life had turned into a huge ball of chaos.

I opened the bottle of whiskey and downed a sip.

Gross. How does anyone drink this?

I lit a cigarette. Sitting near the window with the bottle wedged between my legs, I listened to the choir of crickets chirping. Each sip of the whiskey began to taste better...or maybe I just couldn't taste it anymore?

It might have been the six cigarettes I smoked within a few hours, or maybe the half bottle of whiskey I drank...but I'd become lightheaded, and my vision wasn't clear. I braced myself against the wall and that's the last thing I remember.

***

"I'm leaving town in a few weeks. I just wanted to let you and your mom know. Ya'll have both been so supportive." Whitney stood at the foot of Beau's bed. "Have you seen her today?"

"No, not today. So, you decided to move to Texas with her?" Beau's emotions were running wild since Charlotte's visit, and he planned to tell her about Isabella, but he was shocked she was moving away from Sedipar with a woman she just met weeks ago.

"It just feels like the right thing to do. With everything crashing around me here...I just need a change. I need to get out of Sedipar." Whitney's defeat was evident.

"Nothing is 'crashing' around you, Whitney. I don't think leaving is going to fix things. In fact, I know it's not. I get that Charlene needs you, but you have friends here...a life...what about all of us?" Beau grabbed his football and tossed it in the air. "You just met her. You don't know much about her other than she deserted you. Why would you move away from your friends and family who have been here for you?"

"I lost my best friend. She won't even look at me anymore. I've made my parents angry since I chose Charlene. I can't win. Your mom has been the *only* positive thing in my life – besides your friendship." Whitney watched each rotation of the football. "I know I don't know much about Charlene, but my heart longs to get to know her better while I have the chance."

Beau continued to toss the football in the air.

"You really love that sport, don't you?" she said smiling.

"Yeah, it's kinda been my life." He threw the football on the floor. "But that's over at least for this year."

Beau stood up from the bed and stretched. "I get it. But, I still don't think leaving is the answer."

Whitney sighed.

"I do need to tell you something about my mom." Whitney watched Beau as he paced the floor.

"For starters, Charlotte doesn't hate you...she's not even mad at you." Beau still had trouble believing what Charlotte told him...but he knew she wouldn't lie. "Whitney, Mom has been manipulating this whole thing. She's the reason Charlotte is...well was...mad at you."

Whitney tilted her head and shrugged. "I don't understand. How has your mom manipulated us?"

"Charlotte told me everything. The way Mom talks to her...the way she's treated her...and how she told Charlotte that you slept here the other night--which you did--but that we were a 'thing' and were getting closer. Mom's the one driving the wedge between the three of us." Beau slapped the wall. "I asked you if Mom seemed weird to you the other day. She's been plotting all along...against me and Charlotte."

Whitney stared down at the floor. "I...I haven't noticed that she's been different. I don't know what to think. Your mom hasn't been the nicest toward Charlotte, but do you really think she's capable of stooping so low as to purposefully break ya'll up?"

"It's hard to swallow...I know...but I'm going to find out...from the source." Beau was eager to confront Isabella about everything.

***

"Nessie...Nessie...wake up!" I faintly heard my name and felt vigorous shakes on my arm. "Wake up, now, Nessie!"

As I came to, Dad was standing over me.

"Thank goodness, you're awake." I watched as Dad leaned over me and shut the bay windows. "I've been looking all over for you. I left work early today, and you weren't at the lake house. I figured you were here since Isabella is working at the hospital. You've let half the mosquitoes in Sedipar into your room. What on earth were you thinking!?" Dad was furious.

I felt groggy...and his voice seemed to echo like he was talking through a tunnel.

"What's going on?" He pulled the curtain back near the baseboard and found the bottle. "Ah, I see...you had a little party last night."

I buried my face in my hands and looked away from him.

"Nessie! Explain yourself! You don't get to look away and not say anything." Dad demanded a response from me. I knew he wasn't backing down.

Last night was so perfect. Besides the mosquito bites that plagued me from leaving the window open all night, it was nice being alone and zoning out. Waking up to Dad yelling at me demanding answers coupled with feeling groggy...not so fun.

Agitated, he threw the pack of cigarettes at me. "These yours?"

"I guess so." I didn't look at him when I responded.

"Nessie, how many times have I told you how dangerous these are for your health? I know I've shared the dangers of nicotine with both you and Beau. What has gotten into you?" Dad crossed his arms becoming impatient for answers.

"Well? Do you have anything to say for yourself?" he asked.

"I don't know what you want me to say. Yes, I smoked those cigarettes. I'm the only one here to smoke them, *right*? And yes, I drank your whiskey, Dad. There...is that so terrible? I sat here alone and had a few drinks and smoked a few cigarettes." My tone was dry. There wasn't much emotion left. I didn't care if he was disappointed in me.

"Well, yes, it's terrible. You smoked a half a pack of cigarettes and drank my whiskey. You're fifteen!" Dad gripped his hands on my desk chair and continued. "I'm getting you some help."

Dad grabbed my arms. "No more of this."

I was exhausted...my body limp...between the 'high' I got from the cigarettes coupled with the liquor...I was still drunk. I couldn't fight him.

***

Jackson was more than angry that Allison told Kent he had seen Isabella near the file cabinets and startled her.

It was inevitable Charlotte was going to hear about it soon, and she would pull away from him. He planned to visit Beau and tell him how he felt about Charlotte.

Beau was surprised to see Jackson walk into the room. "Where've you been? I haven't seen you since the accident."

Jackson felt uncomfortable immediately knowing he hadn't been the best friend to Beau.

"Sorry, Coach has us practicing a lot lately – getting ready for the fall." Jackson shook his head. "I'm sorry. I shouldn't talk about football. My bad."

"It's fine. Really. I've had a lot of time to think in here, and I'm okay with it. Besides, that gives me more time with Charlotte." Beau watched Jackson's face as his eyes darted across the room.

"I know you say you're okay with it, but we miss you on the field. It just isn't the same." Jackson's head hung low staring at the floor knowing he was lying.

"Blaine said you're doing a good job in my place. I knew you would step right in and get the job done. Happy for you man!" Beau wasn't really happy about it, but he attempted to make Jackson comfortable.

"Thanks, that means a lot coming from you." Jackson avoided eye contact with Beau.

The room became awkwardly silent.

Beau reached for the tv remote searching for a distraction when Jackson finally spoke.

"Look, I wanted to come by and check on you. Things are different now. On the field, I finally feel like I mean something to the team besides just sitting on the sidelines. I'm sorry this happened to you, Beau. I don't mean to sound like I'm not. It's just...it feels so good to be on that field." Jackson realized he sounded selfish.

Beau breathed deeply attempting to frame his response. He couldn't believe how cold and selfish Jackson was being. "That's great, man. Glad to hear you're happy." Beau laughed to himself and continued. "You know, I really don't care anymore. All I want is for me and Charlotte to be together. Spending time with her is all that matters to me. You can have the quarterback spot."

Jackson rubbed the back of his neck. Hearing Charlotte's name made him feel uncomfortable. He didn't respond.

"You surprised or something – to hear me say that?" Beau questioned him.

"Oh, no, I'm not. It's just...everyone has been wondering about where it goes. You know...since the paternity test." Jackson felt Beau's focus center on him.

"Man...you're really something. I'm not sure I can keep swallowing the crap you keep throwing at me." He was engulfed with rage. "You come in here, a month and a half after the accident, and give me pity for you having to ride the bench. On top of that, you throw being quarterback in my face – knowing what I've been through. I thought we were better friends than that, Jackson."

Jackson remained quiet, trying to focus on anything other than Beau.

"You can't even look at me. Why did you really come by? I know you didn't waste your time coming by to check on me or tell me how much you love football." Beau stood in front of Jackson demanding an answer.

Jackson shrugged, biting his lip, and responded, "I'm here because I love Charlotte. I've always had a thing for her Beau --but like usual--you got the girl...you got quarterback. You always get it all."

Beau clenched his fist, his breaths becoming more rapid hearing the words 'I love Charlotte'. "What in the hell did you just say!?"

"You heard me." Jackson didn't back away. "I said I've always wanted to get closer to her...and lately I've been able to. And I think she enjoys me being around."

Jackson waited, as Beau, now inches away from him, pushed him into the wall. "She enjoys being around *you*. What in the hell does that mean?" Beau began to realize what Blaine had told him was true. "I heard you were trying to get closer to her...easy enough, huh, when I'm laid up here in this room. I didn't believe it. I thought you were a better friend. Get out of my room before I do something I'm gonna regret."

Jackson moved away from the wall and turned before leaving and said, "She kissed me, you know. Twice. I think the feeling might be mutual."

Beau picked up the football from his bed and fired it at the door. "I'm sure she really enjoyed it, asshole. I'll find out if she did."

***

I woke up once Dad put me in the backseat of the car. "Where are we going?"

"You'll see when we get there. Sleep this one off." Dad focused on the road ahead.

I faded in and out and noticed we had stopped at Callaway's. I wanted some water so bad. I fumbled to find the door handle and the door slightly opened – then Dad shut it. "Buckle up, Nessie. Here's you a Gatorade."

The drive to wherever we were going was horrible. My headache embraced the quiet, however I knew the quiet wasn't good. I felt myself dozing off again as the sunlight pierced my face through the window. That's when Dad decided to talk.

"I saw Owen in the pharmacy. He was helping at the checkout." Dad's eyes locked with mine as he continued. "He said he hasn't seen you in a while...that you've been avoiding him."

I didn't have the energy to defend myself nor to explain why I'd been so distant with Owen.

Dad didn't care if I responded. He rambled on about how Owen was my best friend. And how could I give that up so easily for such trash like Tennie Adams...now I'm wasting my life away with bad habits I learned from them.

Yeah...yeah...yeah.

I never responded. About thirty minutes later, we pulled into a gravel drive. I picked my head up from the seat and read the sign attached to the open gate, A Brighter Day Ahead.

"No, Dad...are you serious? A rehab facility!?" My mouth hung open, and I froze in the seat. "No way! I'm not going in there. Take me home!"

"You don't have a choice. I already gave you two chances. You're on a bad path. This is going to be your home for a few weeks." Dad pulled into the circle drive and met the clinical staff at the front of the car.

I watched the staff nod as Dad talked and they smiled my way as I sat in the car. I looked away not making eye contact.

I saw them start walking over to the car.

He's really doing this...he's gonna leave me here.

When they opened the door, one of the staff members grabbed my arm.

"No way! I'm not getting out of this car! I'm fine...I can fix this. Dad! I can fix it myself. I don't want to stay here! Please...please...don't leave me here!" I begged and pleaded – tears streaming down my face – for Dad to save me.

He couldn't look at me.

As I entered the sliding doors, I peeked over my shoulder and watched him drive away.

***

"Nessie, I didn't know you were..." Isabella rounded the corner surprised to see Dad.

"What in the hell are you doing here? I thought you were Nessie." Isabella leaned against the kitchen counter.

"There are some things we need to talk about, Isabella. Maybe you should sit down." He motioned for her to move to the living room. She didn't budge.

"Since when do you care about me? I'm perfectly fine right here." She crossed her arms over her chest glaring back at Dad.

"Nessie isn't here, by the way. I've been worried about her lately." Dad proceeded to walk through the last week, explaining my behavior, the drinking bouts, Tennie, and Brice, and the icing on the cake -- taking me to rehab.

"You didn't tell me any of this when it happened!? How dare you! You challenged me when I made a decision for Beau without you and made me look like a fool in front of my staff at the hospital. And you do the same thing with our daughter!" Isabella turned away.

"Yes, you're right. I didn't tell you. But I'm telling you now. If you could have seen her this morning...she was in bad shape. She's headed down a bad road. I had to stop it." Dad sat on a bar stool across from her.

Isabella attempted to walk away when Dad stopped her. "Oh, there's more. There's a lot more. So, don't run off."

Isabella's brow raised as she walked back toward the counter facing Dad. "Well?"

"It's time I call your bluff on everything, Isabella. You've had your 'glory days' of winning. That's over now. I hold the cards, and you've lost the game." Dad smirked thinking how good it felt to see her squirm.

"What on earth are you talking about, Tucker? My *'glory days'*?" Isabella chuckled. "You've lost your mind!"

"No, not quite, but you lost your hand big time in this *game* you've been playing." Dad continued on. "I'm not going to dance around it. I don't owe you anything. I know what happened with the paternity tests. Just admit what you did."

She froze at the mention of the words *paternity test*. "Excuse me! What do you mean by that!?"

"Now isn't the time to play dumb with me. I know you did something with them. Just spit it out." Dad tapped his fingers on the table – he knew that annoyed her.

"Would you stop it already!!" she snapped. "I have no idea what you're talking about, Tucker. You come into *my house* and accuse *me* of tampering with the..."

"For starters, let's be clear...it's my house. And...tampering? I didn't say tampering, Isabella. I said I knew what 'happened' with them. Can you tell me more about it though?" Dad's eyebrows raised and he smiled. "And you were saying..."

Isabella groaned. "Ugh, you're a fool! You think you can turn on your special 'attorney charm' with me? I have nothing to say to you."

"What do you think about your license being revoked for tampering with confidential medical results?" He grinned knowing that would get her attention.

"You wouldn't...that's low!" Her eyes were cold and narrowed on him.

"Not as low as you - tampering with your own son's life...my life...Mason's life...his girlfriend's life! What in the hell were you thinking!?" His stare fixated on her.

She couldn't look him in the eye. "What do you want?"

"I want you to admit you did this! And you know I want the house. I want you to leave – preferably soon. I've signed over my part of the clinic to you. You can sell it and move for all I care. I just want you out. You're nothing but poison to this family and this town." Dad could have continued, but he knew it would fall on deaf ears.

She sat in silence. Her hands cupped her face as if she were crying – Dad knew better.

She quickly became enraged thinking about Jackson's visit to the clinic the other day. "That damn Beale boy! He started this didn't he!?"

"No, he didn't. *You* did all of this." Dad anticipated she would implicate others.

"He thinks he saw something...he didn't see anything." Isabella's cold stare didn't stop Dad from responding.

"Oh, he saw enough! We put the missing pieces together. Just admit it, Isabella! You switched the kits!" Dad yelled.

Isabella knew he was not going to be convinced. She certainly could not afford to lose her license to practice. "Fine. It's yours. Give me a few weeks to get settled somewhere else. I do have one other request or the deal is off." Her eyes met his and she continued, "Beau can never know that it was me. I couldn't live with it."

"That's insane, Isabella! I have to tell him what happened otherwise we don't have a leg to stand on for the second paternity test. You know how it works." He wasn't surprised she asked to keep it between them.

"Then, the deal's off. I'm not moving out of here. This house is as much mine as it's yours." She attempted to stand firm, but she knew he held the cards.

"That doesn't matter. Once the news gets out that you tampered with the tests, your license will be revoked to practice medicine, you won't have a job. Would you like me to continue?" Dad was enjoying this – revenge was sweet.

"What an asshole you've become! You would really do that to me?" she questioned.

"Are you kidding? Have you forgotten that you slept with my best friend in high school, kept it from me all these years, lied about Beau not being my son – made me feel sorry for you as if Mason forced himself on you..." Dad shook his head and laughed. "You're not going to find pity from me, Isabella. I'm washing my hands of you, for good."

"*Okay...okay!!* I get it. I'm a terrible person. *Whatever!* I'll move out. You can have the house. But you *cannot* let this get out. I made a terrible mistake. That Callaway girl is not right for my Beau...our Beau. I was simply trying to protect him." She shrugged, walked closer to Dad, and reached for his hand.

"No, we're not doing this. I'm not here to comfort you. Beau will find out – he has to – the second paternity test has been scheduled. We were waiting for him to get out of therapy. Now with this news, it's a moot point, but we'll need to prove the first results were wrong. I can't believe you stooped so low...however, I'm really not surprised. And 'that Callaway girl' has a name you know-- it's Charlotte." Dad backed away from her.

"Mason is an evil man...you know that, Tucker. He lied to you as well. I'll never accept *her* as family. It won't happen." She sighed, reluctantly admitting defeat. "Do what you feel you need to. I'll figure things out. I always do."

"Yeah, that's what I'm afraid of," Dad said as he slammed the door.

Chapter Fifty-One

Exposing the Truth

"I've called several times, and no one is answering. Tennie, I'm worried about her." Brice paced the floor of their living room.

"I'm sure she's fine. Besides, why are you worried? I thought you washed your hands of her?" Tennie noticed Brice's stare. "Well, at least it sure sounded like you did the other day when she bolted up outta here," she said as she finished washing the dishes.

"Yeah, I just don't like seeing her that way. She's better than that." Brice sighed. "By the way, why in the hell did you tell her about the detention center?"

Tennie smirked. "She told you! I knew she would call you out on it!"

"It's not funny, Tennie. You think people are puppets that you can pull strings and manipulate. Besides, it wasn't your place to tell her."

"She would've found out eventually." Tennie jabbed. "You didn't plan to tell her because you didn't want her to judge you."

"Whatever! Nessie isn't like that. I did plan to tell her – just not on our first date!" Brice looked at Tennie daring her to say anything else.

"She's not any better than us! You know that." Tennie threw the dishtowel at him and rolled her eyes. "You put her up on a pedestal just because she's a Corbin. She's not innocent in this either by any means. She made those choices. Maybe she's fed up with being so 'straight and narrow'. She may not want to change."

Brice shook his head. "Nah, Nessie's not like that. She's had a lot going on lately with Beau, her mom and dad – I was so hard on her. I have to find her." Brice grabbed his keys and ran out of the door.

"Where's he going in such a hurry?" Trisha asked as she stumbled down the hall in her nightgown.

"Nowhere, Mom. I'm working a double today at The Dixie. I'll be home late. Don't wait up for me." Tennie laughed to herself knowing Trisha waiting for her was a joke. She slammed the door.

***

"Look, Beau, this is going to be difficult to hear. I'm sorry I'm the one having to tell you this, but..." Tucker sat across the room from Beau struggling with the right words to tell him that his mother was the root cause of most of his anguish.

Beau stared back waiting for him to explain.

"I just...I thought it would be easier to tell you this, but it's very difficult." Dad rubbed his chin. "There's just no easy way to say it."

"Dad, just say it! C'mon, already! After everything I've been through over the last month or so, just tell me! I can handle it." The pitch in Beau's voice raised slightly.

"It's your mother, Beau." Dad shook his head. "She's been the one..."

"Dad, I know already." Beau cut him off.

Dad stared at Beau confused. "What...how do you.... Did she come by here?" Beau had piqued his curiosity.

No, she didn't come by. Charlotte told me everything the other day."

"Charlotte told me how Mom has been treating her. She's been manipulating us this entire time. It was hard for me to believe Mom could be so cruel, but I trust Charlotte...she's telling the truth. Mom hurt her."

Beau swallowed the lump in his throat and continued. "Charlotte tried to come by and see me...several times. She wanted to see me and all this time Mom kept pushing her away." Beau felt tension build within him just thinking about it.

"Oh...wow...yeah, I'm sorry. I'm sorry for Charlotte. She's a sweet girl. Is she okay?" Dad was somewhat relieved that Beau was aware of how Isabella felt about Charlotte...but he had more to share.

"I guess...I mean...Mom was pretty ruthless to her. I'm trying to convince Charlotte it doesn't matter what Mom thinks. I wanted her here." Beau sighed.

"I'm glad you and Charlotte were able to talk. I know you both care about each other, a lot." Dad smiled.

"Son, while that was part of why I'm here...unfortunately there's more." He stood and walked toward the window and faced the outside. "It looks like we have to get that second test after all. It appears we have cause to support the second test. I found out the tests were left unsupervised for a period of time."

Beau stood up from the bed and approached Dad. "I thought we had already planned to go when I get out of here?"

Dad shook his head in agreement and turned to face Beau. "We did and we will. However, we didn't have much of a leg to stand on in court. Now, we do."

Beau was confused. "I don't understand. What happened?"

Dad placed his hand on Beau's shoulder. "You may want to sit down for this one."

Just as he was about to reveal the truth to Beau, Isabella appeared at the door. Her face was long, and it was obvious she'd been crying. Dad sighed...head hanging low...and looked back at Beau, who hadn't noticed her standing by the door.

"The test kits were stored in my filing cabinet in my office. Allison kept them secure for the majority of the day, however, she mistakenly left the cabinet unlocked. The janitorial service was in the building unsupervised as usual – restocking supplies and cleaning the restrooms – dumping trash bins in offices etc. Since the office was unsupervised for a few hours coupled with the fact that the cabinet was left unlocked...it's a bit of a stretch...but I think we have a case to discount the first test or at least challenge it." His jaw tightened at the disgust he felt for caving. Again.

"Dad! That's the best news I've heard lately! Why do you look sad? Did I miss something?" Beau hoped there wasn't more news that might diffuse his happiness.

"No, you didn't miss anything. It's great news!" Dad smiled and nodded once to Isabella still leaning against the wall.

"When I get outta here, that's the first place we're stopping." Beau clapped his hands fiercely and smiled. "Finally! Something positive!" As he turned back toward the door, he saw Isabella staring back at him.

"Well, it *was* positive for a minute. What do *you* want?" Beau asked dryly.

"I need some time with you, Beau...to explain." Isabella's tone was soft and low as she waited for his response.

"Yeah, Mom, I've been waiting to hear your side of all of this. And, don't lie to me. I'm tired of the games." He stared coldly back at her.

***

Rehab was terrible.

No incoming calls...no outgoing calls. The food was subpar...concrete walls...stupid gowns. Therapists working to 'make you better'--withdrawals from my 'normal life'. And most of all, I missed Brice terribly.

I fumbled with the patient bracelet that adorned my wrist. *How in the world did I end up here?*

I certainly didn't belong amongst the raging alcoholics and drug abusers. I kept repeating this to myself as I watched several patients battle with withdrawal as their bodies responded with tremors and seizures. How could something that once provided amazing peace turn against you so cruelly?

Rehab provided me with a lot of time to think – since I was alone- with the exception of my counselor. I longed to feel the same peace, independence, freedom--again. It was not the same solace when four walls constantly crash around you 24/7.

The counselor assigned to my case didn't cut me any slack. The more I longed for that feeling of belonging to something that didn't suffocate me, she denied me steps forward.

"How long do I have to be in here?" I'd become demanding and belligerent.

"However long it takes for you to realize that you're sick and you need and want help. 'Want' is the main one. And when it clicks. It will just click." My counselor was dry and matter of fact...just like Isabella. *Ironic, right?* That made me despise her even more.

"You may not think you have an addiction, but using starts in the very spot you're in right now – using occasionally turns into a desire you can't turn off." She paused waiting for me to comment.

I rolled my eyes.

She continued. "Do you know we found traces of THC in your blood sample? Do you want to tell me about it?"

My silence didn't bother her.

I didn't respond. I was angry. I knew I needed to put out more effort and comply – in order for me to leave this dreadful place. Once again I found myself travelling down a path of conformity...and it made me nauseated.

My counseling sessions typically ended with me attempting to tell my counselor what she wanted to hear, but she read me right off the bat. "Try again tomorrow, Nessie. You're not fooling me today," she'd say as she stared writing on her stupid notepad, never making eye contact with me. "I've seen it and heard it all. You can do this...you just have to tell yourself you can."

Eye roll.

As I walked back to my room, I thought about Brice. I needed his touch more than anything. If there were anything that would persuade me to acknowledge my 'sickness' and move forward, it would be him.

I have to get out of this place.

***

"I'm going to let you two have the room," Dad said with a half grin toward Beau.

"Thanks. You don't have to leave, though. I want you to stay." Beau pleaded for him to remain in the room for support.

"I would, but I think your Mother needs some time alone with you. I think it would be good. I'm going to grab some lunch at The Dixie for us." Dad walked by Isabella without making eye contact.

She tugged on his arm and attempted to pull him closer to her.

He shrugged her off. "No, don't even. I said what needed to be said." Dad kept walking.

"Thank you, Tucker. I don't know what to say..." Isabella's tone was lighter and softer than it had been in a long time.

"Nothing...don't say anything. Just talk to him." Dad replied.

Isabella approached Beau to hug him, and he backed away.

"No, Mom. You don't get to do that. I have so many questions for you, and you aren't leaving this room until you answer them." He was angry, and she struggled to look him in the eye. "No more games. I know what you've done. I can't believe you would stoop so low."

"Now, Beau, not everything is as it seems. Please give me a chance to explain!" She pleaded for him to listen, but he ignored her. She sat poised in the chair across from his bed.

"Charlotte didn't do anything to you. All she did was love me. She actually cares about me, and I care about her - more than anyone else in this world. I love her. You were so cruel to her and to me--keeping her away when I needed her the most." Beau breathed in deeply and stood over her.

"Can I say something, please?" Isabella looked up at him towering over her. "I admit I was a little *strong* in my approach with Charlotte. However, I think she has blown this somewhat out of proportion. I wouldn't say I was *cruel* toward her by any means. That sounds so awful." Isabella lightly laughed and shook her head in denial.

"I want to protect you. That has always been my job as a mother to protect you. You may not see it now, but she's not good for you. And no matter how hard you try to convince me, I'll never see it. She's a Callaway, and well they just aren't good people."

Beau sat down on the bed in front of her and replied, "Mom, I don't care if you like Charlotte or not. We're going to be together. You don't have a say in this. You never did before...but you tried to keep us apart and took advantage of me being in the hospital. I don't even know who you are anymore. Who would do something like that...to their own son?"

Isabella sat quietly and crossed her arms. Their eyes locked for a moment, and she responded, "A mother that cares about her son and wants only the best for him. Charlotte Callaway isn't the best for you. Besides, you can't be together anyway for goodness' sake. You're related!"

"Well, that's where you're wrong!" Beau stood up from the bed. "How long were you standing at the door when Dad was here? Did you hear what Dad said about the second test?" Beau asked.

"No, honey, I didn't." Isabella feared where this was going, however, she was relieved that Dad didn't expose the truth about her tampering with the kits.

"I'm doing it to prove that Mason is not my dad. And, we have proof we can take to court that will make the first results null. If we can make the court agree there was a moment of time the kits were discoverable – in this case, the janitors were unsupervised – then we might have a leg to stand on." Beau watched as Isabella's lips pressed together and she rolled her eyes.

Beau continued, "Mom, you don't have to like Charlotte, but you aren't going to stand in my way anymore. We'll be together, and you can make the choice of being a part of my life, which includes Charlotte, or not."

Isabella stood up quietly and gently caressed Beau's cheek. With a half grin she replied, "I just can't allow it...not a Callaway...being part of my family."

As she neared the door, Beau shouted firmly, "That's your choice, Mom. Honestly, you don't have much family left!"

***

"Quit moping around, Brice. She obviously lost interest. Just let her go." Tennie doodled on the receipt booklet while leaning on the order counter at The Dixie.

"I didn't ask your opinion. I just want my po-boy so I can get outta here." Brice was getting annoyed with Tennie. "It's funny though...one day Nessie is your best friend...and the next she's not worth the words."

Tennie laughed. "Really...that's funny to you? You know I don't have friends, Brice. It was kinda cool to watch her let go and express herself. But, eh, she's really not someone I would choose to hang around in the end."

Brice shook his head. "I knew that. I told Nessie not to get sucked into your 'world'. Obviously, she didn't listen to me."

Tennie quickly turned around at the sound of the words, 'Order up!'. "Here's your po-boy. Take your food and mope somewhere else!"

As Brice walked away from the order window, he crossed paths with Dad.

"Mr. Corbin," Brice nodded at him and quickly looked away.

Dad acknowledged him with a slight nod and kept walking to the order counter.

Brice kept walking and sat on one of the benches to eat.

Tennie screamed the order into the microphone as Dad walked back toward Brice.

"You mind if I take a seat?" Dad motioned to sit across from Brice on the worn wooden picnic table bench.

"No, sir." He finished swallowing the bite of his po-boy and wiped his face.

Dad leaned across the table and asked, "You heard from Nessie lately?"

"No sir, I haven't." Brice dodged his stare.

"You know I do this thing for a living? So I can tell when someone is either lying or keeping something important from me?" Dad made steady eye contact.

Brice's palms became sweaty. He threw his napkin to cover his food. Dad made him nervous.

"Sir, look, the other night...I didn't know she was at--" Brice was sure he was going to curse him for Nessie staying over at his place.

"That has nothing to do with you, son. Well...outside of leaving her in the middle of the road...but I get it. Nessie is smart. She can make decisions for herself. She made a very bad decision that night." Dad sighed as his fingers splayed covering his eyes. "That night doesn't top what I know happened the following days."

Brice's pulse began to race.

Brice suddenly became overwhelmed with anxiety fearing Dad would interrogate him until he caved.

"I don't understand what's with you kids today - drinking, smoking, and cutting up all hours of the night. Back in the day..." he shook his head and stopped talking. "I guess I shouldn't compare it, should I?"

Brice remained still. His lunch had become cold. The sweat from his palms made imprints on the top of the wooden table.

"Order up, Corbin!" Tennie yelled from the window.

"See you later, son. And, I knew you hadn't heard from Nessie. I was testing you. I appreciate the truth. Anyway, she hit rock bottom. She's in a rehab facility a few towns away. She needed some help." Dad tapped the corner of the picnic table and walked away.

Brice's head fell down into his hands. *"Rehab!? Dammit, Nessie. What have you done now!?"*

Chapter Fifty-Two

Shattered Secrets

"Owen! Can you get the door?" Charlotte yelled from her upstairs bedroom.

Owen reluctantly got up from the couch. His eyes remained fixated on the television hoping not to miss the part of the show he'd been waiting for.

"Yeah, I got it. At your service Queen Charlotte!"

"Haha, Owen, very funny. Just get the door. It's probably Jackson." Charlotte finished putting the final touches on her makeup.

She was going to use tonight to tell Jackson that she and Beau had talked and intended to be together if at all possible.

"Hey Owen. What's been up?" Jackson attempted the cool football handshake and remembered that didn't work with Owen.

"Hey," Owen responded as he rushed back into the living room.

As Charlotte proceeded down the stairs, Jackson commented, "You look great!" He smiled and extended his hand to grab hers.

She smiled back. "Thanks, Jackson, that's sweet," and reached for her purse avoiding his hand. "Let's go! I'm starving!"

***

As Jackson and Charlotte pulled out of the driveway, the phone rang. "Ugh, can I just have ten minutes to finish this show!" Owen ran to grab the corded phone on the side table. "Hello?"

"Hey, Owen. It's Beau. Is Charlotte there?" Owen put the handset against his shoulder. "No, she's not here."

"Do you know when she'll be back?" Beau questioned. "I really need to talk to her. If she's at Stella's then I'll just call there."

"No, I don't know any of that…not sure when she'll be back. I can tell her when she gets home." Owen didn't want to lie. He decided to tell Beau where she was. "She just left with Jackson going somewhere."

The phone went silent and a few seconds later all Owen heard was a dial tone.

***

"I've missed this place!" Charlene wandered around AELs reminiscing. "We always sat back there in the corner. What a fun time in life!"

"Well, it looks like it's ours today," Trisha said as she plopped down in a chair. "I'm exhausted and need some breakfast."

"How are you two ladies this morning?" the waitress asked as she watched the dining floor fill up with more customers.

"The usual…I'll have the usual." Trisha muttered with a smile.

"I'll have the same then!" Charlene handed the menus back to the waitress. "Goodness, this place is still hopping like the good ole' days, isn't it?"

"Sure is! Nowhere else beats the good ole' home-cookin!" Trisha reached for a cigarette in her purse. The pack was empty. "Shit...I'm out."

"You know you should lay off of those. They're not good for your health." Charlene took a sip of her coffee and waited for Trisha's snarky response.

"I know...I know...you sound like Brice. He's always looking out for me." As Trisha glanced around the dining area she locked eyes with Isabella as she walked toward the cashier.

"Dr. Corbin!" Trisha waved Isabella over to their table. "You got a minute?"

"Good morning," Isabella's poise intimidated Charlene. Actually, everything about her intimidated Charlene – since high school.

"Charlene...I haven't seen you in years. I heard you were back in town." Isabella's response was flat and emotionless while standing with her arms crossed.

"Yes. I made it back here after all this time. It's so good to be back home." Charlene's fingers traced the rim of her coffee mug avoiding eye contact.

"You called me over for something, Trisha?" Isabella's eyes focused on the clock on the wall. "I need to get back to the clinic."

"Oh, yes, I did. I'm not sure if you've heard, but Charlene came back to town because she's...well...sick." Trisha grabbed Charlene's hand and squeezed it.

Charlene took a deep breath in and her eyes widened.

"Trisha, I know you care, but Dr. Corbin is extremely busy. She doesn't need to worry herself with me." Charlene caught Isabella's eyes narrowing on her.

Isabella knew Charlene was sick and dying. She couldn't resist probing. "Well, what exactly is going on with you?"

Charlene glared at Trisha and responded. "I have stage four cancer. I have a few months left to live."

Isabella nodded. "I assume you have exhausted all avenues for treatment?"

"Yes...yes, I have. There's nothing anyone can do at this point. Trisha knows that." Charlene squeezed Trisha's hand. "She's just being a good friend--hopeful for a different outcome."

"Dr. Corbin, you know so many wonderful doctors. Is there anyone you would recommend for a second opinion?" Trisha ignored Charlene and continued. "I'm just asking for a second opinion."

Isabella glanced back at the clock. "I'm sorry, but I've got patients waiting for me. Let me check with a few of my colleagues, and I'll let you know something soon. A second opinion is always worth pursuing."

As they watched Isabella leave, Charlene sat back in her chair and released Trisha's hold on her hand. "Goodness, Trisha, you should've just let it go."

"What on earth do you mean by that? Why would you want to let it go?" Trisha noticed Charlene had become agitated.

"It's nothing. Thank you. Thank you for being such a good friend." Charlene leaned closer to Trisha and smiled. "I just don't think a second opinion is a good idea. I'm tired Trisha. I just can't do this much longer."

"That's exactly why you need a second opinion. There must be alternatives for you to consider--to prolong your time here with us. I'm not letting you ignore any opportunities Isabella comes up with. If anyone can get you answers and help--she can!"

Trisha noticed Charlene had become distant and quiet. "Did I say something wrong?"

Charlene knew Trisha would be persistent. "You didn't say anything that a true friend wouldn't say. You've always been like family to me. I don't know how or why I deserve you as a friend."

"Well of course I care. We've been through so much together. You just seem disinterested in allowing Isabella to help."

Charlene's eyes darted around the dining area hopelessly seeking an escape.

"Charlene, I've known you for way too long. What in the hell is going on? Tell me!" Trisha was becoming annoyed.

"I can't do this anymore." Charlene burst into tears. "I don't know where to even start."

The waitress attempted to come over to their table, and Trisha motioned her away.

"Oh, Charlene, what's going on? You know you can tell me anything." Trisha moved closer, placing her arm around her. "I'm here for you. I can help you...but I have to know what's going on."

Charlene's lips trembled as she attempted to respond. "I'm just exhausted, Trisha."

"I'm sure you are. Your body has been through so much."

Charlene looked at Trisha. "That's not what I meant. I'm exhausted from all the lies. I can't do it anymore."

Trisha was confused.

"I'm not sick, Trisha. I'm not dying of cancer. I've lost everything--my job, home, and now my family--the only family I ever had that cared about me." Charlene's face flooded with tears.

"You mean...you...lied to all of us? You're not sick? But you said you wanted to meet Whitney before you..." An inferno of rage was building inside Trisha, however, she refrained from lashing out.

"Yes, I did. None of it was true. I didn't have anywhere else to go. I thought Aunt Barbara and Uncle Carl might offer to take me in if

I persisted in taking Whitney back to live with me." Charlene stared back at the floor. "I never dreamt Aunt Barbara would be so cold. I guess I deserved it."

Trisha sat back in her chair with a look of disgust. "How dare you! How dare you come back into our lives and lie about something so serious. Dammit, Charlene...I thought you were dying!"

"I know, and I'm truly sorry. I didn't know what else to do. I feel horrible about it." Charlene tried to apologize, but Trisha cut her off.

"You should feel horrible. What a terrible thing to do! Especially to your friends and family and to Whitney. I know I'm not the perfect mom by any means, but I would never lie about something like that." Trisha shook her head in disbelief.

"All I can say is that I'm sorry. I know I've made a mess of everything." Charlene pushed away from the table. "I need to let Whitney know. I've probably lost her forever."

***

Jackson pulled into The Dixie and parked near the back of the parking lot.

Charlotte looked around to see who was hanging out. Whitney and Stella were sitting under the pavilion of The Dixie.

"Let's go. You know, I'm not really hungry anymore. Let's do something else." Charlotte smiled.

"I thought you were starving," Jackson casually responded.

Charlotte glanced over his shoulder and saw Whitney walking closer to his Jeep. "Never mind, it's ok. We can stay. Just forget I said anything."

Jackson smirked, "Good, because all that talk about being hungry has my stomach growling wanting food!" As he opened the door to his Jeep, he saw Whitney approaching from behind.

Ah, that's why she wanted to leave.

The moment Charlotte saw Whitney approaching her, she became more irritated.

Whitney tapped on the window lightly. "Hey, Char, we need to talk. I can't keep doing this."

Charlotte rolled down the window continuing to stare blankly ahead. "It's not a good time, Whit."

Whitney didn't back away. She placed her hands on the frame of the door and continued, "I don't care if it's not a good time. We need to talk. You're my best friend. We can't keep ignoring each other like this."

Charlotte missed their talks--their friendship. She needed her best friend now more than ever.

"Jackson, will you order our food? I just need a minute alone," Charlotte quickly asked Jackson and then turned back to Whitney. "This isn't what it looks like...I mean...Jackson and me."

Whitney backed away from the door. "That's completely your business."

Charlotte snapped, "But there's no *business!* We're just friends. End of story."

"Okay, *okayyy,* I didn't mean anything by that. I just meant that...Char...this has gotten weird. We can't talk and be normal...like we used to. I hate the wall between us. Besides, I found out some things I think you should know."

Charlotte's eyebrow raised eager to regain her friendship with Whitney, but her pride stopped her from letting her guard down too quickly. "Like...that you and Beau are now a *'thing'*?"

"What? No, that's absurd! Char, no! Me and Beau are just close friends...like it's always been. There's *nothing* going on between us. *Nothing!*"

"Yeah, Beau told me that. I just wanted to hear it from you." Charlotte fidgeted with the frayed hem on her blue jean shorts.

"Char, you have to believe me. Yes, I went by there to check on him and visit. I did spend the night in his room – all completely innocent – I swear!" Whitney still felt compelled to defend herself.

"I know...I get it. I hoped deep down in my heart it wasn't true, and that you were a better friend to me than that." Charlotte opened the Jeep door and stood in front of Whitney. "Why didn't you say anything when Isabella was being so manipulative and cruel towards me? That's why I'm still mad at you. You followed her around and fell into her trap. That hurt me."

"I'm sorry. I didn't mean to hurt you. And I'm sorry I didn't see that side of Mrs. Issie. She's always been great to me, and I admit it was hard for me to see it. But, I never meant to hurt you. I know you and Beau should be together. Ya'll both mean so much to me, and I want nothing more than to see you both happy." Whitney grabbed Charlotte and hugged her.

Charlotte smiled. "I missed your friendship more than anything."

"Not as much as I've missed yours. I have *so* much to tell you." Whitney was eager to fill Charlotte in on Charlene.

As they walked back arm in arm to The Dixie, Stella ran up to them. "The Trio is back!!! OMG...I've waited like forever for ya'll to fix things." Charlotte and Whitney laughed as all three approached Jackson.

"Our food is almost up. You wanna eat here or take it to go?" Jackson hoped she would choose the latter desperate to have her alone.

Charlotte had waited for this moment for a while – having the Trio back together felt so good. She didn't want to hurt him, but she preferred to hang out with her friends.

"Jackson, um, would you mind if I took a raincheck?" Charlotte hoped he wouldn't make a big deal. They were just hanging out as friends--so she thought.

"It's fine. We can do it another time." Jackson grabbed the bag of food from the counter and weakly smiled. "I know you've been waiting to talk. I'll call you later."

Charlotte smiled back at him as she was eager to catch up with her friends.

Well, she didn't hesitate at all, Jackson thought as he walked back to his Jeep alone.

Stella watched Jackson walk away with his head hung. "Poor guy. Is he gonna be okay?"

Charlotte caught a glimpse of him getting into his Jeep. Their eyes connected briefly, and she looked away. "Yeah, he'll be fine. We were just hanging out. He wants it to be more than what it is. We're just friends."

"Well, at the lake the other day it didn't seem like that!" Stella pursed her lips.

Charlotte gave Stella an evil stare and mouthed, *Stop!*

"What happened the other day at the lake? I saw you two leaving town in his Jeep. I'm not going to lie...I was a bit curious." Whitney noticed Charlotte's face drop and realized quickly she shouldn't have said anything.

"Uh, no...we're not going to gang up on Charlotte." Charlotte glared at Whitney. "We may be talking again, but I don't deserve that."

"I'm sorry. I shouldn't have said anything. It's just that, we all know he likes you," Whitney replied.

"Yeah, I know he does. And, honestly, when I thought me and Beau were over, I considered dating him. He's a great guy, really, and he's super cute. But he's not Beau." Charlotte smiled and quickly remembered the hurdle she faced--the paternity test. "Ugh, that stupid test...I can't be with Beau regardless."

"Char, there's something else I want to tell you. Please don't get mad...I'm telling you this because I want to be completely honest with you." Whitney took a deep breath and continued. "Beau knows about Jackson."

"What!? How? I mean...what does he know?" Charlotte was furious.

"Well he knows because he asked me if I knew if you and Jackson were talking. I couldn't lie to him Char! I promise I only told him that I saw you and him in town that day. I told him I didn't know anything else...which is the truth...because I don't! I think Blaine told him he saw Jackson close to you that night at the Abyss. I'm sorry, Char, I am!" Whitney watched as Charlotte rose from the table.

"I can't anymore. I just can't. I need more time." Charlotte walked away from the table.

"Char, I didn't tell him anything other than I saw you in Jackson's Jeep. He asked me about what Blaine told him! Please stop and hear me out!" Whitney pleaded as Charlotte kept walking away.

Stella followed closely behind. "Char, I can take you home."

"Thanks, Stella, yeah, that'd be great. I just can't be around her right now. It's too much." Charlotte's eyes met Whitney's and she looked away.

"Char, one thing," Stella asked.

"Yeah, what is it?" Charlotte replied.

"Go easy on Whit. And before you attack me...just hear me out. She's had a rough month – not to say you haven't. She's needed both of us to get through it – she's missed your friendship. And she needs us now more than ever." Stella backed out of the parking spot.

"I don't know what's going on with her, but she's gotten *way* too close to Beau for my comfort, and she keeps prying in my business. I don't need her to explain things to Beau. I can do that myself," Charlotte replied. "Speaking of Beau, can you drop me at the therapy center?"

***

"I'm home!" Whitney yelled as she entered the living room.

"Hey, honey, we're in the back," Barbara shouted.

"I'm going upstairs to rest. I'm exhausted," Whitney went up the stairs.

As Barbara came into the living room to meet her, she heard Whitney's door slam.

"What on earth is going on with that girl?" Barbara shook her head as she walked back to the back porch. Just as she opened the screen door, the phone rang. "Hello, oh, hi Isabella. Yes, I have a minute."

Isabella had made a point to stay out of the Charlene debacle up until this point, however, at Trisha's request and moreover due to her close relationship with the Taylors, she'd made a connection with an oncologist in New York. "He's rearranged some things next week to see Charlene. I'm happy to pay for her flight there to help out."

"That woman makes my blood boil!" Barbara replied. "Why in the world are you finding her an oncologist, Isabella?"

"Not that it matters, but you know when it comes to the medical profession…I'm all in." Isabella had anticipated Barbara's response.

"It's Charlene. Remember how much I did for her back then? And she moved on without a blink in her eye." Barbara shook her head with disgust.

"Yes, I remember, however, Trisha and Charlene caught me at AELs, and Trisha practically begged me to help her. I get that *all* of the time, you know. I have connections outside of Louisiana...good connections. If I can get her a second opinion, well, I can't deny her for Whitney's sake." Isabella was motivated to help Charlene mainly for Whitney. She'd already been through so much.

"I get it...I guess. Have you spoken with Charlene?" Barbara asked coldly.

"No, I haven't. I was going to call her today and let her know. She needs to decide soon though so we can arrange travel plans." Isabella paused.

"Well, I'm staying out of this, and I'm not paying for her travel expenses. I'm sorry. I know I sound harsh and cruel, but she's 'taken us to the cleaners' one too many times!" Isabella knew she would never convince Barbara this was a good idea.

"I would love nothing more than for her to be cured so Whitney has more time with her, but I'm just having a hard time with it. I know I need to get over it for Whitney." Barbara sighed.

Isabella noticed Barbara's tone soften. "I understand, Barbara. No one expects you to help. You've already done so much adopting Whitney and taking care of her. She's a great girl, and I'm honestly doing this for her."

"I'll give Charlene a call. I'll let you know what she decides." Isabella hung up the phone.

***

Later that afternoon, Charlene appeared on the front steps of the Taylor's home.

Barbara noticed her pacing the front porch and met her outside.

"Charlene, why didn't you knock?" Barbara asked as she held the screen door open.

"I planned to. I just...can I come in?" Her face was expressionless.

"Sure, I needed to talk to you anyway," Barbara replied as she closed the door behind Charlene. "I just made a fresh pot of coffee."

Charlene paced the living room floor. "I won't be long. No need for coffee."

"Well, alright then. You're beginning to scare me a little the way you're pacing and all." Barbara thought, *This reminds me of the day she came to ask us to adopt Whitney.*

"I do have something to tell you. Is Uncle Carl around?" Charlene softly asked.

"No, he's not. He's helping in the field today." Barbara replied anxiously. "Did Isabella call you?"

Charlene's voice cracked as she replied, "Yes, she did. How'd you know?"

"No, you've been in this town long enough to know that not much happens without me knowing. Besides, Isabella is a family friend – always has been – and she called me before calling you." Barbara was tired of dancing around the topic. She pointedly asked, "Well are you gonna go to that appointment next week?"

Charlene's eyes became misty while swallowing the lump in her throat. "No...I can't." With her head hung, waiting for Barbara to unleash her fury, she waited.

"Why in the hell would you not take this opportunity!? I don't understand!" Barbara was frustrated and stood with her hands on her hips waiting for Charlene's response.

Charlene looked at Barbara and quickly looked away. The shame that had built up within her was almost too much to bear, but she knew she had to tell her she wasn't sick. "I can't because...well...please promise you will hear me out Aunt Barbara."

Barbara's patience with Charlene had met its limit. "Girl, if you don't spit out what you're holding in...I'm going to lose it!"

Charlene stared at the floor as the words "I'm not sick" slowly left her lips.

"What did you just say? I know I didn't hear...you're not sick? What in the hell!" Barbara threw her hands up in the air and breathed in deeply before continuing. "What do you mean 'you're not sick'?"

Tears welled in Charlene's eyes as she forced herself to tell the truth. "I lied, Aunt Barbara...about being sick...about dying...the whole thing. I lied about all of it." Her eyes darted avoiding Barbara.

"You little...no good...get out! Get out of my house!" Barbara yelled. "Get out! Now!"

Charlene didn't budge. "Can I please explain? Can you please give me that...then I'll leave."

Barbara shook her head furiously. "No, you've had one too many chances from me! I knew you were up to something from the moment you came back here. You can't just pop up into people's lives and destroy them. Get out! Now!" Barbara forcefully opened the front door and motioned for her to leave.

As Charlene walked past her, she turned. "I don't have any money Aunt Barbara. I don't have anywhere to go...to live." Charlene pleaded as tears rolled down her face. "I was hoping by inviting Whitney to live with me...well...you wouldn't allow it...and *maybe* offer for me to live here...with ya'll."

Images of the past raced in her mind as Charlene pleaded for help. *This is all too familiar.* Barbara stood her ground not allowing Charlene to manipulate her again. "No, I can't do this again. You're not going to do this to me...to my family again! And you certainly aren't living with us!"

Charlene glanced over Barbara's shoulder and saw Whitney standing on the staircase. "What in the world is all the yelling for?"

Barbara froze and replied, "Whitney, honey, it's best if you get on up to your room. I mean it."

Whitney continued down the steps ignoring Barbara's request.

Barbara's tone became more direct. "Whitney, I'm not going to tell you again. Go back to your room. Now!"

Whitney stood behind Barbara at the base of the stairs and replied, "No, Mamma, I'm not. Something is going on here...and I want to know what it's about. And it must be bad because all that yelling woke me up."

Barbara rolled her eyes and turned to Whitney. "Why can't you just let something alone? Please let the adults take care of things." Barbara grabbed Whitney's hands. "I'll handle this. No need to get in the middle of it."

Whitney released her hands from Barbara's and questioned Charlene directly. "I'm not a child. What's going on? I want to know."

Charlene stared at Whitney. Barbara interjected. "Don't you even dare to open your mouth!"

Whitney placed herself between Barbara and Charlene. Facing Charlene she questioned, "Tell me, please."

The tension between Barbara and Charlene was too much for her to take. She broke down.

"I can't do this anymore! I'm stuck in the middle of all of this." Whitney paused as tears flooded her eyes. "None of this is fair to me! I've been dealing with all of this alone – playing tug of war with both of you! How is that fair? Did either of you think about my feelings and what I'm going through?"

Barbara immediately reached for Whitney to hug her. Whitney resisted. "No, Mamma, I don't need it now. It's too late. I have every right to know what ya'll are so upset about."

"Oh, I'm sorry I did this to you!" Charlene blurted. "It's all my fault...the tension between you and your mamma. I'm sorry."

Whitney wiped her tears and approached Charlene. "Just tell me then. Tell me what all of this is about."

Charlene reached out to grab Whitney's hand. Whitney let her. "Honey, I want more than anything to tell you, but I've caused so much grief and pain by coming back home. I can't do this anymore! Just promise me one thing that you know I love you more than anything."

Before Whitney could respond, Charlene bolted out the front door and ran toward her car.

Barbara pushed Whitney aside and yelled from the front porch, "I can't believe you're leaving me with the mess to clean up! How dare you!"

Charlene didn't look back as she made her way down the driveway.

Barbara continued screaming, "You're worthless, Charlene...worthless!" and slammed the front door.

Whitney stood in the doorway staring blankly at Barbara. "Honey, sit down. It's time you learn the real truth about your birth mamma."

Chapter Fifty-Three

Breakthrough

Beau was in the therapy room when Stella dropped Charlotte off to visit him. She waited in his room hoping Isabella wouldn't show up.

She paced around the room anxious to tell Beau about Jackson...her side of the story...and come clean. The room was freezing so she snuggled into the chair next to his bed rubbing her legs together to keep warm. Her eyes wandered hoping he would come through the door any second.

Why is it so cold in here!? she thought to herself as she grabbed Beau's letter jacket to cover up with.

As she snuggled underneath the jacket, the lingering smell of his cologne overcame her. She closed her eyes and imagined him holding her close, her leaning into his chest, and him kissing her softly. Her hands found warmth within the inside pockets of his jacket.

What does he have stuffed in the pockets? Charlotte's hands pulled each of the dried, pink roses she'd brought to him when she visited. *He found them...and kept them...all of them.* She smiled.

She closed her eyes again and let her mind wander back to their hoco night. *That was the best night ever. It seems everything fell apart after that.*

"Charlotte! Hey," Beau softly whispered as he stood in front of her lightly tapping her to wake up.

Charlotte jumped.

"Hey, sorry, I guess I dozed off!" She hoped she hadn't said anything out loud while reminiscing. "All finished with therapy for the day?"

"Yeah, I'm done. They said I only have a few more sessions here and should be able to go home." Beau smiled at the thought of sleeping in his own bed.

"That's great news!"

"I see you found my jacket. You cold or something!?" Beau said jokingly.

"Haha...real funny! Yes, you could hang meat up in here. Geez!" Charlotte replied as she released the roses back into the pockets.

Beau sat on the bed and faced her in the chair. "I'm so glad you came by. Did Owen tell you I called you earlier?"

Charlotte hadn't been home to talk to Owen. "No, I haven't seen him."

"Yeah, about that...he told me you were with Jackson." Beau stared at Charlotte.

"I was...for a little while...and that's why I'm here now." Charlotte leaned forward. "I wanted to explain everything myself...to you...so you heard all of it from me, not someone else."

Beau fell back on the bed. "Not anymore of this...please...I don't know if I can take anything else."

"I have something to tell you. I want to be honest with you," Charlotte persisted.

"Fine, just get it out." Beau longed for just one visit with her to be normal like it was before. He sat up in the bed.

"It's about Jackson." Charlotte was blunt. "I don't like him. I never had a 'thing' for him...if that's what you're thinking. Whitney said you asked her about me and him. Why didn't you just ask me? Why'd you have to go behind my back – asking my best friend?" Charlotte waited for him to answer.

"First, I tried calling you...remember? You weren't talking to anyone. I know why now, but I didn't then. I just assumed you had moved on. You know he came to see me the other day?" Beau became irritated at the thought of Jackson's visit.

"Wait...Jackson came to see you? Why?" Charlotte questioned.

"Why do you think? He hasn't been here once since I had the accident." Beau became more agitated thinking about what Jackson said.

"I'm sorry, Beau. Judging by the look on your face, his visit must have been about me." Charlotte's face became flushed thinking about Jackson being in the room with Beau. "What'd he say?"

"He told me he's always wanted you. He told me he kissed you...and you kissed him back. Is that true?" Beau's face was long.

"No! That's not true...well," Charlotte thought back on that day at the lake and continued, "Maybe I did. But I promise I was confused. You have to believe me. I thought you had moved on! I thought you were with Whitney and had forgotten me. It just felt good to have someone want me...to be close to someone. But the kiss meant nothing."

Beau had hoped her response would be different. Something inside him knew Charlotte was telling the truth and that the kiss meant nothing to her. It still made him mad--the thought of Jackson kissing his girlfriend. After all, she trusted him when he told her about Whitney. "I want to believe that it didn't mean anything to you. I do. So, why were you with him again this morning?"

Charlotte shrugged her shoulders. "I don't know, honestly. Beau, even if Isabella liked me we still couldn't be together. You're my…I can't even say it out loud…it's too weird. I can't continue to pretend we can be together as much as it hurts."

"That's where you're wrong, Charlotte. There's still a chance on this paternity test thing." Beau loosened his grip on the edge of the bed and leaned toward her. "I called to tell you that the paternity kits could have been tampered with…at least Dad said we can prove that in court now…so we have cause to get another test done. I'm going straight to the testing facility once I leave this place."

Charlotte's eyebrow raised. "What do you mean 'tampered with'?"

"The file cabinet was left unlocked the night Mrs. Beale and Mom were at the law firm. The cleaning crew came in and Mrs. Beale didn't remember to lock it. The court may find that the kits were unsupervised. Dad seems to think the judge might allow the new test now." He leaned closer to her and softly caressed her cheek. "We'll be together, Charlotte. You're the only girl for me."

"Wow, that's a lot to absorb…I mean, how did ya'll find this out?" Charlotte was trying to piece together the information. "Who would have tampered with them?"

"Yeah, it's a lot. Dad told me. I don't know. Maybe the kits got mixed up. I'm just focusing on getting out of here and getting that test done." Beau smiled. He noticed Charlotte did not seem as excited. "What's wrong? I thought you'd be excited like me. You do still want to be with me…don't you?"

"Really, Beau! Do you even have to ask me that? I'm here aren't I? I just don't want to get our hopes up. That's all. The test results may come back the same as the first…and that means we still can't be together. I don't want to go through that again." Charlotte hated to sound negative, but it was the truth.

"I've told you all along I felt like the test results weren't right. I just felt it...can't explain it. We'll know the truth in a week or so when I get outta here." Beau stood up from the bed and grabbed his football. Tossing it in the air, he looked at Charlotte and asked, "Just please tell me you don't have a thing for Jackson. I need to hear you say it again."

Charlotte's mouth dropped. "I already told you, Beau. I don't have any feelings for him. Yeah, I kissed him. And I don't know why I kissed him...but I don't see him like I see you. I was caught up in the moment. I guess it felt right at the time. And then today...I promise I went with him as friends. He's fun to hang out with but apparently, he thinks there's more to it." Charlotte walked closer to Beau. "Until I saw Whitney at The Dixie and she told me that you were asking questions about me and Jackson...I felt right then that I needed to come here and explain it to you." Charlotte grabbed Beau around the waist. "I don't like him that way, Beau. I promise. It was just something that happened."

Beau wanted to brush her away, but he couldn't.

"I'm trying...real hard, Charlotte. I am. You know he came here and threw all of this in my face. He made it seem like you wanted him, and you enjoyed it. I've never seen that side of him before. It was like some pity party for Jackson. He even made me feel bad about being quarterback...like I stole that position from him!"

As he paced the floor, he noticed Isabella at the door and walked toward her. Shaking his head with frustration he yelled, "No! I don't have time to deal with *you* right now," and slammed the door in her face.

Charlotte's mouth dropped.

Isabella turned her back in despair.

***

Whitney was a complete mess. She had nowhere to turn. Stella was on vacation. Charlotte was mad at her again. The only friend she thought of was Beau, and she knew better than to visit him after the confrontation with Charlotte. She didn't want to make things worse.

Barbara had told her everything from the beginning. Charlene was a complete failure and liar.

Whitney drove towards following the windy back road. Tears rolled down her face as she realized the last few weeks of worry were for nothing. It was all based on a lie. *How could she just walk away again like that...without saying a word to me!? She's such a coward!*

As Whitney's car approached the stop sign at the end of the country road, she slammed her hands on the steering wheel and screamed, "Ugh...is anything ever going to go right for me!?"

She turned left heading away from town, and something compelled her to pull over near the embankment of Bayou Fueob and park. She got out of the car and found a shady spot under a cypress tree near the water's edge. It was a humid summer day. The sweat beaded on her forehead just after five minutes of sitting.

The water was calm other than the occasional ripple from a turtle jumping into the water from a log. A few cars passed slowly, and she waved letting them know she was okay. But she wasn't really okay. She'd lost everything...she was alone. Again.

Just as she stood up from the ground, she heard a truck pull up. It was Blaine.

"What in the world are you doing down there, Whitney!?" Blaine asked as he rounded the front of his truck.

"Nothing, Blaine. Now's not a good time." She longed for her friends to support her. Blaine was not the person she'd hoped for.

"I saw your car and thought something happened. I just stopped by to--" She cut him off.

"I'm fine," she snapped, "I don't need your help. Besides, you couldn't help me with this anyway."

"Try me," Blaine said as he walked closer toward her. "What's going on?"

Whitney turned away from him. "It's nothing you'd care about. I mean it. I'm not in the mood. Besides, don't you have some girl to chase or something?"

Blaine laughed under his breath. "That's funny, really, but no, I don't. I'm being serious, Whitney. I want to help. I can listen at least?"

Whitney turned and her eyes narrowed. She laughed out loud. *Baaahhhaaa.* "That's the funniest thing I've heard you say! Blaine Ferrell can listen to someone other than himself? Yeah right!"

Whitney continued laughing as Blaine stood on the bank with his hands in his jean pockets. "Yeah, yeah, I get it. Real funny." He quickly retreated to his cocky demeanor and continued, "You know what...you're right. Forget it!" He started walking back up the embankment. When he reached the top near her car, he turned, and she was right behind him.

"Did you really mean it...you *want* to listen?" Whitney wasn't sure why she was asking him and giving him a chance other than he was all she had at the moment. She stood with her arms crossed.

"Yeah, Whitney, I want to listen. Something has you parked on the side of the road staring at the bayou, sweating your ass off!" Blaine reached his hand out to caress her arm.

She backed away. "No, it's not going to be like that. I don't need you to comfort me. I need you to listen."

"Okay, I'm sorry. I get it." He backed away. "Wanna take a ride and talk? It beats sitting in this heat."

Whitney debated it for a moment and replied, "Sure, just for the A/C though. Nothing else."

Blaine smiled as they walked back to his truck.

***

Blaine drove the winding back roads and ended up at the Abyss. They sat on the tailgate under the shade of the oak trees and talked. Whitney explained everything that had happened from Charlene's lies to Charlotte avoiding her.

"I had no idea...Whitney. I'm sorry. I can't believe she just left like that without explaining anything." He watched as her head sank with despair.

"It's just been horrible the last few weeks, Blaine. I feel like everyone has left me. I didn't have anyone to talk to about this. Stella is on vacation, Charlotte is avoiding me, and my Mamma is crowding me. Hell! My own birth mother lied to my face! I still can't believe someone could be so cruel – especially to their family!" Whitney wiped the tears as they rolled over her cheeks. She caught Blaine staring at her, taking in every word.

"What? Why are you staring at me? It's normal for people to cry, Blaine. It's how you express yourself!" Whitney replied sarcastically.

Blaine suddenly became overwhelmed with emotions listening to Whitney talk about Charlene and how cruel she'd been to her...how she lied the way she did. His mind raced back to the night of the accident and thought, *I've been holding on to this secret all this time. I've done the same thing to Beau.*

He pulled himself closer to Whitney. She immediately leaned away. "No, Blaine. I told you. I'm not interested. We're just talking, remember?"

His hands cupped her face and softly replied, "I know. I just wanted to tell you that I'm so sorry. I know it's long overdue...but I am. I'm an ass, Whitney." He pulled his hands away and slid off the tailgate. "I've been a complete asshole to you since the pregnancy and miscarriage, and now you're dealing with this."

Whitney stared at Blaine trying to figure out who this guy with all the emotion was in front of her.

He moved closer placing each hand on the side of her legs on the tailgate. "I just want you to know that I am sorry. For all of it. For everything I said...everything I did...ignoring you...all of it!"

Whitney didn't respond. Emotions flooded her. *He apologized? What do I say? Is this some pity party or joke?*

"I...I don't know what to say, Blaine. I mean, the miscarriage...I'll never be truly *over* but I'm past the hurt part. You're right. I managed it without you. You were hurtful and cruel and cold...and I told myself I'd never forgive you." Whitney's eyes locked with his. "But I'm going on a whim here and accepting your apology. I can at least give you that. And...thanks for being here for me today."

Blaine shook his head as he stepped away from the tailgate. He rubbed his chin while pacing the ground. "I can't keep doing this. I just can't. It's killing me inside not to tell someone."

Whitney scooted off the tailgate. "What is it? Well, tell me!"

"I need to talk to Beau. I need to go tell him now before I change my mind. Will you come with me?" Blaine rushed back to the driver's side door. "Please come with me."

"Okayyy, you're scaring me. Can you please just stop for a minute and explain it to me?" Whitney pointedly asked while standing at the back of the truck.

He shut the driver's door and walked back to her. He put his arms on her waist and pulled her close to him.

Her mind told her to back away, but her heart and body savored the smell of his cologne and his strong hold on her. He leaned closer to her ear and whispered, "I'm so sorry. I never stopped caring for you, Whitney. I blamed myself for all of it – I still do. My pride didn't allow me to say it, but I'm saying it now, and I mean it. You didn't deserve the way that I treated you. If you let me, I want to make it up to you."

Whitney buried her face in his chest, and she closed her eyes thinking how hurt she was after the miscarriage - alone and afraid – and how angry she was at him. While Blaine was the source of her emotional distress, deep down she still cared for him.

His tone was soft and comforting. It was different. He was different.

She looked up at him as tears welled in her eyes. "I do want you to make it up to me."

He smiled and gently kissed her lips then pulled away.

"Something in what you said about your birth mom got me thinking. I have to tell Beau...I've got to tell him that I'm the reason..." Blaine slammed his hand on the tailgate and cursed, "Dammit! How do I tell Beau that I'm the reason he ran off the road that night?! How do I do that?"

Whitney was shocked and stood in silence as Blaine continued.

"It was me, Whitney. Me!" Blaine beat his fist on his chest. "I was drunk leaving the party that night, and I guess I blacked out in the curve. I ran him off the road!" Whitney had never seen Blaine so emotional before.

"Blaine, calm down." Whitney grabbed his hand, surprised when he clutched it back tightly.

"I can't calm down. I did this to my best friend. Worst part is...I lied...well kept it from him. It's been eating away at me. I can't do this anymore." Blaine's eyes were wide and his breathing was rapid.

"Just take some deep breaths...it's going to be okay. I'll drive you to see Beau. I'm sure he'll understand. I think you need a minute to calm down." Whitney walked with him to the passenger side, and he got in.

"I'm sorry for unleashing all this on you. I didn't mean to turn the focus on me. I'm really sorry you had to go through everything alone. I will understand if you can't forgive me."

"Stop it...stop apologizing. I've already forgiven you, Blaine. You're different – something has changed with you. I see it. I like it." Whitney softly kissed his lips. "It's going to be okay. We are going to be okay!"

As she walked around the back of the truck she sighed and thought to herself, *Maybe we both needed each other more than we thought after all.*

Chapter Fifty-Four

Burdens Released

"Corbin! You have a visitor!" the guard called as Dad entered the room.

I'd 'earned' visitation for whatever reason, and I watched Dad's eyes search the room anxiously waiting to see me.

You put me here! You could see me anytime you wanted if you wouldn't have left me here!

"Dad," I said flatly as I walked up to the table.

He stood up from the chair and attempted to hug me.

"No, don't do that." I stopped him mid-hug.

"Okay, I get it. You're mad at me." He sat back in the chair.

"Why did you come?" I couldn't look him in the eye.

"I was worried about you and wanted to check in," he replied.

"Oh yeah...well if you were so worried about me, why would you leave me here? Look around, doesn't it feel like *home?*" I knew my response was sarcastic, but I didn't care.

"Nessie, worrying about you and this place feeling like home are two completely different things. You needed help. I brought you here to get that help. End of story."

"I don't have anything to offer you. I can't help you with anything. I've been locked in here because *you* put me here." I couldn't stand the sight of him right now.

His eyes widened, and he became more defensive. "I'm not here for you to offer me anything or help me. I wanted to check on you, Nessie. We all miss you and want you to get better." Dad paused obviously hoping I would respond.

I remained silent and rolled my eyes.

"Brice asked about you. He was worried since he hasn't heard from you." Dad knew mentioning Brice would pique my interest. And it did.

"What did he say?" I quickly asked.

"He was just worried. I told him you were here and that I brought you." Dad folded his arms on his chest.

"Really? Great, now he thinks I'm an addict or something. Thanks, Dad!" I slumped in my chair.

I've lost the one good thing in my life.

"No, actually, he was glad I brought you here. He knows you need help." Dad leaned forward toward me. "We all know you need help. This behavior just isn't like you."

"You don't know what I need, Dad," just came out of my mouth. "You never have." I felt guilty the minute the words rolled off my tongue. But it was true. He didn't know what I needed. Everyone has a breaking point, and I'd hit mine. "I would say I'm sorry, but I'm not."

"What has gotten into you with all this lashing out? I've never seen you act this way before." Dad's tone had softened. "How can I help you?"

"I don't need anyone's help. I've navigated life without much guidance so far. I'll find my way out of this." I wanted to tell Dad that our family is ultimately what put me in here – the burning desire to feel free and weightless from all the problems that weighed me down.

"Nessie, you can't do this alone. I'm here to help you. I put you here to get you better, and I want you to come back home to us." Dad looked up at the clock on the wall noticing only five minutes remained for his visit. "I did want to give you an update on things outside of here...if you want to know?"

I shrugged my shoulders. "Whatever."

"Beau is almost finished with therapy. So, that's good news, and come to find out, the paternity test can be taken again. I can explain the details..." The words kept rolling off of Dad's tongue – all about how great life was for Beau – as I sat in silence staring blankly back at him. "Charlotte and Beau seem to be friends again..."

I could feel the rage building inside me hearing about how perfect Beau's life was, and I blurted out, "Seriously! You say you want to help me...you come here to visit me...and all you can find to talk about is how great Beau's life is going!" I stood up and backed away from my chair.

Several patients around me stopped talking and stared.

"This is exactly why I'm in here, Dad. This right here." My finger pointed at the source of my frustration. Him.

"I'm in here trying to find peace and direction...and all you talk about is how perfect Beau's life is! Did you ever stop and think maybe my life wasn't so good outside of here? Sure, I could have anything and everything I wanted, but if you and Isabella would've stopped caring so much about your work and your precious son and focused a little more time on me, maybe you would've seen that I needed something more...something money could never buy."

Dad stood up and walked toward me attempting to console me. I pushed him away.

"No! I'm not asking for it now! It's *way* too late for that! The sad part is I finally found an 'out' – an escape from always feeling like I always had to fix everything – and look where it got me."

I turned away from Dad and motioned for the staff to open the door.

"Nessie! Don't leave things this way. Honey, I'm sorry!" Dad yelled across the room.

I didn't turn around. There was nothing more to discuss. It felt like a weight had been lifted off my chest. A burden that once defined who I thought I should be for everyone else had now been released.

***

Whitney held Blaine's hand tightly as they walked down the hall of the therapy center. She'd never seen Blaine so nervous.

"Hey, ya'll," Whitney said as she knocked on the open door to Beau's room.

Beau and Charlotte were sitting together on the sofa when they came in.

Charlotte glared at Whitney, but her expression relaxed when she saw Blaine following her into the room.

Beau looked at Charlotte confused. "What in the world are you two up to?" He asked. "I never thought I'd see you together again– at least this close."

Charlotte watched as Whitney grabbed Blaine's hand again and leaned against his side.

I'm so confused. What in the world is going on? Are they together now?

"Man, you look like you've seen a ghost! What's up?" Beau noticed Whitney staring at Charlotte. Whitney quickly looked up at Blaine as he stared blankly at the wall. She nudged him.

"One of ya'll better start talking. Ya'll are acting all weird! And, are ya'll back together or something!"? Beau looked at Charlotte and grinned.

Whitney finally spoke up. "Blaine needs to tell you something." Whitney's elbow nudged Blaine again.

He sighed and took a deep breath in. "Yeah, man, I gotta tell you something. I just don't know how to tell you."

"Look, if you don't know already, I've been blasted with all kinds of information since I've been locked away in this place. I won't lie though. I'm getting tired of it. Can't we just go back to being teenagers and talking about stupid stuff?" Beau stared at Blaine. "Just say it already."

Blaine released his hand from Whitney's and sat on the bed. Whitney followed him and sat closely beside him. His heartbeat was rapid, and his palms were sweaty.

"Blaine...it can't be that bad! Is it about Coach? Football? You're killing me, man! Just spit it out!"

"No, it's not about any of that. It's about the night of your accident." Blaine grabbed Whitney's hand. He swallowed deeply and continued. "There's no easy way to tell you this. I've been struggling with it since...since I remembered...I wanted to tell you when I visited...but I couldn't find the way to do it."

"Blaine...what already? I'm going to lose it!" Beau's tone was firm.

Blaine looked at Whitney and then back at Beau. Charlotte reached for Beau's hand anticipating the worst.

"I ran you off the road that night. It was my fault, Beau. You're in here because of me!" Blaine blurted out. With each word it felt as if a weight was lifted from him - until he felt Beau's punch.

Smack! Right in the jaw.

"OMG, Beau! Why'd you do that!" Whitney screamed as she stood up and lightly touched Blaine's face.

"I'm fine!" Blaine said as he brushed her hand away. "I deserved it."

"Damn right you did! I have so many questions, but damn you! How could you keep this from me!?" Beau clenched his first, still facing Blaine.

Charlotte's hands covered her face in shock.

"I'm sorry, man. I know I should've told you sooner. This is all on me." Blaine wiped the blood from his mouth with his head hung. "I'm sorry, Beau. I am. I didn't want to keep it from you...I just didn't know how to tell you. Hell...I didn't remember until one of the guys talked about the party that night. Then, it all came back to me."

Charlotte reached out to grab Beau's hand hoping he might release his clenched fist. "Beau, c'mon, he's telling you now. Calm down, okay?"

Beau pushed her hand away continuing to stare Blaine down. "We're better friends than this. You ran me off the road...you could've killed me...and you kept this to yourself because you didn't know how to tell me!? That's low...real low."

Blaine remained silent as Whitney sat by his side. She glanced at Charlotte thinking they had just had this same conversation about being better friends.

"I think we all just need to take a minute to breathe," Charlotte said trying to calm Beau down. "C'mon. I know it's a lot to take in. Let's talk through it."

"If you think I'm going to sit here and *hash things out*...you're mistaken." Beau sat and leaned forward resting his arms on his legs. "Why'd you decide today was the day? Huh? What made today so special?"

Blaine looked at Whitney and grabbed her hand. "Whitney...she's the reason."

Beau was even more confused. He shook his head and laughed while poking fun at Blaine. "So, the girl you got pregnant, ignored when she dealt with a miscarriage and haven't had *anything* to do with since then...made you come today and tell the truth? Good try. No girl will ever make you do anything you don't want to do."

Blaine, keeping a tight hold on Whitney's hand, tried to explain. "She didn't make me do anything. And I've...well...we've had time to talk through all that's happened, and we're in a good place."

"Well, I'm sure glad you both are in a good place, now. That's just perfect. Isn't it Charlotte?" Beau sneered and laughed. "Aren't you so glad babe that our friends are happy?"

Charlotte's gaze wandered around the room. Beau was angry. She knew he was just lashing out.

"Whitney told me about her birth mom...and--" Beau cut Blaine off.

"Yeah, I've known about that for a few weeks. Funny you just found out." Beau could feel Charlotte staring him down. He looked at her and grabbed her hand. "I haven't had time to fill you in on that and honestly it's not my business to share. I figured Whitney wanted to tell you."

Charlotte's gaze danced between Beau and Whitney. "Well, is someone going to tell me about your birth mom?"

Whitney released Blaine's hand and walked over to Charlotte. "I planned to at The Dixie...but...well...you left to come here."

"Well, I'm here now. So...you found out who your birth mom is?" Charlotte felt even more hurt that Whitney hadn't told her. *That must be what Stella meant by going easy on her.*

"Yeah, I met her. She came back a few weeks ago unexpectedly. Alot has happened since she came home." Whitney's eyes lowered and she fidgeted with the keys in her hand.

"This still doesn't make any sense. How does Whitney's birth mom have *anything* to do with telling me the truth!" Beau persisted.

"Because she has lied to Whitney over and over again!" Blaine's tone raised. "I can't live with being a liar like that! I realize I've hurt Whitney...and I could have hurt you...or you could have--"

"*Could* have hurt me!? Look at me Blaine! You did hurt me! You could've killed me! I've been in this stupid hospital room most of my summer! I can't play football..." Beau stood up from the sofa and got in Blaine's face.

"Get the hell outta my room. Now! I don't want you around. You're nothing to me! Nothing!" Beau's jaw clenched, and his eyes filled with rage. "Now! Get out now before I do something I might regret."

Blaine backed away and Whitney moved closer and grabbed his hand as Beau motioned to the door.

"I'm sorry, Beau. I just want to say, Blaine has changed. He sees things differently now. I wish you would hear him out and give him a chance."

"No, I can't. Get out! Both of you!" Beau yelled.

As the door closed, Beau screamed, "What in the hell? He caused all of this! My best friend did this to me and kept it from me!"

Charlotte ran to his side and wrapped her arms around him. "I know you're hurt. I get it. I'm here for you. I'm not going anywhere."

Beau hugged her back tightly. "I'm glad. I need something normal in my life at this point."

***

"Tucker, you can't just let her get away with it. I mean, she manipulated the test results!" Allison was shocked that Tucker didn't expose Isabella. "She doesn't deserve a 'pass'. She broke the law! How can you allow her to do that!?"

"I know. I just couldn't do it to Beau. I had everything planned out – to tell him the truth about his ruthless mother – and I caved. I couldn't do it, Allison." Dad paced around the conference room feeling regret for not telling Beau the truth. "I couldn't break him. He would never talk to Isabella again if he knew the truth."

"I still think he has a right to know. We have seen what that woman is capable of." Allison was still in shock that Dad was able to get Isabella to confess that she tampered with the kits.

"I can't believe she was honest with you." Allison waited for Dad's reply. "Tucker, you okay?"

"Yeah, I'm fine." Dad rubbed his chin. "It bothers me that she knows Jackson said something to us. I told her to leave him out of this."

Allison became troubled. "She better not bring Jackson into this!"

Dad was most concerned about Beau finding out the truth. "You can't say anything to anyone – even to Kent. This stays between us – you got it?"

Allison knew there was no way she would be able to keep this secret from Kent. "Sure, yeah, I get it." Allison sighed.

Chapter Fifty-Five

Liberated

A few days had passed since Dad visited me. All my time was spent thinking while staring at the wall. I'd been 'sober' now for almost two weeks.

It's not like I was a drug addict...the whole sober reference just sours me.

My counselor continues to tell me that the cravings are real and how I should combat them. Honestly, I don't crave alcohol or cigarettes...any of it. I crave the relief from the weight and pressure they provide. I've tried to explain that to my counselor, and she doesn't get it.

On paper, it appears I'm in a positive emotional state to leave the facility and enter 'back into the world' in a few days. While my discharge papers seem to tell the story that I've achieved the level needed both physically and mentally that warrants my invite to return home, I'm really no different.

The burning inside me still rages to find my place--not necessarily for a drink or a smoke. I certainly didn't find that answer in this stupid rehab facility, and I'm doubtful I'll find it outside. I'm not sure what

I long for. I haven't found it yet – other than when I was with Brice. I thought he was 'that place' for me.

Snap out of it, Nessie. You really screwed it up with him.

"Did you contact your family? You know, they have to pick you up from here in a few days." My counselor asked.

"No, I haven't. Can you just do it for me? I really don't want to speak to any of them." She gave me *that* look. "C'mon, please."

"You're really supposed to do that Nessie – to show growth." I knew she was ready to get rid of me. She sighed and responded while rolling her eyes, "Whom should I call?"

"Can you call my friend...Owen? Does it have to be immediate family? They just aren't that close to me like my best friend is."

I lied. I'd avoided Owen. *Would he even come if they called him? He was still my best option.*

"I'll have to get approval from your parents...but I don't see why not if they approve. I'll let you know." As the counselor left my room, I drew my legs up to my chest and looked around.

The walls were solid white and bare. On top of the desk was a pen and stack of paper with envelopes that were in the same position as when I arrived. *They expected me to write my family who put me here. Yeah right!*

I knew I had to get over it eventually – the fact that Dad brought me here. I thought back to the way I acted when he visited. I know I was rude to him. H*e deserved it, didn't he?*

Regardless, I knew I had to let go of the 'blame game' if I wanted to stay out of this place.

I dozed off and awoke to my counselor tapping on the door. "You're going home in two days. Owen Callaway will take you home. Any questions?"

"No, that's good...and thank you." I felt a small weight off me knowing my trip home wouldn't be explaining myself to Dad. Owen wouldn't talk to me...if he actually would show up.

***

"Finally! It feels so good to breathe in fresh air and be out of that room!" Beau walked hand in hand with Charlotte to her car.

"You got it back?" Beau questioned realizing he hadn't asked about her car since the accident.

"Yep, a few weeks ago. Mr. Beale did a great job. It's like new!" Charlotte smiled as she opened the driver's door.

Beau stopped briefly before getting in. He leaned on the roof and smiled. "I'm lucky to have you."

Charlotte blushed and she smiled. "Let's go get this test out of the way."

Tucker met them at the testing facility. "Let's get this done. Long overdue." Beau's hands clasped tightly with Charlotte's as they walked inside."

***

"You're back! How was vacay?" Charlotte asked as she walked to meet Stella after Whitney and Blaine left.

"Girl, it was great! I can't wait to tell you all about it, but first, you gotta tell me what's going on...I mean...Whit and Blaine sort of told me what happened after I pried it out of them."

"Yeah, it's bad. Beau's not in a good place with Blaine. He says he will never forgive him." Charlotte watched as Beau grabbed their food from the counter. "It's not like him to hold a grudge. He's had so much happen to him lately...I don't blame him for being angry. I just hate to see him like this."

"Hey, Stella, you made it back to town?" Beau smiled as he sat next to Charlotte.

"Yes! Good to see you. So, they finally let you break out of there!?" Stella laughed.

Reaching around Charlotte and pulling her close he replied, "Yes, it feels good."

Knowing Stella was going to pry more about the whole Blaine and Beau situation, Charlotte attempted to change the subject. "We have some good news...well, we hope. We went by the testing facility and Mr. Corbin and Beau gave their sample for the paternity test. We're hoping to get the results in a couple days. Dad is going tomorrow."

"That's awesome, ya'll. I know it's been a long time coming. It's so great to see you both together again." Stella smiled.

"Well...we aren't technically together..." Charlotte wanted to be clear. "We're waiting on the paternity test to see," she grabbed Beau's hand and continued, "but we both have a good feeling about it."

"I get it. Those gut feelings mean something you know...it's going to work out!" Stella was happy to see them together...at least talking again.

Stella's smile quickly left her as she saw Jackson pull into the parking lot and park next to her car. Noticing Charlotte tense up, Stella thought, *Well this sure has been the most interesting day at The Dixie.*

Beau released Charlotte's hand as Jackson approached, daring him to start something. Jackson looked directly at Charlotte but kept walking to the counter.

"Beau, I want to talk to him. Just finish eating." Charlotte stood up and followed Jackson.

Reluctant to let her go alone, Beau sat down...his eyes fixated on both of them.

"Hey, Jackson. Look, I need to talk to you." She stood behind him as he stared at the menu.

He didn't respond.

"It's not like you don't know what's on the menu, Jackson. I need to talk to you. Look at me!" Charlotte was quickly becoming more agitated with him.

"Oh yeah, well, I'm pretty sure I don't want to hear it, Charlotte. So, just save your breath." Jackson responded coldly still facing the counter.

As he put in his order, Charlotte stood behind him with her arms crossed waiting for him to turn around. "You gotta face me at some point."

Jackson spun around and laughed. "You're something, you know. I don't get it." Shaking his head, he turned back to the window.

"What don't you get, Jackson? I'm listening." Charlotte was becoming even more angry.

"You! I don't get you!" he shouted back at her, and Beau stood up.

Charlotte put her hand in the air motioning to him she was okay.

"What? You don't get that you took our whole hanging out *way* too seriously?" Charlotte rolled her eyes.

"Oh, so you think kissing a few times, which you seemed to enjoy by the way, is just '*hanging out*'?" Jackson laughed and grabbed his food.

"Yeah, about that. Beau told me that you told him I kissed you back, and I seemed to like it. How dare you tell him! I planned to talk to him about it. That wasn't your place, Jackson. Yes, I kissed you...and it was okay...but I knew the whole time in my heart that it should be Beau. I was confused and lonely." Charlotte looked back at Beau then back at Jackson.

"Must be nice to flirt around and make someone feel like you like them – and then dump them when things get better for you. I don't need you to explain. I get it...I just thought we might have had something." Jackson pushed her aside and walked toward his car. As he passed the table he pointed at Beau. "She's yours man...all yours...just like it's always been. At least I still have football."

Rage overcame Beau as he jumped over the table. Drawing his arm back to punch Jackson, he felt Charlotte's touch. "Don't stoop to his level, Beau. Just let him go."

As much as Beau wanted to punch him for being so cruel, he backed away.

Jackson laughed as he jumped into his Jeep. *So, you got the girl back, but I'm quarterback, Beau. I hope you like sitting in the stands this year.*

Chapter Fifty-Six

Defining Moment

"Corbin, you got all your things?" my counselor yelled as she knocked on my door.

I won't miss her voice.

"Yeah, give me just a sec!" I was so tired of being under someone's thumb.

As I gathered the few things I came in with, I leaned against the door. Something came over me – hearing her soft reply, "Just take your time," a surprising sentiment suddenly filled me with emotions.

While the walls had quickly closed around me since Dad dropped me off, the room had become my solace similar to reading. It's funny how it hit me as my time was up. I hadn't recognized before how much I needed an 'out' – before it was reading or writing in my journal which turned into drinking and partying. The required quiet time to reflect annoyed me, and I'd combated it the entire time I'd been here.

At that very moment, it hit me, *I've been the sole source of everything that weighed me down. I allowed it.*

My counselor knocked again, then entered. "You ready? I think your ride is here."

"Yeah, yeah...I think I am," I replied following her from my room.

As we walked to the entrance of the building, she stopped me and smiled. "It clicked didn't it?"

I looked back at her confused and then thought back to my first day here. I grinned. "Yeah, it did. It finally did."

As I walked through the sliding doors I searched for Owen's car. "He's not coming," I said to myself and sat on the bench. I looked around the parking lot, but he was nowhere to be found. I sat for about five minutes and decided I'd wait inside where it was cooler. As I gathered my things and began walking back to the entrance, I froze.

Brice pulled up into the first row of guest parking and got out.

What's he doing here!?

He leaned casually against his car with his hands in the pockets of his jeans. He didn't wave...nor say anything...he just stared at me.

Move, Nessie. Go to him.

My inner voice was screaming, but my body was motionless. Finally, I mustered enough courage to move closer.

As I got closer, he grinned and shrugged his shoulders. "So, I'm obviously not Owen. You surprised?"

Feeling ashamed of how I'd treated him, I tucked my hair behind my ear and looked down at the pavement. I knew I looked terrible and wanted to hide under a rock.

"No, you're not. Where is he?" I asked dryly.

"I'll explain. Just hop in. It's hot out here!" Brice opened his door and stood waiting for me to get in.

I hesitated.

"Well...you coming? I doubt you want to stay here or do you?"

"*Really?*" I replied sarcastically. "It's just that...well...I haven't seen you--" Brice cut me off.

"Just get in, Nessie. We can talk on the way home." Brice's tone was different than before.

The drive was odd. I wasn't sure what to say – how much he already knew – and how much he wanted to know.

He broke the silence after the first few miles. "Owen is leaving for boarding school tomorrow. He's going abroad to Europe."

"What!" I exclaimed. "When did he decide...why is he going...?" I had so many questions.

"Yep, he decided a couple of weeks ago that he needed a change. That's all I know. Your Dad asked me to come pick you up since Owen was busy." Brice couldn't help but notice my irritation with the news. "You okay?"

"No, not really. I mean...I've been kinda rude to him the last few times I've seen him. Since the accident, I've brushed him off." I stared out the car window feeling ashamed. "And now...he's gone. He was my only friend..."

"I'm sure he understood...I mean, you're family has been through a lot this summer." Brice was careful in his response.

"Yeah, I know. But I was really mean. He tried to help me, and I pushed him away. I just couldn't be around him. Mason and Isabella created this entire mess and even though Owen wasn't responsible, I blamed his family."

I couldn't help but feel like I made Owen leave.

"He's still in town?" I hoped that he was home so I could talk to him.

"I'm not sure. His flight was leaving from Baton Rouge today. I don't know what time Mrs. Callaway was taking him." Brice didn't have any more details.

"Ugh...how could I have screwed up so bad...with everything!" I rubbed my fingers across my forehead and closed my eyes.

Brice's hand grabbed mine. His touch was exactly what I needed although I didn't deserve it.

I looked back at him and smirked. "Thank you. I missed that."

He smiled, and I felt relieved that he seemed to still be interested.

"I've missed you too, Nessie. But..." Brice looked my way and then focused back on the road.

"Awe, but...what? That's never good. Don't ruin the only good moment I've had in several weeks." I went to release my hand from his, but his held became stronger.

"It's only bad if you let it be. We need to talk about what happened and what it means...for us." Brice's tone became more serious.

"I know...I was cruel toward you as well. I shut you out...and I'm sorry." A tear welled in my eye as I continued. "I hated it in there, Brice. I blamed Dad for throwing me in there. I wasted my time staring at the blank walls and blaming everyone else. I didn't think I had a problem."

"Nessie, you passed out at home...your Dad found you passed out. And you got wasted with Tennie and ended up in my room! You don't think you had a problem?" Brice's tone wasn't accusatory, but it still bothered me.

"Will you let me finish!?" I snapped. "I'm sorry, I didn't mean it that way. I'm just trying to sort through everything."

"I get it. But I'm not going to let you go back to that. Whatever drove you to feel like getting wasted – that needs to be your past." Brice was blunt. "I mean it. I'm not doing this again."

"Well, you don't have to!" I snapped again. "Why are you beating me up? I feel like I'm a prisoner back in that rehab facility! And, like you have room to talk!"

Brice pulled the car to the side of the road and faced me. "Look, I'm not 'beating' you up! I just need to know if you're through with all the drinking...and mostly, are you done hanging out with my sister? I want you to know that I didn't lie to you about me being put in the detention center. It wasn't the right time to tell you. I've moved past that and grown from it. That's exactly why I hated seeing you fall into Tennie's trap. I moved past all of that. I'm clean and want to stay that way. The way you were acting around Tennie – that's not you. I want to put it all in the past, and concentrate on you...well, us." Brice gently caressed my arm.

His touch still mesmerized me. I closed my eyes and tried to block it out and focus...but it was no use.

Why was I angry at him? I'd lost my train of thought.

I leaned in closer hoping he would kiss me, but the moment I leaned forward, he sat back in his seat. "Just tell me you're done with it, Nessie, all of it."

As mad as he made me for pushing me away, I knew I'd hurt him, and he deserved answers.

"I know I've hurt you. I'm sorry for that. I need to tell you something. Back to what I was saying before...staring at the walls...I had a lot of time to think and unfortunately, I didn't see it clearly until this morning. While I've blamed everyone else for my unhappiness, just a moment ago something hit me as I left that stupid room...a defining moment when I realized it's been *me* all along, Brice. I've played the victim in this and that's exactly the reason I sought something that made me feel good...and free. I thought if I fixed everything for everyone I would be noticed."

I pulled myself closer to him leaning on the console. "I need you now more than anything. I searched recklessly to find something that uplifted me over and above the weights that continued to drag me down…weights that I put on myself. You're what was lost in me. I didn't need Tennie or any of the other stuff – I needed you the entire time."

Brice's hands cupped my face as he gently kissed my lips. His soft lips touched mine and for an instant, I was floating in space – similar to the night at his house. He held his lips to mine, stroked my cheek softly, and whispered, "I was lost without you, Nessie."

I melted hearing those words as his kiss became deeper. I pulled away briefly as his hand grabbed mine.

"What's wrong?" he questioned.

"Nothing. Nothing is wrong. Everything is exactly how it should be!" I smiled back at him. "I'm just ready to get home!"

Chapter Fifty-Seven

Worth the Wait

"It's so great to finally be home!" Beau plopped on the sofa and watched the ceiling fan spin round and round.

"So good to have you home, Beau." Isabella quickly took the opportunity to catch him in the living room.

Beau stood up from the sofa. "I'm not ready to talk to you, Mom. I need more time."

Isabella watched as he walked back into the kitchen. "You may never understand why I did what I did, but I always wanted the best for you. We obviously have different paths in mind." She followed him and grabbed his arm motioning to turn toward her. "Beau, just please let me say this."

Beau turned around and decided to let her talk. "Five minutes and then I'm heading to pick up Charlotte."

She smiled and released her hold. "Look, a lot has happened since the accident. You've been through so much."

Beau became impatient. "I know all of that, Mom. Remember, I lived it. Just spit out what you want to tell me."

Isabella refrained from snapping back at him. His comment would've typically resulted in a ten-minute shouting match. But this time it was different. As Beau waited for her angry, belittling comeback she said, "I'm truly sorry, honey. I'm sorry about keeping you and Charlotte apart. I can see that it hurt you and that you truly do care about her."

Beau was shocked. He didn't know what to say. He stood in silence. Smiling she replied, "Well say something!"

"I...um...that caught me off guard. I never expected you to say anything close to that." Beau didn't believe her and questioned her motive. "What do you want, Mom? I mean, a week ago you said you would never accept Charlotte, and now, you're saying you do. That doesn't add up. What's going on?"

"Why does it have to be like that? I'm simply trying to apologize to you. That's all. Nothing is going on. I'm not saying that I *like* her nor that I'll accept her like I would've accepted Whitney, but if that's who you choose, I'll live with it."

"Oh! Geez, okay, you'll live with it!? You act like me seeing Charlotte is such a huge burden for you! Your five minutes is up." Beau grabbed his keys and headed for the carport door. "Oh, and by the way. It's my path to choose not yours!"

Isabella sighed. "I also wanted to tell you I gave your dad the house. I'm going to live in Dr. Dawson's cottage for a little while until I decide what to do next. I felt it was right to give him his family's home." Isabella leaned against the kitchen island waiting to see if Beau would respond asking her to stay.

"Good!" Beau yelled and slammed the door.

***

Dad waited for us to arrive at the lake house. He ran outside to meet us as Brice's car pulled into the driveway.

Deep breath, Nessie. Deep Breath.

Brice leaned over and kissed my cheek while softly whispering, "You've got this. Just make it right."

As soon as I stepped out of the car, Dad bear-hugged me. He wouldn't let me go.

"Nessie, I'm so glad to see you. I've sure missed you!" He stepped back from me, then came back for another hug. Brice grabbed my bag from the car and walked toward us.

"Thanks, Brice, for picking her up," Dad said continuing to lock eyes with me.

The words 'I'm sorry' danced inside my mouth but wouldn't roll off my tongue.

Dad didn't seem to be phased by my involuntary silent treatment. I wanted more than anything to tell him how terrible I felt when he left the facility that day...but I just stood there...staring.

"Let's go inside and get out of this heat!" Dad motioned for us to follow him.

When I walked into the kitchen, I froze. My journal was sitting on the kitchen counter. "Why...why is this here!"

Dad turned around and smiled. "I brought it here for you."

"Dad, this is *my* personal journal! How dare you take it out of my room!" Every ounce of 'I'm sorry' had left me. My tone was harsh.

"Nessie, calm down. I didn't read it. I simply brought it here. I thought you might like to devote some time to writing again." He smiled and looked at Brice. "You know I wouldn't pry into your personal things."

I snatched it off the counter and handed it to Brice. "Burn it."

Brice's eyebrow raised and asked, "Burn it, really?"

"Yep, burn it. That's the old Nessie. That part of me is gone." I smiled and turned back to face Dad. "And...I'm sorry. Something came over me when I saw that journal...brought back memories of the old me that I've left in the past."

"No worries. I'm just glad you're home," Dad replied.

"I'm not finished." I sat on the barstool and leaned on the kitchen island. "I'm sorry for how I treated you when you came to visit. I blamed you and everyone else for putting me there. I've accepted that was on me...one hundred percent me."

Dad grinned. "I appreciate that, Nessie. That means a lot. Seems like you may have gotten something out of that facility after all."

"No, not really. I didn't get much out of it to be honest." I shrugged my shoulders.

Dad had a confused look on his face. He looked at Brice and then back at me. "Hmm, well, they had to have seen improvement, or they wouldn't have released you."

"I'm fine, Dad. Really. Nothing within the walls of that facility could've helped me...nothing. I wasn't overdosing on drugs; I'm so far from an alcoholic. I didn't fit in...at all. I spent most of my time in my room, staring into space, my brain spinning about how I was going to get out of there and come home. I kept telling myself nothing was wrong with me. I was angry at all of you." I looked at Dad and then glanced back at Brice. "I blamed you and Isabella for everything."

Dad interjected, "Nessie, I took you there for help. I found you passed out drunk in your bedroom. You could have fallen out the window of your room. It had to stop. You just took it too far."

"I know. But that's not why I blamed you. Yeah, I was mad, no doubt, that you took me there, but this morning I figured out who was really to blame, and it was me." It felt so liberating to say it out loud. "Yes! The source of my angst and drive to feel free and weightless...to not care...to be wild--was built on my own preconceived notion that everyone...relied on me. I put that pressure on myself."

Dad had a weird look on his face, but he didn't interrupt me.

"I've always felt like I've missed something in life...you know...like a part of me was non-existent. I've tried telling you this before, but it never resonated with you. I've always longed to feel needed, wanted and loved – not just for the benefit of others – but for my own happiness. I've been missing that, until I met Brice."

I reached out my hand to grab his, and he walked closer. His arms wrapped around my waist as I leaned my back into him. "Brice is what I never had...the 'high' that I searched for. I don't have a drinking problem. I'm definitely not the wild and crazy party girl that surfaced the last few weeks. Brice gives me that same feeling, lifts me higher than the clouds, and most of all, makes me feel needed."

Dad's head hung low. "Nessie, I had no idea. You've always been the strong one of the family, and I knew I didn't have to worry about you as much – but I loved you! It didn't mean I didn't worry about you or care for you, but I knew you handled things. I guess I really messed up."

"No, Dad, it's okay, really! I had to find it myself...and I did. And I'm happy." I looked back at Brice, and he kissed me softly.

"Okay, enough of all of that kissing stuff. It's going to take me some time to get used to that!" Dad smiled – I cherished it.

It had been a while since he was happy – since we were both happy.

***

"I can't believe it's here! The results are in from the paternity test!" Charlotte and Beau walked into the courthouse hand in hand.

Me, Dad, and Brice stood outside the courtroom waiting.

"Where have you been?" Beau asked as he walked up. He had a confused look on his face seeing me and Brice holding hands.

"It's a long story." I replied. "I'll fill you in later. Today is all about you."

As we walked into the courtroom, I saw Isabella sitting in the front row. I quickly pulled Brice to the opposite side, and we took a seat near the aisle.

Dad followed Beau and Charlotte and sat a few seats down from Isabella. She glanced his way, but he ignored her.

Mason and Melissa entered the courtroom and sat in the seats directly behind us.

The judge came in shortly after, and the bailiff handed the results to the judge.

"Well, I'll be! Hmmm, that's interesting." The judge looked out at the courtroom and said, "Well, here we find ourselves again in the court of law to decide the paternity of Beau Corbin. It seems we did this months ago, and it was put to rest. The court was recently provided evidence of a possible breach in the test results from the first test, therefore I've allowed the parties involved to retake the test at a facility I've chosen. Moreover, the requirements were to use a facility with an in-house lab and controlled environment. All parties have conformed to the requirements and the samples from Mr. Tucker Corbin, Mr. Mason Callaway, and Beau Corbin have been obtained."

I must have zoned out. I was too keenly awaiting the results, and I missed them.

But as I looked around the room I saw smiles, laughter, and hugs. It was evident by the happiness surrounding me that Beau received the news he'd longed for. The first test was false.

Brice took my hand and smiled. "It's all working out like it should. I'm happy for them." He pulled me closer and held me tightly. "Just like it worked out for us."

Dad walked past us and waited his turn to hug Beau. Charlotte wouldn't take her hands off him, and Beau was more than okay with that.

"Son, it feels so good to call you that! This has just been too much on us." Dad wiped his eyes and hugged Beau. "I'm glad you kept fighting for this. You went with your gut."

"I'm happy he listened to his gut as well," Charlotte said as she thought back to how she wanted to give up. She looked up at him and smiled. "I'm so thankful you didn't give up on me...on us...on this. I love you, Beau Corbin."

Beau smiled and kissed her.

"Alright, you two, that's enough of all that." Charlotte heard Mason through the rest of the noise surrounding them. He reached out his hand to Beau. "You knew it all along...it didn't feel right."

Beau shook his head. "Yeah, I did."

Mason shook Beau's hand and looked at Charlotte. "I'm happy for both of you."

Charlotte ran to Mason and hugged him. "Thank you, Dad. I'm happier than I've been in a long time."

Mason shook Dad's hand and smiled. "I'm glad Beau was persistent. I'm happy for ya'll."

Dad smiled back and replied, "Me too!."

Mason didn't want to detract from the celebration, but his curiosity got the best of him. "Tucker, there is one thing about all of this I would like to know. How did you find out the kits were left unattended?"

Dad looked down at the ground and hesitated before responding. "You know...the cleaning crew came in that evening and Allison didn't remember locking the cabinet." Dad hoped the explanation would suffice.

"Hmm, that's interesting. How did this come about now? It has been months since the paternity test." Mason wasn't giving up that easily.

"I can't really talk about it now, Mason. Maybe we can catch up later?" Dad wanted to end the conversation.

"Yeah, sure, but something seems odd about all of this. I would like to hear more when you have time." Mason shook Dad's hand again.

Isabella stood in the back of the courtroom keenly watching Mason and Dad's conversation.

As everyone left the courtroom, she caught Beau and Charlotte walking to the exit.

"Beau, can I have a minute?" she softly asked.

"Sure, Mom," Beau replied.

Isabella looked at Charlotte then back at Beau and smiled. "So, you got the news you wanted. I'm happy for you."

"Thanks, we're happy this is over." Beau wrapped his arm around Charlotte and kissed her cheek. "Charlotte's all I ever wanted, Mom. She means everything to me."

Charlotte smiled embracing Beau's strong hold on her.

"I know. I just wanted to say I'm happy for you." Isabella grabbed her purse and walked out of the courtroom.

Charlotte sighed. "She'll never come around, will she? She'll never accept me."

Beau shook his head as they left the courtroom. "Do you even care if she accepts you at this point? Most people don't accept the way she treats everyone. You're not losing much not being accepted' by Isabella

Corbin!" Beau stood in front of her and wrapped his arms around her waist. "Everyone else is happy for us...I'm happy for us. Besides, you couldn't get rid of me if you wanted to!"

He reached into his jean pocket and pulled out a small, dried pink rose. "Your favorite color, right?" He smirked.

Charlotte smiled. "You know that's my favorite color!" She pulled his lips close to hers and whispered, "I love you so much."

***

"I heard the paternity test results were coming back today," Whitney said as Blaine unloaded hay bales from the trailer.

"Yeah, that's good." He wiped the sweat from his forehead. "I don't really want to talk about Beau."

"I get it. I was just making conversation." Whitney wished Beau and Blaine would resolve things.

Blaine grabbed a few more bales of hay and dropped them at the end of the trailer. "You think Beau is going to tell the police what happened?"

"No. He wouldn't do that." Whitney seemed surprised he even asked.

"Why the hell wouldn't he? I mean...I ran him off the road and he's pissed at me." Blaine threw his gloves on the trailer and took a break. "I don't know...it just keeps bothering me. I wish he'd talk to me."

"Maybe you should try to talk to him again," Whitney replied while sitting on the tailgate of the truck.

"Yeah right. You saw how mad he was at me." Blaine went back to throwing hay bales into the barn.

She changed the subject to lighten the mood. "You need any help with that? I feel bad just sitting here watching." She jumped down off the tailgate.

Blaine stopped and grabbed the water cooler. Laughing, he replied, "I've never seen you *want* to do anything related to manual labor."

"Well, that's mean!" she said jokingly. But, he was telling the truth. She hated to sweat other than when cheering.

"It's true, and you know it. Besides, I just like having you here...it's nice." Blaine leaned on the hay bales and smiled. "I might just turn you into a farm girl after all."

"Not happening!" Whitney laughed as she followed him into the barn. When he finished stacking the hay bales, he came closer to her – drenched in sweat – and tried to hug her.

"Don't you dare do it, Blaine!" she yelled as he wrapped his muscular, sweaty arms around her waist.

"Too late!" His arms enveloped her body, and she became lost in his hold on her.

He felt her arms wrap around his waist, and she looked up into his eyes. "I'm not sure where this may go, but it feels right...being with you."

Blaine ran his fingers through her blonde hair. "Yeah, it does feel right. I can tell you where this goes."

"Oh, you can, huh?" Whitney replied sarcastically and laughed.

"Yeah, I know exactly where this is headed." He lightly kissed her lips and whispered, "To the pond!" He picked her up and threw her over his shoulders. "Hold on babe!" he yelled as he took off running toward the pond.

"Blaine! Put me down! I can't...get in the...water! I don't have my bathing suit on!" Whitney struggled to get the words out as he pounded the ground. She laughed knowing he didn't care about her having a bathing suit.

At the end of the wooden dock, he stopped and let her down. "Okay, I won't do it. I just thought maybe you'd like to cool off."

His face became serious like he planned to kiss her again and she relaxed.

"Yeah, that sounds nice...I just don't have my swimsuit!" Whitney smiled at him anticipating his kiss.

"Yeah, that's too bad...because you're going in!" With one push, she fell back into the water and Blaine followed.

"Oh, you're so mean!" she said splashing water in his face.

He laughed. "Okay, I'm sorry. But doesn't the water feel better than standing out in the heat?"

She swam over closer to him. "Yeah, it does." She wrapped her arms around his neck and her legs around his waist.

He smiled and leaned closer to kiss her. "This is much better...don't you think?" He kissed her softly and pulled her body closer to his.

Her heartbeat wildly as his hands caressed her body and his kiss became deeper. She could kiss him all day and never come up for air.

He pulled back and gazed into her eyes. "I want it to be different this time, you know. We rushed things last time...and well...you know the rest."

Whitney placed her hands on his shoulders and poked out her lip being playful. "I know, but I was enjoying that kiss." She smiled. "I'm with you, though. I want to take things slow as well."

***

Stella picked up lunch for her mom and dad at AELs. As she waited for her food, she saw Jackson pull up in his Jeep.

She sat down at an empty table to wait on her order and hoped Jackson wouldn't see her.

To her dismay, as soon as he entered the door, his eyes locked with hers.

"Hey, Stella. You here by yourself?" Jackson asked anxiously scanning the restaurant.

"Yep!" Stella coldly replied.

"Where's everyone at?" he asked nervously.

"I have no clue. I'm just picking up lunch, and I'm headed home," she replied hoping they would call her order soon.

"Hmm, okay. Have you talked to Charlotte lately?" Jackson continued to pry for answers.

Stella had met her limit. "No, Jackson, I haven't talked to her. Have you? Let me answer that for you: no, you haven't. And the reason I know that is because she doesn't want to talk to you!"

Jackson stepped back from the table, "Geez, Stella, I just asked if you talked to her. I know I was rude to her the other day at The Dixie."

"Rude!" Stella laughed and shook her head. "You were more than rude! I wouldn't be talking to you either!"

Stella knew Jackson didn't have anyone else to lean on, but he sure wasn't going to lean on her. She was standing her ground.

"I just heard my name...my order is up." Stella stood up from the chair and laughed to herself. "You know, it's funny; when I wanted you to notice me and spend time with me, you didn't. Now when I'm over you and you don't have anyone else you think I'll be your friend."

Jackson stared back at her with a blank look on his face.

"Well...you're wrong!" She snapped her finger and turned away from him.

She smiled as she left. *That was harder than I thought it'd be. But, he doesn't deserve me or my time.*

Chapter Fifty-Eight

The Twilight Zone

"Here's another round," Trisha said to her table of regulars. "Tonight's my last night bartending so my tips better be good!"

"Oh yeah, I heard you decided to go with Charlee up to Mississippi to open a bar there. We sure will miss seeing you here."

Trisha smiled. "I'll keep em' coming tonight." She winked at them and made her way back to the bar.

Two men had been sitting at barstools near the end of the bar most of the evening.

"Can we get another round?" They motioned with their beer mugs.

Trisha gave them both a fresh mug. "I don't recall seeing either of you here before. Ya'll travellin through?"

"Yes, ma'am. We're from Texas and on our way up to Tennessee for a business opportunity." One of the men elbowed the other cueing him to stop talking.

"After this round, we'll take our check." The large burly man stood up from the barstool. "Where's your restroom?"

Trisha pointed to the corner and noticed Charlene coming through the door. "You're an hour late!"

"I know...I'm sorry." Charlene hurriedly put on her apron and grabbed a tray.

"Thanks for covering tonight...even though you're late," Trisha said with a smirk.

As Charlene rounded the bar, she froze. *Could it really be him? It couldn't be.* When she walked closer, he glanced her way and spit out his beer.

Oblivious that Trisha was watching her every move, Charlene approached the man on the barstool. "What in the hell are you doing here?"

"I guess I should ask you the same question!" he replied.

"I live here...well I'm from here and have been visiting." Charlene put the tray down on the bar. "So, why are you here? For business?"

He took a long sip of his drink. "Man, that's some cold beer! I think I might have one more."

Charlene sat on the barstool next to him and continued to press. "Are you gonna ignore me or tell me why you're here in my hometown?"

The burly man came back and seemed annoyed seeing Charlene. "You're on my stool. Get up!" His voice was deep and unfriendly.

She ignored him still waiting for an answer.

"We're just passing through. We won't be here long." The man motioned to Trisha to cash him out.

"Well, where you headin off to?" Charlene's questions were beginning to annoy Trisha.

The burly man leaned on the bar and faced Charlene. "We aren't headed anywhere that's your business. So back off."

Charlene realized she'd hit a nerve and walked away.

They cashed out their tab. As they walked out of the bar Charlene mumbled, "I'll catch up to you again soon...very soon."

Trisha walked up behind Charlene. "What in the hell was that all about? You know them?"

"Yep, sure do. Just a few ghosts from my past that's all." Charlene smiled as she gathered empty bottles from tables.

Trisha knew the gleam in her eye meant she had something up her sleeve. *What are you up to now Charlene?*

***

"You were in rehab? What in the world, Nessie!" Beau was shocked as I explained the last two weeks of my life.

"Yep, the old man put me there," I jokingly said, then looked at Dad and smiled. "You know I'm kidding."

Dad smiled. "I hope so."

"I've got to hear more of this story...you crashed in your room with the windows open in the middle of July!" Beau found the story amusing. "My sister...Nessie Corbin...drinking...what!?"

I didn't know how to react, so I laughed along with him. I really didn't feel like going down memory lane.

Dad interjected. "While it may seem funny looking back on it...it was very serious at the time."

My lips pressed together tightly as I knew what that tone meant. We had said enough.

"Dad's right. It wasn't a joke. It was real. The main thing is I'm better now." I grabbed Brice's hand and pulled it around my waist. "Everything is perfect now."

For once, living in this house might not be too bad.

Beau and Charlotte were together...the way it was supposed to be. My relationship with Brice was still new; the butterflies in my stomach...my heart racing when he held my hand...becoming weightless when he held me and kissed me. I never wanted those feelings to end.

Dad was moving back in the house slowly which meant Isabella was moving out. I think that made me smile the most. I know that sounds so cold and heartless, but we all needed space from her.

"Who's staying for dinner?" Dad asked and we all knew we better say, 'yes'. "I've got some white perch I planned to fry. I've got plenty, so bring your appetites."

We left him in the kitchen prepping for dinner and walked out onto the patio in the back of the house. Charlotte and Beau followed.

I'd been waiting for the right time to ask Charlotte about Owen.

"Brice, come help me with these chairs," Beau said as they walked across the yard to get them.

Charlotte sat down on the rocking chair. "I can't believe school is about to start again. I'm not ready."

It felt weird talking to Charlotte. We were in the same grade...but she never really paid much attention to me before. Small talk made it worse.

"Me either." I didn't know how to ask what I wanted to know.

"You heard Owen's gone?" Charlotte asked glancing my way.

"Yeah, actually, I was hoping we could talk about him." I'd been eager to understand more about why he left.

"It's different around the house without him. He never really made himself known much, but it just feels weird with him not being there ya know." Charlotte watched as Beau and Brice raced back to them with chairs on their back. She laughed. "That's just like Beau, huh? Always a competition."

"Yeah." I laughed. "You're right. Living with him you realize he's going to win everything, so I finally got smart and just quit trying!"

As they made their way back up the steps, I yearned to hear more about Owen. "So, why'd he decide to go abroad?"

"Ah, the million-dollar question no one really has the answer to!" Charlotte pulled her hair back into a ponytail. "He's always wanted to do it, I'm just not sure what pushed him over the edge to do it now."

"Who's doing what now?" Beau repeated jokingly.

"We're talking about Owen and why he decided to go to boarding school...across the globe!" I hoped deep down he didn't leave due to the way I'd treated him.

"Ohhh...someone seems a little bothered that he left." Beau poked fun at me.

"I'm not *bothered* by it. I'm just curious why he decided now was a good time. He talked about it a lot. In fact, we had a pact that after senior year we might go abroad for the summer." I smiled as memories flooded my mind of our friendship. "I guess all of that is out the window now."

Beau straddled the armrest of Charlotte's chair. "Why are you asking all these questions? Aren't ya'll like best friends? Wouldn't he have told you all this before he left?"

I gave him 'that' look. "No, Beau he didn't tell me." I could feel my pulse begin to race. "He didn't tell me because I was not talking to him. Okay, there! I said it!"

Charlotte looked at Beau and he shrugged his shoulders. Brice grabbed my hand and squeezed it lightly. "You okay, Nessie?"

"Yeah, I'm fine." It didn't feel normal having this conversation with Beau and Charlotte; they'd never been interested in talking to me...as friends.

"Look, whatever happened, that's your business. I get it. You know Owen about as well as I do being his twin, and well...he doesn't make changes easily. So, you know he thought this one through." Charlotte's response seemed genuine.

"Thanks. Just, if you talk to him...tell him to call me...to check in." I pressed my lips together as I thought, *I really wished we could have met up before he left town.*

***

Jackson dreaded going back to school. He stopped by the firm to get Allison to sign his physical form for sports.

"I've ruined things with Charlotte for good. I know she loves Beau, but I felt like we really connected."

"Jackson, you need to let her go. It's the right thing to do. I do feel sorry for Melissa and Mason having to deal with Isabella." Allison sighed and continued, "Trust me, Jackson. There is someone out there that will be over the moon crazy about you." Allison hugged him and walked to open her office door. "Are you going to the clinic to get the physical today?"

He sighed, "Yeah, I have to. It's due tomorrow back to Coach. But, I dread seeing Dr. Corbin."

"She probably won't mention the paternity stuff. I think she got the message from Tucker." Allison hoped Isabella wouldn't stoop that low.

"I hope she doesn't, but I have a feeling she is going to ask me about it." Jackson walked out of the office dreading the clinic visit.

***

"Really, Mom! You are leaving to start some new bar thing...out of state!" Tennie yelled as Trisha sat on the sofa doing what she did best, smoking her cigarette.

"Yep, Tennie girl, that's what I'm doing. You're eighteen. You have a job...you're practically an adult--or should be!" She relaxed on the sofa as Tennie put up groceries in the kitchen.

"You can't just leave me and Brice here alone. They have laws for that you know!" The fury inside Tennie raged as she slammed the cabinet doors closed. "I just don't get you, Mom."

"What's there to 'get'?" Trisha laughed until a coughing spell ensued.

"And the cigarettes, Mom. They're slowly killing you. You smoke a carton a day at minimum." Tennie rolled her eyes.

"You and Brice will be just fine. Besides, I don't do much around here anyway. I'm always at the bar working. I'm hardly even here." She extended her legs across the coffee table and closed her eyes. "We're heading out in two days. You can have my room if you want it!"

"Ughhh...I can't!" Tennie stormed out the front door.

She met Brice as he pulled up into the driveway.

"What happened now?" Brice knew something was wrong based on the look on Tennie's face.

"It's *your* mom...she's completely lost it! She's leaving in two days with Charlee to help him start the new bar in Mississippi." Tennie looked at Brice waiting for him to blow up.

"She can't do that! She can't leave us here alone. You've misunderstood her or something." Brice opened the door to the living room hoping to drill Trisha about leaving them.

He quickly slammed the door.

Tennie lit a cigarette and offered him a drag. "She's passed out."

"Yep," Brice replied and shrugged. "Maybe she should leave. Every time I come home I feel like I'm living in the twilight zone."

Chapter Fifty-Nine

Silver Lining

"Gone? She can't leave town, Brice!" I looked at Dad for reassurance. "That's not legal, right?" I exclaimed.

"No, Nessie, she can't legally do that...at least with Brice since he's a minor." Dad looked at Brice and back at me. "What's Tennie doing?"

"She's eighteen, so she's fine. I mean, she's definitely mad at Mom for leaving...but we couldn't make her stay. She thinks she's going to make it big in this new bar...the bar owner, Charlee, is making her manager or something." Dad saw the desperation in Brice's face and heard it in his tone.

"Brice, you can stay here, son, until we get things figured out." He didn't hesitate to offer.

"Oh, no, sir, I can't do that. I can figure out something." Brice's pride got the best of him.

"No, you're staying here. We have an extra room...and it's yours for now. I'm not taking 'no' for an answer." Dad's tone hardened.

Brice smiled and grabbed my hand. "Thank you, Mr. Corbin. That means a lot to me. I'll do whatever I can around here to help."

"Well, you can start with the laundry and dishes. It seems neither of my children thinks that they have to do chores." Dad walked toward the pantry and Brice headed to the sink. "Brice! I was kidding! Sit down!"

***

It was the first week of school and everyone dreaded going back. The only exciting thing about the week was the football jamboree on Friday night.

School was different without Owen. I still hadn't heard from him. I wished he would call me. Even with Brice by my side, I still longed to close things with Owen. He deserved an apology. Maybe one day he would call.

While I missed Owen's friendship, it was nice having someone who was happy to see me between classes – sometimes sneaking in a quick kiss – and talking about what we were planning for the weekend. This whole relationship thing was very new to me, but I soaked in all of Brice's attention.

Before we got to my third-hour class, his hold on my hand tightened and he stopped me. "Hey, I wanted to tell you something. It's been on my mind for a while. I've been back and forth about it...and I wanted to hear what you thought."

"Yeah, sure, tell me!" I was unsure what it was about.

"I...I think I'm going to try out for baseball again this year." Brice had tossed the idea around so much in his head he was tired of thinking about it.

"Brice! Yes, that's great! I know how much you miss it. I definitely think you should try out." The bell rang, and I realized I was now late. I blew him a kiss and ran to my class.

***

Beau and Blaine had one class together this year, and Beau was dreading it.

Blaine walked in and took a seat near the back of class like usual. Beau was already sitting on the right side of the room near the teacher's desk. He didn't make eye contact.

Noticing he had five minutes before the bell rang, he walked over to Beau's desk.

As soon as Blaine attempted to sit down behind him, Beau got up and walked out of the classroom.

Blaine followed.

The bell rang and the halls were empty. Skipping class was something Blaine was good at, but Beau always followed the rules.

He's probably in the locker room.

Blaine opened the boy's locker room door and saw Beau sitting on the bench throwing a football in the air.

"Me leaving the class meant I didn't want to talk to you." Beau's tone was firm as his eyes followed the twirl of the football in the air.

"I know. I get it. I know you don't want to talk to me. And I get it. Just hear me out." Blaine sat down on the bench across from Beau. "I need to ask you something."

Beau continued ignoring him. His hands squeezed the football.

"Look, I'm sorry man. I know I said it already, but I'm truly sorry. I have so much guilt inside...I wanted to tell you once I remembered...I did. I just couldn't find the right time." Blaine was sincere for once. Beau heard it in his voice, but it didn't quiet the anger that raged inside of him.

"Oh, I'm glad you finally felt responsible enough to tell me!" Beau yelled as he threw the football against the lockers. "Aggghhhh...Blaine...man...you messed everything up for me. You could've killed me! And you're sitting here with all this guilt that you didn't tell me. That's messed up!"

Blaine opened his arms exposing his chest. "Hit me. Take it out on me. I deserve it. Just punch the shit of out me."

Beau's jaw tightened and he imagined whaling Blaine down to the floor, but he backed away. "No, it's not going to be that easy. I don't trust you anymore. I don't want you around me...or Charlotte...or my family. You're nothing to me, Blaine. You got that!? Nothing!"

Blaine looked at the floor and then back at Beau. "Can I just ask you one thing, please? I know I don't deserve you to listen, but I need to know."

Beau stood with his arms crossed over his chest. He nodded.

"Am I gonna go to jail for this? I mean, I deserve to and all, I just want to be prepared for it." Blaine waited for what seemed like minutes for Beau's response.

Beau grabbed the football from the floor and tossed it to Blaine. With a sarcastic grin he said, "I guess we'll just have to see what play I call."

***

"He's living with me right now, but he can't stay with us forever. I trust the kid...I do...he's nothing like Trisha, but he's dating my daughter!" Dad explained to Allison as they worked through lunch on a case.

"Oh, my, I can't even imagine. How could she just up and leave town like that!?" Allison tried to make sense of Trisha's actions.

"She's never been a good mother. Honestly, I'm surprised those two kids made it this far." Dad took another bite of his sandwich. "Brice seems to be a good kid. Tennie is nothing but trouble."

Allison continued sorting the various files while he made notes for his opening argument. Something about Brice's situation unsettled her. *How could a mother leave her children?*

***

"Why are you quitting cheer?" Charlotte asked Whitney.

"It's just not something I want to do this year...that's all." Whitney knew Charlotte wasn't going to be happy she was quitting.

"That's not good enough. You *love* cheer! I'm not buying that you just don't want to." Charlotte stepped in front of Whitney's car door. "You're not leaving until you tell me the real reason."

Whitney fidgeted with her car keys stalling to answer.

"Whit! You know I'm not gonna' leave until you tell me. It's not because of the guys not talking is it?" Charlotte figured that was the reason.

"No! I wouldn't quit cheer over the guys...no...that's stupid." Whitney laughed. "It's really just...well...I like spending time with Blaine at the farm, and when he doesn't have football, I want to spend time with him."

"He will always have football...you know that! And you're going to be at the games anyway. I still don't believe you." Charlotte crossed her arms and stared at Whitney. "And, I need you on the squad. We've been doing this since elementary school, Whit. Stay on the team...if not for you for me."

Whitney pressed her lips together holding back the answer she knew would not sit well with Charlotte. "I just don't want to do it anymore. That's it...honestly. I want to focus on school and Blaine. It's just different now, everything is different."

Charlotte's head tilted and her eyes narrowed. "Did you just say *focus on school*?"

Whitney laughed. "Yeah, Char, I did. It's true. After all this with Charlene...I just want to be successful at something, have something to be proud of."

"That's great, I mean...I'm shocked as I never thought the two words focus and school would come out of your mouth, but I'm glad for you." Charlotte pushed herself from Whitney's car and hugged her. "No matter what happens we'll always be friends...right?"

"Yeah, of course." Whitney smiled knowing things were going to be somewhat normal between them...like old times.

***

"We can't just bring him into our home...it's not that easy, Allison." Kent walked back into the shop office.

"He doesn't have a home! His mother left him with his irresponsible sister. Tucker agreed to let him stay with them, but he said it can't be long term."

Allison's heart broke for Brice. She was having a hard time swallowing the fact Trisha just up and left. "He's a good kid, Kent. He deserves more than this."

Kent sat back in his office chair. "I know he's a hard worker. Hell, I've been giving him extra hours here the last two years to help him make ends meet. I want to help him. I do. But, I don't want to have to deal with Trisha."

"I need to get back to the office. Just think about it, okay?" Allison always had a way of getting what she wanted. Kent knew she wouldn't stop until they helped Brice.

"I'll give it some more thought. Love you." Kent loved everything about Allison – but most of all – he loved her caring and giving nature. "Have a good day, honey."

As she walked out of the shop into the parking lot, she noticed Brice pulling up. She waved and smiled. *That poor kid has so much to give...he deserves a chance.*

***

Isabella stared at the four walls of the 600 square foot cottage Dr. Dawson insisted she move into. The décor was nothing like she was accustomed to, but this was the only place available to her on short notice. Dr. Dawson's love for antiques spilled over into the cottage – no telling how old some of the pieces were.

I'll stay here for a while and let things settle at home. I can always focus on the clinic. I know Tucker needs more time. He'll come around...I know he will.

She longed to be back together with her family. Things had changed...she'd softened. And she hoped that Dad would see it as well. After all, he could have told the truth about her switching the results which would've been a complete disaster – both professionally and personally.

Maybe he does still care about me? Maybe we still have a chance to be together. Or will he use this against me...holding it over my head? I have to make sure no one finds out what I did with those tests.

***

"There is more to this story than Tucker is letting on." Mason swirled the ice cube in his whiskey glass. "Something isn't adding up, and I'm going to find out what it is."

"Honey, let it go! Charlotte is happy, Beau is happy. We need some happiness around here." Melissa sat across from him on the sofa, folding clothes.

"I know, but I can't let this go. My gut told me from the beginning that Isabella had something to do with this. I can't help but think that Tucker is still protecting her. I don't know how or why, but I'm going to find out!" Mason couldn't let it go. "I'm going to find out the truth. We all deserve to know what happened to those test kits!"

***

I sat on my bench in my bay window staring blankly at the silhouettes of the grand live oaks as the sun found its resting place across the bayou. Surprisingly, for a Louisiana mid-August night, the air was pleasant, so I opened the bay windows to soak it in.

As I closed my eyes, the chirps from the crickets filled my ears. Their melodious 'song' made me smile. I hadn't felt this much peace in a long time.

While things were not perfect – not by a long shot – I was happy, Dad was happy, and Beau got his girl back. Things were moving in a good direction.

It felt good to be home. I finally felt at peace.

As I made my way back to bed, I caught a glimpse of my journal lying on my nightstand and smiled.

Brice must have saved it. I told him to burn it! I'm glad he didn't listen to me.

It had been a while since I opened it up.

As I picked up the journal, a piece of paper fell out of it onto the floor.

Intrigued, I picked up the folded paper and opened it.

To Nessie...From Dad...there's always a silver lining...

"The world breaks everyone, and afterward, many are strong at the broken places."

—— Ernest Hemingway

I smiled. Dad had placed this note in my journal and brought it to the lake house for me with intentions I would read it. I read the quote over and over again. Such a simple statement packed with deep meaning.

The world will break everyone at some point...in some way...and if you choose to heal...to recover...you will be stronger where you once felt broken and alone.

I tucked the note from Dad back into the journal and smiled. I looked out of the bay window and noticed the moss dangling from the sweeping branches of the live oak dancing in the light breeze that made its way from Bayou Fueob. I became entranced by the graceful sweep of the wind on the moss until I was interrupted by Mason's voice.

"Tucker! We need to talk about this whole paternity test!" Mason yelled as he knocked on the front door.

I closed my eyes seeking quiet...peace...like the soft breeze on the moss. I tried to embrace it tightly, but it faded.

So many things were still unsettled.

A storm was brewing, and things were far from being normal in Sedipar.

Chapter Sixty

The Blame Game

"Tucker! I know it's late, but we need to talk!" Mason beat his fist against the front door. "Open the door!"

"Alright, I'm coming!" Dad yelled from the foyer. "Give me a minute!"

As soon as the door opened, Mason flew by. "Something's not right Tucker. I don't want to sound accusatory, but I think you're covering for Isabella."

Dad smirked and laughed, closed the front door, and calmly replied, "*You* think I'm protecting the woman who lied to me about sleeping with you in high school which destroyed my family?"

"Well, when you put it that way, no. But something doesn't add up. And I know you were a part of it!" Mason wasn't leaving until Dad gave him an answer.

"Want one?" Dad reached out his hand toward Mason offering a drink.

"No, I just want answers. Damn! You Corbins are thick-headed!" Mason paced the floor.

"Just sit down." Dad sighed knowing he'd have to share something with Mason to get him out of our home. "Allison didn't lock the cabinet when the cleaning crew came in that evening. I'm not saying one of the staff tampered with the kits, but we can't assume they didn't."

"Why are you telling me this? I know that already. Isabella's name is written all over this!" Mason wasn't backing down. "She manipulated my daughter's relationship with Beau. I know she had something to do with the tests."

Dad stirred his drink with his finger. "Isabella was in the office that evening with Allison. They enjoyed a few too many glasses of wine, and Allison passed out." Dad waited for Mason's response.

"So, Isabella was there, in the office, unattended. I knew it! I knew she must have had something to do with this!" Mason clapped his hands together with excitement.

"No, Mason, she didn't have anything to do with it. I told you – the cabinet was left unattended overnight. Isabella stayed with Allison until Jackson picked her up." Dad struggled to lie to Mason. But he knew what would ensue if Mason found out the truth.

Intrigued by Mason's visit so late in the evening, I entered the living room with Brice by my side. "Hey, Mr. Callaway. Have you heard from Owen?"

Mason looked my way and smiled. "No, Nessie, we haven't heard from him in almost a week." He quickly focused his stare on Brice and then back at Dad.

I paused and wondered, *What on earth is so important for him to come by so late?*

Brice followed me into the kitchen with a confused look on his face. "What's he doing here?"

"I don't know. Your guess is as good as mine." I folded my arms across my chest and watched Dad and Mason whispering in the other room.

***

"What's wrong, babe?" Blaine asked as Whitney sat next to him on the truck's tailgate. Her body was close to his, but her mind was thousands of light-years away.

"Nothing," she softly muttered, resting her head against his shoulder.

"You don't have to go to the jamboree if you're not feeling it." He jumped off the tailgate and positioned himself in front of her. His thumbs lightly caressed her cheeks as his hands cupped her face. "As long as you're waiting for me when I come out of the locker room – I'm good with you missing the game." He kissed her softly and then gave her space.

"No, I'm not going to miss it. I just feel weird not cheering this year." She sighed and fidgeted with her keys. "Besides, Charlotte is still acting weird toward me. We're talking some, but it isn't the same."

"Babe, just go talk to Charlotte. I know she wants you back on the team. Just show up in your uniform. She'd be happy." Blaine knew how much cheering meant to Whitney, but he also understood why she was avoiding it. Between her mom leaving town coupled with the tension between him and Beau, she needed something positive like cheer to keep her happy. "Go back to cheer, babe. You love it. It makes you happy."

Whitney pulled his body closer between her legs and smiled. Looking up at him she said, "You make me happy. You're all I need."

He smiled and kissed her forehead softly. "Well, as much as I don't want to let go of you, I gotta' go before Dad kicks my butt. I've got one more cornfield to cut."

She watched him run to the tractor he'd left idling near the barn. "I love you Blaine Ferrell," softly rolled off her lips.

***

"Jackson Beale," the nurse yelled while holding a chart. "Second door on the right. We need to get your height and weight."

Jackson had dreaded this appointment knowing Isabella was going to put him on the spot about the paternity test. He'd avoided it as long as he could. Coach wouldn't allow him to play in the game without it.

"Just sit here until we have an open room," the nurse said as she finished recording in his chart.

Just as the nurse left the room, Isabella appeared in the doorway. "Come with me," she said dryly.

"Yes, ma'am," he replied as he followed behind her. Her demeanor didn't surprise him as she never made anyone feel comfortable.

Once in the exam room, she shut the door and reviewed his chart. "It seems you are a healthy boy. Your weight is on target, and your blood pressure is normal. Let me check your reflexes."

She continued through the motions of the physical jotting down information into his.

"Here you go. Just bring this to Coach. You should be good to go." She handed him the paper and walked toward the exam door.

Jackson was relieved that the appointment had gone so smoothly until he saw her turn toward him. As he scooted off the exam table, his eyes met hers.

Her cold eyes pierced his soul. "I expected more from you, Jackson. You're a smart boy. Smart boys don't cross me."

Her evil grin penetrated him as he stood in silence unsure of how to respond.

"It seems you've tried to get close to that 'Callaway girl'." She watched as his eyebrow raised, but he remained silent. "I don't know what you boys see in her. If she's anything like her father...well...I wish Beau could see through her."

Jackson remained silent with his hands clasped waiting for her to let him escape.

She moved closer to him and softly touched his shoulder. "Jackson, I know you wanted her to notice you and to be your girlfriend. What a perfect way to break her and Beau up. The truth will come out sooner or later. Everyone will know that you're the reason Beau's fairytale romance with that *girl* almost ended."

Jackson brushed her hand from his shoulder and shook his head. "You're insane! No one is going to believe I tampered with the tests! Besides, I saw *you* by the filing cabinet. Several others know the truth too."

"Tampering? Who said anything about tampering? Oh, you poor boy. It must be hard keeping that secret bottled up inside. You have *so* much to learn. I'm not worried about any of that. Diffuse all of this noise surrounding the paternity test and your secret is safe with me. If you make this worse for me, I promise I'll make your life a living hell." She casually walked toward the exam room door and paused before exiting. "Do I make myself clear, Jackson?"

He stood motionless trying to dissect what had just happened. He nodded his head, and she slammed the door.

Chapter Sixty-One

Friday Night Lights

Game day seemed different with Beau sitting on the sidelines. While the hall walls remained plastered with Beau mantras, the vibe was much different knowing he wouldn't be the Mustang quarterback this year.

"How you feelin' about tonight?" Charlotte asked as she slid her hand into his while walking into school.

"I'm okay. I mean...there's not much I can do anyway. I'll be there to support my team." Beau kissed her hand and pulled her closer to him. "Besides, I get to watch you cheer the entire game now."

Charlotte grinned at the thought of Beau focusing one hundred percent on her.

As they entered the school doors, Blaine stood arm-in-arm with Whitney as the football team circled them.

"Blaine, dude, you ready to tear apart the Bears tonight?" A team member shouted cockily as his outreached fist waited for Blaine's bump back.

"Yeah, sure thing, dude. The game is ours!" Blaine yelled as Whitney leaned in closer and smiled.

"Just be safe out on that field. The team ya'll are playing is rough. I need you back home to me in one piece." Whitney smiled, nestling her head on his chest, inhaling his cologne.

Blaine placed both hands on her hips and lightly kissed her lips. "Babe don't worry about me. Just be sure you are waiting for me on the sidelines after the game."

"I can do that!" she replied biting her lip hoping he would kiss her again. Noticing Charlotte and Beau standing inches away, she knew her moment with Blaine being alone was over.

Beau made his way through the crowd of football players as they chanted hoping he would partake in the makeshift pep rally they had created in the hallway. Charlotte followed closely behind holding his hand tight.

Jackson leaned up against the wall standing away from the crowd. Charlotte's eyes met his as they walked past and then quickly darted toward the floor.

By habit, the team attempted to raise Beau into the air, but he resisted. "Ya'll know I can't play tonight or rather the entire season."

The team continued to chant louder, and the hype was heard by students down the hall. "We don't care man! You're still our QB Beau...we'll always choose you," a few team members shouted as they raised Beau into the air and paraded him around.

Jackson pushed away from the wall – annoyed that he wasn't recognized as the quarterback.

Charlotte watched, smiling as the team carried Beau up and down the hall; the way it should be. She noticed Jackson walking briskly ahead of the team toward the main hall.

As she started to follow the crowd, she caught Whitney staring her way and their eyes locked. Whitney raised her hand to wave and smiled. Charlotte lifted her hand in a half wave.

"Ugh, see, Blaine. She hates me. I knew it. She's still mad about cheer." Whitney crossed her arms on her chest.

"Babe, I already told you what you need to do about cheer. Just show up. It'll fix the tension between ya'll." He quickly kissed her cheek and continued, "I gotta follow the team. Maybe this is my chance to talk to Beau."

She watched as Blaine trailed behind the crowd hoping to get the chance to make amends with Beau. She sighed knowing it likely wouldn't be that easy.

***

"Char, have you talked to Whit about rejoining the cheer team?" Stella questioned as they sat in homeroom.

"Girl, I've tried several times, and she won't budge. I gave up, but I'm worried about her. She's putting all of her focus on Blaine now, and we all know where that road will take her." Charlotte doodled on her notebook thinking about how Blaine easily dropped Whitney last year when he found out she was pregnant and miscarried.

"I'm worried about her as well. She isn't thinking clearly. I know she's been through a lot with her mom, but quitting cheer - something that she loves - doesn't feel like the best choice." Stella sighed and started chewing on the end of her pencil.

Charlotte turned to face Stella. "You have to convince Whit to come back to the team. The girls need her for stunts. The football team needs her fiery spirit, and...well...I need my friend."

"Girl, I get it. If she wouldn't listen to you...I doubt she will listen to me. But I'll try." Stella's brow raised as Whitney entered the classroom.

Sitting at the desk in front of Charlotte, Whitney was reluctant to talk.

As the bell rang, Whitney felt a light tap on her shoulder. "Hey, Whit, we need to talk after class," Charlotte whispered.

Whitney glanced over her shoulder and smiled while nodding as the World History teacher asked the class to open up their books to begin the lesson on Egyptian culture.

The lesson seemed to take hours and finally, the bell rang.

"Whit, meet me at my locker okay? I'll walk with you to our next class." Charlotte lightly touched Whitney's arm as she walked past her.

Whitney knew that Charlotte wanted her back on the team – hence the reason she wanted to meet up at her locker. She gathered her books and backpack and walked into the hall.

Charlotte switched out her books for the next class and shut her locker door. "You scared me!" Charlotte gasped placing her hand near her heart and giggled.

Whitney's lips pressed together tightly as she smirked. "I know why you're doing this, Char. I'm not changing my mind. I'm not doing cheer."

"Whit, you need this, and we need you! You can't just quit on the team like this!" Charlotte knew Whitney's decision had been made from the lack of concern on her face.

"I'm sorry, Char. I am. But I *don't* need this. I have longed to find my place, to feel wanted, to have a purpose...and I feel that with Blaine." Whitney watched as Charlotte rolled her eyes. "Stop it! He's changed, Char! You can't see it because you're jaded by Beau's hatred of him, but he's different now."

Charlotte stood facing Whitney holding her books tight against her chest. "You're right Whit...I don't see it. I don't see it at all. He was so cruel to you before. How in the world did you even forgive him? We were here for you...your team...and friends. Now, all of a sudden, we don't mean anything?"

"It's not like that Char, and you know it. That's not fair." Whitney knew Charlotte wasn't going to let it go.

"Maybe so Whit, but you left the team. You left me. We didn't deserve that. I hope Blaine is worth it." Charlotte said pointedly as she walked past Whitney. "We don't have to walk to class together. I'd rather be alone."

Whitney hated arguing with Charlotte and thought their friendship meant more than Blaine and Beau's disagreement. Sighing, as she walked toward class, Blaine startled her with his strong hold on her waist and then felt his lips touch her cheek.

"Hey, babe," Blaine said as he secured his hold on her from behind. He squeezed his arms around her attempting to pick her up and she stopped him. "Not now Blaine. I can't!" She turned around and faced him. "I can't right now. Me and Char just..."

Blaine interrupted her. "I get it. You don't have to say anything else. What can I do to help?"

"Nothing. She just needs time." Whitney couldn't help but smile seeing Blaine so focused on her. "Well, come to think of it...it would help if you and Beau made up."

Blaine grunted. "Yeah, I know. I'm trying. He won't even look at me." He pulled her back in closer to him. "I'm just glad I have you."

"Yeah, me too." Whitney closed her eyes embracing everything about him holding her close.

***

Jackson threw a few passes before the game and kept checking the sidelines for any sign of Beau. He was the team's leader now, and he had worked hard to fill Beau's shoes as quarterback. No one seemed to care.

As he continued warming up, he glanced into the stands and saw Stella and Whitney sitting together. He raised his hand to wave at them and quickly retreated as Stella rolled her eyes and turned away.

"Hey, babe, come wish me luck!" Blaine yelled from the sidelines. Whitney made her way down the bleacher steps to meet him.

Stella watched as Blaine's arms wrapped around Whitney with his helmet in hand. "Get a room you two!" she yelled from the bleachers and laughed.

As Blaine made his way back onto the field, Beau walked up behind her. "You could do so much better, Whitney."

"Beau, shut up! I got crap from your girlfriend this morning, and I don't need it from you!" Whitney pushed her way through the crowd to her seat by Stella in the stands.

Beau followed and sat behind them. "I'm sorry…I shouldn't have…" Whitney cut him off. "No, you shouldn't have. Blaine makes me happy. We needed each other."

Beau didn't agree. "Look, I'm not getting into this here at the game. But, if you want to be with someone that almost killed one of your best friends – well fine by me."

Whitney whipped her hair from her shoulder and turned. "Beau Corbin! Ugh! I don't even know what to say!"

"Just watch the game, Whit." Beau leaned forward clasping his hands while focusing on Charlotte.

"You need to talk to him, Beau. Ya'll are better friends than this. The bad part is, ya'lls stupid fight is causing me and Char to argue.

Ya'll need to swallow your pride and just fix things." Whitney waited for Beau's response.

"Did you just say, 'stupid fight'?" Beau tried hard to control his anger. "There is nothing stupid about Blaine being drunk and running me off the road. I can't believe you! He's the reason I'm sitting in these stands and not out on that field."

Whitney took a deep breath before turning around to look at Beau. She knew she had hit a nerve. Her words came out wrong. "I'm sorry. I didn't mean the reason you are mad is stupid. I just hate ya'll not being friends."

Beau watched as Blaine and Jackson made their way onto the field as the announcer began thanking the sponsors for the game over the speakers. "I can't do this. I'm outta' here."

As he made his way through the crowded bleachers, Charlotte caught a glimpse of him leaving and yelled his name.

When he made it to the bottom of the stairs, he looked out onto the field again and then at Charlotte. He shook his head and walked down the steps away from the field.

Charlotte dropped her poms and ran after him. "Beau! Wait!" she yelled running behind him. He stopped at the end of the sidewalk and turned.

"I can't do it, Charlotte. I thought it would be easier, but I just can't." She leaned into his chest not saying a word. He hugged her and softly pushed her away. "I just need some time alone. Go back to the game. I'll meet you at The Dixie after. I promise."

"Beau! Don't do this! If you leave, then I'm leaving with you!" Charlotte followed behind him.

"No, your squad needs you, and I need to be alone." Beau grabbed her hands and held them up to his lips, kissing them. "I love you and appreciate you wanting to come, but I need to clear my head. I'll see you at The Dixie later, okay?"

Charlotte watched as Beau sped away in his Corvette. As his taillights disappeared, she turned to face the stadium. She could hear faint chants of 'Cor-bin, Cor-bin!' from the stands. When she stepped onto the track, the announcer's words pierced her heart. "This first jamboree game is in honor of Beau Corbin, star quarterback of the Mustangs, who was injured last year and unable to play this season. Let's win this thing for Beau!"

Charlotte's eyes became misty as she scanned the crowd in the bleachers watching as everyone searched for Beau. She was the only one that knew he'd left. Everything he lived for was on that field. He'd lost something special…a piece of him that nothing but time could heal.

***

The game was a total disaster. Jackson had too many dropped passes to count, and the Mustangs lost 25-3. Coach threw his clipboard and headset onto the field and stormed to the locker room. The fans exited the bleachers silently and the only sound heard across the field was the stomping of feet on each step leaving the stadium.

Jackson walked off the field with his head hung. Kent and Allison met him at the fence and patted his back. "You had a bad night son. Just shake it off. You'll do better next time." Allison attempted to hug him across the fence, but he stopped her. "No, Mom, I gotta get into the locker room before Coach finds something else to yell at me about."

"Then, we'll see you at home."

Jackson turned back quickly and replied, "Don't wait up. I'm sure we're going to be in here a while."

Walking toward the locker room, he crossed paths with Charlotte and paused. He didn't know what to say, so in true Jackson fashion, he continued walking.

"Oh, so it's going to be like that, huh?" Charlotte stood with her arms crossed on her chest. "You don't deserve to be angry with me after what you did."

Jackson threw his hand in the air as he kept walking. "I don't have time for this now, Charlotte. I need to get in that locker room so Coach can chew my ass out for losing the game."

"Figures," Charlotte mumbled under her breath as she watched him retreat behind the door. She yelled as she walked away, "You'll never apologize. Your ego is too big."

Chapter Sixty-Two

Uninvited Host

We hadn't seen Isabella in several weeks, and we all hoped that would become the norm. It was nice not having to walk on eggshells in my own home or hibernate in my room to avoid interacting with my family. Things were different now – without her. As much as I wanted my life to be free of Isabella, I knew better than to believe she'd let go that easily.

"Well, good to see you too Nessie," Isabella said as she slyly maneuvered her way through the carport door.

"I...I was just leaving. No one is home." I hoped Brice wouldn't spoil my lie and appear from around the corner.

"Oh, I see. Where's Tucker?" Isabella placed her purse on the kitchen counter.

"I'm not sure...he said he..." I thought I hid my eye roll, but she immediately cut me off.

"Whatever. It doesn't matter. I'm going to cook dinner this evening for everyone. I miss my family, and I think we need to be together." Isabella made her way around the kitchen opening the refrigerator and the pantry. "This is terrible. Everything is bare."

As Isabella grabbed her purse from the counter, I breathed a sigh of relief at the thought of her leaving. Just as she rounded the corner of the bar, she paused and turned back toward me. "I'm going to get a few things at the store. Tell your father to expect dinner this evening."

I sarcastically saluted her as she pranced out the door.

"What was *that* all about?" Brice asked as he appeared from the hallway.

"Just the usual crap – typical Isabella stuff. She wants to have dinner here tonight…family dinner." I laughed at how silly that sounded.

Brice made his way closer to me and leaned on the kitchen bar. "What do you think your dad is going to do? Maybe I shouldn't be here."

"No, you don't get off that easy." He smirked as I pulled him closer to me. "Besides, you live here, remember? She doesn't."

Brice held me close, and I didn't want the moment to end. I longed for him to keep his strong hold on me in hopes of drowning out everything else. I imagined the storm that was about to brew up once Dad found out she had been here.

I closed my eyes and thought, *Dad is going to blow a gasket when he hears about this.*

***

"Isabella called me earlier and invited us over to their place for dinner. I find that a bit odd. Do you?" Allison asked as she folded the laundry.

"Did you talk to Tucker?" Kent knew Isabella had to be up to something.

"No, he was out of town most of the day, and I had to leave early for an appointment. She called me after I'd left for the day." The more

Allison recalled the conversation with Isabella the more worried she became.

"I'm going to call Tucker. He needs to know what he's coming home to. I bet he's still at the office tidying up after the case he had today." Allison reached for the phone and dialed the office. After several rings, the answering service picked up.

"Honey, why don't we drive over to the Corbin's?" Kent knew Allison wasn't going to like that idea, but he suggested it anyway.

"What's that look for?" Kent asked anticipating what Allison's facial expression meant.

"I'm not driving up to their home...especially when Tucker likely has no idea she's invited us. I'm not stepping in the middle of that mess. No way." Allison picked up the basket of clothes and walked down the hall. "I'm going to get a bath instead. Why don't you fix us a glass of wine, and we can stay home and watch a movie? I picked up a few rentals from Kountry Video that were new releases."

"I guess so," Kent mumbled as he picked up the DVD rentals and shrugged as he read the titles, 'When a Man Loves a Woman,' 'Dumb and Dumber,' and 'Pulp Fiction.' "She probably wants the romantic one," he continued mumbling as he walked to the kitchen to pour two glasses of wine.

"I think we need to ride over and protect our friend against whatever Isabella has up her sleeve." Kent handed Allison a glass of wine as she relaxed in the tub.

Allison enjoyed a sip of her wine and replied, "I guess so, but it feels strange just showing up. Tucker is our friend, I know, but I'm really afraid of walking up to something we shouldn't be a part of."

"So, it's settled. We're going...and then we can watch that sappy romance movie you picked out," Kent said laughing as he walked back into their bedroom.

***

Dad's flight was stuck on the tarmac in Atlanta for two hours causing him to miss his connecting flight. He left a message on the answering machine at home, but no one bothered to check the messages. Beau had been at Charlotte's house most of the afternoon, and Brice and I spent the afternoon washing my car.

As Brice put the bucket and soap in the garage, I took the liberty of 'accidentally' spraying him with the water hose.

"Oh, you're gonna' get it now," Brice laughed as he tossed the bucket and ran toward me. In a desperate attempt to escape, I blasted him with the hose again, but he overtook control and drenched me.

Soaking wet and feeling defeated, I found an opportunity to wrap my arms around his neck and steal attention from the hose. "You got me. I give up!" I whispered in his ear.

I heard the nozzle drop on the ground and felt his strong hold on my body. His hands softly cradling my face, he whispered, "You started it!" He kissed me lightly and laughed - then picked up the nozzle, and drenched me again.

As I ran toward the house to escape, I saw Isabella's car pull up into the driveway and rolled my eyes. *She wasn't kidding about dinner tonight.*

"What in the world is going on here?" Isabella questioned as she stepped out of the car. Staring at Brice, she ordered him to give her a hand. "Brice, make yourself useful and come grab these bags for me."

"Yes ma'am," Brice replied as he briskly walked over to her car. I stepped in his way and stopped him. "No, Isabella. We don't need your dinner, and Brice isn't hauling in your groceries. What are you up to?"

Isabella leaned on her car door and scoffed, "Young lady, you do not speak to your mother with that tone. I may have moved to the cottage for a while, but this is still my home and my family." She slammed the door and continued, "And I'm cooking dinner whether you like it or not."

I rolled my eyes and gave Brice a look, and he understood not to follow her. She nodded toward her car and looked at Brice, and I quickly interjected. "Isabella, we had plans already to go out to dinner tonight. We won't be here."

"I told you earlier that I was cooking dinner, Nessie. You can reschedule your plans with *that* boy. This is your family." Isabella coldly replied and walked toward the house.

Brice locked his hand in mine. "Nessie, look, I think you need to spend time alone with your family. Ya'll have been through a lot. I've got some things I can work on at the shop tonight while ya'll have some family time."

I laughed uncontrollably and then realized Brice didn't think it was funny. "How long have you known our family? Family time is not what you think." Brice stared at me with a concerned look.

"Stop it, Nessie. It's not funny. Ya'll have been through a lot lately." His expression didn't change.

"Yeah, I get it. We have. But, you have *so* much to learn about my family. We aren't like what everyone thinks. We don't have dinner around the table, hold hands, and sing kumbaya. It's one hundred percent the complete opposite." I released my hand from his and twisted my shirt to release the water from it. "Even before all of this- we weren't that kind of family. Dad is going to shit when he sees her here. I've got to make her leave before he gets home."

As we walked into the carport, I saw headlights appear in the driveway. "Who is that?" As the car got closer, I realized it was the Beales.

Isabella must have invited them to the 'family dinner'.

***

"Why are you here?" Beau approached Isabella as she set the groceries on the counter.

"Well, hi, Beau. How was your day?" Isabella smiled slyly.

"Cut the crap, Mom. Why are you here?" Beau wasn't budging. Charlotte walked up behind Beau and latched her hand in his.

"Hi, Charlotte, good to see you. Are you staying for dinner?" Isabella asked, ignoring Beau's question.

Charlotte was surprised that Isabella acknowledged her by her name. Beau released his hold on Charlotte's hand and stood in front of Isabella putting his hand on top of the bag of groceries.

"You heard me. Cut the crap. What's going on?" Beau demanded an answer and stopped her from unloading the bags. "We don't need you to cook dinner – just go back to the cottage."

"Beau, that's enough!" Isabella scoffed. "While I don't live here anymore, this is still my home. I thought it would be nice to spend some family time together." She smiled at Charlotte while walking past him to place a few items in the fridge. Charlotte turned away. Isabella always made her uncomfortable.

"Who the hell is driving up? I hope it's Dad, and he tells you to leave." Beau moved closer to the front porch windows to get a better view of the car. "It's Mr. and Mrs. Beale. I hope Dad is okay." Charlotte followed Beau as he opened the front door and walked onto the porch.

"Hey, Beau...and Charlotte. I hope we're not..." Allison attempted to apologize, but Beau cut her off.

"Hey, Mrs. Beale, Mr. Beale...is everything ok? Is Dad ok?" Beau had become worried.

"Oh, yes, Beau, everything is fine. Your dad should be home by now." Allison's eyes narrowed on Kent. "I brought this coconut pie from AELs for dessert."

Standing on the steps of the front porch, Beau was even more confused. "A pie? Okay, what's that for?"

"Didn't Isabella tell you she invited us for dinner?" Allison had warned Kent they were walking into a mess, but he didn't listen. She glared at him, and he knew she was right.

Before Kent could defend himself, Isabella appeared at the door and welcomed them inside. "I'm so happy ya'll made it! Come inside and have a glass of wine."

Allison reluctantly followed behind Isabella as Brice stopped Kent. "Mr. Beale! I need to finish a few things at the shop and thought tonight would be a good time. Is it okay if I put in a few extra hours?"

I grabbed Brice's hand, squeezing it tightly, desperate for him to stay home with me and help me navigate the incredibly awkward night that faced me. He knew what the squeeze meant and turned my way. "You need to be here for your dad. I'll only be a few hours at the shop. Okay?" He leaned in and kissed me, smiled, and turned back around to face Kent.

"That's fine. Just be sure to lock up the garage when you're done." Mr. Beale smiled and wrapped his arm around me. We started walking toward the front porch when another car's headlights blinded us from the driveway.

"Great...who else did she invite?" The words came out of my mouth so quickly that I didn't have time to apologize. "I'm sorry. I didn't mean it that way. I don't mind you and Mrs. Beale being here. It's just that..."

"Nessie, you don't need to explain. I insisted we come over to let Tucker know what he was walking into. We didn't plan to stay for dinner." Kent shrugged and continued walking up the porch steps.

I watched as Brice's taillights faded into the distance. He was the one person I needed to save me from Isabella's wrath. I closed my eyes and looked up toward the clear night sky. I took a deep breath in hopes of finding some level of peace to help me cope with her.

"Nessie, what on earth are you doing out here in soaking wet clothes?" I recognized the voice but wasn't ready to leave the peace I'd suddenly found standing in the darkness enveloped by the quiet.

The Taylors had made their way up the walkway, waiting for my reply.

"I washed my car earlier…and…I guess I got carried away. Let me help you with those." Attempting to distract them from asking more questions, I walked with them into the house.

Beau met me at the front door as soon as I entered with Whitney's parents and whispered, "Nessie, what in the hell is going on? First, Mom shows up and wants to cook dinner and have family time. Now, we have guests – like it's a party or something. Dad is going to flip out when he gets home."

"Where is Dad anyway?" I asked, curious why he hadn't made it home.

"No one has heard from him. Mrs. Beale said he should have landed earlier this afternoon. Maybe he's still at the office." Beau felt Charlotte's hand clasp into his as she leaned her head on his shoulder.

"This is all weird," she whispered.

"I know. I've got to warn Dad before he walks into this mess." As the words left his mouth, we saw headlights coming down the driveway. Dad's car stopped in front and parked.

"I've got to change. I'll be right back." I ran upstairs to change out of my water-soaked clothes.

Beau walked outside to give Dad a heads-up that Isabella was hosting a party inside.

As I came down the stairs, Dad stood inside the doorway – speechless. He watched Isabella from a distance bouncing around the kitchen, catering to her guests. I walked closer to him and grabbed his hand hoping to calm his nerves or at least minimize the lash out. Beau walked into the kitchen in an attempt to warn Isabella, but she brushed him off.

Fury raged inside Dad, and he couldn't retain it any longer. "What in the hell are you doing in *my* home? You have no right to be here!" Dad threw his briefcase on the dining table and lunged toward her in the kitchen as she attempted to sip her wine. He took the wine glass from her hand and threw it on the floor. *Crash!*

"Tucker, my goodness, what has gotten into you!?" Isabella stepped away from him as the Taylors and the Beales moved into the living room away from the altercation.

"What in the hell do you mean...what has gotten into me!? What the hell has gotten into you? You are in *my* kitchen, entertaining *my* friends, cooking, and acting like you still live here. This is *not* your house – you are *not* welcome!" Dad moved closer to her in sync with every step she took away from him. "You don't get to come here when you choose and pretend like nothing happened between us. Isabella, we are over! You don't belong here. Get out!"

Everyone remained silent. Kent and Allison attempted to quietly retreat through the carport door, but Dad raised his hand to stop them. "No, you two aren't leaving." He then pointed directly at Isabella and flatly said, "She's leaving – now!"

Isabella rolled her eyes and scoffed. "Oh, Tucker, please. They aren't just your friends – they are my friends as well. And this is my home too. I realize you aren't ready for this. I thought a dinner with a few friends and our family might help. It's not healthy for any of us to continue like this." She grabbed her purse and walked toward the carport door.

"Isabella, nothing about you is healthy. You're damn right I'm not ready for this. I never will be. We are over. I thought I made myself clear?" Dad was pointed and direct.

Isabella smirked. "You did, Tucker. I thought perhaps our two children might appreciate their parents getting along in the same room – even though we aren't physically together any longer."

I thought my burst of laughter was contained, however, the evil grin from Isabella told me it wasn't. "I'd say I'm sorry, but I'm not." My eyes locked with Isabella's, and I continued, "I have no desire for the both of you to get along in the same room. It's been refreshing with you not living here."

Dad looked at me and shook his head. "Nessie, that's enough! There's no reason to speak to your mother that way."

I crossed my arms across my chest and shrugged. Beau and Charlotte appeared next to me.

"Just go back to the cottage, Isabella. I'll finish dinner. You've done enough." Dad began tossing the ingredients into the saucepan and opened the oven.

"So, just like that, huh – you can just kick me out of your lives." Isabella's voice was low.

Dad looked around the room at his audience as everyone's eyes darted from the obvious. "No Isabella, you did this all by yourself. Now get out! We're over…for good!"

Isabella cockily walked to the door and replied, "Whatever Tucker. You say that now. You'll come around."

Chapter Sixty-Three

Homecoming With a Twist

"Well, that ended just like I figured it would," I said walking through the door of the garage. Brice was lying on a mechanical creeper underneath a truck.

Smiling, he pushed himself forward. "I'm sorry, Nessie. I hoped it would be different."

"No, it's okay. I've wasted too much time on her tonight. I didn't come here to talk about it. I missed you." I positioned myself next to him and leaned against the step rails on the truck he was working on.

"Come see," he said as his hands grabbed my waist and twisted my body onto the creeper with him. "This is much better," he smiled and kissed my neck.

The events of the evening began to leave me as his lips found their way up my neck and to my lips. His arms wrapped tightly around my waist leaving little room between our bodies. My breaths became shallow thinking where this moment might take us, and I heard him whisper, "You're so beautiful, Nessie. I hate seeing you upset."

"Just keep kissing me and holding me close," I found his lips as my hands removed his button-up uniform top and caressed his exposed biceps. My heart felt like it was going to explode from my chest as his fingers began to dance along the waistline of my jeans.

"Nessie, you sure about this?" his eyes penetrated mine.

I sat up, straightening my position on top of him, and smiled as my fingers played with the buttons on my blouse. Kissing him I replied, "Does this answer your question?"

He kissed me back and smiled, "I don't think I can-not here, Nessie. We're in a shop...on a creeper!" He sat upright.

"Well, I think it's kinda' hot..." I bit my lip waiting for his response.

"I can't. I mean...I want to more than anything, but not here." He kept a strong hold on my waist as his head fell into my chest. I felt his lips softly kiss my collarbone as he swept my hair over my shoulder. I closed my eyes savoring his hold as my fingers traced the wet imprints left on my skin. My fingers ran through his hair as my heart began racing anticipating his next move.

Suddenly he released his hold on me and looked toward the rollup door of the garage. "Did you hear that?"

"What?" I asked as I playfully nudged him to lie back down. "I didn't hear anything."

"Someone knocked. Stay here...let me go check it out." He jumped up and walked toward the garage doors. He peeked out into the front parking lot and didn't see anything. "I don't see a car. That's weird because I know I heard someone knocking."

He walked closer to the front door of the office, and I gasped. "Owen!"

"Huh? Owen!? Where?" Brice opened the door to the office and saw Owen peeking into the windows.

"Hey, um, we had a flat and walked to the shop hoping maybe someone would be here." Owen walked closer to Brice standing outside the office door.

Intrigued that Owen was home and by the word 'we,' I found myself behind Brice, buttoning my shirt.

"We?" Brice questioned as there was no one else in sight.

"Yeah, my friend...Aubrey. She walked back to the car to grab a few things. She'll be back in a minute. Can you fix the tire?" Owen remained focused on Brice. I know he saw me through the panes of the office door window, but he didn't make eye contact.

"Yeah, sure, c'mon inside. I'll grab a few things. About how far are you down the road?" Brice asked. I backed away allowing Brice to pass, my eyes still focused on Owen.

Owen answered, still looking away from me. "We're about half a mile that way," he replied pointing, watching her walk up to him. Finally, Owen turned toward me, with one arm wrapped tightly around *her*.

A lump appeared in my throat as I struggled to find the right words to welcome him home. It was awkward. Brice saved the moment, appearing with his tool set and keys to the wrecker truck. He lightly kissed my cheek. "Wait for me, please."

I smiled. "I'm not going anywhere."

I looked over Brice's shoulder toward Owen and to my surprise his eyes locked with mine.

He's gotten so hot! I thought to myself and quickly looked away.

"Let's go. It shouldn't take too long." Brice motioned for them to get into the wrecker. She latched hands with Owen, *my* Owen, and they drove off into the dark.

***

Earlier that day, Owen smiled as they began the final descent into New Orleans. "We'll have to drive the remaining way once we land in New Orleans." She smiled anticipating her arrival in Louisiana. "I hope your family likes me."

"Are you crazy? They're going to love you! Besides, haven't you heard about people in the South? Everyone is always welcome." Owen laughed to himself thinking how ironic that sounded. He left home months before because he didn't feel welcome – even in his hometown.

When they landed, Owen found a payphone and called home hoping Melissa would answer. "Hey, Mom! We landed...but you can't tell anyone. I want it to be a surprise!"

"Owen! Oh, my goodness, son! I've missed you so much! I can't wait to meet your friend!" Melissa smiled through her tears of joy.

Owen waited a moment for Melissa to calm down. "Mom, really, I know you're excited, but I want to surprise everyone. Please don't say anything. We're driving in from NOLA today and should be there this evening."

"Oh, Owen, this is wonderful. We've all missed you so much! I won't say a word." Melissa was overjoyed at the thought of Owen being home. "Nessie is going to be thrilled to see you."

"I don't want Nessie to know I'm home, Mom." Owen's voice turned cold.

"Well, Owen, honey, that doesn't make any sense. Why wouldn't you want your best friend to know you're home?" Melissa was confused.

"It's a long story that I don't feel like getting into. I'll see you in a few hours." Owen hung up the phone.

Taking Aubrey's hand, he smiled and said, "Let's get going. I can't wait for you to meet my family."

***

"Well, that didn't take long." I was shocked Brice had returned so quickly.

"Yeah, Owen helped me, so we got the spare on in no time," Brice replied as he put away the tools.

"Who was she? Did he introduce you?" I couldn't wait any longer to find out who she was.

"I don't know. He didn't elaborate. Her name is Aubrey though – if that helps?" We hadn't been together very long, but Brice could already read me. "Does it bother you he brought someone home?"

I snapped. "No! Why would you say that!? It doesn't bother me. I just asked a simple question if he introduced her. Gosh!"

Brice continued putting the tools up and set the keys on the desk as he leaned back on the edge. "Come here." He smiled with his arms outstretched toward me.

I stood still with my arms crossed on my chest. "Why would you say something like that?"

"Oh, c'mon, Nessie. I didn't mean anything by it. But I can tell it bothered you. I get it. He was your best friend." Brice pushed himself away from the desk and walked toward me. "You ready to head home? I'm done here for the night."

"Yeah, I am," I harshly replied. He attempted to grab my hand, and I threw mine out of his. "I'm just not in the mood anymore."

"Nessie. I have to ask. Did you expect Owen to move away from here and not meet someone? If anything, I would've thought you would be happy for your friend. Unless there is something I don't know about?" Brice hit a nerve.

"How dare you insinuate that me and Owen...we're just friends...well *were* friends. I can't believe you right now!" I snapped back at him.

"Well, by the way you're acting, anyone would assume you had feelings for him." Brice stood staring at me defending his position. "Why hide it if you did? That's in the past now."

"What an asshole! You don't know anything about me and Owen! For you to stand here and assume that I felt something else other than friendship for Owen - how dare you!" I couldn't look at him any longer. I grabbed my purse and darted for the door. I felt his hand grab mine.

"Wait, I'm sorry." His hand softly caressed mine attempting to apologize.

I needed space. Seeing Owen at home...with another girl...was too much for me to absorb. *Why did I care that he had brought a girl home?* For some reason, fury raged inside of me.

"I need space, Brice. I need time to think, and you're not helping accusing me of having feelings for Owen." I pulled my hand away from his.

"I don't think you need space, Nessie. Seeing Owen triggered something – I saw it. Just be honest with yourself and..." I cut him off.

"Really!? You're telling me to be honest with myself - coming from the guy who wasn't honest with me when we first met about being in a detention center and getting kicked off the baseball team!" I paused and took a deep breath waiting for him to respond.

"That's not fair, Nessie." Brice's tone was flat.

"Why not? You can accuse me, but when I bring up things from your past it's not fair?" I shook my head.

"You know why, Nessie. We'd just met. So, the girl I want to be with and want to get closer to – I tell her things I'm not proud of? I'd moved past that. I didn't see a reason to tell you, and I don't understand why you're so damn worried about it still!" Brice picked up a wrench and slung it into the corner of the room.

I jumped.

"Dammit...you make things so complicated!" he yelled.

"Oh, that's what it is? It's complicated!? It's called caring about someone enough to be honest with them." I realized once I said it how harsh it was.

"Caring!" His body stiffened, and his hands tightened into fists. "You're one to talk! You hate your mother – you barely have a relationship with your brother – and your dad..."

"Stop it!" I screamed. Fighting back tears, I continued, "Well, maybe I should uncomplicate your life and leave." I turned my back to him and opened the door. "Looks like you lost your place to stay too. I need some time, Brice." I slammed the door behind me.

***

Brice never imagined he would be back home – at the trailer park. He wasn't surprised to see that Tennie was having a party. The front porch was overridden with empty beer cans and cigarette butts.

"Well, it must be a ghost!" Tennie's voice echoed through the loud music as Brice entered the living room.

"Tennie, I'm not in the mood." He pushed her away as he attempted to make his way to his bedroom.

"Well, they weren't shitting us when they said you had become all 'high and mighty' living over there at your girlfriend's place. Why'd you come home?" Tennie followed closely behind him. "I'm talking to you, little brother."

"Yeah, I hear you. I'm not in the mood. Make your friends go home." He slammed his bedroom door in her face. He listened as she cackled down the hall.

Moments later the music blared with chants of 'shot...shot...shot' as the crowd partied until the early hours of the morning.

***

Somehow Brice fell asleep amidst the noise. It was early morning, and he awoke to several police officers kicking down the door of his room.

"What in the hell!?" Brice jumped from his bed.

"Young man. Do you live here? Is this your residence?" The officer stood boldly in front of Brice demanding an answer.

"Yes...yes sir. I do." Brice sat back on the bed as his hands cupped his face.

"Stand up, son. You're under arrest for possession of narcotics with intent to distribute. You have the right to remain silent. You..." The police officer continued as Brice tried to make sense of what was happening.

"Sir, I have no idea what you are talking about? Possession? Where? Distribute?" Brice continued to question as the officer handcuffed him.

As they entered the hall, he noticed Tennie leaning against the trailer wall smoking a cigarette, smiling slyly.

"Tennie! What did you do!?" Brice yelled as he walked past her handcuffed.

She whispered in his ear and grinned. "Someone had to take the fall. You were sleeping. I guess you aren't so 'high and mighty' after all, are you?"

"You'll never change, Tennie," Brice shouted as he attempted to lunge toward her.

"Oh, c'mon, Brice. We don't change. This is our life. I guess you should've stayed over in 'richville'." Tennie was ruthless.

Brice became enraged as his chest bowed up to Tennie. Gritting his teeth, he replied, "This isn't over. You'll get yours soon."

"Maybe," she grinned and took a long drag of her cigarette. "It doesn't matter though for me – now does it? I don't have much to lose." She put the cigarette out in the ashtray and plopped down on the recliner laughing hysterically.

Chapter Sixty-Four

Jailtime

"That should keep her out of my home!" Dad put the last lock on the exterior door and shut it behind him.

"You changed all the locks?" I asked seeing the smile of satisfaction on his face.

"Yep. She won't be able to surprise us like that again." Dad kissed the top of my head. "Where's Brice? I didn't see him on the sofa this morning." His eyebrows raised as he picked up his coffee mug.

"It's nothing like that Dad...before you even get started on me." I knew what he was thinking.

He smirked and threw his arms from his side, "Hey, I was just asking."

"We fought. I'm not sure where he is." I didn't want to tell him about Owen or details about the argument. I wanted to go back to my room.

"Well, that happens sometimes. Ya'll will figure it out. I'm heading out to the office for a few hours. I'll be home later. Tell Beau the keys for the new locks are on the bar." I appreciated Dad not prying since I was still trying to dissect how a perfect evening alone with Brice had drastically turned into a nightmare.

I turned to walk upstairs when the phone rang.

"I got it," Dad said as he opened the carport door and reached for the handset on the kitchen wall. "Oh, I see. Well, I'll be at the office within fifteen minutes. We can discuss it then."

I knew Dad was hiding something, by the way his lips parted, then quickly pressed them together. He adjusted his tie and smiled.

"What was that about? Everything okay?" I knew something was wrong, and he wasn't going to tell me.

"Oh, yes, no reason to worry. Just a little mix up I'm sure. I'll see you this evening." Dad didn't give me a chance to respond. He quickly closed the door behind him.

I sighed and thought about the fight I had with Brice. *I wonder what he's thinking. Maybe I should call him? How can you do that Nessie? You don't know where he is.*

***

"I can't believe ya'll are considering adopting him!" Jackson couldn't understand why his parents were interested in adopting Brice. "I get it, Dad. I know he works for you and all...but living here, with us? Maybe ya'll should save the entire trailer park!" He knew he'd hit a nerve with his last comment.

"Jackson! That's enough!" Kent had enough of his snarky comments. "You don't have a voice in this decision. I understand you don't agree with us, but that doesn't give you any right to cast judgment."

"I'm not casting judgment. I'm speaking the truth. If you open the door for Brice to live with us, he's going to bring his trashy sister Tennie with him and that'll be the end of it." Jackson stared out the window of the car as Kent parked in front of AELs.

"Enough, I said!" Kent raised his voice louder this time. "Can we talk about something else over breakfast?"

Allison gave Jackson 'the mom look' and he knew he'd better stop talking. "We need to hurry. Ya'll know AELs fills up quick for breakfast."

To Jackson's dismay, Allison found the first table open – right next to Charlotte and Stella.

"Hi, girls!" Allison greeted them as Kent pulled her chair back for her to sit.

Jackson took the seat with his back turned to the girls. The waitress topped off the girls' coffee and came over to take their order. "I'll take two specials, and Jackson, what are you getting?"

"I'm not hungry. Coffee is good." Jackson fidgeted with the menu, avoiding eye contact with his parents.

"Son, what has gotten into you? You never turn down breakfast." Kent waited for Jackson to respond.

"I'm just not hungry." He looked up at the waitress and said, "Just a coffee please."

It was awkward, with Kent's constant stares at him hoping to understand his defiant behavior to the faint whispers coming from Stella and Charlotte's table, he longed to be anyplace other than AELs. He finished his coffee and stood up. "I'll be in the car."

In sync, he stood up at the same time Stella rose from her chair. Their eyes met and Stella's quickly darted back to Charlotte. "I'll see ya later, Char." She grabbed her purse and walked toward the cashier. Charlotte, avoiding eye contact with Jackson, stared at the remnants of bacon on her plate.

Jackson followed closely behind Stella. "I'll get your ticket." He grabbed her ticket before she could respond and handed it to the cashier.

"Uh, no...you won't," Stella replied desperate he would leave her alone. "I don't need you to pay for my food."

"I know you don't, but I'd like to." Jackson paid for her meal and followed Stella outside.

"I don't know what that was all about Jackson, but you need to stop." Stella stood with both hands on her hips.

"Look, I know I haven't been the nicest to you...and we usually disagree more than agree...but I was hoping we could change that." Jackson stuffed his hands in his pockets and stared at the ground. His eyes danced wildly attempting to avoid her usual, cold stare.

She watched him as he waited for her response. A part of her wanted to rush over and comfort him. She knew deep down he needed a friend – after all, he didn't have anyone else.

Finally, after not hearing a response, his beautiful, dark brown eyes met hers and he smiled. Her heart began to race, and her breathing became more rapid. She took a step closer to him, and then quickly backed away.

"You haven't been nice to me, Jackson. You avoided me last year when I tried to get close to you. Now, you've got some little pity party going on, and I'm the only one who will talk to you. I'm sorry. I can't." She turned and attempted to walk away. He reached out his hand and softly touched hers stopping her from leaving.

"Stella, please. I just need someone to talk to. My parents want to adopt Brice and..." Jackson was surprised when she didn't pull her hand away from him.

"What!? Adopt Brice?" Stella turned to face him – her hand still locked in his. "What are you talking about?"

"His mom took off and left them. Brice is a minor, and he can't live with Tennie. Mr. Corbin has been letting Brice stay at their house, but my parents want to give him a home." Jackson released her hand and raised both of his into the air. "I'm just not good with it. He's not like us, and he brings trouble with him."

"Yeah, I agree that Tennie is trouble, but Brice seems to be better now. Nessie seems to think so. Besides, what does 'He's not like us' mean?" Stella fought the urge to grab his hand again.

"I don't know. He's just not one of us. That's all. And, he will bring Tennie's baggage with him. My parents don't see any of it. Dad only sees the side of him from the shop. It's more to it than that." He raked his fingers through his hair. "I just don't get it. I should be enough."

Stella pressed her lips together. "Ah, well maybe that is what all this is about."

Jackson stared at her with a confused look. "What?"

"That last comment you made…about you being enough." Stella straightened her stance and folded her arms across her chest. "Maybe you don't want to share the attention?"

Jackson's eyebrows raised – his eyes widened. "Really! Attention! No way! That's crazy! You're not helping!"

Stella saw Charlotte walking out of AELs and yelled, "Bye Char!"

Charlotte raised her hand in the air and waved without turning around.

Jackson laughed under his breath while shaking his head. "She can't stand me. She can't even look at me."

Stella rolled her eyes. "I would be mad at you too. And as for helping you, my advice is to get over the Brice thing and help him out – do something good for once." As much as Stella knew this was the perfect opportunity for her to get closer to him, her gut told her to give it more time.

She turned to walk away from him, and he reached for her hand again. "Stella, you wanna' hang out today? I could use a friend, and I think we have more in common than you realize."

She became annoyed and shrugged. "No, Jackson. I have some things to do at home. Besides, you need to tell your mom and dad that you're willing to let Brice live with ya'll." She nodded her head back towards the entrance to AELs and quickly raised her hand to wave at Allison and Kent. She smiled at Jackson and walked away.

***

I drove around town later that morning hoping to run into Brice, and he'd want to talk things out. As much as my gut told me not to go by the trailer park, my car found its way to the entrance.

I knew it! His car was parked in front of the trailer.

"What are you doing here?" Tennie answered the door in a half-buttoned plaid shirt with a cigarette dangling from her pursed lips.

"I'm looking for Brice. Can you tell him I need to talk to him, please?" I asked nicely.

She exhaled smoke into my face and laughed. "Brice! Yo, Brice!" she yelled over and over again while laughing uncontrollably.

Before I had the chance to wedge myself between her and the door, she blew smoke in my face again and said, "Oh yeah! I forgot. He's not here. You just missed him! The police picked him up a couple of hours ago," and she slammed the door in my face.

What!? The police!? Why!?

I fell to my knees on the porch and stared at the duct-taped hole in the front door. My hands cupped my face as tears welled in my eyes.

What have you done, Brice?

Music blared from the trailer walls as I jumped in my car and drove to see the only person I knew could help me-Dad.

***

"Sir, do you accept a collect call from Sedipar Parish Detention Center?" Kent heard as he placed the receiver to his ear.

"Yes, yes I will," Kent replied unsure of who would be on the other end of the line.

"Mr. Beale, hey, it's Brice..." Brice stuttered unsure of how Kent would react.

"Brice, hey, a collect call...? What's going on?" Kent watched as Jackson plopped in the recliner next to him, listening intently.

"It's a long story, Mr. Beale. I'm sorry I called you. I just...I just don't have anyone else to call." Brice sounded defeated. "I was arrested this morning."

"It's alright. It's going to be okay. Tell me what happened." Kent whispered attempting to avoid Jackson from eavesdropping.

Jackson huffed. "Arrested, huh!?"

Kent brushed him away.

"Mr. Beale, I only had three minutes to call someone. I can't explain over the phone, but Tennie set me up. She did this."

"Brice...you there?" Kent heard only a dial tone.

"Dammit!" Kent slammed the phone down.

Allison jumped and rushed over to him. "What in the world was that all about?"

"Brice was arrested!"

Jackson couldn't wait to interject. "I'll tell you what it's all about. It's that sister of his...trying to pin something on him. See...I told ya'll. She's bad news, and she's gonna' bring Brice down with her."

"Dammit, that's enough Jackson!" Kent's anger had escalated, and Jackson realized he should back away. "I'm going down to the detention center where they're holding him."

"I'll call Tucker and let him know. Let us know if you need anything when you get there, okay?" Allison hugged Kent and then dialed Dad's number.

***

"Drug bust, huh?" Dad was eager to obtain more details from his colleague who'd left several messages at his office.

"Yeah, they raided the bar last night. Trisha was arrested with the two ring leaders of the operation. They were running illegal drugs and other weapons through the bar. It didn't take the police long to figure it out." Trisha had asked for Dad's counsel once they brought her into the jail, and Dad's colleague knew he'd appreciate a heads up.

"I can be up there tomorrow at the earliest," Dad sighed as he hung up the phone. He stared at the walls of his office hoping what he'd heard was only a dream. The ringing of his office phone startled him.

"Law firm," he answered and heard the distress in Allison's voice. "Allison, slow down! What is it?"

"Tucker, I'm sorry to be the one sharing this with you, but it's Brice. He's been arrested." Allison waited for Dad to respond.

"What in the hell!" He sat back in his chair while running one hand through his hair. "Arrested...did I hear you right?"

"Yes, Tucker, that's correct. I don't have the details, and Kent is on his way there now." Allison paused to catch her breath.

"I'll meet him there." Dad gritted his teeth thinking about Trisha and shook his head. "Allison, if you can come down to the firm there's something I need you to do for me."

"Sure, I'll be there shortly. I can start gathering information on what happened last night – maybe from Tennie..." Dad cut her off.

"No, that's not what I need. I'll get the details from Brice. I need you to call the Mississippi DEA and get any information you can on Trisha Adams. She was arrested last night in a drug bust at a bar. I don't know much else other than she asked me to defend her." Dad hung up the phone.

Allison sat in silence tightly closing her eyes. Jackson knew something was wrong. "You okay, Mom?"

"Yeah, honey, I'm fine. Shocked a little bit...but okay. I have to go into the firm today." Allison scurried around the living room to find her keys and darted out the door.

***

"Adams! You have a visitor." The guard escorted Brice from the holding cell to a room down the hall and pointed, "In here."

Brice felt some relief seeing Kent in the corner of the room. When the guard shut the door, he stopped in place as Dad appeared from the opposite corner.

"What in the hell happened, Brice?" Dad questioned.

"I didn't do anything, sir. You have to believe me. I was sleeping...and all I remember is the police coming in my room...and..." Brice was telling the truth, but sadly the facts were against him.

Dad placed both hands on the table and leaned across staring at Brice. "Sit down."

Brice clasped his hands and rested them on the table.

"They've got quite a bit of evidence suggesting you were dealing drugs out of your home. No one else had anything on them, including your sister, which surprises me, but witnesses pointed back to you as the seller." Dad paused hoping Brice had proof he could use to defend his case. "And why in the hell were you back at that place? Why weren't you at my house?"

Brice shook his head and replied, "Tennie did this. She's behind all of it!" He pounded the table with his fist. "She told me when the police handcuffed me that it was easy to pin it all on me."

Dad looked at Kent and then back at Brice. "Why were you there in the first place? You shouldn't have been there. None of this would have happened." Dad became angrier with each breath, but seeing that Brice was scared and confused, his approach softened. "How can we prove it?"

"I don't know. Her friends do whatever she says so they aren't going to talk." Brice pushed the chair away from the table and stood. "It's a long story why I went there. I'd rather not talk about it...if that's okay. It has nothing to do with what happened. It was the only place I had to go. Mr. Corbin you have to believe me." Brice rubbed his chin and mumbled, "There has to be something...someone - Tennie is smart, but she doesn't think things through."

"Will they allow bail?" Kent asked hoping he could bring Brice home.

"I doubt it, but I'll ask." Dad left the room to find the deputy.

"Mr. Beale, I'm so sorry. This wasn't me. I promise. I need my job...I need it so bad...this wasn't me...you have to believe me!" Brice pleaded with Kent.

"Look, Brice, I want to believe you...I do. I know your sister is nothing but trouble. Why in the world were you even there? I thought you were staying with the Corbins. What happened?" Kent kept prying.

"It has to do with Nessie. That's why I didn't want to tell Mr. Corbin. We had an argument...well disagreement...and she told me to find somewhere else to stay...so I did." Brice sat back in the chair and slouched, crossing his arms over his chest. "I knew it would be trouble going home, but I had nowhere else to go."

Kent shook his head. "No, that's where you're wrong, son. You always have a place – my house." Kent jabbed his finger into his chest. "That's right-you call *me*. Don't ever think you can't call me, you hear? Going home is nothing but trouble."

Dad came back into the room with the deputy following behind. "You've made bail with one stipulation. You have to stay with Kent with full supervision. And if you're caught stepping one foot on your property, they will haul your butt back here before you can count to three. You got it?"

"Yes, sir." Brice felt some sense of relief knowing he wasn't going to have to spend the night there. He looked up at Kent waiting for affirmation that he could go home with him. After all, he did just say to call him.

"Well, I guess it's time to go home, Brice," Kent responded quickly knowing there was no other option. "I just need to make a call."

When Kent left the room, Dad leaned on the table staring at him. "Now, are you going to tell me why you weren't at my house? What made you go home?"

Brice, swallowing the lump in his throat, replied, "Your daughter, sir. Nessie told me I needed to find another place to stay."

"Hmm, well, I'm not sure the reason she told you that you weren't welcome, but I'm sure she'd be disappointed to know you went back home and ended up here." Dad tapped the table with his fingers as he thought about how he'd tell me.

Before Brice could give more details, Kent motioned from the door for him to leave.

"Stay out of trouble, kid. I mean it. You go to work, school, and Kent's house. If you need to go elsewhere, Jackson should bring you. We'll figure out how to get you out of this...and find the truth." Dad patted Brice's back and followed him out the door.

***

The door to the firm was locked since it was the weekend. In a panic to talk to Dad, I'd forgotten the code. Mrs. Beale opened it after several minutes of me knocking furiously.

"Nessie, what can I do for you?" Allison softly asked.

"Where's my dad?" I ran past her toward his office. "I need to talk to him."

"I'm sorry, but he's not here. He's at the..." Allison paused thinking she should not be the one to tell her about Brice.

"He's where? He said he was coming here to work on something...and he got a call before leaving home...and I could tell something was wrong. I need to find him! I need his help!" I fell to the floor in tears. "It's Brice, Mrs. Beale. He was arrested. I don't know what happened! I feel so helpless!"

"Oh, dear, come see." Allison sat next to me and placed her arms around me. "I wasn't sure if you knew. I didn't want to be the one who told you. But your dad and Mr. Kent went to see him."

I wiped my tears. "Dad knew about this! He didn't tell me!? How could he not tell me!? That's the call he got this morning, and he left the house without telling me." I was furious.

I got up from the floor and stormed down the hall. Before I reached the front door, I saw Dad unlock it and walk inside the office.

"Nessie, hey. What are you doing here?" He glanced my way and saw the devastation on my face. "Why are you so upset? Are you okay?"

"No, Dad, I'm *so* far from being okay. I know about Brice. Why didn't you tell me!?" My voice was cracked as I struggled to not yell at him.

"How'd you find out? I just got word, Nessie. That's where I've been. He's getting released now...and going home with Kent." Dad put his briefcase on the receptionist's desk and encouraged me to sit down. "There's nothing you can do right now for him. I know you're worried about him. Rest assured I'm going to do everything I can to clear him of this."

I wiped my tears from my cheeks and looked up at him. "What does 'clear him of this' mean? What did he do? I thought you said he was released with Mr. Beale."

"It's complicated, Nessie, and I shouldn't be sharing any details on the case with you. I know Brice and you are close, but I can't share that information. He can if he chooses...that is...if you are speaking to him?" Dad's eyebrows raised as he questioned the status of our relationship. He knew more than what he was letting on.

"Yeah, I mean, we're talking." I looked at the floor to avoid Dad's stare.

"Nessie, I know you told him to find somewhere to stay. He told me." Dad said blankly.

I sighed. *Great. What else did he tell you?*

"I'm not getting into a discussion about my relationship with you. Brice felt comfortable to give you all the details about our argument, but I'm not privy to any details on why he was arrested." Frustrated, I stood up and walked to the front door. "I need to get out of here."

"Nessie! He didn't..." I raised my hand in the air, cutting him off.

"It's fine. He probably doesn't want me in his business anymore. I'm fine." I knew I wasn't fine. My heart was exploding inside wondering what had happened...why he was arrested...what he was feeling...was he still angry with me. Filled with varying emotions, I walked outside the firm and screamed.

Chapter Sixty-Five

Torn

Melissa prepared a breakfast feast for Owen's return home. Mason wasn't back from the camp and Charlotte was still sleeping. Per Owen's request, she hadn't told either that he was coming home.

"Geez, Mom, are you planning to feed an army!" Owen was in awe at the table covered with food.

Melissa smiled as she set the biscuits and gravy in the center of the table. "I can't wait for your dad and Charlotte to find out you're home. I'm going to wake Charlotte up! I can't stand it any longer."

Aubrey walked up behind Owen and wrapped her arms around his waist. "Avez-vous bien dormi?" she asked yawning. "I'm sorry! It's hard...I need to lose my French. I meant, did you sleep well?"

Owen snickered. "You're English is getting better! I did sleep well, but it looks like you didn't." Aubrey grinned as she peeked around him and saw the table filled with food. He watched as she searched the table for familiar favorites from back home. "Les Jambon? Pourquoi? Pour petit déjeuner?" She covered her mouth and apologized again.

Owen smirked. "It's ok. I understand you, but no one else will! Yes, our breakfast table looks a little different than what you are used to. But Mom made sure to have baguettes with jam...your favorite."

Melissa woke Charlotte up and she followed behind her closely, walking down the stairs. "Mom, this better be good – waking me up before nine in the morn..." As she reached the last step of the staircase, she saw Owen standing in the foyer. "Owen! You're home!" Charlotte said running toward him with outstretched arms. As she got closer, she watched as Aubrey stepped out from behind him.

"Oh, okay, so you brought someone home with you?" Charlotte was confused and knew her comment was uninviting. "I'm sorry...I didn't mean it like that, but I'm shocked that you're home...and you have a friend with you?"

Owen chuckled. "Sounds like you missed me!?"

Charlotte replied, "Eh, just a little bit, I guess. You look so sophisticated without your glasses. What happened over in France?" They hugged as Aubrey took a step back waiting. Charlotte stepped back from Owen and smiled. "Who are you, and what did you do with my brother!?" She was impressed with his new style of clothing. "What's with the clothes?"

"Nothing," Owen smirked.

Owen immediately pulled Aubrey back closer to him and introduced her. "This is Aubrey, my friend. We met through host families, and she had an interest in visiting the States. Mom agreed. So, here we are!"

"Hi, I'm Charlotte...you do speak English...?" Charlotte quickly became embarrassed for asking.

Aubrey smiled. "Yes, I do. I struggle with some words, but I'm getting there. It's nice to meet you."

Melissa encouraged everyone to move into the dining area just as Mason entered the front door.

"I'm starving! Something smells goo..." Mason paused seeing Owen standing in the center of the dining room. "Son! What in the hell are you doing home!?" He rushed over to Owen and pulled him in closer to hug him. "How didn't I know about this!?" He asked directing the question to Melissa.

"Well, now, that isn't important. Let's enjoy breakfast as a family." Melissa's eyes widened at Mason, and he understood to let it go. "Most importantly, you need to meet our guest, Aubrey, Owen's friend."

Aubrey appeared from the corner of the room, and Mason shook her hand. "Does she speak English?" Everyone in the room laughed.

"No, Dad, she can't understand anything you are saying." Owen latched his hand into hers and asked. "Papa veut savior Si vous parlez anglais?"

Aubrey smiled and nodded her head then turned to Mason. "I do speak English, sir. I'm sorry Owen fooled you."

Everyone but Mason burst into laughter. "That's not funny! Ya'll are ruthless. It's nice to meet you Aubrey and welcome to our home. It seems you've already got acquainted with the mischief that surrounds me daily." Mason chuckled.

As everyone began fixing their plates, the home phone rang. Melissa ran into the kitchen to answer it. "Charlotte, honey, it's Beau on the line."

"Alright, I'll get it in my room," she answered while running up the stairs and shutting the door behind her.

"Have you heard the news?" Beau couldn't get the words out fast enough.

"News about what?" Charlotte questioned.

"Brice. He was arrested early this morning." Beau paused.

"What in the world!? Do you know why? Does Nessie know?" Charlotte sat on her bed in disbelief.

"I don't know what happened. All I know is Nessie came home upset saying he was arrested. She's taking it hard. She doesn't want to talk to me about it. I was wondering if maybe you could come talk to her?" Beau waited for Charlotte to respond.

"Why me?" Charlotte wasn't convinced that she was the right person. "I'm sure she's not going to want to confide in me. We aren't that close of friends."

"I know that, but she's refusing to talk to me about it. I can't listen to the drama and crying anymore." Beau hoped Charlotte would give in.

"I can't do it. I feel bad for her, but we aren't that close. She probably doesn't want me in her business anyway." Charlotte paused hoping Beau would understand.

"I get it. Just thought I'd ask. I'll see you tonight?" Beau had planned to pick her up around seven o'clock to ride around town.

"Yep. I'll be ready." Charlotte made a kiss sound into the phone. Before she hung up, she remembered to tell him about Owen. "Oh, guess what!? Owen's home!"

"What!? That's awesome! When did he get back?"

"Late last night, I guess. I had no idea he was coming home. And he has a 'friend' with him."

"A friend?"

"Yep. A *girl* friend. She seems nice. He said they met through host families, and she wanted to come to the States. Mom agreed."

Beau became silent.

"Beau, what's wrong?"

"Nothing. I just worry about Nessie. She's already in a bad mood about Brice. Now, Owen's home – with a girl. This is only going to make things worse."

***

I didn't feel like company, and I didn't want anyone, including Beau, nosing around in my business. Even though we'd become somewhat closer through all the drama with Isabella, we still weren't close enough for me to confide in him. I didn't have anyone to vent to.

Brice had been arrested. And Owen was home - and as much as my mind told me to block it out, my heart screamed how hot he'd become. He was different – a more relaxed, yet confident Owen.

My mind shifted between both of them – my defiant boyfriend and my best friend – both had my heart for different reasons – at least that's what I told myself.

I lay in bed, tossing and turning, hoping Brice would call. Every thought of Brice made me smile, him holding me, kissing me, and then Owen's face crashed it all.

I pulled a pillow over my face and screamed as loud as I could.

I've messed things up big this time. I'm alone. I feel like I'm trapped again in that stupid rehab place – locked within the confines of cinderblock walls – except I'm not.

My hand grazed over my journal and for a split second I thought about leaving my ranting on a few pages, but it ended up in the corner of my room. I didn't feel like writing. I didn't feel like talking...well...maybe only to Owen...to find out what made him leave and then come back...with a girl...a gorgeous one at that.

Ugh. You're so stupid, Nessie.

The phone rang, and I jumped. I reached for the receiver, and it stopped ringing. Minutes later I heard light tapping at my door. It was Beau. "Nessie, it's Brice...on the phone."

My heart sank. *Brice...what do I say to him? What if he wants to break up? Ugh...Nessie...just talk to him.*

"Okay...you can hang up!" I yelled as my hand shook holding the receiver.

"Nessie, hey," his voice was cool and calm – one of the things about him I loved the most.

My hand was sweating. I'm not sure why I was so nervous to talk to him. My heartbeat raced, and I mustered the courage to respond, "Hey."

"Look, I can't talk long, but I wanted to tell you...where I've been. I'm so sorry I haven't called."

My eyes closed, and I inhaled deeply. *I already know where you've been. But, I don't know what you did to get there.*

"It's a long story, Nessie, but Tennie set me up. I'll figure things out, but I wanted to let you know that I'm okay. Mr. Beale is letting me stay with him until things get straightened out."

I tried to respond, but I was at a loss for words. Ironically, I'd longed to hear his voice and ask him what happened. Now, I had him on the other end of the line, and I couldn't get the words to come out.

"Nessie, you there?" Brice's tone raised.

"Yeah. I'm here." I responded flatly.

"Okay, well, I just wanted to let you know I was okay...that is...if you were worried." His voice softened.

"Yeah, I'm fine. I just...I want to know what happened." I couldn't resist any longer.

"I gotta go. Mr. Beale is waiting for me. Can you meet up later tonight at The Dixie?" The eagerness in his tone made my heart flutter. *He called...so he must still want to be around me...and cares about me.*

"Yeah, that sounds good. I'll meet you around seven-thirty tonight."

"Wait. I forgot. We can pick you up."

"We?" I was curious who else he'd invited.

"Yeah, I have to get Jackson to bring me everywhere – your dad's orders."

"Oh, alright, then, I'll see ya'll at seven-thirty." I hung up the phone and smiled.

***

Later that afternoon, Aubrey had fallen asleep in the den. "The jetlag is rough on her I guess," Owen's eyes darted between her and Melissa on the other side of the room. "Thanks for letting her stay with us, Mom. That meant a lot to me."

"Oh, honey, I'm just glad you are back home. And, now that you're home I will tell you that I didn't like you being over there one bit! I missed you terribly! If it took Aubrey wanting to come to the States to bring you back to us, then I'm happy to welcome her to our home for as long as she wants." Melissa walked across the room and sat down in the recliner next to him.

"What is it, Mom? You have that look like there's something else." Melissa smirked. "Yes, there is just one thing...and I don't want you getting mad at me for asking." Melissa peeked around him to be sure Aubrey was still asleep.

"It's Nessie. What happened between ya'll?" Melissa knew as soon as she mentioned my name Owen would shut down.

"Mom, I've told you. We just grew apart. She moved on, and I moved on as well. We're different people now." Owen stared at Aubrey and lightly moved her hair that had fallen on her cheek. He smiled. "We just clicked, you know, a lot like Nessie and I did, but different."

Melissa sighed at the thought of me and Owen never reconnecting. "I can tell you like Aubrey, but Nessie was your best friend since childhood. Just promise me you will at least talk to her."

"I can't promise that. I don't know what I would say. The last time we spoke she brushed me off and told me to leave her alone. The next thing I knew, she and Brice were a thing. And rehab!? What in the world? She's like a completely different person." He fidgeted with the frayed ends of his jeans.

Melissa frowned.

"Mom, it's fine. I'm over it. I'm over her. I've moved on. Really. I'm happy. Besides, Nessie seems to have moved on as well – at least it seemed that way the other night at the shop." Owen leaned back in the chair and closed his eyes hoping Melissa would stop asking him questions.

Chapter Sixty-Six

Failed Attempts

"I'm starving Blaine! Hurry up and change so we can beat the crowd at The Dixie." Whitney tapped her fingers on her steering wheel as she yelled from her car window.

"Alright, alright. I'm moving as fast as I can." He yelled while jogging over from the barn. He tore off his shirt and threw it over his shoulder in an attempt to cool off. She watched as each bead of sweat rolled down his perfect chest.

"I'm going to leave you," she yelled again as he got closer to her car, "if you don't hurry up!"

"No, you won't. You can't be without me for another minute." He smiled at her, attempting to lean into her car to hug her.

"No! Blaine! You're all sweaty!" Whitney locked her door anticipating his next move.

"Don't worry, babe. I just wanted a kiss." He leaned in casually placing his lips on hers and smiled. "I love kissing you. You're perfect in so many ways." He backed away from her car and headed for the house.

She honked the horn. "Hurry up! I'm giving you five minutes or I'm leaving!" she yelled jokingly. She knew in her heart Blaine was the one. She smiled as her fingers traced her lips where his had touched hers.

***

Beau made a pass through The Dixie parking lot before finding a place to park.

"What are you doing...circling. There's Stella – stop the car!" Charlotte gave Beau a confused look when he didn't stop. "Well, are you gonna park?"

"Yeah, yeah, I am. Just give me a second." Beau scanned the parking lot – no sign of Blaine. "Okay, we're good. I'll meet you over by Stella, and I'll order our food."

She figured out why he was circling the parking lot. "Beau. C'mon. You are going to have to face Blaine one day. This is a small town. Ya'll can't keep avoiding each other."

He knew where this conversation was going and didn't want to fight with her, so he leaned in closer to kiss her. She didn't fall for it.

"Don't try to cut me off with a kiss, Beau Corbin. You have a lot of nerve!" She playfully pushed him away and hopped out of the car. "I'm starving. Get me a burger with a soft-serve cone...and some curly fries!"

Beau shook his head smirking and replied, "Yes ma'am," and walked to the order window while Charlotte walked to meet Stella.

***

"Well, if it isn't Mr. Big Shot...Mr. QB...oh wait! I forgot. You can't play this year! How stupid of me!" Tennie slapped her hand on her forehead and smiled.

"Cut the crap, Tennie. I need two burgers, with curly fries and a soft-serve vanilla cone." Beau threw some cash on the counter. "Keep the change."

Tennie counted the bills, stuffed the remaining loose change in her apron, and sarcastically replied, "I promise I won't spend it all in one place."

As she put in the order, Beau backed away from the counter hoping to ignore her.

While he waited for their food, he scanned the parking lot again waiting for Blaine to appear. Stella and Charlotte walked over toward him and noticed Jackson pulling up.

"I don't care to talk to him either," Beau looked back toward the window hoping their food would be ready. "Tennie! We need our order to go now." Beau yelled through the order window, but there was no sign of her.

Charlotte nudged Beau and pointed toward the back of The Dixie. "She's back there smoking."

"Dammit! We gotta get out of here, Charlotte. I can't be around Jackson either." Beau took Charlotte's hand and turned to walk back to his car. "Forget the food. We'll drive into town."

Charlotte stopped Beau. "Why is Nessie with Jackson?"

As Jackson stepped out of his Jeep, Brice and I jumped out from the back seat.

"What in the hell? Nessie has no business hanging around that asshole, Jackson!" Beau became furious and threw Charlotte's hand away from his.

Jackson approached with a sly smirk. "I didn't want them to be here with me. This is all my dad's problem." He looked back at me and Brice and laughed. "My dad has fallen off his rocker. We have a convict living in our house."

Brice clenched his fists as Jackson walked by Beau.

"Order up, Corbin!" Tennie yelled from the window.

Stella quickly ran up to Tennie and asked for to-go bags.

Charlotte found her way behind Beau and attempted to calm him down. "Stella has our food. Let's go."

He ignored her – staring at me.

"Nessie. Why in the hell are you with Jackson?" Beau was pointed and cold.

"Excuse me? Why do you care?" I responded and rolled my eyes. Brice latched his hand tightly with mine.

"Beau, we're with him because I..." Brice tried to soften the mood, but Beau wasn't entertaining it.

"I know, Brice. You were arrested. We all know. My sister can do what she wants," he paused and looked at me and continued, "but I can't believe after all the things Jackson did to me and Charlotte that you would step foot in his vehicle or even be close to him."

"It's not like that Brice...at all. You heard him! He doesn't want us around, but he's the only way Brice can go anywhere." I looked at Brice and sighed. "It's the only option we have to see each other." Brice squeezed my hand tighter.

"Whatever! I gotta get out of here!" Beau threw his hands up in the air and turned back to Charlotte. They walked back over to another group of friends that had parked near his car.

***

We followed Jackson to the order window, and I stopped. "What's wrong?" Brice asked.

"I don't want to see Tennie. I'm so mad about this whole thing...and I know she's behind it." I knew I'd have to face her one day soon...but I wasn't ready to do that tonight."

Brice walked up to the order window and put our order in. I watched as Tennie taunted him. Brice just laughed it off. He was better than me. I would have jumped over the counter and strangled her for what she did to him. We all knew the truth would eventually surface, and the charges against Brice would be dropped.

***

Jackson caught Stella alone in the back parking lot near her car.

"Jackson, look, I don't want to talk about it. I'm sorry you have to share your life with Brice for a while. That's not my problem." She attempted to walk away, but he grabbed her hand and pulled her back.

"I need you, Stella. I know I said it the other day, but I want to say it again. I was horrible to you this past year. I admit it. I was confused...and thought I wanted Charlotte...and now I know that..." He was rambling until Stella cut him off.

"Oh, so I'm last choice." Stella was pointed and flipped her hair at him. "Surprise, Jackson. Stella Atkinson is never last."

He kept his hold on her hand, and she tried to release it. "Let me go. I don't have anything else to say to you."

He held her hand even tighter and moved closer. "You don't understand. I need you, Stella. I need to tell you something I've been holding in for a while."

Something in his voice or his hold on her made her soften. "You...need...me?" Stella felt her heart race and she inhaled deeply. "I...I don't know what to say."

He pulled her closer to him and whispered in her ear. "Don't say anything. I need you to...listen...be a friend...we can take things slow...you know...at first." Jackson's tone had become soft, and he ran his hand softly through her hair pushing it behind her ear.

Her head rested on his chest – instantly wanting more. She closed her eyes as his fingers softly traced her neckline and he gently kissed her shoulder.

The noise from the parking lot grew louder, but his soft, sweet kiss mesmerized her, and she became lost in his hold. She wrapped her arms tightly around his waist. With her eyes closed, he pulled her chin up and traced her lips with his fingers as they danced playfully across her lips. He leaned in closer to kiss her...a moment of bliss...she'd waited all year to be in his arms.

Suddenly, he became distracted by the noise coming from the crowd and slowly pulled away.

"You're a drunk loser, Blaine. No one wants you around. You're wasting your time, man. I have nothing else to say to you." Beau's fists were raised in defense. "Get outta' here. Now!"

Stella placed her hands on Jackson's chest, looked up at him, and smirked. "Maybe we can catch up later?" She glanced toward Beau and Blaine and noticed Charlotte and Whitney on opposite sides of the crowd pleading for the guys to stop fighting. A circle of friends from school surrounded the guys enticing them to fight.

Jackson stared at the crowd and then back at Stella. "Come with me to the Abyss." He looked back at the crowd and then at the ground. "It's not like anything good is happening here."

"I really would like to, Jackson, but I need to check on Whit and Char." Stella took a step back and held both of his hands. "Raincheck?"

"No, I'll wait for you. I'll be in my Jeep." He waited for her to agree before walking away.

"Okay, just give me a few minutes to check on my friends, and I'll meet you." She walked away unsure of what had just happened. She felt a range of emotions – excitement that Jackson was interested in her to worry that he was using her because he was alone.

"Char," she ran and hugged her friend. "Make them stop fighting. Geez, they have to stop."

Charlotte yelled at both of them to stop, but they both ignored her.

"I messed up, Beau. I owned it. What else do I need to do for you to forgive me?" Blaine pleaded with Beau hoping he would calm down and reason with him.

"You messed up! You owned it!? I'll tell you what else you need to do, man. You need to leave me the hell alone. I'll never forgive you for what you did. You ruined my football career. Hell, you could have killed me!" Beau remained defensive - not relaxing his fists. "Get out of my face, Blaine. I should punch you right here...right now."

Whitney walked up from behind Blaine and stood between them and facing Beau said, "Well, if you punch him you're gonna' have to punch me too."

Blaine pulled on Whitney's arm to move her behind him and she pushed his hand away. "No, I'm not moving."

Beau laughed. "Whitney, I'm not going to hit you. Although someone should knock some sense into you for being with him."

"Beau, Blaine apologized. He's truly sorry for what he did. Ya'll have been friends forever. You can't ignore that." Whitney glared at Beau hoping to reason with him. Charlotte smiled at Whitney and walked up behind Beau.

"Beau, maybe you should just listen to him. Give him a chance to explain." Charlotte's hand rested on Beau's shoulder as she hoped she could calm him down.

Beau shifted his stance and spat at the ground. Shaking his head in disbelief that his girlfriend and best friend were taking Blaine's side in all of this, he replied, "I don't owe him anything."

Whitney leaned back against Blaine as Charlotte stared at her feeling hopeless.

***

As we waited for our food, Brice talked about his arrest. "I can't believe Tennie would stoop so low," I shook my head as Brice explained to me what happened.

"Really? It's Tennie we are talking about." Brice laughed. "She only cares about herself."

"Yeah, I guess I can believe she's capable of setting you up." I smiled and leaned my head on his shoulder. "I miss you. And I'm sorry."

"No need to be sorry. It was late, and we both had a long day. We said things we didn't mean. Let's forget about it." Brice moved his arm to pull me closer next to him. "I can't lose you, Nessie. You're the one good thing in my life that is going in the right direction. I'm not letting you slip away."

Our eyes locked, and I smiled. In my heart, I knew his words were genuine. He was the one thing that was right in my life as well. "Hey, who said I was slipping away?"

He tapped his fingers on the table hoping to avoid answering.

"Brice? What'd you mean by that?" I wasn't letting him off the hook that easily.

His head hung low and remained quiet.

I elbowed him. "Brice! You can't say something like that and not explain. What'd you mean by it?"

"I don't know really. It just came out." He leaned back and ran his hands through his hair. "Maybe just being arrested – in jail – everything feels like it's crumbling apart. I don't deserve to have you."

"Hey, look at me." I pulled his chin to look my way. "Nothing is crumbling. We are going to find a way to get you out of this." When I leaned in closer to kiss him, I caught a glimpse of Owen and his new girlfriend coming up to the order window. I pushed away from Brice.

"What's wrong, Nessie?" Brice continued staring at me – his lips longing for mine to meet his.

"It's nothing. I just..." I didn't need to finish responding. Brice watched as Owen and Aubrey walked by us laughing and holding hands as they approached the order window.

Brice slammed his hands on the table. "Seriously! I'm not going to compete with him, Nessie."

I wasn't sure what to say. I stared at Brice blankly for a minute. His eyes met mine and locked. I could see how broken he was inside – with everything falling apart in his life – and now this. His eyes widened waiting for me to respond.

He stood up from the bench and faced me. Leaning forward, he placed his hands on the table as if to barricade my body. Every ounce of my being wanted him to hold me, to escape into a deep kiss and not look back, but he didn't move.

My words were blocked. My eyes quickly darted to Owen upon hearing her laugh uncontrollably. They seem to be so incredibly happy.

"Nessie!" Brice slammed his hands down again on the table.

I jumped. His jaw clenched, and every second I remained quiet seemed to cause even more tension between us.

I watched as they casually passed by us with their food, her hand conveniently placed in his back pocket and his arm perfectly wrapped around her waist. He glanced my way and quickly turned back to her.

I don't even recognize him anymore. He's somehow...cooler...nothing like the old Owen.

"Nessie, I'm outta' here. I can't do this." Brice backed away from the table and walked back to Jackson's Jeep.

"Brice! Wait! I'm sorry." I yelled, but he threw his hand in the air.

"See if Beau can bring you home," he yelled from Jackson's Jeep.

"Please let me explain!" I couldn't stand fighting with him. I needed him now more than ever, and he needed me. Why was it so hard for me to explain to him what I was feeling?

Did *I* even know what I was feeling? I was confused seeing Owen - happy with another girl. And whether I wanted to admit it to myself – a small part of me wished I were her.

Chapter Sixty-Seven

There's Your Motive

Mason waited for Isabella outside the clinic before it opened. As she pulled into the parking lot, she was startled to see him standing near the entrance.

"What in the hell do you want?" she scowled, slamming her car door.

"Well, great to see you as well!" Mason replied sarcastically.

"I don't have time for you or whatever this is about. I have a full clinic today." She brushed past him and unlocked the door.

He followed her closely as she made her way into her office.

Slamming her bag on the table, she threw both arms in the air. "What is it, Mason? What do you want? Since you didn't hear that I'm busy."

Mason laughed as he pretended to admire her credentials pasted across the walls of her office. "It's quite impressive – a small-town girl – not much going for her – pregnant at a young age – but somehow finds a path to become a doctor."

Sitting poised now in her chair behind her desk she responded, "I'm admirable. I know. It's called being determined. Now, what do you want?" Isabella was getting more annoyed with him.

"Oh, I didn't say you were impressive – I said *it's* impressive." Pretending to admire the awards that lined her bookshelf, he turned to her. "You don't impress me a bit. However, your cunning and manipulative ways never cease to amaze me. That's what I meant." He grabbed one of the awards and slammed it on her desk in front of her.

Startled, she flinched and replied, "That's enough! How dare you come into my clinic and...," she stood up and leaned forward toward him.

"And what? What am I doing?" Mason smirked knowing he'd hit a nerve.

"I don't know why you're here. I have patients to see. If you came here to remind me how much you despise me – I'm not interested. Now, get out!" She walked over to her office door and opened it.

He shook his head looking down at the floor. "You might want to shut that door."

She rolled her eyes and leaned back against it to close it. "Well, whatever it is...just spit it out!"

He walked over and stood inches from her face. "I know what you did that night at the law firm...with those tests. It has your name written all over it."

Isabella inhaled deeply, pretending to remain calm, but her mind was exploding with worry. "I didn't do anything with those tests!"

Mason backed away to give her space as she darted toward her desk.

"Ah, a little defensive. Did I hit a nerve?" Mason smirked.

"You ignorant man! Nerve! You have some nerve – bombarding me at my clinic – accusing me of tampering with the tests – how dare you!" Her hands planted firmly on her hips, she grabbed her stethoscope and walked back toward her door. "It's almost eight o'clock – the clinic opens soon. I need to go."

"I'm not finished, Isabella. I'm not leaving until you tell me what you did. No one believes that the cleaning staff mixed up those samples merely because the cabinet was left unlocked. That's a ridiculous assumption. You know it, and Tucker knows it. Ya'll may have fooled everyone else, but you sure aren't fooling me!" Mason stood between her and the door. "Now admit to what you did, and I'll get out of your way."

Isabella knew there was no other way around it. Mason was not backing down. "Fine! I'll tell you what happened. But you have to promise me that it ends here...in this room."

Mason was amused. "Oh, so you admit to tampering with them and then it all just goes away?" He laughed and then his jaw tightened. "No, I'll tell you what's going to happen. You are going to admit to how you tampered with those tests, and I'll decide what happens next. Do you not recall how you manipulated your own son...my daughter...you lied about me and our 'so called' relationship long ago and ruined your marriage. You think we should all let that go?"

Isabella was fuming inside, but knew Mason expected her to blow up at him. Instead, she mustered together a half smile and asked him to sit down.

"I'll explain what happened, but the reason I'm asking you to keep it between us is that others will be hurt by this news. It's not about me." She watched as Mason sat across from her.

"Alright, I'm listening." He leaned in, arms resting on his knees, intrigued by what was to come.

"Jackson altered those tests. I caught him in the cabinet that night." The words rolled off her tongue easier than she thought they would.

Mason stood up. "Oh, you've got to be kidding me! Jackson! No way it was Jackson. You're wasting my time."

"Mason! I'm telling the truth. Sit back down." Isabella's eyes followed him as he sat in the chair.

"Allison drank too much that night, and I stayed with her waiting for Jackson to pick her up. Allison was passed out on the sofa when Jackson came to get her later that evening. He was left unattended for a bit while I was freshening up in the ladies' room. When I came back to check on Allison, I found him with the file cabinet open. I guess Allison must have told him where she'd stored the tests. The key was in the cabinet door." Isabella paused, her eyes focusing on Mason.

Mason shook his head and sighed. "I still don't believe it. Why would Jackson be interested in tampering with those tests? It doesn't make sense. You, on the other hand, had every reason to do it!"

"Mason, I'm telling you the truth. Jackson had motive. He's had feelings for Charlotte for quite some time and this was the perfect opportunity to break her and Beau's relationship. Think about it." Isabella paused again hoping Mason would accept her story. "There's your motive!"

"I don't know. That's a lot to take in. It's certainly not what I expected. Tucker knows this?" Mason became infuriated thinking Dad had lied to him.

"Yes, Tucker knows. Jackson is just a kid, Mason. A teenager with a crush – you know – we all did foolish things in the heat of the moment." She leaned forward to touch his hand, and he pulled it back.

"You're pathetic. Don't touch me." Mason stood up and walked toward the door.

"You promised to keep this within these walls, remember. I gave you the information you wanted. Now, let it rest." Isabella sat poised in her chair waiting for his confirmation that he'd remain quiet.

"I didn't promise anything, Isabella. I've got to think about this more, and I want to talk to Tucker." Mason slammed her office door behind him.

She fell back in her chair hoping this would be the end of it. Maybe Mason would do the right thing and let it go.

***

"You Corbins just don't know right from wrong do you?" Mason said while forcing his way into Dad's office.

"What in the hell are you talking about, Mason?" Dad stood up from behind his desk. "You can't just bust into my office like this. I have staff working."

Mason plopped down on the sofa.

"Have a seat, Mason. Make yourself at home." Dad's sarcasm didn't phase Mason.

"Quit with the bullshit, Tucker. I know all about the tests. I just left Isabella's office. You're a liar." Mason's nostrils flared as he leaned forward toward Dad.

"What in the world? What do you mean 'you know all about the tests'? I told you what happened. They were left unattended." Dad walked around his desk and stood in front of Mason. "You just can't let things go can you."

"Let things go? I don't understand. What's there to let go?" Mason tilted his head questioning Dad.

Dad looked away. "I just meant that you should be happy with the last test. We know the truth now."

"Oh, yes, I see, protecting your ex-wife still." Mason chuckled. "She still has a hold on you doesn't she?"

Dad turned to face Mason and pointed his finger at his face. "Mason, that's enough! I have no feelings for that woman after what she did to our family. She's nothing to me...not that it is any of your business."

Mason stood up realizing he'd likely overstayed his welcome. He stood with his arms crossed over his chest. "You see, I came here to tell you that I know Jackson switched the tests. Isabella told me everything. I just wonder now what I should do with this information."

Dad stood motionless. His jaw dropped as he rubbed the back of his neck. "She told you...Jackson...switched the..."

"Yes, Tucker. Jackson wanted to split up Charlotte and Beau. There's your motive. And *you* knew about it and lied to me." Mason pointed his finger in Dad's face.

"Now just wait a damn minute. I didn't...," Dad caught himself mid-sentence.

"Oh, now you're going to lie to me that you didn't know it was Jackson. C'mon, man. It's pretty low to blame it on the cleaning crew. That never made sense to me. Now it does." Mason turned and walked toward the door as his pager beeped. "Ah, that's the pharmacy. I have to get back."

Mason left his office before Dad could tell him the truth.

Chapter Sixty-Eight

Like Mother, Like Daughter

"Adams, you have a visitor. First door to your right." The guard pointed as Trisha walked into the room in handcuffs. She sat down, rested her hands on the table, and asked, "It's not good for me is it?"

Dad shook his head. "No, it's not, Trisha. They have you on multiple counts, and they aren't allowing bail. This will go to court, and you will likely lose. There's not much I can do for you."

Trisha sighed and asked, "Do you happen to have any cigarettes? I'd die to have just a few drags."

Dad reached into his pocket and threw a pack on the table. "I figured you'd want these."

"Thanks. I appreciate you coming, Tucker." She fumbled with the pack of cigarettes until Dad put one between her lips and lit it.

"I recommend you work with the state defense attorney. He can represent you at no cost - unlike me who would have to charge a minimal fee. I have my doubts that..."

"What...that I can't afford you?" Trisha laughed through the cigarette smoke. "You're right. I can't. I can't afford anything. I put my only savings into setting up the bar." She held the cigarette between her fingers while staring at the cuffs. "I've lost it all."

He couldn't help but feel sorry for her even though she'd created this mess herself. "I've got to head back home tonight. I'll get things set up with the state defense attorney. He'll take care of things from here."

He watched as Trisha stared blankly at the wall.

"Is there anything I can help you with back home?" He asked hoping she would mention Tennie and Brice.

She shook her head no and asked for help lighting another cigarette. She inhaled a long drag and smiled. "I thought this was my ticket out of Sedipar -a town that has done nothing but bring me bad luck. I thought a fresh start, with new friends and a steady job was all I needed. Now look at me." She raised her handcuffed hands and shrugged.

Dad frowned – agitated by her selfishness. "Trisha, do you even care about your kids back home? You're sitting here feeling sorry for yourself and *you* are the sole reason you are in jail. You willingly accepted the risk of dealing with illegal drugs...and see where it got you."

She took another long drag of her cigarette and laughed. "My kids, seriously? They haven't called me one time since I left. Tennie's old enough to take care of things. Brice is practically an adult. They'll be fine. They never needed me much before."

Dad sighed and grabbed the handle on the door. "Well, just so you don't worry about them - Brice was arrested a couple of days ago. He's living with Kent and Allison Beale until we get things straightened out. He didn't have any place to go since you abandoned them."

"I didn't abandon those kids! They're practically adults." Trisha shook her head. "That figures. That boy! What's he done now?" She turned in the chair to face Dad.

"Tennie. That's what he did. He went home to Tennie, and she turned on him." Dad slammed the door behind him.

***

Tennie hadn't been to school in over a week. She was failing all of her classes. There was no one to call at home since Trisha had left town – and was now in jail.

She slept in until about ten in the morning and found the trailer a mess from the party she'd held the night before. As she made her way into the living room, she stepped over a few friends that had passed out on the floor.

One guy sat on the couch struggling to keep his head up. She laughed as she plopped down beside him. "A little too much fun last night, huh?"

"Yeah, girl, you throw a wicked party. You got any more of those pills you were handing out last night?" More pills were the last thing that he needed, but Tennie only looked out for herself. She pulled out a bag from her pocket. He threw a hundred-dollar bill on the coffee table, and she snatched it up. He stuffed the bag into his pant pocket and passed out again.

She waited until he was asleep a few minutes and stole the bag from his pocket knowing he wouldn't remember any of it, and he'd pay her again.

"Sucker," she said laughing to herself as she walked into the kitchen.

"Damn you, Tennie! Give him back his money." She heard a voice coming from the living room. She turned with a sly grin.

"Go back to sleep. You didn't see anything." Tennie was pointed.

"Damn right I did. I saw you take back those pills. That's messed up, Tennie. You took his money – like you always do." The voice became louder as her slim, six-foot, tattooed friend walked toward her. "We're all tired of your shit, Tennie. You think we don't know what you've been up to?" As he walked by the guy on the couch, he nudged him to leave. "I'll meet you at the truck."

Tennie laughed. "Oh...so you think you got me, huh? Well, it's my house so get the hell out!" She motioned with the spatula in her hand for the front door.

"Give me my hundred back. I'm not leaving until you pay me or give me the pills." He stood in front of her wedging her between him and the stove.

He pulled his shirt back revealing a pistol in its holster. "Now you don't want things to get ugly, so either give me my damn money or the pills. It's your choice."

Tennie slammed the spatula down on the counter. "I can't believe you! You've been hanging out with me for a long time, and this is how you treat me?"

"Cut the shit, Tennie. For the last damn time - give me the money or the pills." His voice became stern – his face full of rage. His hand reached for the pistol as her hand followed his to stop him. "I've had about all I can take of your shit."

"No need for all of that." She smiled playfully at him and wrapped both arms around his waist. "You could hang around for a little fun. I don't have to be at work until later this afternoon."

"Not today, Tennie." One hand secured her neck and the other grabbed his gun. Lightly tracing her cheek with the end of the pistol, his jaw clenched, and he said, "Pills or the money, Tennie. What's it gonna be?"

She threw the bag of pills on the counter.

He quickly snatched them and shoved them into his pocket. He withdrew the pistol from her face and smiled. "I see why Brice can't stand you. You better hope he doesn't find out what happened the other night, or your ass is going to jail."

"Oh yeah, well the only two people that know about it are you and me...so, keep your damn mouth shut!" Tennie's finger stabbed his chest. "That's our little secret."

He smirked. "Yo, Brice is smart Tennie. You better watch out for him. He's been asking around town ever since they released him. I hear he's living with his boss now."

As he closed the door, she slammed her fists on the table and yelled, "Dammit. Everyone always seems to save Brice. I've got to make sure he doesn't find out the truth."

***

"Brice, tell your sister that she has one more unexcused absence and she's expelled." The assistant principal knew it didn't matter anyway. Tennie wasn't coming back to school.

"I'm sorry. I can't tell her. I don't see her much anymore. I'm living with the Beales. But, you can find her working at The Dixie most days." Brice waited to be excused.

I saw him at the end of the hall and hoped he'd stop to talk to me. I waited by his locker, but he casually walked past me staring straight ahead.

He's going to have to talk to me. He can't keep ignoring me like this.

After the last hour of school, I hoped we could talk in the parking lot. I purposely parked next to him, but by the time I made it outside, he was already in line to leave school.

I bet he has to work today. Maybe I should just go by there and corner him. No, Nessie, that will push him away more. Just give him time. Ugh, I can't stand this!

I didn't want to give him time. I needed him more than ever now – and he should need me.

Ugh! Owen messed everything up! Why did he have to come back home? Things were going good until he showed up.

***

As soon as Brice got to the garage, Kent sent him on a call with the wrecker truck. "It's about fifteen minutes out of town. It seems the truck broke down on the side of the road."

Brice drove out of town and found the truck parked on the edge of the highway. When the owner stepped out of the truck, Brice stopped. "Man, what are you doing out here? You must be lost. You got a drug run in these parts?"

"Cut the shit, Brice. I'm not in the mood." The guy walked around to the front of the truck.

Brice laughed. "I don't care if you're in the mood or not. You need my help – I don't need yours." Brice opened the driver's door as wide as it would go and looked at the seat of the truck. "Yeah, I figured you'd do a better job hiding this stuff...you know...so the police can't find it easy."

The guy came up from behind Brice and pushed him out of the way. "It's not mine. My friend left it in here when we broke down.

Another friend of ours picked him up because he couldn't take the chance of getting caught with drugs. He's still on probation."

Brice glanced sideways and shook his head laughing. "You expect me to believe you!? That's the biggest pile of crap I've ever heard. I know they're your drugs."

"Whatever, who cares? Look, I get you're all pissed at Tennie for what happened the other night. I'd be pissed at her too. I need your help though..." Brice cut him off.

"What do you mean 'you'd be pissed at her too'? Why'd you say that?" Brice pinned him against the truck.

The guy raised his hands hoping Brice would back off. "Look, I didn't mean anything by it. You got arrested – and everyone saw how Tennie acted toward you when the police took you in. That's all I'm saying. You need to chill, dude."

Brice retained his hold and replied, "Quit lying! You know something, and you damn well better spit it out." Brice's teeth were clenched and his hold on his collar tightened. The silence made him angrier. "You must have forgotten that I have a little piece of information on your younger brother that might interest the police."

The guy's eyes widened as he knew exactly what Brice was referring to. "You wouldn't. You promised it was taken care of."

"Yeah, it was. I did time in rehab for it – for him – so he wouldn't get in trouble. He owes me – and you're gonna' make things whole." Brice released his hold slightly and waited.

"Brice, dude, if I knew something I'd tell you. Honestly, I don't know anything." He felt his body bang against the side of the truck again.

"If I find out you're lying to me, I have a wide-open door to Mr. Corbin." Brice backed away from the truck. "I'll tell him everything, and they will take your brother away from you so fast you won't know what hit you."

"Okay, alright...just give me a few days. Let me see what I can find out." He straightened his shirt and waited for Brice to respond.

"Two days. That's it." Brice walked back to the wrecker. "Get rid of those drugs, and let's get this truck back to the shop."

Chapter Sixty-Nine

Queen of Denial

Dad knew Isabella would be at AELs for lunch. He planned to confront her about the conversation she'd had with Mason.

"I knew you'd be here." He took a seat across from her.

"Tucker, to what do I owe the pleasure? Are you finally ready for me to move back in with my family?" She sipped her tea slowly.

He laughed. "Not quite. I told you that is never going to happen. Mason told me he came by the clinic a few days ago." Dad didn't waste time getting to the point.

"Oh, yes, I recall him coming by the office. He was insistent that I had something to do with those horrid tests." She laughed to herself. "I wonder where he got that idea?" Her eyebrow raised as she waited for him to respond.

"C'mon, Isabella. It's me you're talking to. I know you did it, remember?" Dad motioned for the waitress to come over. "I'll take a coffee. Black."

"I have to get back to the clinic. What exactly did you want, Tucker?" Isabella knew why he was there, but she wanted him to verbalize it.

He looked at her with disgust. "You know what in the hell I want. You need to tell Mason you lied to him and make things right before anyone finds out."

The waitress came back with his coffee, and he asked for it to go. Jamming his finger on the table he said, "Make it happen, Isabella. Tell the truth for once."

Isabella replied cunningly, "Oh, Tucker. You're such a fool." She casually took another sip of her tea and continued, "I already told the truth. Jackson is behind all of this mess."

***

Dad stopped by Callaway's Pharmacy hoping to talk to Mason.

"Hey, Tucker. How's your day going? Can I help you with anything?" Melissa moved from behind the counter.

"Hi, Melissa, it's going okay. Thanks for asking. Is Mason around?" Dad quickly responded.

"He sure is. He's in the back. I'll give him a buzz to let him know you're here." Smiling, she paged Mason.

Mason approached the front of the store and paused when he saw Dad. "I'm busy, Tucker. I don't have time to..."

"Oh, you're going to want to hear what I have to say," Dad stepped closer to him and continued. "It's about the tests. It's time I tell you the truth."

Mason nodded. "I knew it! I knew you were hiding something the entire time!" He laughed and continued. "But you're too late. Remember, Isabella beat you to the punch. I know it was Jackson."

Dad noticed several customers in line one aisle over and whispered, "Maybe we should talk about this in your office?"

"Of course, that's fine, but there really isn't anything to talk about." Mason followed Dad's lead into the office.

Dad leaned against the wall with his arms crossed on his chest. "Mason, I thought you knew Isabella better than that. You trust her...what she's saying about Jackson?"

Mason walked around his desk and sat in his chair. "No, I don't trust her, but she's given me the only piece of information that makes sense. I challenged her on it, and well, I think I do believe that Jackson had something to do with it. He had a motive to break up Beau and Charlotte."

Dad grinned. "She's really good! I can't believe you fell for her story. Mason, she did it. She switched the tests...and she admitted it to me." Dad breathed a sigh of relief with every word that left his mouth.

Mason stared at Dad with a confused look. "Why are you telling me this now? I asked you several weeks ago – confident that you were hiding something – and you lied to me. Why should I believe you now?"

"You should believe me because it's the truth. Isabella was there that night with Allison and they both had too much to drink. Unfortunately, Isabella took advantage of Allison as an opportunity to be alone in my office. She switched the results in hopes of tearing Beau and Charlotte apart. I found out and confronted her, and she denied all of it."

"How do you know that it was her? You weren't at the law firm that night, right?" Mason asked pointedly.

"You're right. I wasn't there; however, Allison and Jackson were. Allison had suspected something was going on but couldn't put her finger on it. She later questioned Jackson about Isabella being in my office. He lied at first but later admitted to seeing her near the cabinet.

I confronted Isabella and had plans to reveal everything, however, she pleaded with me to keep this from Beau." Dad paused.

Mason shook his head. "I can't believe you would protect her – lie for her."

"Mason, you'd do the same to protect your family. I did this for Beau and Nessie. I didn't do it for Isabella." Dad waited for his response.

"Yeah, I guess I can see that, but she's ruthless. How could she do that to her son? And now she's blaming an innocent kid who had nothing to do with it."

Dad shrugged. "I know. I just confronted her at AELs demanding her to tell you the truth and make things right. She's still denying she had anything to do with it. So, I wanted to clear the air with you."

Mason stood up and reached his hand out to shake Dad's. "You're a good man, Tucker. You're better than me, though. I don't think I could have lied for her...not after the lives she's ruined over the last year."

Dad was relieved and extended his hand to Mason's. "I wouldn't be praising me too soon. You heard me say she's still in denial and blaming Jackson. We have to stop her. We can't have the town thinking Jackson did this."

Mason grinned. "I'm in. Whatever it takes. She isn't going to destroy anyone else in this town. I'll make damn sure of that." Mason rubbed his hands together eager to get started on a plan.

"One more thing, Mason. Let's keep this between me and you for now. Isabella is smart and resourceful. We should keep this between us." Dad's eyebrows raised hoping Mason would agree.

"Yes, I can do that." Mason patted Dad's shoulder as he walked past him to the door. "She's not going to know what hit her," Mason said laughing. He turned and faced Dad and smiled. "Let's do it at Christmas on the Bayou. There will be a huge crowd...she won't expect it."

Dad grinned knowing she deserved every bit of humiliation that was coming to her, but a small piece of him knew it wasn't going to be easy. "Yeah, let's think it through some more, but that's a good start."

Dad watched Mason walk back to the pharmacy area whistling the entire way.

Chapter Seventy

Shocking Truth

"Come with me to the Abyss, please," Jackson attempted to hold Stella's hand while walking to their cars after school.

She pulled her hand back quickly. "I can't. I promised Mom I'd go shopping after school and have dinner in town."

Jackson exaggerated his bottom lip by poking it out and smiled. "Well, maybe later?"

Stella grinned and turned away knowing his innocent, dark brown eyes would talk her into saying yes.

His hands lay perfectly on her hips as he pulled her back to him and whispered in her ear, "C'mon. Please. I just want to talk. That's it."

His hold on her felt amazing...something she'd longed for...it was getting harder to resist him. "Okay, maybe I can talk Mom out of dinner. I'll meet you at the Abyss around six thirty."

He lightly kissed her cheek and smiled. "Thank you. I just need to get something off my chest. I can't hold it in any longer."

Stella quickly turned to face him. "Well, that sounds intriguing. What kind of dark secrets are you hiding?"

"You'd be surprised," Jackson replied with a sly smile. "I'll see you in a few hours."

She bit her lip as she watched him walk back to his Jeep.

***

As confident as Stella seemed, she was nervous being alone with Jackson at the Abyss. Most of her memories there were spent trying to get his attention only to be ignored by him. She pulled up next to his Jeep and saw him sitting on the front bumper.

"Hey, you came!" Jackson seemed surprised as she walked around the side of his Jeep.

"You didn't think I'd come?" Stella replied jokingly.

He ran his fingers through her hair playfully as his eyes locked with hers. For a moment, he imagined leaning in and kissing her, but he resisted. "I haven't been down to the embankment in forever. Wanna' take a walk?"

She latched her hand lightly in his and replied, "Yeah, sure. I'd like that."

As they made their way onto the embankment, they found a rotten log, perfect for a makeshift seat.

"I used to come here a lot. It's a good, quiet place to think about everything, you know." He picked up a couple of rocks and tossed each into the water. "You ever skipped a rock before?"

"Boy, look at me. I thought you knew me better than that. You're lucky you got me down here." Stella laughed.

He laughed at her reaction, leaned forward while clasping his hands, and snickered, "Yeah, I figured that."

She scooted closer to him on the log and leaned her head on his shoulder. "So, what's that secret you're dying to tell me?"

Shaking his head he replied, "It's not like that. It's more than a secret. It's what comes after the secret."

Stella could see he was struggling with sharing whatever had him so distraught. "Jackson, you don't have to tell me if you're not comfortable. But I'm here to listen and help you...only if you want to."

He reached for her hand and stroked hers softly. "I do. I need to tell someone. Every day it's eating away at me. It won't stop."

Stella's curiosity was getting the best of her, however, she recognized how difficult this was for him. "Just take your time. We can sit here all night..." About the time she said this, something scurried from the bushes behind them, and she screamed. "Okay, well maybe not all night!"

"It's probably nothing. You scared?" Jackson taunted her.

"Normally I'd pretend like I wasn't jaded, but whatever that was needs to stay away from us. Wild animals aren't my thing." Stella stared as Jackson's eyes focused on the ripples in the water.

"I don't know the best way to tell you this. I've replayed this a thousand times in my mind, and each time it rolls off easily. I'm struggling with it now that you're in front of me." Jackson paused noticing Stella's intense stare. "What?" he asked softly and smiled.

All sorts of things were going through her mind. She knew the secret couldn't be about her. They hadn't spent much time together. Her heart wanted him to fall in love with her, but she knew this bliss wouldn't last long. "It's nothing." She smiled back at him. "I...I just like being here for you."

He pulled her closer to him on the log and wrapped one arm around her. "If I tell you this, you have to promise to keep it between us."

Her fingers latched within his. "Of course. I promise."

He inhaled deeply and closed his eyes. "That night the tests were supposedly tampered with – I know who did it."

Stella pushed back from him surprised. "You didn't, did you!?"

Jackson's eyes widened. "Are you serious? No! I didn't do anything. But I saw who did it."

Stella placed her hands over her mouth. "Oh, no, I'm sorry. I didn't think..."

"Yeah, you did!" He laughed.

She slapped his arm playfully. "Stop! I didn't mean anything by that. You just caught me by surprise."

"Well, if you think that surprised you...when you hear who was behind all this mess...you're gonna freak out." Jackson bit his lip.

"Well, tell me already. I have to know now." Stella had become impatient at this point.

"Isabella. She did it. I caught her by the file cabinets." Jackson felt a surge of relief. "It feels so good to get that off my chest!"

Stella jumped up from the log. "No way! Beau's mom!? Are you sure!?"

"Yes, I'm one hundred percent sure. I saw her near the filing cabinet the night Mom drank too much. Later, I confronted her, and she tried to pin it on me saying my motive was to be with...well...Charlotte." He looked up at her hoping the part about Charlotte wouldn't upset her.

With crossed arms over her chest and looking away from him, she replied, "I knew it! It always comes back to Char!"

"No, Stella, it's not like that. I have zero feelings for Charlotte. That's in the past. I'm over all of that. You have to trust me." Jackson felt hopeless at this point.

Seeing his desperation, she knelt in front of him. "Look, I trust you. It just brings up a lot of memories hearing you talk about her...the way you treated me..."

He softly cupped his hands around her face. "I know, and I'm so sorry for that. I want to make it up to you. You're the only one who has given me a chance and stood by me while my other friends have ousted me. I need you."

Her fingers wrapped around his wrists as he kept her face close to his. "Thank you for the apology. That makes it a little better. As far as the needing me part...we just need to take it slow."

He kissed her forehead, and she stood back up facing him. "So, what's next? Does anyone else know?"

"Mr. Corbin and Mom know – that's it. Well, and now you." He stood and stuffed his hands in his pockets. "Mr. Corbin blamed it on the cleaning people because he didn't want Beau to find out the truth. I get it...but now with Isabella turning things on me...I don't know if I can keep it quiet any longer."

Stella was in denial. "I just can't fathom how she could do this to Beau." She sat back down on the log. "What are you going to do?"

"I don't know. A part of me wants to tell Beau all of it...but he probably wouldn't listen to me. And is it the right thing to do? I mean...I would be pissed if my mom did something like this. I'm sure he's gonna' feel the same way." He turned and faced the water. "Dammit! I just wish I knew what to do."

"I'll tell you what to do." She approached him from behind and made him turn around to face her. "You're going to tell Isabella that she's lying, and that you will tell Beau if she doesn't make things right."

Jackson laughed. "Really? Do you know Isabella at all?"

"Yeah, kinda. I know she's ruthless and gets what she wants." She rolled her eyes.

"She's not going to back off. She's manipulative and is pinning this all on me." He threw a rock into the water. "Damn her. She's caused all this mess."

Stella knew there had to be a better path than exposing Isabella and putting him at risk of losing Beau's friendship for good. "Maybe you don't have to do anything. Didn't she tell you she'd remain quiet as long as you kept this to yourself?"

"Yeah, but what good does that do? I have to live with this forever – eating at me every time I see Beau – knowing what his mom did. Keeping it from him is the same as lying to him." He threw his hands into the air. "If I do expose Isabella, there's a chance she will turn this on me, and others may believe her. After all, there is no real proof she tampered with the tests – it is only my word that I saw her – and her confession to Mr. Corbin."

She could see the turmoil on his face. "I'm sorry, Jackson, that you're stuck in the middle of this. I don't know how else to help."

He found his way closer to her, extended his arms, and pulled her into his chest. "This. This is how you can help. Just being here for me like this."

She closed her eyes and savored the moment – a moment that she never thought would happen – a moment that she could lose just a quickly as she gained it.

Chapter Seventy-One

The Next Best Thing

Who would have guessed that Owen shared his passion for reading with his new 'girl' friend – similar to what we shared? What I hoped was a rumor had become reality as I watched them paw over each other from across the library. It was nauseating the way she flirted with him, and it was obvious how much he adored her. I rolled my eyes at them – especially Owen.

How dare he share our special library moments – what our friendship was built on – with a girl he hardly knows.

After a few minutes of spying on them, I couldn't stomach it anymore. I opened my novel and attempted to get lost somewhere other than my physical environment.

My eyes darted every few minutes to them across the library. As much as my gut told me I should ignore them, my heart longed for him to talk to me.

Ugh. This sucks. I can't keep doing this...avoiding him isn't working.

Without giving it much thought, I rose from my chair and casually approached them. Her arm was latched under his and her hand rested on his thigh. She nuzzled her head against his shoulder as I approached. It was awkward to say the least, but it was too late to turn back.

Owen glanced up from his book and then at Aubrey. His fingers played with the edge of the pages flipping them repeatedly.

I stood still for what seemed like minutes and realized I would have to say something. "Hi, I'm Nessie. I'm..."

She cut me off. "Yeah, I know who you are. I saw you at the shop the night we had a flat." She closed her book and glared at me then back at Owen. "Pourquoi est-elle là?"

Owen smirked back at her. "Je ne lui ai pas demandé de venir."

They both laughed and stared coldly back at me.

Fury built inside me. *Why was he being so rude to me? And her...she barely knows me.*

"Je suis venue vous dire bonjour," I replied snarkily and watched both of their jaws drop. "That's, I bet you're surprised I know French."

Aubrey stood from behind the table. "So...did you need something?" She tilted her head and crossed her arms on her chest.

I'm not sure what had gotten over me. I had mustered the courage to walk over to them, and once I was in front of them – I froze. The old Nessie was back-retreating into a passive state. But the rage building inside of me to charge at her coupled with the desire to spend time alone with Owen, sparked something in me to finally mouth the words, "I'd like to talk to Owen alone."

She burst into laughter and planted both hands on the table. "So, you want to talk to Owen...alone?" She glanced back at Owen, and he refused to make eye contact with either of us.

In that moment, I saw a glimpse of the old Owen. He was unsure of himself – avoiding confrontation.

The Owen I fell in love with as a friend – my Owen.

I rolled my eyes back at her and focused my eyes on him. Her apparent distaste for me invigorated me to be more forceful. I sat on the edge of the table directly in front of him. "Owen. Look at me. You can't keep avoiding me."

Aubrey sat down next to him and whispered something in his ear.

He smirked, shook his head, and quickly kissed her cheek.

"He says he doesn't want to talk to you. He doesn't have anything to say." Her fingers made their way up his neck and playfully ran through his tousled hair. "Is that right, baby?"

Baby? Ugh! Make me puke.

I scooted in closer to him and placed my hand on his book. "We have to talk. We need to talk. Are you just going to let *her* speak for you!?" Expecting Aubrey to intervene, in a most sarcastic tone I said, "And *we,* doesn't include *you, baby,*" I scoffed.

Owen stood up from his chair. He didn't find any of it amusing. "Whatever you have to say – say it in front of me and Aubrey or don't say it at all. She's not going anywhere."

I remained seated on top of the table, surprised by his response.

Aubrey's sly smile made me even more angry. "So, what do *we* need to talk about?"

Owen's hand latched into hers.

"Yeah, Nessie. What's so important that you need to talk to me now? It's funny that before I left town you didn't have anything to say to me. Come to think of it – you brushed me off like I'm doing to you today. Karma is something – isn't it?" Owen's laugh was hateful and spiteful. *What happened to my friend?*

"I didn't brush you off, Owen. Not like this. I needed space. Don't you remember what my family was going through!?" I struggled to get the words out clearly as my emotions were all over the place.

He smirked and replied, "Yes, I remember what we *all* were going through...not just what *you* were going through. Remember, my family was just as much a victim in all of that mess as yours was. But you found someone to confide in other than me. The next best thing, right? Brice." Owen looked around the library and stared coldly back into my eyes. "Where is he right now, Nessie? Huh? Where is he when you need him most?"

Various responses flooded my head, but none of them were formulated into vocal responses. I just stared back at him-speechless.

"I can answer that! He's not here," Aubrey mouthed laughing.

"No, he's not. And you're not going to use me anymore, Nessie. I'm not playing the second string for your attention. I don't need it, and I don't want it." He raised Aubrey's hand to his lips and gently kissed it. "I have all I need right here." He turned, her hand still in his, and they walked away.

A tear rolled across my cheek, and I quickly wiped it away.

He's not going to belittle our friendship – especially with that ruthless girl. Who had Owen become?

***

"How's Nessie doing?" Charlotte asked as she sat next to Beau on the sofa.

"Good, I guess. She's like any normal sister. She doesn't talk to me much." Beau reached to pull Charlotte closer to him, and he tickled her.

"Stop...I'm serious...that's not funny!" Charlotte finally escaped his hold. "I'm worried about her. Be serious for once. She's upset about Owen and Aubrey. She wasn't ready for that."

Beau leaned back against the cushions on the sofa. "Do we have to talk about my sister's problems? I want to spend time with you – not try to fix everything for Nessie – when she doesn't want me to help."

Charlotte smirked realizing how cute he looked – all sad that he wasn't getting the attention. She straddled his body, her legs on each side of him, and playfully replied, "You're handsome like this – you know – all vulnerable – in your feelings."

His hands cupped around her back securing her on his lap. "Oh, really. You think I'm vulnerable?" He laughed as he threw her on the sofa with her back pressed against the cushions. "Now tell me who's vulnerable!?"

Charlotte giggled as she tried to release from his hold. She attempted to push him away, but he resisted and let his body press against hers. "Just kiss me – no talk about my sister or my family – I want to concentrate on us."

His lips met hers as her legs wrapped around his waist.

"I missed this," he whispered as her breaths became shallower.

"Me too," she replied as each kiss became more intense.

Their moment of intimate bliss ended with me – once again – interrupting them. I threw my keys on the counter hoping to make the smacking of lips cease.

"Dammit, Nessie. Really!" Beau yelled.

"It's my house too, Beau. You have a room." I rolled my eyes and sighed.

I grabbed a snack from the pantry and attempted to go to my room. Charlotte met me near the kitchen and stopped me.

"What's going on with you and Owen? Have you talked to him?" Charlotte asked pointedly.

I shrugged. I didn't want to get into anything with her about Owen. I'd had a bad morning – seeing him with Aubrey – I wasn't ready to talk about it – especially with Charlotte.

"Okay, well I was hoping maybe you'd had a chance to catch up with him…being that he left town without saying goodbye." Charlotte's eyebrows raised.

"Fine. I did talk to him. Well, I tried to talk to him. It didn't go as I expected." I was trying my best to avoid reliving that moment, but Charlotte kept pressuring me.

"Oh! Well, at least you got to talk to him." Charlotte giggled as Beau's hands grabbed her waist and pulled her back against him. He brushed her hair off her neck to expose her ear and whispered, "Are you through trying to save my sister?"

She turned around to face him placing her hands on her hips. "That's so selfish of you." She smiled playfully and turned back toward me.

"I'm sorry it didn't go as you expected. I know deep down he misses your friendship. You're all he talked about…" She didn't get another word in.

"Stop! Okay!" I slammed my hands on the counter. "I don't care if I was all he talked about. He made it very clear he's moved on with her."

Charlotte was surprised at my lash-out. "I…I'm sorry, Nessie. I didn't mean anything by that – I just know he valued your friendship. That's all."

Beau stepped in front of Charlotte. I hit a nerve when I yelled back at Charlotte. "Nessie, none of this is our fault. You need to take things up with Owen. Quit attacking Charlotte. She's just trying to help. She was worried about you."

"Whatever!" I grabbed my bag and attempted to leave the conversation.

"You can't just mope around here and expect everyone to give you space." Beau stopped me before leaving the kitchen.

In my most sarcastic tone I replied, "Thanks, Beau, you're such a great brother. I know you care." I gently tapped his shoulder and smiled. "I didn't know you were so worried about my happiness." Holding my hands over my heart I continued, "That means so much to me."

"Really, so that's how it's gonna' be?" Beau backed away from me. "I don't care about your happiness. You're right. What I care about is my girlfriend wasting her time thinking about how to help *you* when her focus should be on our relationship." Beau pointed his finger toward me. "You made this mess. You ousted Owen when Brice showed you an ounce of attention. You made Owen leave town, and now you're mad because he moved on. Figure it out, Nessie. But don't drag the rest of us into it."

My mouth dropped open. "You asshole. You have no right to say any of that. You didn't know the friendship we had – you couldn't have cared less about me or Owen. And don't bring Brice into this! Stay out of my life!" Beau had overstepped and so had Charlotte. I ran up to my room and closed the door.

Chapter Seventy-Two

The Betrayal

The next day at school, Stella and Whitney worked on the Christmas decorations in the Sophomore hall. Most of the student council was attending a leadership convention which left Stella and Whitney in charge of decorating the school.

"How are things going with you and Blaine?" Stella asked as she twisted the red and green streamers.

Whitney smiled. "Things are going great. He's not the same Blaine as before. I keep pinching myself thinking it must be a dream." Whitney grabbed the other end of the streamers. "He's really sweet – has been so supportive and focused on me. I needed that so much with everything that happened with my mom."

"I'm so happy for you, Whit. I'm not going to lie though. I had my doubts. I mean it is Blaine we're talking about." Stella laughed.

"I know. I had doubts as well, but he swept me off my feet the right way this time. And we're taking things slow. He hasn't pushed me to move faster." Whitney's heartbeat faster just talking about him.

"Do you love him?" Stella knew the answer based on the way Whitney talked about him.

"I think I do. I think he's the one. We just connect, you know, in a way I never thought we would. It feels amazing to be with him, and when I'm not with him, I'm constantly thinking about him." Whitney sat back down on the floor. "Now, enough about my love life. What's going on with you and Jackson?" She nudged Stella jokingly.

"Uh, nothing is going on! What are you talking about?" Stella focused on the next row of streamers.

"Oh, please. We all saw ya'll at The Dixie the other night talking alone. It looked like he was trying to get close to you." Whitney knew not to press Stella too hard, or she would shut down.

"Oh, yeah, that was nothing." Her eyes locked with Whitney's and she knew that wasn't going to be enough. "Okay...okay...so we have been talking more – only because he doesn't have any friends."

"It didn't look like he was being forced to hold your hand." Whitney smirked.

Stella burst into laughter. "Stop it! That's none of your business."

"Oh, c'mon, Stella, spill a little. It's good to see you happy – and we all know you've been interested in him." Whitney noticed Jackson coming down the hall. "Speaking of..."

"Speaking of what?" Stella turned around and saw Jackson standing behind her. "Oh, hi! How...how long have you been standing there?"

Jackson knelt close to her. "Long enough to see ya'll have a mess going on here." He laughed.

Stella felt a surge of relief. "Whatever, we know what we're doing!"

Jackson stood up and made his way through the decorations lying on the floor. He turned around to face them before rounding the corner of the hall, "Stella, I'll see you after school?"

She smiled back at him and caught Whitney making kissy faces at her.

"Yeah, I'll meet you at your Jeep," she replied as Jackson walked away. "Girl, you have to quit all that. We're not like that." Stella didn't like the attention.

"Oh, please, Stella. It's written all over his face! He soooo wants to be with you. Just let him in. I think ya'll are good together." Whitney picked up the remaining decorations. "We better get this picked up before we get trampled when the bell rings."

As they picked up the large tote of decorations Stella asked, "Whit, you really think we are good together?"

"Yessss! Girl, he's totally into you...and you've been crushing on him for a while." Whitney's eyes lit up. "Do you think we didn't notice? C'mon, girl. We all saw the way you looked at him – begging for him to notice you."

Stella sighed. "So it was that obvious, huh?" She laughed. "I want to be with him more than anything, but a huge part of me can't get past the reason he finally talked to me in the first place. He's alone, Whit. He needed someone – and I'm the only one who would talk to him."

Whitney couldn't believe what she was hearing. "Girl, really? Do you believe that you're his last resort? Jackson is smart and knows what he wants. When have you ever known him to back down from what he wants? He's the most disciplined, straightforward person I know."

"I don't know. It's hard not to think that way, but you're right – he's always got a plan – and knows what he wants." Stella jumped as the bell rang for the next class. "Besides having a plan – he's super cute."

They giggled as they grabbed a different tote full of decorations and headed for the cafeteria.

"What's the deal with the polar bear decorations this year?" Whitney picked up a handful of polar bear ornaments adorned with a Coca-Cola bottle. "I don't get it."

Stella shrugged. "It's what the secretary chose for the cafeteria this year."

The girls laughed and joked as they spread Christmas décor on the tables and the food line.

As they placed the final polar bear on top of the milk and juice cooler, Whitney couldn't help but ask, "Stella, what drew you to Jackson?"

Stella smirked. "I don't know...I mean...he's super cute...we all know that...but he intrigued me for other reasons."

"Like what?" Whitney sat on one of the cafeteria tables.

Stella sat next to her. "He's smart and seems to know what his future will be. He's confident and strong."

Whitney leaned on Stella. "You're lucky, you know. I'm happy you found each other. It seems like we are all getting what we wanted...to be with the person that makes us happy."

"Yeah, I agree!" Stella noticed Whitney's tone soften. "What's wrong?"

Whitney shrugged her shoulder. "I don't know. I guess it's just Blaine and Beau. Yeah, we're all happy, but it doesn't mean anything if we can't all be friends. I wish they could fix things between them."

Stella hugged Whitney. "Girl, we have to get them all back talking. It's not just Beau and Blaine, remember. Beau can't stand Jackson. What can we do to bring them all back together?"

Whitney's hands cradled her face. "I have no clue – but we need to figure something out."

Stella smiled. "I think I might know of something we can do." She slid from the edge of the table and said, "I just need to talk to Jackson."

***

Stella approached Jackson as he leaned cockily onto the door of his Jeep. "Hey!" she said playfully, smiling.

"Hey back to you." He reached out his hands on her waist and pulled her in closer to him. "I've been waiting for a while. What held you up?" His hands fell on her hips with his thumbs tucked into the rim of her pants.

His touch felt amazing, and she was drawn into his chest. Her face nestled in his cologne-soaked shirt hoping the moment wouldn't end.

A few friends passed by his Jeep yelling out the window, and the moment was over.

"I was with Whitney finishing up decorations in the cafeteria." Stella took a step back from him, but he kept his hold on her. "Can I ask you something?"

"Sure, ask me anything. What's up?" Jackson's fingers softly found their way under her shirt and caressed her back.

She inhaled deeply and continued. "Whit and I were talking – and – well – we need the boys to get back together."

Jackson pulled his hands away and stuffed them in his pockets. "That's a good way to ruin a perfect moment." Smirking, he continued, "Oh yeah. Ya'll *need* us to get back together, huh? You do know Beau can't stand me?"

"Yeah, I know, and he can't stand Blaine either. That's why...and hear me out okay...I was thinking...maybe we should tell Blaine about Isabella and the tests so..."

Jackson pushed himself away from his Jeep. "Hell no! Are you crazy!?"

"Jackson, please hear me out!" Stella pleaded with him. "Give me a minute to explain."

"Stella, nothing you say is going to sway me to tell Beau the truth. Besides, he doesn't want anything to do with me and wouldn't listen if I tried." Jackson leaned back against his Jeep. "Can we talk about something else?"

Stella was insistent. "No, I want to finish telling you why I think we should tell Blaine."

"You're something, you know." He shook his head and smiled. Throwing his hands in the air he said, "I'm all yours. Let me have it."

Stella grinned knowing she'd won him over. "We can use Isabella as a way for you and Blaine to gain Beau's trust. Telling Beau the truth about his mom is huge, and I know Beau will see that both of you care about him as a friend and couldn't keep this terrible secret."

Jackson stared at Stella and rubbed his chin. "I get what you're saying, but I don't know if I can tell him."

Stella grabbed his hand. "You'll find a way, Jackson. This is the chance for you and Blaine to make things right with him."

"I can't do it. Isabella is ruthless, and I don't trust her. The minute the truth gets out, it's going to explode into something much bigger than Beau forgiving us." Jackson opened the door to his Jeep. "I'm sorry, Stella. I know you want me to do this, but it's not going to happen."

She backed away from his Jeep.

"I thought we were going to hang out this afternoon?" Jackson asked as he stepped into the driver's seat.

"Maybe a raincheck? I'm sorry." She pressed her lips together noticing his disappointment.

"So, it's like that? You're mad that I won't say anything?" He grabbed the steering wheel and glared at her.

"No, Jackson. I'm sorry. It has nothing to do with that. I forgot Mom needed me to pick her up in town from the dealership. Her car was having some issues this week." She knew he didn't believe her.

"Okay, well, I guess I'll see you tomorrow," Jackson said dryly as he left the parking lot.

"What's his problem?" Whitney asked as Jackson's tires spun out in the gravel lot.

"Who knows!" Stella threw her hands in the air.

"Does it have something to do with why you left the cafeteria in a rush to find him?" Whitney pressed Stella.

"I guess, it kinda' does." Stella started walking toward her car. Whitney followed closely behind.

"He's mad that I couldn't hang out with him this afternoon, that's all." Stella wanted to tell Whitney the truth, but she knew it would risk her relationship with Jackson.

She unlocked her car and turned around thinking Whitney was behind her. Instead, she saw Blaine standing in the middle of the parking lot, Whitney behind him, throwing his hands and yelling back at Beau. She sighed.

"Guys, ya'll have to stop this!" Whitney yelled as she attempted to calm Blaine down.

Charlotte kept a firm hold on Beau's arm. "Beau, ya'll stop it. Enough!"

Beau stepped closer to Blaine with clenched fists and punched him in the face.

Blaine didn't flinch. Blood fell from his nose, and he wiped it away laughing. "That's all you got! You can do better than that!"

"No, Beau! Stop it!" Charlotte yelled trying to intervene.

Beau pushed her away. "Stay out of the way Charlotte before you get hurt."

Beau drew up his fist and punched Blaine again – this time in the eye.

Blaine stood motionless and laughed again. "Well, I guess I deserved both of those blows. Are you finished?"

Stella walked closer and yelled, "Ya'll stop it! This is crazy!"

The girls huddled together watching as Blaine stood in front of Beau with outstretched arms, "I'm right here, man. Keep hitting me until you get it all out."

Beau's stance remained stiff with his chest thrusted out. "I'll never get it all out." He threw one more punch that busted Blaine's chin.

Whitney screamed and ran toward him. "Blaine, are you okay?"

"Yeah, I'm fine," he replied wiping the blood from his chin with his arm. He spit blood in front of him toward Beau. He grabbed Whitney and said, "Let's get out of here."

"I can't. Mom is expecting me at home. I'm late as it is." Whitney kissed his cheek and whispered, "I'll call you when I get home."

Charlotte ran to Beau hoping to keep him from following. "Just let him go." She pulled his hand up and noticed it was busted up. "Beau, your hand is bleeding."

"It's fine. It's worth all of it to hit that son-of-a-bitch. I've had it with his tough guy 'I can take it' attitude. He got what he deserved." Beau breathed in deeply, grabbed Charlotte around the waist, and walked toward his Corvette.

Stella walked back to her car arm in arm with Whitney.

"This has to stop, Stella." Whitney wiped a tear from her cheek. "Blaine's poor face…all bloody…," she cried as tears rolled off her face.

Stella knew what she needed to do. She knew in her heart she shouldn't tell Whitney, but her gut told her nothing would change – and this was their only hope. "I need to talk to you and Blaine tonight. Do you think ya'll can meet me at the Abyss around nine?"

"What? Why do you want to meet at the Abyss so late?" Whitney asked.

"That thing that I had to talk to Jackson about earlier – that's why." Stella responded dryly as she opened her car door.

"Well, what's it about?" Whitney's curiosity was peaked.

"You'll find out tonight. And bring Blaine with you. This is the only chance we have to smooth things over between the guys." Stella waited for Whitney to acknowledge her. "Well?"

"Yeah, sure. I'll let Blaine know. Nine o'clock at the Abyss," Whitney replied as Stella revved her car and drove away.

***

Blaine and Whitney got to the Abyss around eight-fifteen to light a fire. A cold snap had come through and temperatures were in the low forties.

"That should be good," Blaine said as he tossed another piece of wood on the fire. Whitney sat on the tailgate of his truck.

"She didn't give you any more details…she just asked for us to meet her here?" Blaine attempted to make sense of it.

"Yeah, she wouldn't tell me anything else."

"Come here," Whitney motioned for him as he stood near the fire. The flame highlighted his busted chin and bruised eye. He found his way between her legs dangling from the tailgate. Saddened by the bruises on his face she softly said, "I can't believe he did this to you." She softly rubbed her fingers near his eye and gently kissed his chin.

"I'm fine, babe. I told you not to worry about it. It's just a cut and a little bruise. I get more beat up on the field!" His head hung low as she ran her fingers through his hair.

"I'll always worry about you, Blaine. You shouldn't have taken that from him. You didn't deserve it." She held his face between her hands and pressed her lips against his.

"Thank you," he said as she kissed him repeatedly.

"Thank you for what?" she asked as he pulled her off the tailgate.

"Just thank you...for being here for me...for having my back...I...I love you, babe." Blaine's lips parted and then found their way to hers once more – this time a much deeper kiss.

Before she could respond, headlights appeared in the distance.

"That's Stella." Whitney pulled away from his hold and smiled. "Maybe we can continue this when she leaves?"

***

Stella stood with her back to the fire.

"What's this all about," Blaine questioned as he sat on the tailgate next to Whitney.

"It's about Beau – and a way to get ya'll to be friends again – hopefully." Stella stood by the fire warming her hands.

"Well spill it! We're waiting!" Blaine looked at Whitney and smiled. "I'm all ears!"

"This isn't easy for me, guys. Jackson asked me to keep this between us. I feel like I'm betraying him – but after what I saw today in the parking lot between you and Beau – and the way Beau feels about Jackson – it has to stop." Stella turned around to face them.

"Stella, just take your time." Whitney scooted off the tailgate and walked closer to her.

"It's just that...well, Jackson would have said something but he's afraid of what Isabella might do." Stella rambled on more and Blaine cut her off.

"Look, Stella, you gotta' slow down. It's just me and Whitney. Take your time." Blaine pushed himself off the tailgate and stood on the other side of Stella.

Facing the fire, Stella told the story of what happened that night at the law firm - from Isabella switching the tests, Isabella denying her involvement and pinning it on Jackson, and Dad covering it all up. As the words left her mouth, she felt a huge weight lifted off of her but immediately felt remorse for not being true to her word with Jackson.

"Holy moly! Did I hear you right that Mrs. Issie switched the tests?" Whitney was in shock. "No way she would have done that to Beau!"

"Whit, it's true. She admitted it to Jackson, Mrs. Beale, and Mr. Corbin. It's true." Stella continued staring at the fire.

Blaine ran his fingers through his hair and sat back down on the tailgate. "Are you sure you have this right? Mrs. Corbin was behind all of this mess?"

Stella was getting agitated and second-guessing whether she should have said anything. "Yes, dammit! It was her! For the third time...Isabella...Mrs. Issie...whatever you want to call that ruthless woman...she did this...she's behind all of it!"

Blaine and Whitney watched as Stella screamed into the night air. "She did this to all of us! She blamed Jackson...broke apart friendships...she's a horrible person!"

Whitney ran to her side. "Stella, it's okay. We believe you. It's just a lot to take in."

Stella pushed her away as tears rolled down her cheeks. "Jackson didn't want me to say anything. He confided in me. I've betrayed his trust. He'll never forgive me."

Blaine felt uncomfortable and backed away. He'd never seen Stella show emotions – much less cry. She always acted tough.

"It's okay, Stella. We'll figure this out. We'll figure it all out together." Whitney hugged Stella tightly.

"I just want it to be over. Jackson is fighting with this every day. It's not fair to him. He didn't want to say anything in fear Isabella would turn it all on him." Stella couldn't control her tears.

Whitney struggled to fathom how Isabella could have been behind this, but she didn't challenge Stella. "I'm sure there's reasoning to this. Once we get more details, I'm sure things will get straightened out."

Stella pushed away from her and wiped her tears. "No, Whit, it's straightened out. She did this to *all* of us. Her reasoning was to break up Beau and Charlotte -don't you see?"

Whitney tucked in her top lip and shook her head.

"You think she didn't do this – don't you?" Stella muttered.

"I don't know what to think…I mean…it's just a lot to take in that's all." Whitney didn't know what else to say. She wanted to believe Stella, but Isabella was like family to her. She watched as Stella turned and walked back toward her car.

Blaine grabbed her arm and stopped her. "Hey, I appreciate you looking out for me…and Beau."

Stella turned around. "Well, I'm not sure what good it did. Whitney doesn't believe me. That's exactly what Jackson was afraid of."

Whitney pushed herself between them. "No, Stella, I do believe you. I will admit it's hard to swallow – but I believe you."

"You shouldn't have doubted me! I came very close to not telling both of you. But this is the only way I can see for Beau to give you and Jackson a second chance. If ya'll go to him with this, maybe he'll come around and things can get back to normal again between all of us."

They walked back toward Blaine's truck to sit near the fire.

"So, what do we do next?" Blaine asked looking to the girls for answers. "I don't know how to approach Beau with this. The last time I was honest we all know how that ended."

"This is different, Blaine. This doesn't have anything to do with you." Whitney reassured him. "You have to tell him the truth."

Stella remained silent – staring at the fire. Whitney noticed she hadn't said much the last few minutes. "You okay?"

Stella's heart was in the right place telling Whitney and Blaine, but she felt terrible for betraying Jackson. "No, I'm not. I have to tell Jackson. He needs to know I didn't keep his secret."

"Are you sure you want to do that alone? I mean...me and Blaine can come with you for support?" Whitney could see the devastation on her face. "Let us come with you and we can tell him together."

Stella reached for Whitney's hand and smiled. "Thanks, Whit. But I've got to do this alone. Jackson has to choose to forgive me or not." She turned to walk toward her car and then paused. "Wait for me to tell Jackson, okay, before ya'll tell Beau. Please."

"Of course, Stella." Whitney's brows drew together, and she smiled. "Just let us know, okay. We're all in this together."

Chapter Seventy-Three

The Only Way Out

"Brice, someone is out front waiting on you," Kent yelled from the office. "There's not going to be any trouble, is there?" Kent eyed the slim, six-foot, tattooed guest who stood at the entrance of the shop.

Brice threw his tools on the ground and wiped his hands on a rag hanging nearby. "Alright, I'm coming." He yelled, peeking out the garage doors. "Shit," he mumbled to himself and responded, "No sir, it's fine."

When he exited the office, he quickly shut the door. "Man, why are you here? You shouldn't be here. I'm working."

"Yo, my man Brice. Why are you so worried, bro? I thought you'd be happier to see me." He pressed his hands together and rubbed them laughing. It was the guy that Brice had towed a few days ago.

"Yeah, I told you two days. It's been three." Brice motioned for him to walk with him around the shop. "Follow me. You're gonna get me in trouble – showing up here while I'm working."

"Relax, bro. It's chill. You get breaks don't you?" The guy lit a cigarette.

Brice immediately pulled it from his mouth and stomped on it. "You've got some nerve showing up here. I can't be seen around you – remember – I got arrested – for drugs. And you reek of drugs."

"Awe, bro, that's no way to treat an old friend. Wasn't too long ago you were hangin' with us." He brushed some dirt off of Brice's shoulder. "Now, you're all high society and shit." He lit another cigarette and glared at Brice daring him to snatch it. "Don't even think about it."

Brice started to get concerned Mr. Beale would come looking for him. He peeked back around the corner, and the office door was shut. "Look, man, what'd you find out? I gotta get back to work."

He took a long drag of his cigarette and smirked. "Yeah, I got you something – but you're not going to like it – or what you have to do with it."

Brice wasn't following. "What do you mean – what do I have to do with it? Just tell me what you found out!"

"Alright, alright." He took one more drag of his cigarette and stepped on the butt on the ground. "It was Tennie. Your sister set you up."

Brice's face tightened, rubbing the nape of his neck he replied, "No shit, man. I know she set me up. I need proof."

"Relax, bro. Yeah, I got you. I have two fellas that owe me. They said they'd tell the police the drugs were Tennie's. They've had enough of her lies and stealing from them. She was selling earlier that night, and they know where she stashed the rest when she heard the cops were on their way." He waited for Brice to respond.

"Yeah, she stashed it on me...in my room." Brice wasn't buying that he had enough information to get the sentence reversed. "I need more than that. This isn't enough."

"You're not hearing me. My buddies know where she hid her stash. You didn't have her stash – she planted a piece on you." He laughed. "You must not know your sister that well. She's got a huge business going out of that trailer."

Brice leaned up against the shop wall and yelled, "Dammit! Tennie – getting me mixed up in this mess."

The guy smirked at Brice. "No, bro, she's the mess. The way I see it, you've got two witnesses who will vouch for you that the drugs were hers. Why are you so worried?"

Brice shoved his hands in his pockets. "I don't know. I'm just paranoid it won't work. What if they can't prove she planted them on me?"

"Well, that's the part you're not gonna' like...where my brother comes in. He saw her plant them on you." The guy looked at the ground.

"No way, I'm not implicating your brother – he's my friend – I'm not taking a chance he'll get in trouble. That puts him at the trailer." Brice moved away from the wall. "It's like déjà vu."

"It's the only option you got. The way this plays out - my guys go in and tell the police where the drugs are, my brother tells them he saw her plant them on you – and your sister goes to jail. I don't see any risks." He looked up and saw Kent standing near the corner of the shop.

"What if they start investigating you again and things turn sideways? Huh? I'll never forgive myself." Brice knew there was always a risk. "And you're brother – isn't he still on probation?"

"No, it lifted a few weeks ago. So, he's cool. Don't worry about us. It'll be fine. We owe you this," he smiled as Kent started to approach them and stopped. "Brice, it's time to get back to work. Break's over." Kent watched as the guy brushed Brice's shoulder.

"So, you do get breaks after all." He laughed as he walked by Kent. "Have a good day, sir."

Kent nodded at him.

Brice followed Kent into the shop. "Brice, what in the hell was that about?"

Brice shrugged and replied, "My way out."

Kent wasn't convinced. "Son, by the looks of that guy, the only way out he's got is not what I have in mind for you." Kent leaned against his desk. "Whatever he was telling you – it can't be good."

"It's the only way I have to get out of this mess. I believe him." Brice explained to Kent what the guy had told him.

"Hmm. I see. And you're sure you want to put your sister behind bars? You know that's where this ends...and you lose your home." Kent hated to be blunt but wanted to state the obvious.

"I hope the trailer burns down. Mom's in prison, and Tennie's right behind her. I can't be part of any of that anymore." Brice grabbed his tools and walked back onto the shop floor.

Kent yelled, "Hey Brice."

Brice paused and turned and faced him.

Kent smiled and said, "I'm behind you one hundred percent. Just let me know what I need to do to help."

Chapter Seventy-Four

Divulged Secrets

"I thought I might find you here," Stella stepped out onto the green turf.

Jackson tossed the football between his hands smiling. "I'm glad you found me."

"Do you spend all your free time out here on this field?" Stella asked jokingly.

"Considering my home life is a wreck with a brother I didn't ask for – yeah – I'd say I spend every, single, minute of free time- right here on this field."

"Take five," he yelled to his teammate across the field.

He dropped the football as she approached and pulled her close, his arms wrapping around her waist. "And, it's nice when a beautiful surprise like you walks up."

"Oh yeah," Stella played along pursing her lips as she admired his abs screaming from his fitted t-shirt.

"I have a few more plays to practice, and then, maybe we can go grab some breakfast from AELs?" Jackson picked up his football. "You want to help me with some runs?" He playfully ran backwards with the football.

"Uh, no! Do I look like football material?" Stella placed her hands on her hips and laughed.

He tossed the football at her suddenly.

She flinched and it jammed her index finger. "Owww!" She shrieked in pain, holding it tightly as he ran over to her.

"I'm so sorry! I didn't mean to..." He felt terrible. "Here, let me see it."

"It's okay. I don't want to take pressure off it. It's throbbing so bad." She brought both hands up to her chest while he pulled her close to his in tandem.

"Come here. I'm sorry." He kissed the top of her head and wrapped his arms around her. "Let me see it."

She slowly pulled her hands apart as he carefully traced the side of her finger with his lips. "Is that better?"

She smiled wistfully and gazed at him. "Yes, that's much better."

His fingers found their way to her chin and his lips found hers. His kiss was deeper this time – not like the time before – and his hold seemed stronger.

Each touch of his lips on hers made her body weak. Her lips parted wider allowing his tongue to briefly meet hers. For a moment she forgot they were standing in the middle of the football field and why she'd come out in the first place. She attempted to block all reasoning and focus solely on his deep kiss and hold, but something inside her kept screaming 'You need to tell him'.

Regretfully, she slowly backed out of his hold on her.

"Did I do something wrong? Was it too fast?" Jackson was worried he'd pushed her away.

She bit the side of her lip and grinned. "No, Jackson, I loved it. I just need a minute."

He felt relieved and reached for her hand. "Take all the time you need."

She watched as he threw a few more passes with his teammate and met her on the sideline bench afterward.

"Ready for breakfast? I'm starving!" Jackson put on his windbreaker and waited for her to stand up. Seeing that she wasn't moving, he laughed saying, "You know breakfast isn't served out here, right?!"

She looked at him with a twisted smile, and he knew something wasn't right. "Are you going to tell me what's going on in that head of yours?"

She stood up abruptly from the bench. "I don't think I can, Jackson. This is gonna' be much harder than I thought."

His eyes widened as he grinned. "My kissing skills need work?" He laughed.

Her hands covered her nose and mouth as she shook her head. "No! Jackson. It's nothing like that. I didn't want you to stop kissing me. But, I have to get this out."

He became more concerned seeing her demeanor become serious. "Well, tell me!"

She paced around the bench unable to stand in one place.

He could tell she was nervous.

"Stella, c'mon, just tell me. You're killing me with suspense over here." He sat on the bench hoping she might take a seat next to him.

She stopped in front of him with her arms crossed on her chest. "It's about Beau. And, well, you and Blaine."

Jackson's eyes seemed to pierce through her as if he knew what she was about to say but he smirked and replied, "What else could be going on between the three of us?"

Stella inhaled deeply and closed her eyes wishing she would've kept her mouth shut after Jackson told her about Isabella. It was too late now. She'd have to persuade him not to hate her.

"It's nothing else, Jackson. It's…about the paternity test…and Isabella." Her eyes focused on his as she sat down next to him.

"We've already been through this. I'm not opening a can of worms – the secret isn't getting out. I only told you because I trust you and needed to get it off my chest." He watched as her head fell between her legs, propping her head up with her hands. He moved her hair away from her face so he could see her. "Stella, tell me what's going on."

Her eyes locked with his. "I told Blaine and Whitney – I told them the truth."

Jackson jumped from the bench. "You didn't! I can't believe you told them after I asked you not to!" He kicked the football across the field and screamed.

She followed him onto the field. "I'm sorry! I don't know what else to say. I know you didn't want anyone to find out, but I can't stand to see what happened in the parking lot the other day. Blaine and Beau are at odds with each other, and Beau has no idea what you've done to protect him. I'm tired of it! I'm tired of the fighting."

He swung around to face her. "You're tired!? Oh, that's good, Stella. I know it's been *so* hard on you." With his teeth clenched, his hands waved crazily in the air yelling, "I can't believe you did this to me."

She backed away from him.

"Get away from me. I can't stand to look at you. I confided in you – and you broke your promise. I can't be around you." He picked up his keys from the bench and walked away.

She followed him closely, still attempting to get through to him. "I did this for you – for our friends – can't you see that? I know I betrayed your trust, and I'm so very sorry for that. But this is the only way Beau will consider forgiving both of you. Don't you see that?"

He turned around and pointed at her directly and replied sarcastically. "The only thing I see is a liar."

Stella's chin dropped to her chest. "I'm sorry. That's all I can say. I didn't mean to hurt you."

He turned and walked toward his car. "Well, you did hurt me."

"I was only trying to help."

"It wasn't your place to help."

She persisted and followed him – unable to give up. As he opened the door to his Jeep and hopped inside, she wedged herself between him and the door. "We're going to tell Beau and Charlotte the truth. We'd like you to be a part of that. I know you can't see it now, but it's the right thing to do. Beau needs to hear it from you. Please come with me."

He cranked his Jeep, forcefully grabbed the door handle, and slammed the door yelling through the window, "No, you made this mess. You clean it up."

***

"Did you tell him?" Whitney pressed Stella for answers as Blaine waited for their food at The Dixie.

"Yeah, I did, and it was horrible." Stella didn't want to relive the nightmare she'd played out a thousand times in her mind – it ended worse than she expected. "He doesn't want anything to do with me. I betrayed his trust."

Blaine set the food trays on the table and rubbed his hands together. "Dig in, ladies."

Both girls stared at him and grinned. "How can you eat in a time like this?" Whitney questioned him.

"You both know me well enough. I love food – especially these burgers. Now, dig in before it gets cold." Blaine began unwrapping his burger as the girls kept staring at him.

"She told Jackson – and he won't talk to her now." Whitney's tone was softer.

"I hate that Stella. You did the right thing telling us. Jackson will come around." He grabbed a handful of fries and shoved them into his mouth.

"Blaine, it's like you haven't eaten in days – slow down!" Whitney nudged him giving him 'the look.'

"What's the next step? I started all this mess – so when are we going to tell Beau and Charlotte?" Stella was ready for all of it to be over.

"So, Jackson doesn't want to be there when we tell them?" Whitney asked for reassurance.

"No, he said it's my mess, and I can fix it. I just don't get him. I told ya'll the truth because I chose my friendship with all of you over my relationship with Jackson – is that so wrong? I guess I hoped that he would see that I did this because I care about him." Her eyes lowered and stared at the burger in front of her and pushed it aside. "Blaine, you can have it. I don't have an appetite."

"Stella, this isn't all on your shoulders. We all have a part in this and so does Jackson whether he wants to be involved or not. Once Beau hears the truth and how Isabella was framing Jackson, I know he will forgive him." Whitney hoped that would be the case.

"It's not Beau he's worried about, Whit. It's Isabella. She's turned all of this on him, and he's afraid it will be his word against hers." Stella stood from the table. "I need to get home."

"Wait, Stella, what's the plan? When should we tell Beau and Charlotte?" Whitney asked.

"Ya'll figure it out and let me know. I just need to be alone."

They watched as Stella left the parking lot. "I'm worried about her. She finally got close to Jackson, something she'd waited so long for, and she lost it." Whitney looked at Blaine attempting to reach Stella's burger. She slapped his chest. "Blaine! For once can you stop thinking about food!"

"What!" he laughed. "I'm hungry, babe. She said I could have it. Besides, you are going to figure this out anyway and tell me what I need to do."

Whitney sighed, stirred a fry in her ketchup, and mumbled, "I'm not sure what the right approach is with Beau. But we need to do something soon. Who knows what Jackson is thinking and what he'll do."

***

Half-time of the homecoming game - the stadium was packed, and everyone was filled with anticipation of naming the Senior king and queen. The game was a blowout. The Mustangs were winning 42-7 - the opponent struggled to make plays against our second string. Coach had lost several players due to the homecoming court and hoped for a victory like this.

Charlotte waited patiently as the Freshman maids walked onto the field. She glanced back at Beau, standing tall next to Dad. He winked at her, and she smiled. Arm in arm with Mason, she stepped out onto the track, and the crowd in the stands cheered.

Moments later, Beau appeared near the edge of the track with Dad by his side. Beau refused to invite Isabella. As odd as it looked with Dad walking next to him – he decided to go with it. The crowd cheered as he stepped out onto the track. Why wouldn't they? It's Beau Corbin! The crowd continued cheering as Dad and Beau made their way onto the field.

As soon as their feet hit the turf, it happened. The announcer's words were clear, "Ladies and gentlemen it seems Dr. Corbin is trying to escort her son."

Beau cringed as he heard the announcer and then her voice from behind. "Beau, dear, you can't be escorted by your father!" She found her way through the crowd. She stood next to him, her arm latched in his, and nodded for Dad to go back to the stands. "I've got it from here, Tucker." She smiled graciously to the onlookers and held onto Beau's arm.

Beau clenched both fists and inhaled deeply. He attempted to pull away from her hold. "I can't believe you would mess this up for me. I don't want you to be here."

"Honey, just keep smiling. You don't want your pictures to turn out with a frown next to your mother, now do you?" Isabella smiled as if everything was perfect.

Beau gritted his teeth and forced a smile hoping to dodge any more attention on them.

Dad slowly walked back through the crowd and stood on the track.

As Isabella and Beau found their spot on the 35-yard line, Jackson, escorted by Allison, found his way onto the field."

Isabella's stance stiffened as she watched him parade onto the field. She muttered under her breath, "Quarterback, heh. He got that chance only because you were hurt."

Beau stood tall, ignoring her comments, hoping no one else had heard.

Blaine was the last one to enter the field.

Once the Senior king and queen were named, the court walked off the field onto the track and began making their way to the makeshift stage.

Isabella released her arm from Beau's and placed both hands on his face. "My boy. I'm so very proud of you."

Beau immediately placed his hands on hers removing them from his face. "No. You don't get it. I don't want you here. I didn't invite you. I don't care if you're proud of me."

Isabella laughed out loud hoping it would distract eavesdroppers. "Oh, Beau. Your wit continues to amaze me." She threw her nose into the air and whipped her hair around to face Dad. "How about a picture...all three of us together?"

Dad's eyes narrowed as Beau searched for a distraction. He found Charlotte in the crowd and walked over to her.

"Isabella. Just go." Dad's voice was calm, and his fake smile didn't fool her.

"I'll go whenever I damn well please," she scoffed and walked past him only to run into Jackson. "Excuse me, I'm sorry," she proceeded to apologize until she realized it was Jackson she'd bumped into. "Oh, it's just you. Get out of my way." She pushed by him and stopped briefly, turned to him, and said, "You clean up nicely. Who would have thought such a deceitful young man could present himself to be reputable?"

Jackson felt rage inside of him stir. He caught a glimpse of Stella as she walked down the steps onto the track. The sight of her made his blood boil even more. He watched as Isabella continued making her way through the crowd poised, and collected, as to make known she was a part of Beau's life.

Jackson walked over to Blaine and watched as he helped each of the girls up the steps of the stage. Blaine reached for Charlotte's hand to help her, and Beau interjected. "I got her. I'll help her." Blaine took a step back. Jackson stood behind locking eyes with Isabella as she approached them.

Beau jumped off the opposite side of the stage once Charlotte found her seat.

"Don't you just look beautiful, Charlotte." Isabella said flatly while looking directly at Jackson. "Jackson, don't you think Charlotte looks stunning this evening?"

Charlotte pretended not to hear her and searched for Beau in the crowd hoping he didn't hear her comment. He was near the concession stand.

Jackson swallowed deeply and turned away unsure of how to respond.

"Oh, don't be shy, now. We all know you had a little 'thing' for her. How couldn't you? Look how beautiful she is." Isabella continued patronizing Charlotte hopeful to make Jackson nervous.

"You look beautiful this evening as well, Dr. Corbin," Blaine attempted to derail the conversation from Jackson.

"Why, Blaine, you're so full of it. I threw this old thing on so quick…" She pressed her hands on her hips. "Oh, who am I kidding." She said smugly and looked around her for affirmation. She caught Jackson's eyes dart from hers and then stared at Charlotte. "As much as I've enjoyed the night with my Beau, I have to get back to the hospital."

Jackson breathed a sigh of relief as she walked past him and out the gate of the stadium. He stared into the distance hoping she wouldn't return. Everything around him became still and quiet as the words 'you know you had a little thing for her' ran over and over again in his head. He felt his breath become shallow as Isabella's face clouded his mind. He knew she would continue to taunt him. Maybe Stella was right. He felt someone grab his arm and he jerked it away.

"Hey, relax, it's Whit," Whitney said softly. "You almost passed out. You okay?"

His hands rested on his knees as he tried to slow his breathing.

"Man, you good?" Blaine squatted next to Jackson.

Jackson nodded. "Yeah, I'm fine." He stood and quickly realized his apparent 'blackout' had captured the attention of everyone around him. "I'm fine. I'm good. I just got dizzy for a minute."

Beau and Charlotte watched Jackson as he walked near the edge of the stage. Halftime was almost over, and the crowd was retreating into the stands. He noticed his friends – staring intently back at him - Blaine standing close to Whitney on the field, Beau near Charlotte on the stage, and Stella on the track. Everyone else had gotten distracted by the football team regaining the field – except for his friends. They stared at him with concern.

He muttered to himself, "I can't keep doing this," as his focus shifted from each of his friends and finally to Stella. In that moment of time, he realized no matter what he did, Isabella would be at his heels. He had to escape.

The football team reclaimed the field as Jackson made a b-line for the parking lot.

***

After the game, Beau and Charlotte were talking near his Corvette. They watched as Stella approached them followed closely by Whitney and Blaine.

"Let's go," Beau said to Charlotte as their friends approached.

Charlotte shut his car door. "C'mon, Beau. Maybe it's best if we stay. At some point, ya'll have to talk."

Beau shook his head. "I don't have anything else to say to him."

"Hey, Beau. Look, can we talk for a sec?" Blaine shouted as he walked toward them.

Beau smiled sarcastically and replied, "No, not really. I don't have a sec. I need to get on the road before you try to run me off again."

"C'mon, Beau. Enough! We all need to tell you and Char something." Whitney was tired of the games.

Beau leaned back against his car with Charlotte right by his side. "Alright. I'm listening."

Whitney turned to Blaine and Stella. "Go ahead. One of you tell him."

Both remained silent.

Beau became irritated and fidgeted with his keys. "Let's go Charlotte. I'm not playing games with ya'll tonight."

Blaine stepped forward and blurted out, "It was your mom, Beau. She tampered with the tests."

Everyone's eyes widened as all focus was on Beau.

"What did you just say?" Beau asked as he approached Blaine.

"The paternity test. It wasn't the cleaning people – it was your mom." He waited for Beau's attack realizing that wasn't the delivery he'd intended.

Beau stepped back and leaned against his car – speechless. Charlotte was confused and asked, "How...how do you know it was her?"

Stella answered, "Jackson saw her by the filing cabinet, Char."

"I...I don't understand. Dad said it was the cleaning people. Mom isn't nice by any means, but to switch the tests, that's so messed up." Beau shook his head in disbelief. "Is this some kind of joke!?"

Whitney intervened. "I wish it were a joke, Beau. It's the truth. I had a hard time believing it myself, but Blaine's telling the truth." She looked at Charlotte standing near Beau. "Char, I'm sorry. I hate this for both of you, but at least now ya'll know the truth."

"So, all of you...each one of you...knew my mom did this to me and Charlotte and no one bothered to say anything?" Beau became agitated.

Charlotte looked at Whitney and Stella and asked, "Ya'll knew about this and didn't tell me? How could ya'll keep this from us?"

The girls rushed up to her. "No, Char, we haven't known long. We promise."

Beau approached Blaine. "How long have you known about this...and you better not lie to me."

Blaine tucked his chin into his chest. "Just a few days. I know I'm the last person you want to talk to, but can you hear me out?"

"Whatever, man. It's not like it's going to be the truth." Beau spit at the ground. "Go ahead."

"Jackson has been under pressure from your mom since he approached her. He didn't see her do it..." Beau cut Blaine off.

"Oh, so now, ya'll aren't sure if Mom did it or not?" Beau laughed. "C'mon, babe, let's get out of here."

Stella yelled with her hands planted firmly on her hips. "No! Stop it!" Stella stood between Beau and his car. "I'm tired of this shit! We are all going to stand here like grown people and work this out. I'm exhausted from being friends with both sides of this and frankly, I'm not going to stand by watching our friendships fall apart over something Isabella Corbin created. Nobody is going anywhere until we straighten all this out!"

"Okay, Stella, we get it. Calm down. We're gonna' work this out," Charlotte turned to Beau and made him respond.

"Yeah, alright. We'll work it all out." He stared toward Blaine.

Stella continued, "Okay. That's progress. Now, let me outline it all for you. Jackson has been manipulated by your mother. I know that must be hard to fathom, but it's true. In fact, she's trying to pin it all on him. That's why he's been reluctant to say anything."

Beau rubbed his chin. "Why did he feel pressured by her? That's crazy."

Charlotte chimed in. "You didn't hear her tonight, Beau. You were at the concession stand. She made jabs at Jackson like she's done to me. She made comments to him…you know…about me…and…"

"Wow. I don't know if I can take much more of this." Beau threw his arms in the air.

"I still want to know how all of you knew about this and me and Charlotte didn't. Huh? Can anybody explain it? And why now? Why tell us now?" Beau leaned back against his car again.

"Jackson wanted to tell you, and he told me a few days ago because it was eating at him. I told Whitney and Blaine hoping we could come to both of you as friends and tell you together. I know this must be so hard to hear." Stella avoided bringing up Jackson.

Beau looked around the parking lot. "Where is Jackson? He's been knowing the longest about this. Why isn't he here with ya'll?"

Silence.

"Where's Jackson? I want to ask him what he saw." Beau's emotions were rampant.

"He's struggling with the truth, Beau. You have to believe me that he wanted to tell you so many times, but he was scared – of your mom.

He told me in confidence, and I betrayed him by telling Whit and Blaine. He's having a hard time with this and left the game early." Stella bit her lip and waited.

"I need to find him. He needs to look me in the eye and tell me to my face!" Beau looked at Blaine and Whitney and back at Stella. "I don't know what to think or say. It's a lot to take in. I need to find Jackson."

Chapter Seventy-Five

Confronting the Obvious

The streetlights on Main Street were adorned with Christmas wreaths and red bows. Everyone in town was focused on the festival that Saturday evening - Christmas on Bayou Fueob. The prior year's festival was canceled due to rain, so the town was eager to kick off the celebration.

Beau had planned for the night to be special with Charlotte, but first he needed to clear his mind and talk to Jackson.

Beau drove up to the gym at school and parked behind the weight room next to Jackson's Jeep. As he rounded the corner inside, he saw Jackson sitting on a bench.

"Hey, you got a minute?" Beau asked walking closer.

"Yeah, I got a minute." He wiped the sweat from his neck with a towel. "By the look on your face - you must know."

Beau stopped a few feet from him and nodded. "Yeah, I know."

Jackson stood up and threw the towel over his shoulder – his eyes focused on Beau.

"I want to hear it from you. All of it." Beau was pointed.

"Didn't Stella tell you? She couldn't wait to tell Whitney and Blaine about it. So much for trusting her." Jackson set the weights on the bench press.

"Yeah, they all told me after the homecoming game. They said you've known for a while." Beau sat on the weight bench next to Jackson.

Jackson slammed a weight down on another. "That's about right. It's always my fault." He mumbled under his breath.

"You're not going to get any pity from me, man. I'm all out of care at this point. I just came here for the truth – from you." Beau stopped Jackson from loading the next weight. "You owe me this. I want to hear it from you."

Jackson took a few steps back and replied, "You know everything. What's left for me to tell you?"

Beau's tone was flat. "C'mon, Jackson. My mom did this. I want to hear it directly from you since you didn't want to tell me in the first place."

"Dammit, Beau." Jackson slammed another weight onto the floor. "Bro, I did want to tell you. I wanted to tell you so many times – but your mom is ruthless. Did they tell you that she is pinning this all on me? I'm not going into why because it's not important, but she's committed to making sure she's not implicated for it."

Beau nodded. "Yeah, they told me. And I don't want to relive the reason she's pinning it on you, but you should've come to me and told me."

Jackson shrugged his shoulders. "It's easy to say that I should have told you. It's your mom, man. Every time I thought – now's my chance – the thought of her pinning this on me stopped me."

"Regardless, I want to know what you saw." Beau wasn't backing down.

Jackson sat on the bench and relived the moment again for the hundredth time. "I didn't see her physically tamper with anything. I startled her when I picked up Mom. She was near the exact cabinet where the tests were locked up. That's why I didn't say anything to Mom or your dad since I didn't know if she did anything at all. For all I knew, it could've been the cleaning crew."

"Wait a minute...Dad knows?" Beau's tone deepened. "Dad knows that Mom did this?"

"Shit, man. Don't drag me into your family drama." Jackson stood up and paced the floor. "This is exactly why I didn't want to say anything. It's like a bad dream that won't end."

"Well, too bad, Jackson. You're tied up right in the middle of it and there's no going back." Beau stopped his pacing. "Tell me! My Dad knows?"

"Yeah, your dad and my mom both know. They're the only ones other than Isabella." Jackson watched as Beau's face became long and he sat on the bench to recollect himself.

"How could Dad keep this from me? He...lied to me about the cleaning crew. That was just some stupid excuse – he made me believe..." His words and thoughts were all over the place. "How could he lie to me...just like Mom did?"

"Look, man. I'm in this deep enough as it is. I can't be part of the family drama. You have to work all that out with your dad. I've done enough damage and honestly just want this to go away." Jackson grabbed his gym bag. "I'm outta' here man."

"Oh, you just want it to go away!?" Beau jumped up from the bench and stood inches from Jackson's face. "This isn't going away until I find out the truth. You are just as much a part of this as I am. So, get ready, Jackson." Beau turned around and slammed the door behind him.

***

Dad was out of town most of the day golfing with several friends from college. Mason had called several times during the day only to get the answering machine.

Dad arrived back in town around six thirty that evening and met Mason at the law firm.

"I've been calling all day, Tucker. We need to talk about Isabella. It's time we set something in motion to expose her." Mason's eyes were cold and dark, and his breath reeked of bourbon.

"Settle down, Mason. There's no need to rush this. We need to think this through so no one else gets hurt." Dad threw his keys on his desk and plopped into his chair. "I'm exhausted from traveling. Can we please talk about this tomorrow?"

"Hell no! We're doing this, Tucker, tonight." Mason slammed both hands down on Dad's desk. Jabbing his index finger onto the desk he sternly shouted, "It happens tonight."

Dad ran his fingers through his hair and sighed realizing Mason's drunkenness was likely provoking his immediate need for retaliation on Isabella. "Mason, go home. You're drunk. We have plenty of time to think about the appropriate way to do this."

Mason laughed. "You're not hearing me, Tucker. Tonight! It happens tonight – at the festival." Mason's eyes brightened. "Just think about it. It's the perfect opportunity. The entire town will be there – I want everyone to hear what a terrible, miserable person Dr. Isabella Corbin is!"

Dad stood up from behind his desk. "Mason, no. That's a terrible idea! You're forgetting that other people are involved in this besides Isabella. Beau and Nessie don't know anything about this. I've kept it from them to protect them. You can't do this!"

Mason became belligerent. "I most certainly can, and I will. This is the last time Isabella Corbin is going to step on me. I will have the last word, and the entire town of Sedipar is going to see her the way we know her – a miserable, pathetic liar."

Mason stumbled out of Dad's office.

Dad followed closely behind pleading for Mason to let him drive him home. "I'm calling Melissa. You're in no shape to drive."

Mason laughed. "Tucker, no need to call anyone. I'm not driving. The festival is only a few short blocks away. I'll see you at the 'show' later…" He continued laughing as he stumbled out the door of the law firm.

Chapter Seventy-Six

Christmas on Bayou Fueob

Beau picked Charlotte up around six thirty that evening. "You look more gorgeous than ever – if that's even possible." He reached for her hand as she walked from the front porch toward his car.

Her eyes met his and she smirked. "Awe, you're so sweet, but I'm way underdressed. I need to go change." She attempted to turn back to the house when he stopped her.

"You look perfect, and you dressed for the occasion – a festive Christmas sweatshirt." He pulled her close and softly kissed her lips.

She gave in. "Okay, but why are you so dressed up then?" Holding both of his hands, she took a step back and admired his neatly pressed button-up red shirt and dark jeans. "You look pretty handsome yourself, but you're way overdressed for this festival!"

"It's the only thing that was clean. Quit worrying about it! Let's go!" Beau tried to change the subject. "Do you want to get dinner before the festival?"

"No, I'm good. Maybe we can grab something later tonight. I'm sure they will have food on Main Street." The small bells jingled on her sweatshirt as she repositioned herself closer to him leaning on the console. She laughed, "These stupid bells are going to annoy me!"

At the end of her driveway, he stopped and put the car in park. He stared into her eyes and smiled. "I love you more than anything. I think you look perfect tonight so quit worrying. I'm just glad I get to share Christmas with you – like this."

His hands framed her face as his thumbs lightly caressed her cheeks, and he kissed her. The smallest hint of his cologne captivated her as his kiss became deeper. As his hands found their way to her waist, headlights illuminated his car.

"What in the world," Beau pulled away as they both raised their hands to shield their eyes. "Oh, it's just Nessie."

I waved as I passed the two lovebirds thinking, *How many times am I going to catch them making out!?*

He slowly pulled out of the driveway with one hand entwined in Charlotte's.

***

Blaine and Whitney walked hand in hand down Main Street stopping at a few of the local vendors to shop. "This is so magical!" Whitney smiled as she spun in circles looking up at the Christmas lights that decorated the town.

Blaine stopped her spin – his arms wrapping around her waist. "I love seeing you happy like this."

She placed both hands on his chest and smiled. "I'm so happy. I don't see how things could get any better."

The crowd pushed by them as they became lost in each other's stare.

She closed her eyes and nestled her face on his chest. "I want to stay in this moment forever with you- the lights, music, everything. Can we just freeze time?!"

He didn't say a word – he didn't have to. His arms squeezed around her body holding her close. Holding her was all he needed. She completed him in every way. Standing on the sidewalk amid the crowd, the world stood still, until a voice interrupted their moment. "You two going to stand there all night latched to each other or come and enjoy this band?" Stella stood a few feet away laughing.

"I guess we should go see the band," Blaine murmured as his lips touched hers.

"Yeah, you owe me several dances – homecoming night – remember?" She hadn't forgotten that dreadful night freshman year when everything seemed so perfect but ended up as a disaster. She longed for Blaine to sweep her off her feet and dance with her, but he chose drinking and the after-party instead.

"Oh, do I?" he laughed as he twirled her around a few times walking toward Stella. "I think I can do that."

"Where's Jackson?" Whitney asked seeing Stella alone.

"He's still not talking to me since the other night. He'll come around at some point – hopefully." Stella grabbed Whitney's hand. "Let's go check out the band!"

As they approached the top of the embankment, the music from the band softened as they prepared for a break. The crowd cheered and clapped as the band exited the stage. "Awe, they're taking a break." Stella frowned.

A crowd remained in front of the center stage and laughter filled the absence of music.

Stella saw Beau and Charlotte standing alone near the opposite end of the stage and motioned them to come over.

"It's probably not a good idea to be around them tonight." Beau tugged at Charlotte's hand, and they walked toward the edge of the bayou.

Stella sighed. "I sure thought things would be different after we told him what happened. I guess he needs more time."

"He'll come around. He can't keep avoiding us." Whitney held onto Blaine's waist as she looked up at the garland of lights hanging overhead. "The town did such a great job, ya'll. It's so beautiful!" She continued rambling on about the elves, candy canes, and other decorations and realized Blaine's focus was still on Beau. "Blaine – don't you love it?"

"Uh, oh, yeah, babe – I love it!" Whitney knew by his flat response that something else was on his mind. And she knew that something was Beau. "Hey, he's gonna' come around. I promise you. Enjoy the night, okay?"

He took her in his muscular arms and twirled her around, her legs kicking up in the air. "I'm enjoying the night!" Her hands rested on his shoulders and slowly wrapped around his neck as he carefully released her body against his.

He noticed Jackson standing at the top of the stairs. "Ladies, I'm going to grab something to eat. Ya'll want anything?"

"No thanks. I'll get something later." Whitney saw Jackson and hoped he'd come talk to Stella.

Stella smirked and replied, "No, but you can tell Jackson I won't bite him. He can forgive me anytime he wants." She rolled her eyes and turned back to face Whitney.

***

"Hey, man, what's up?" Blaine nudged Jackson.

"Nothing, just seeing what's up in town, that's all." Jackson watched as Stella kept turning around looking his way. He shook his head. "Did you come up here to tell me I need to talk to Stella?" He followed Blaine to the food booth.

"Nah, I'm hungry! But, since you mentioned it – she is hoping you'll come talk to her." Blaine attempted to coax him to forgive her. "You know, apologizing isn't the end of the world. I learned that the hard way."

Jackson stopped walking. "What in the hell do I have to apologize to her for!?"

"Calm down, man. I didn't say you *had* to do anything." Blaine ordered a corn dog from the food vendor and turned to face Jackson. "She did the right thing, Jackson. You know she did. It was going to come out eventually. Just go be with her – give her another chance."

Jackson scratched his jaw. "Who are you? What happened to tough guy Blaine – macho superstar football player? What's with all this 'apologize' and 'be with her' stuff?"

Blaine tore a ketchup packet open with his teeth and squeezed a line on the corn dog. "I'm a new man, Jackson. What can I say!?" He laughed as he took a bite of his food and kept talking. "You have to find the girl – and not just any girl – the right girl."

Jackson snickered. "You sure you're alright, man? Just seems weird– all this mushy stuff coming from you."

"I'm serious." Talking with his hands, Blaine shoved the corn dog at Jackson.

"Watch out with that thing, Blaine." Jackson pressed his hands on his button-up shirt. "Get that ketchup on me and it won't matter that you're all mushy anymore!"

"Whatever. I'm serious though. I found the right girl – almost lost her by being an ass – she's the reason I'm happy." From the top of the stairs, Blaine watched as Charlotte made her way closer to the girls. Beau was a few feet behind her talking to a few players from the football team.

Jackson stood next to Blaine as they watched the girls hug and laugh – just like old times – like they never missed a beat. "That, my friend, is how it should be." Blaine took the last bite of the corn dog and ran down the steps to Whitney.

Blaine's arms secured tightly around Whitney's waist as his lips kissed her neck. Smiling he said, "Ladies, can I steal my girlfriend for a minute?"

"Blaine, Char just came over. Can it wait a minute?" She tilted her head against his and poked her lip out playfully.

"I guess." Blaine knew what she was doing. Beau had walked up behind The Trio, and she knew they'd have to talk to one another or stand there awkwardly.

Beau glared at both Blaine and Jackson and then stared at the ground.

"Beau, my uncle is here selling beer. I know he'd give us one or two." Blaine hoped that might entice him.

"Nah, I'm driving. You shouldn't drink either, Blaine. Remember what happened last time?" Beau was pointed.

Blaine crossed his arms over his chest. "I only offered to have a chance to talk. I don't want a beer. I haven't had one since several months after the accident."

Beau responded sarcastically, "Well, good for you Blaine. I'm glad you're finally responsible."

Blaine moved closer to him. The Trio took a step back. Charlotte snapped, "Oh, no. We aren't doing this again. Ya'll stop it!"

Beau took a step back and smirked as he glanced at Charlotte and smiled. "Don't worry, babe, I'm not going to start anything here tonight. Blaine was just leaving."

Blaine took Whitney's hand and backed away.

Stella caught Jackson's stare. He quickly turned away. "Great!" she muttered to herself. "Just great!"

***

As Owen and Aubrey walked along Main Street, she was mesmerized by how our quaint, small town could be transformed into a Christmas wonderland.

The live oaks were glittered with soft, twinkling white lights that left the most perfect impression on the water.

As they walked onto the bridge over the bayou, Aubrey leaned over the edge to take a peek below. "Look how beautiful!" She was taken aback by the luminaries set alongside the bayou bank.

She caught my stare as I made my way toward the bridge.

Owen stood behind her closing the space between them. His arms covered hers as they took in the beauty of Bayou Fueob. She looked my way and with a playful laugh, she grabbed his arms and pulled them around her waist.

Closing her eyes and feeling his hold on her, she blushed, as her fingers locked within his. "It's such a beautiful night." She closed her eyes and welcomed the warmth of his body against hers as the damp air crowded them.

When I noticed them holding each other close, I turned around.

"Where are you going, Nessie?" Aubrey shouted.

I stopped and inhaled deeply. *Nessie, you can do this. Be the bigger person.*

Without turning toward them, I responded, "I thought I forgot something in my car."

Owen didn't say a word. Aubrey's eyes remained focused on me – watching my every move.

I was stuck. I wanted to go home, but I didn't want *her* to think she got the best of me. "Oh look! I found it in my purse." I walked toward them with my head down. As I got closer, I looked his way and said, "Hi, Owen."

In that brief moment, his stare was different and his eyes locked with mine. I felt something. *Did he feel it too?*

He responded with a half-smile, "Nessie. I'm glad you stayed."

Aubrey spun around and watched as I walked by.

I smiled thinking, *He's glad I stayed! So, he does still care about me.*

I glanced back at them and noticed Owen leaning on the rail. Aubrey stood with her arms crossed staring down at me.

I smiled to myself. *Maybe she's not all that he needs after all.*

***

Kent and Allison's home was at the center of town. The Christmas wonderland that surrounded them was pure bliss as their home was in walking distance to all of it.

Brice tagged along with them as they made their way across the street and down to the stage.

I hadn't spoken to Brice in weeks since he got mad and left The Dixie. I hoped to bump into him tonight.

"Brice, why don't you grab us a few of the bowls of gumbo?" Kent handed him a twenty-dollar bill.

"Yes sir." He hesitated, "Thank you, Mr. Beale, but I can get mine."

"It's Christmas, Brice. It's on me!" Kent laughed as he walked hand in hand with Allison to grab their drinks.

My favorite supper during winter was gumbo. Even if I wasn't hungry, the blend of roux, sausage, chicken, and onions bubbling on the stove drew me in every time. I stood in line waiting for over five minutes behind all the growling tummies waiting to warm their bodies with the juice from the gumbo.

As I moved up in line, I saw Brice with several bowls. His beautiful eyes locked with mine.

My body froze, and my breathing became shallow. I didn't know what to say, so I stood there – silent.

After what seemed like minutes, yet it was only seconds, his eyes left mine -he walked away – not saying a word.

You're going to have to talk to me at some point, Brice Adams. You can't keep avoiding me.

Chapter Seventy-Seven

Mic Drop

Despite what everyone hoped for, we all ended up crowded in a tiny space in front of the stage. That's what happens in a small town. There is no escape. There is no hiding.

The band was coming back in about five minutes, and everyone was patiently waiting to continue their party. I longed for the band to turn the miserable quiet into a distraction – a distraction from both Owen and Brice.

The Trio had gathered near the middle of a makeshift parquet dance floor as Blaine, Beau, and Jackson were spread thinly around them.

Kent and Allison had found a table in the corner near the stage and were enjoying their gumbo. I could see Brice in my peripheral view, alone, leaning casually against the brick wall with one foot propped against it.

I'd avoided Isabella earlier while in line for gumbo and was more than happy she didn't see me. As I made my way down the stairs, I saw her standing near the front of the stage.

I found a spot near the back of the dance floor and watched as Beau and Blaine faced each other in what looked to be a fight. Quickly, Beau backed off.

Blaine backed away but accidentally bumped into Mason. "Oh, sorry Mr. Callaway. I didn't see you…"

Blaine could smell the bourbon on him. Holding an open bottle of bourbon in one hand and a cigar in the other, he threw one arm around Blaine's shoulder. The cigar dangled helplessly – barely secured between his fingers.

"Well, what do we have here," Mason stuttered.

"Mr. Callaway, maybe you should sit down over there on the bench. I'll help you." Blaine eyed Jackson to help him, but Mason refused.

"Get your damn hands off me, son. I don't need to sit down." He glared at Jackson. "You…you lying coward." Taking a sip of his bourbon followed by a long pull from his cigar, he blew the smoke in Jackon's face.

The girls were still laughing amidst the crowd that was beginning to gather for the band's return. They hadn't noticed Mason.

Blaine leaned closer to Mason and whispered, "Mr. Callaway, you want to go grab a bite to eat?"

Mason raised his voice. This time it was loud enough for those around him to hear – including Charlotte. Beau had made his way near her hearing Mason shouting.

"I'm not going to say it again, son, I don't need your damn help." Mason pushed Blaine aside and faced Jackson. Boastfully he said, "Jackson Beale – star quarterback of the Sedipar Mustangs – you have it all now don't you son?"

Jackson eyed the crowd that began to form around them. "No, no, sir. I'm not sure what you mean?" He swallowed the lump in his throat.

Mason circled him. "Well, it seems you tried to have it all – but you failed."

Charlotte broke through the crowd attempting to deflect. She softly asked with a half-smile, "Hey, Dad, why don't we go upstairs and find Mom."

"Hey, look, it's Charlotte. My beautiful girl." Mason raised his glass and cigar to the crowd. "Isn't my daughter beautiful!?"

Charlotte, embarrassed, muttered with her teeth clenched, "Dad, stop it! You're embarrassing me and yourself! Let's go find Mom."

"Your mom isn't here, Charlotte," he stuttered. Ignoring her attempt to silence him, he turned back to Jackson and smiled. "Yeah, that's right. You couldn't get the girl on your own, so you faked those tests to break my Charlotte and Beau Corbin up." He pointed his cigar in Jackson's face.

Beau stood behind Charlotte as the crowd grew silent. The band was delayed a few minutes which didn't help the situation.

Dad appeared in the distance and saw Mason in the center of the crowd. As he got closer, he saw Isabella approach from behind Jackson.

Jackson shook his head and threw his hands in the air. "For the last damn time – that isn't true!"

Dad watched as Isabella made her way to the stage. Grabbing the microphone from the stand, the crowd paused hearing a loud piercing sound over the loudspeakers.

Isabella stood at the center of the stage and faced Mason and Jackson. "Good evening, Sedipar! I hope everyone is enjoying the evening. I certainly am!" Holding a glass of wine, she continued, "I'd like to take a moment to share a few words about a young man who has struggled with something for quite some time and has decided tonight that enough is enough!"

I looked around as the crowd stared at Isabella – intrigued by what she had to share – and then back at boisterous Mason.

Isabella smiled flatly at Mason – knowing this was her chance to pin everything on Jackson.

She glared at Jackson and smiled. "Tonight, you will witness a confession – one that we have all longed to hear. I commend this young man, Jackson Beale, for being open and honest about what he did."

Whispers floated through the crowd as they searched to find him.

Allison threw her napkin on the table. "What in the hell is she doing?" She searched for Jackson in the crowd. Kent followed closely behind her.

Anger enveloped me wondering what in the world she had up her sleeve. I glanced at Brice and his focus was on Isabella. The Trio's eyes widened and with interlocked arms, drew each other closer. Mason stumbled around spilling the remainder of his bourbon on the dance floor.

Beau stood behind Charlotte – completely still. Blaine looked around the crowd and nudged Jackson. "What's she doing!?"

"Exactly what I told ya'll she'd do." Jackson stared at the ground.

After several minutes of silence, Isabella spoke in her most condescending voice, "Well, looks like we have the attention of the crowd! Jackson come on up, son, and share with the town. Don't be shy!"

Jackson looked up at his friends with wide eyes. Kent and Allison made their way over to him, but he pushed them away. "I got this."

"Son, it's time the truth comes out." Mason stumbled toward the stage mumbling along the way.

Seeing Mason in his drunken state made Isabella nervous. "Someone please help that poor man. He drank *way* too much this evening."

No one listened. Mason struggled to get up the steps onto the stage, but finally made it. "Give me that mic, Isabella."

She covered the mic and whispered, "What in the hell are you doing up here? Get down! You're an embarrassment!"

Mason forced the mic from her hand and smiled. "Now, without further ado, I'm here to share with you what Dr. Corbin has attempted to tell you."

The crowd remained still and quiet.

He pointed to Jackson. "This young man right here, well, he got himself into a little bit of a pickle." Mason chuckled.

Isabella's jaw tightened unsure of what Mason was going to say next.

Jackson started walking away from the stage, and Mason stopped him. "Wait, Jackson, you're probably going to want to stay for this."

Jackson stopped as Kent and Allison surrounded him. "What is he talking about?" Allison questioned.

"You know what this is about, Mom. He knows." Jackson pointed toward his friends and said, "They all know."

Allison covered her mouth. "No, Jackson. How did they…" Jackson stopped her. "I'll explain later. We need to get them off the stage."

Kent had already made it to the front of the stage and pleaded for Mason to get down. "Man, get down from there. We can fix this without the whole town seeing. Get down now."

I suddenly felt a hand lightly graze my arm. It was Dad. "Hey, Dad. Perfect timing."

"I know. I've got to stop this." Dad walked closer to the stage and froze as Mason continued.

Looking at Isabella with a sly grin he said, "The town must remember all of the gossip about who Beau's father was – me or Tucker – and the debacle with the paternity tests." Mason faced the crowd and asked, "Ya'll remember that right?" Several nods of affirmation were seen in the crowd.

"Good! We're on the same page tonight then. Well, it seems those test results were tampered with – and for a while, I thought I had another son. Isn't that the darndest thing?" He stared at Isabella and smiled.

She forced a smile and another sip of wine hoping to hide her anger.

"Come to find out – Beau wasn't my son after all. Isn't it something you think one thing and something different happens?" Mason chuckled. "I'll tell you something. This young man over here...well...he had something to do with those tests."

Kent jumped up onto the stage. "Now that's enough, Mason. Give me the mic, now!"

Mason pushed Kent aside. "Nothing like a father's love – right?" The crowd softly giggled.

"You see, what I was saying is that this young man knew what happened that night. That's right. He saw it with his own two eyes."

Isabella moved closer to Mason and whispered, "Get off the stage, Mason. I know what you're doing. I shouldn't have gotten up here in the first place. We can do this a different way."

Mason wrapped his arm around Isabella roughly. "Just like a mother isn't it to try to save a young man's reputation." He smiled slyly again at her.

"I'm here to tell the truth tonight. You see, Dr. Corbin switched those tests to break up my daughter and her son. That's the truth folks! Then, she pinned everything on this poor young man – and has been lying to all of you – family and friends – all this time."

My mouth dropped.

"How dare you!" Isabella reared back and slapped Mason across the face. "I did no such thing! He's the one who did this and you're turning it on me because you despise me!" Isabella pointed at Jackson and then slapped Mason's face again.

Dad approached the stage and demanded the microphone from Mason. Mason handed it to him with a crisp nod. Isabella stood silent with her arms crossed.

"Well, nothing like airing out dirty laundry on a stage – and right here at Christmastime." Dad looked toward the back of the stage and saw the band. "I think the band is ready to come back on."

The chord of a guitar was heard, and a light tap of a drum.

"Yes, it sounds like the band is ready." Dad put the microphone back on its stand.

Isabella turned toward Mason and Dad. "You cowards! You've always been cowards!" She looked out onto the crowd and smiled at the various onlookers still intrigued by the 'show' and said, "It's all a misunderstanding – that's all!" She walked past Mason and Dad and glared at them. "This isn't over yet."

Dad put his hand out to stop her. "Isabella, it's over. You've lost. I know you want to avoid the obvious, but you're done. Your family, your friends, your patients – all of it – is gone – all because you can't leave well enough alone."

"Tucker, you disgust me. After all of our years together, you can stand by 'this'...*pointing to drunken Mason*...and destroy everything that I worked for? How could you destroy me like this?"

Dad shook his head. "That's your problem right there, Isabella. I didn't destroy you – you did all of this. And the worst part about it is that you aren't concerned one ounce about your son who can't stand to look at you or your daughter who can't call you 'Mom.' The only thing that matters to you is that damn practice – which you've now lost."

Isabella scoffed. "That's your opinion, Tucker. My children adore me. You've turned them against me." She turned toward the crowd and yelled, "He's turned all of you against me!" She lowered her head and left on the opposite side of the stage.

Dad and Kent helped Mason off the stage. Beau was waiting for Dad at the bottom of the stairs with Charlotte close by. "Dad, I didn't think it was true. So, you did know!?"

Dad looked at Beau confused. "You knew about all of this? How?"

"That doesn't matter. What matters is that you knew, and you didn't tell me." Beau's wide stance prohibited Dad from moving.

"Son, not now. It's not the place. I think this crowd has witnessed enough tonight." Dad's attempt to delay didn't work.

Beau wasn't backing down. "No, you tell me now! I can't believe you would keep something like this from me." Looking at Charlotte he continued, "This almost tore my life apart, Dad. I almost lost the one thing that means the most to me – Charlotte."

I stood behind Beau and Charlotte in shock. *Dad knew about this and didn't tell any of us?*

"Yes, son. I knew." Dad looked at Beau and Charlotte with despair. "I wanted to tell you...but your mother pleaded with me...and I couldn't do that to her." Dad paused and stared at the ground. "Nothing good would've come out of it, son."

"Oh, you couldn't do that to her, but you could lie to us. That was easy for you, huh?" Beau threw his hands in the air. "You are no better than she is! I'm done with both of you." He turned and walked away.

As he passed me he said, "They're both all yours, Nessie."

I didn't know what to say. I knew Dad had a reason for keeping it from both of us. Beau would eventually come around – he would have to make amends with Dad.

Chapter Seventy-Eight

A Mess of Things

Whitney grabbed Blaine's hand and followed Beau and Charlotte. "C'mon. They need us now."

Stella waited near the side of the stage hoping Jackson would come talk to her. He stood by Allison quietly as they waited for Kent.

Allison looked around at the crowd and noticed Stella glancing toward Jackson. She nudged him. "I think someone is waiting for you, Jackson."

His saddened eyes raised and locked with Stella's for a brief second. If her heart could've spoken in that brief moment, he would have heard how much she wanted to be with him and how much her heart hurt for him. But he looked away.

"I need to get away from this place, Mom. I can't talk to her right now." He turned and walked back toward the steps.

Stella followed behind him closely. When he reached the bottom step, she lightly touched his hand securing a soft hold. "Hey, you got a minute for me?"

"She has a mind of her own, you know. She never would've done anything she didn't want to. You can't blame yourself for that." Owen stared at the floor.

"Honestly, though, I'm not sure why you're here telling me all of this."

Owen's eyebrows raised.

Brice laughed. "The night you and your girlfriend needed a tow – well – Nessie hasn't been the same since that night."

"What do you mean by that?" Owen shifted his stance.

"I mean just what I said. She's torn, man! Or she's jealous of your girlfriend? Or she missed you and wants answers. I have no idea what's going on in her mind, but I can't sit around and wonder whether or not there is something between us or not. You need to talk to her...not me."

"I saw her last night...at the festival." Owen swallowed hard thinking about how nice it felt holding her close.

That grabbed Brice's attention. "You talked to her last night?"

"Yeah, I found her sitting alone near the bayou bank." Owen wished he wouldn't have mentioned anything now seeing Brice's interest.

"I looked for her after her mom ran off stage, but I couldn't find her. So, she was with you?" Brice clenched his fists thinking about Nessie and Owen being together alone but composed himself.

"Yeah, just for a few minutes. I wanted to check on her." Owen watched as Brice leaned over the hood of the truck.

"Anyway, the reason I came here was to..." Brice cut him off.

"To tell me how close you got to Nessie last night and how I need to back away?" Brice looked forward.

"No, that's not why I came." Owen shook his head and leaned into the hood of the truck. "Nessie needs to decide who she wants to be

Chapter Eighty-Three

Crumbling

"How could you do this to me?" Tennie leaned across the table focusing on Brice.

"Shut up, Tennie. I didn't do anything to you. You got yourself in this mess."

"Alright, enough." The sheriff stood inside the door with a wide stance. "Brice – you're free to go. Charges have been dropped."

Tennie slammed both hands on the table and stood up. "This is such bullshit! He lives in that house too. He used the drugs just as much or more than I did."

The sheriff placed his hands on her shoulders and forced her to sit down. "Miss Adams – it's in your best interest if you refrain from talking."

Brice smiled slyly and placed his hands on the table as he faced her. "It's called a drug test, Tennie. I'm clean. I've been clean. The drugs weren't mine and you know it."

to give you one more chance– to find out if you love me – and I got my answer."

He turned and threw open the door into the main hallway.

I yelled for him, but he kept walking.

I slid down the wall and cried. Ugly cried. What had I done? He was wrong. I loved him for being Owen – my Owen. Nothing would ever change that.

Chapter Eighty-Seven

A Fresh Start

Tennie had multiple charges against her, various witnesses – friends who'd turned on her – and a jury who believed she was guilty. She'd be behind bars for a while.

Kent followed Brice to the trailer to get the remainder of his belongings and grab a few things Trisha had asked for.

"I can't believe I lived in this mess," Brice kicked the door open to find several of Tennie's friends passed out on the floor.

Kent nudged each of them with his boot, waking them up. "Time to get up – and out!" Kent shook his head as they stumbled to the door and left. "Make it quick, Brice. We don't need to be here long."

Brice was relieved to find his room undisturbed. He grabbed his trophies and a few other things from his desk. With mixed emotions, he felt relieved saying goodbye – even though it had been his home. He wondered how everything had gotten so messed up – his mom in prison – his sister in jail – how'd he managed to escape?

My Owen,

If you're reading this it may be too late. You may be on your flight back to France and that's okay.

I couldn't take the chance that you may never hear how I truly feel about you.

As I write this note to you, I'm watching you stand on the pitcher's mound. Who knew you could pitch!?

You seem to be full of surprises.

You are likely wondering why I'm writing you instead of waiting for you when the game is over.

My heart is broken – wary – and cannot take much more defeat – so I'm safe here – behind this pen and paper - writing you.

I've had time to think about me...and you...and the words you said that will forever stain my heart,

'I wanted you all along.'

Owen, I wanted you all along as well – I just didn't know it.

You left Sedipar because of me. You came back for me. And now you've decided to leave again because of me.

I need you.

The void I felt -the freedom I longed for – the love I never knew I needed – was right in front of me the entire time.

I want to be with you – if you'll give me another chance.

I don't have anything else to lose.

P.S. I'd love to study abroad with you. Just not in France.

I folded the note up and walked over to the dugout. Owen's bag was leaning up against the fence. I crouched down and slipped the note into the side pocket of his backpack.

***